SACRAMENTO PUBLIC LIBRARY
3 3029 05882 0960

D0953426

Katie's Dream

Katie's Dream

A Novel

Leisha Kelly

Grand Rapids, Michigan

Published by Fleming H. Revell
a division of Baker Publishing Group
P.O. Box 6287, Grand Rapids, MI 49516-6287

Printed in the United States of America

ISBN 0-7394-4589-8

Scripture is taken from the King James Version of the Bible.

To my own tenderhearted, gentle,
hardworking husband. With love.

And to Debi and the other wonderful church friends
who have helped my family so that I could find time
to write this book.

To everything there is a season, and a time to every purpose under the heaven: a time to be born, and a time to die; a time to plant, and a time to pluck up that which is planted; a time to kill, and a time to heal; a time to break down, and a time to build up; a time to weep, and a time to laugh; a time to mourn and a time to dance; a time to cast away stones, and a time to gather stones together.

Ecclesiastes 3:1–5

Prologue

Samuel and Julia Wortham and their two children had managed seven difficult months since losing their dear friend Emma Graham. On the same night as Emma's passing, the ten neighboring children had lost Wilametta Hammond, their mother. Worthams and Hammonds had endured together. Independence Day in the small town of Dearing, Illinois, afforded them the perfect opportunity for a special day of rest. They didn't know to expect the unexpected.

Bouncing on the seat of a 1920 Ford, Katie finally managed to drift off to sleep just as they were crossing a winding creek. She didn't hear the chug of the engine anymore, or the drone of the driver talking to himself once again. All she heard now was the sweet, gentle voice of someone new. A different kind of mother, perhaps, who would sit alongside a bed and sing a tender song only for her.

ONE

Julia

July 4, 1932

Samuel lay stretched out asleep on the blanket in front of me, missing every bit of the fireworks he'd gotten us all here to see.

"Shouldn't we wake him, Mommy?" six-year-old Sarah begged. "He's missing the show."

"I don't know, honey. Seems like if he can sleep through all this, maybe he needs to."

We were surrounded by all of the Hammond children, and the littlest ones had been anything but quiet. Not to mention the noise of Oliver Porter's firecrackers, bought by that one well-to-do family in the hopes of lifting the spirits of a depressed community.

Kirk Hammond shook his head at Sarah. "Pa says never to wake a grown man when he's sleepin'. Unless his house is afire."

"There are other times," his sixteen-year-old sister Lizbeth maintained. "Like, say, if his pigs are out." She kept on rocking gently back and forth, soothing her baby sister to sleep.

It seemed like far longer than seven months since these kids had lost their mother, and nearly their father too. George Hammond wasn't with us today. He'd offered to stay home and see to the milking, theirs and ours, in exchange for us getting his entire brood into town to witness an extravagance that was rare for Dearing, even before Depression days. Real fireworks. And earlier that day, a tractor demonstration and cattle show. And an automobile race right through the middle of town. The big boys, including our eleven-year-old Robert, had urged Samuel to enter the race, hoping for the three-dollar prize. But Samuel wouldn't enter, because the truck we were using was borrowed.

"They had bigger shows in Pennsylvania," Robert remarked, slapping away at a mosquito.

"I'm sure there are bigger ones in some parts of Illinois," I told him. "But this is a little town, and it's nice for them to do something like this at all."

I looked around us at the square where most of the activities had been held. Glowing lanterns sat at the four corners and at other important spots like the lemonade stand. Some people had brought their own lanterns, so there were shining spots of light among the crowd. It made for a pretty scene, and I smiled.

But Willy Hammond frowned. "It weren't so nice, Beula Pratt and Gussy Welty singin' at the top of their lungs. I coulda done without that." Willy was the same age as our Robert, and they'd both been rather pessimistic lately.

"I liked their singin'," Sarah told him. "'The Star Spangled Banner' is my most favoritest song. An' the rest was good too."

"They were patriotic," Lizbeth agreed. "We're supposed to be patriotic today."

Thirteen-year-old Kirk shook his head. "Well, I didn't unnerstand Mr. Porter's recitation, 'least not all of it. It was too blame long."

"The whole Declaration of Independence," nine-year-old Franky said proudly. "The most important words in our whole country."

"What do you know?" Willy asked. "You're the dumbest kid in the whole county."

Franky didn't reply. He almost never did to such words, which he heard far too often.

"He's not dumb, and you know it," Lizbeth said, defending their brother. "He does fine. You don't have to read to unnerstand stuff, and he unnerstands a lot more than you do. So shut up."

I kept quiet because Lizbeth had spoken out. But usually I defended Franky, though he'd told me more than once I didn't have to bother. I knew he was special, despite his struggle to learn letters. Lizbeth was right about him. He understood most everything he heard and remembered it too. There were times when he didn't seem nine at all, though he was scarcely bigger than Sarah.

Berty Hammond, the four-year-old, on the other hand, was growing by leaps and bounds but tried to act like a baby as often as not, just to get my attention. He scooted his way into my lap and laid his little head on my shoulder, sucking away at his thumb.

"Getting tired, Berty?"

He shook his head, but I knew he was. They all were. It was past dark, and we had quite a ways to go to get home.

The oldest boy, Sam, must have been thinking that too. "We'll have to go purty quick. An' maybe I oughta drive, Mrs. Wortham. Mr. Wortham's dog tired."

"Maybe you should," I told him, knowing he'd welcome the chance. At seventeen, Sam was pretty responsible.

"Can we stay at your house?" Rorey asked, hugging at the doll I'd made for her.

"Not all of you. Your father said that was too much."

"Can I?"

"We'll see." Berty squeezed my neck, and I heard myself sigh. George should have told them who could and who couldn't this time, instead of leaving it for us to decide. It would have been so much easier. George did a lot, but he still left a lot on us and his older children. Especially Lizbeth.

There was a flurry of crackles from the bandstand, where most of the fireworks were being lit. Then one last long burst of light and sound. I put my hand on Samuel's shoulder, knowing the show was almost over. Time to be picking up blankets and getting all these kids home to bed.

He rolled over and stared at me in the darkness. For a moment I thought I saw that look in his eye that he used to have so long ago, when we first got married and he was still having bad dreams. He'd never talk about them then, and he didn't say a word now. He just sat up, and then he stood, ready to get back to the business of life.

Oliver Porter bid everybody a good night in his great booming voice, and all the kids started rising to their feet. Five-year-old Harry tried sneaking away, toward the Humkeys, who had given him a lollipop earlier, but Joey grabbed him by the collar and kept him with us.

Samuel picked up our blanket and folded it neatly. Franky lifted theirs from the ground and wadded it under his arm. Berty didn't want to let go of me, so I held him, thinking maybe he'd go to sleep that much faster.

"I need to stay with Robert," Willy told us. "So we can get an early start fishin' tomorrow."

"Fine," I agreed. "But remember your father said you could only fish till noon. Then you've got to work field."

"Fishin' is work too," Willy protested. "We might bring home dinner."

"That would be wonderful. I hope you do. But you can't fish all day, no matter how good they're biting. You're going to obey your father."

Samuel stood looking out over the park in Dearing's town square, at the stir of the crowd and the swaying cottonwood trees beyond them. I wished I knew what he was thinking. We had so little time to talk anymore. Just managing to get through our days was taking about all the energy we had—working the farm Emma had so lovingly given us, trying to put food on the table and make a decent life for all these kids. It seemed like we were parents to all of them now, not just our own two. And George Hammond let it be that way. He was a decent father. He was trying. But he never seemed to be able to manage without us, even for a couple of days.

"I wish I had some firecrackers," Harry said, trying to squirm away from Joe.

"Thank heaven you don't," I told him. "Hard to say what would happen if something like that were in your hands." More than the other children, Harry was a trial to look after. He'd try anything. Several times. He was absolutely fearless, more than a little reckless, and ornery as the dickens.

"I'd only just blast 'em," he told me. "I'd make a lot of noise and see if I could make your doggy bark."

Whiskers, our dog, barked plenty, at groundhogs and coons. But not at people he knew, especially kids, though Harry tried to get him to.

"You better leave that dog alone," Robert warned him. "One of these days he'll get real sick a' you and haul off and bite."

"Not Whiskers," Sarah said. "Whiskers is a sweetie."

"Come on," Samuel said suddenly. "Let's head for the truck." He took Berty from my arms, swooped him onto his shoulders, and led the way across the square to where he'd parked Barrett Post's truck amidst the other vehicles, most of them years old and held together by a combination of baling wire and ingenuity.

With Sarah holding one of my hands and Rorey the other, I followed him, suddenly feeling bone weary and ready for a bed myself.

As we walked to the truck, young Thelma Pratt made her way through the crowd just to say hello to Sam Hammond and ask him if she'd see him at church on Sunday.

"Uh, yeah. Far as I know," he said, embarrassed by her attention.

I couldn't help but smile. "Have a good night, Thelma," I told her. "Say hello to your mother and tell your sister she did a fine job with her singing."

"Thank you, Mrs. Wortham, I will." She glanced at young Sam one more time and disappeared in the direction of the bandstand.

Kirk jabbed at Sam with his elbow, but the skinny teen shoved his brother away and went walking ahead of us. He'd told me about two weeks ago that he liked the Pratt girl, but he wasn't especially thrilled to have everybody else knowing it.

Close to the stand where they'd been passing out lemonade, I saw Ben Porter and took the time to tell him to thank his aunt and uncle for sponsoring the festivities. Lizbeth thanked him special for not charging us a dime for the popcorn and the ice-cold lemonade. We'd have gone without otherwise.

"I wanna do this kinda thing when I get older," Franky remarked as we went walking on. "I wanna have plenty a' money so I can put it to use every whipstitch doin' stuff for people. It'd be fun, seein' 'em enjoy themselves 'stead a' sittin' and frettin' over tomorrow."

I wasn't surprised, hearing something like this from him, but Willy and Kirk were shaking their heads.

"You ain't gonna have no money," Willy said. "Nobody's gonna pay you for nothin'."

"Willy, that's enough," I warned.

"Well, it's true! Pa says for most any job you at least gotta sign your name!"

"I can sign," Franky said bravely.

"Yeah," Willy said with a laugh. "With half the letters missin', and the other half backwards."

"Do you want me to tell your father how you've been acting?" I asked him.

"I don't care," Willy said boldly. "He won't do nothin'. He thinks the same as me."

Unfortunately, I wasn't sure that wasn't true. But Samuel turned around and faced us, with Berty still bouncing on his shoulders. "I have no doubts about Franky," he said. "He can work with me anytime. And there'll be a lot more people feeling the same way when they see how he works wood. It's not everybody that's got a gift that can be seen so young."

Franky smiled and Willy sulked. And I might have said more, but right that minute, as we were rounding one side of a giant oak, I very nearly ran smack into Hazel Sharpe coming from the opposite direction. Her lantern clattered against my leg, and we both reached out our hands to steady it.

She was looking smaller than ever, her ancient shoulders stooping more all the time. Her nephew Herman was right behind her, carrying one of her chairs over his head. Hazel must have come out to watch the show. I was surprised that she would.

"Miss Hazel! Excuse us. I didn't see you coming."

"I can b'lieve that, Julia Wortham!" She raised her lantern to look us over. "You always got your mind goin' on somethin' besides business. An' here you are out with these Hammonds again! An' them lookin' like a bunch a' ragamuffins! Don't that George have the least bit a' self-respect? Where is he, anyway?"

"Home doing the milking and such," I answered

quickly. "Working hard." Why did she have to cut so with her words, and right in front of the children? None of them looked that bad, just a little dirty and tired, like anyone would after a day like this. And it was dark too, so why would it make any difference? Why did she have to act as though it were her job in life to make people uncomfortable?

"Good evening," Sarah whispered to her; she was echoed immediately by Rorey. But Miss Hazel didn't answer them or even look their way.

"C'mon, Herman," she sniffed. "Sure is late. Didn't know Porter was gonna keep us up half the night."

"Nice show, wasn't it?" I asked.

She ignored me and went walking right on with her usual quick steps.

"Good night, Miss Hazel," I called after her. "Good night, Herman."

"Good night to you," Herman acknowledged with a nod as he hurried along with that chair.

I wondered what it must be like to be Hazel Sharpe's nephew. She had three of them, I'd heard. All with families of their own. But Herman was the only one who came around, every time she called on him, to help her with this or that. It was hard to picture her thanking him, but I hoped she had courtesy enough. I figured he must be a patient sort, anyway. He sure was quiet most of the time, at least around her.

"I don't know why you bother," fourteen-year-old Joe told me when Hazel and Herman were out of earshot. "She ain't lookin' for no conversation from us."

"I'll give it to her anyway," I said. "I'm going to speak to her every time I see her and be just as pleasant as can be. One of these days, she'll crack."

"She prob'ly only done that once in her life," he argued. "When Emma died. Only time I ever seen her soft. She don't like a one of us, an' I doubt sittin' with her at church or throwin' words her way is gonna change anything."

I was surprised at the sharpness of his tone. Joe was usually so quiet and reserved. But maybe he was tired of being put down. "Those Hammonds" Hazel always called them, in her snippety, belittling kind of way. I'd never seen her speak a word to any of them directly. But she'd done plenty of talking about them.

"Maybe it won't change her," I said. "But Emma loved her. And for her sake, I will too. Just because it's right."

Joe shook his head. "She jus' goes 'round spittin' vinegar all the time. Makes me wonder what the good Lord'll say 'bout it, her supposin' to be one a' the church elders."

"That's none of our business," Lizbeth told him. "Except to pray for her."

Holding Harry's hand, Joe moved ahead of us without acknowledging her words. And I understood how he must be feeling. Since Wilametta's death, many people had come to respect Samuel and me for helping the Hammonds, but the kids and their father were pitied as often as not for needing that help. And Hazel, more than any other, had a way of making every word jab like a knife.

We came to the old truck, and Samuel lifted Berty down from his shoulders into the back end. Robert and Willy crowded into the seat, leaving barely enough room for a driver, and Samuel turned to help Lizbeth and the baby as the rest of us drew near.

"You want I drive?" young Sam asked him. "You were looking mighty sleepy."

"I was asleep," Samuel acknowledged. "And you might as well drive. If you're not too tired."

"Oh no. Not a bit."

Samuel knew as well as I did that young Sam loved every

chance he got to drive a motor car or truck. Sam could never understand why his father claimed he wouldn't buy one even if he had the money. George preferred his team of horses, and some of the other boys were the same way, especially Kirk.

I helped Sarah and Rorey into the truck, but Harry scampered up on his own and jumped into the bed with a whoop and a thunk.

"Be quiet!" Lizbeth admonished him. "You're gonna wake the baby."

It was quite a squeeze, getting nine of the children plus Samuel and myself in the back of that truck. Lizbeth was holding Emma Grace, Berty climbed up on Samuel, and the two little girls snuggled as close to me as they could get. As young Sam started the motor, Joe was trying to get Harry to sit down, Kirk was scooting over by our picnic basket, trying to get off to himself, and Franky was sitting staring out over the town like the rest of us weren't even there.

Samuel reached over and took the folded blanket from my arms, at the same time touching my hand warmly. "Nice stars," he said, his dark eyes twinkling in the moonlight.

"Nice day. Thank you for it." I leaned over and kissed him, just a peck really, but Sarah giggled and Harry stomped his feet.

"Quit," Lizbeth warned him again. "You gotta be quiet and sit still."

Going down Harper Street past the boarded-up grocery store made me think of all the other businesses that had closed. The year 1932 was not a good one for Dearing, that was for sure. Even the Farmer's State Bank had locked its doors. I'd heard some people say that Oliver Porter and his family should have been passing out food baskets instead of planning festivities; it would have been more practical. The whole countryside just didn't have enough of anything. Except children.

I fretted a bit because, like many others, we had no money left. We'd spent the last bit a couple of weeks ago for things like cornmeal and flour, and we already needed so many other things, or would soon. I knew George Hammond was in the very same shape, because we were sharing things back and forth just to get by. What would we do for shoes for all these children, before the school year returned? Every last one of them had outgrown what they'd been wearing. And most of their shoes were in awfully bad shape to be passing down.

Looking around at the children's sleepy heads, I was especially glad for the Porters' generosity, because the whole day had cost us nothing but the work Samuel did for Barrett Post in exchange for the use of his truck. Only once did Sarah ask us to buy her something at one of the sidewalk stands, and she wasn't too disappointed when we told her no.

I could remember a long-ago Fourth of July when my own daddy took me to a celebration and bought so much from the street vendors that we could hardly carry it all home. I must have been only six or seven, but I could remember clearly my Grandma Pearl's reaction. "Stuff is nice," she'd said. "But too much will make you weak. What're you gonna do when a trial comes?"

When Daddy's trial came, he didn't face it very well. He'd liked being able to travel with his sales job and then come back and lavish money on me. But when he lost the job, he didn't come and talk it over with Grandma Pearl like he should have. He didn't come back at all, and we spent three months wondering, till we found out he'd been killed in a train accident clear up in Maine. I never did know what he'd been thinking to go there.

I looked over at Samuel in the dim light. He had his head leaned back against the truck's wooden side rail and his eyes closed again. No wonder he was tired. When Samuel lost his job early in 1930, instead of running the way my father had done, he had come out here to Illinois with us and had been working ever since to do all that needed doing—and now for the neighbors too. Emma would have been proud to see him helping George as if they were brothers. Sometimes it seemed like she'd left us the Hammonds as much as she'd left us her house, clearly intending us to treat them like family.

I wanted to snuggle in Samuel's arms the way Sarah was snuggling up in mine. We'd never asked to have so many kids in our charge. But he never complained about it, not ever. I felt like giving him another kiss and telling him how much I appreciated his kindness. But not now with all the children looking on.

"Mr. Wortham?" Franky was suddenly asking in his faraway voice. "Why did God make so many people?"

"What?" Samuel asked, stirred from near sleep as the truck jostled us around a corner and out into the countryside.

"Why did God make so many people? Seems like just a few woulda been enough." Franky had turned around, and I could see the earnestness of his face in the moonlight. "Like maybe he coulda made jus' one town or somethin'," he continued, "instead a' hundreds an' hundreds a' towns. Plus there's years an' years afore we were ever born. That's lots more people."

"What do you know 'bout stuff like that?" Kirk scoffed.

"Nothin' much. That's why I'm askin'."

"I don't know much about it, either," Samuel told them

both. "But I suppose God's got a purpose for everybody, hard as it may be to see."

"Even folks that don't follow him?"

"Even them." Samuel sighed. "But he's got good desires for everyone. It's just that they won't all listen, which is not his fault."

"But there's so many," Franky said again. "I don't unnerstand it. An' it's pretty brave, lettin' 'em have their own way, don't you think? You never know what could happen, right?"

"Franky . . ." Kirk shook his head impatiently. "Why don't you shut up—you're prob'ly keepin' people awake."

"He's not botherin' me," Lizbeth said quietly. "Nor Emmie Grace."

"He's just doing a lot of thinking tonight, Kirk," Samuel said. "No harm in that."

"He's bein' odd. I guess he likes to be odd."

"He can't help it," Joe added. "That's what the schoolteacher said."

"Better to be odd than lazy or disrespectful," Samuel told them. "I've been accused of being odd a time or two myself."

"Really?" Franky asked. "When?"

"Yeah, when?" Rorey echoed from beside me. Harry stood up again, and Joey pulled him down.

"Not so long ago. When we first came here. But even before that, when I was a boy."

I leaned forward. It was so very seldom when Samuel said anything at all about his childhood. But he stopped before he got the story told. "None of that matters. The point is, people have opinions, and they express them often enough, but it doesn't have to have any bearing on what you make of yourself."

"Like Miss Hazel," Joe pointed out. "I guess she figures we're all a bunch a' losers."

"But we know better. And it doesn't have to bother us."

We turned at Hunter's Corner, and I reached across Sarah's back to find Samuel's hand.

"Bessie had fun today," Sarah said about her doll.

"Lacey too," Rorey added, jumping her little doll up to whisper something to Sarah's Bessie-doll.

"We should take 'em swimmin' tomorrow," Rorey said. "Is that all right, Mrs. Wortham?"

"Goodness, not in the pond, Rorey, if that's what you're meaning. You'd scare all the fish the boys are trying to catch. And besides, they'd get filthy."

"Well, how 'bout in the washtub, then?"

I could picture that easily enough, having done it once myself as a girl. But oh, what a mess I'd made of my doll! Her yarn hair coming loose and her pretty dress all a shambles. Grandma Pearl had to fix her nice again for me. "Rorey, honey," I told her with a shake of my head, "it's not good for cloth dolls to be played with in water. You want to keep her looking nice."

"We'll just *pretend* they're swimming," Sarah decided. "That's better than real anyhow, 'cause you can imagine the whole ocean and ride on whales and stuff."

They whispered back and forth across my lap as Harry started fidgeting again. "We're goin' near thirty miles an hour," Lizbeth told him with alarm. "You can't be standing up in the back of a truck."

Harry sat down and folded his arms in disgust. Sitting still was never easy for him. But Franky was staring out over the closest field again, quiet as the sky above us. What a difference between these brothers.

I looked at Samuel, wondering if he thought as much as I did about tomorrow. He used to be the one so troubled by our lack, but now I probably fretted more than he did. I knew I shouldn't. God had been so good to lead us here, to give us a home and a dear friend in Emma Graham. And I'd been strong to believe that God would always provide. But last winter struck me down, shook me terribly, as it did all of us. Losing Emma and Wilametta Hammond at the same time was the worst thing I could ever have imagined. Except losing Samuel. And ever since then, trusting was a little harder.

What would we do from here on out with no money at all? Even with Emma's beautiful farm, how could we manage? George was worried about the crops, we knew that, but there was nothing we could do about it. Our garden was bearing, but not like I'd hoped. There were no jobs for miles, if anywhere, in times like these. Seemed like everybody was looking. Samuel tried so hard to find anything at all. Barrett Post had worked him for a while, but not even the Posts were hiring help anymore. And we had so many mouths to feed. For months now, George and Samuel had been working together, sharing everything alike, from both farms. But it wasn't enough. With winter coming up, what would we have? It didn't look like there'd be enough of anything to store away for the cold weather that was sure to come.

I thought of Emma singing hymns on the way home from church so many times, whether she felt well or not. Whether she had a dime in her pocket or not. She was always being blessed by the littlest things.

I tried to be like her. I tried to be the saint people needed to have around in her stead. But I fell short. I knew I did. In so many ways.

"God will provide." She'd told me that so many times. I used to say it myself, back when we'd had nothing to eat but what I could pick growing in the timber somewhere. What had happened to me? At least we had a roof over our heads. And more family than Samuel and I put together

had ever had before—with the Hammonds, the Posts, and all the church folks. But still, the weight of uncertainty was heavy tonight. At least for me. I knew everything would be all right, and yet I didn't know, all at the same time.

"I don't guess the Lord wants us to have all the answers yet," Franky said suddenly, and I jumped. It was like God speaking directly to me, though I knew the child was probably just talking about what he'd been asking before.

"If we knew ever'thin' already, maybe we wouldn't have nothin' to talk to him about, nor look forward to," he said.

And I marveled. At God and at Franky.

"As high as the heavens are above the earth," Samuel quoted. "So are his thoughts above our thoughts and his ways above our ways."

"Ain't that somethin'?" Franky added. "I guess that means there's a lot we can't figger out."

Why didn't Franky's teacher or his father or his brothers see what a marvel he was? All they seemed to notice was that the poor kid couldn't read and kept to himself a lot. We knew his eyes were fine, so they took him for an oddity, or worse, an idiot.

"What's that mean, 'bout his thoughts above our thoughts?" Rorey suddenly asked, lifting her head. She and Sarah were alike in that. They always heard, even if it didn't look like they were listening.

"It means God knows better than we do," Samuel explained.

"Oh." Rorey turned her attention back to Sarah and the dolls. "I knew that already."

The rest of us grew quiet, and my eyes rested on Franky. He liked to sit and think more than anybody I knew, adult or child. He was obviously bright, able to quote the preacher's sermons or most anything else he heard. Young as he was, he'd loved it when I read *Pilgrim's Progress* to him over the winter, and I knew he understood it better than many grown-ups because of the things he had to say. How could anyone consider him slow, though he still struggled and continued to fail at trying to decipher even the simplest written word?

"He doesn't seem to be learning anything," the schoolteacher had complained to me once. "Doesn't even know an *A* from one day to the next. I just don't know that there's much hope for him."

We'd tried him out at threading needles and sighting birds in the trees. He could see just fine. But he still couldn't read his own name.

So maybe there was no hope for him in that one-room schoolhouse with kids of every grade level right there to watch and laugh as he tried so hard but continued to fail. Lizbeth and I were already planning to keep him at home when the next school term started and do the best we could with him ourselves. It had been the teacher's suggestion. And Lizbeth, who wanted to be a teacher herself, was looking forward to it, though I wasn't sure how she could concentrate on that and keep up with her own studies.

"Mommy, Bessie wants a lullaby." Sarah looked hopefully at me in the moonlight, calling my thoughts back to the bumpy truck ride. "Please, please, Mommy, sing her the sleepy song."

I squeezed Samuel's hand. The sleepy song. I'd made it up a few months back when trying to soothe baby Emma Grace through a bad cold; I hadn't wanted to leave it all on Lizbeth when she was studying for a recitation. George and Samuel had been planting then, putting in long hours, and I'd had most of the children, particularly the younger ones, with me almost every evening.

I took a deep breath, and Sarah brought her dolly closer to me. Sarah was the sleepy one, I knew that. Bessie only needed a lullaby when Sarah was feeling tired but too big to admit it. I patted my little girl's hair. My little angel. She never seemed to mind how much attention I gave to the Hammond children. She'd understood it all along.

"Sing, Mommy," she whispered.

I touched her hair again, and she and her dolly settled across my lap.

> Sleep, baby, sleep, baby, close your little eyes.
> Sleep, baby, sleep, baby, quiet those cries . . .

I sang the whole song, marveling at how it stuck in my memory and in Sarah's fancy. It was nothing special, though Emmie Grace had liked it too.

Rorey snuggled closer against my leg. Both girls were very still. We turned the corner past the Muellers', and I hoped the little ones would drift off to sleep in the short time we had before getting home. Berty and the baby were so quiet that I figured they were probably asleep already, and even Harry had finally leaned his head back against Joe's chest. The older boys wouldn't sleep. I knew that. But just to have some of the kids down already would make it easier when we got home. I still didn't know how many we'd have over with us and how many would be going on home to George. But that really didn't matter. Once they were all asleep, Samuel and I would be alone in the quiet.

Lord, here we are at the end of another day. Guide us, provide for us, tomorrow and all the days to come . . .

I leaned back against the bumpy truck rail until we were on the lane leading up to Emma's old house. I always thought of Emma when we came home from anywhere. She used to say that just getting home was one of the finest blessings this world had to offer. And she was right. In so many ways, we were blessed.

I took a deep breath and thanked the Lord for a house to come home to. I was looking forward to a splash of cool water on my face, a breeze blowing through our window, and Samuel lying beside me.

Whiskers was barking as we came upon the house, and a car, small and dark, was parked to one side of the drive-way, almost surely on Emma's coneflowers. Somebody was there on our steps, sitting in the moonlight as still as a statue. I could feel myself tense up. Somebody was waiting for us, at so late an hour. Something was wrong.

TWO

Samuel

Young Sam parked the truck under the sweet gum tree, just in front of the old Ford someone had driven in. The dog got quiet and came running out to greet us.

I could see the man, whoever it was, as he stood up tall and lean. And for a moment my heart pounded irrationally. The dream I'd had in the park was floating over me again. It could almost be my father standing there, the build was so much the same.

I tried to shake the dream away, to meet the present and whoever it was who had come out so late to greet us. But before I could say anything, a booming voice floated across the yard, out of my past, and set my mind spinning again.

"Is that little Sammy there? Huh? Sammy Wortham?"

He sounded like my father, but I knew it wasn't. Father was dead. It was Edward. My brother. Never in a thousand years would I have expected him to show up at my door.

"Do you know him?" Julia whispered. Dear Juli. She didn't know Edward, except for the little I'd told her. He'd been in the penitentiary most of our married life. She'd never even heard his voice. And I hadn't known he was out.

"It's my brother," I said.

Juli became still as a stone beside me. But Edward was approaching, so I jumped from the truck to face him. "Edward. This is quite a surprise."

"Yeah. I figured it would be." He laughed. "What are you doing in the back of the truck? You come so far up in the world that you got somebody else driving for you?"

"The neighbor boy enjoys it once in a while, that's all." It had been so long, I didn't know what else to say to him. And I didn't know why he was here. Was he just longing to see family again, after all this time?

"Not very talkative, are you, Sammy, old boy?"

"I'm sorry. You caught me by surprise."

"You said that already. Aren't you going to introduce me to anybody? Or ask me in? I'll tell you, that's a long drive. I sure could use a drink and a smoke."

"We'll get you some coffee. But I don't smoke anymore, Edward. Can't help you there."

"Should've had you figured for that. Too good for it, aren't you, Samuel? Mother says you're out here trying to be some kind of saint."

This wasn't starting off very well. Robert got out of the front seat but didn't say a word. Juli climbed down and stood beside me.

"Edward, this is Julia," I said, far from comfortable. What would it mean to my family to have their Uncle Edward here? Already I wondered if my brother had changed at all, and if he would be staying long.

"Good evening," Julia said politely. "It's good to meet you."

"That's generous of you," Edward said with a laugh. "Hard to say what all you've heard."

"You have a brother?" Rorey asked from behind me. "I didn't know you had a brother."

"That your baby Sarah?" Edward asked.

"I'm not a baby," Sarah answered immediately. "But that's Rorey."

In two shakes, Kirk and Joe and Harry had climbed down behind me, and Willy and Sam were out of the front seat and standing next to Robert.

"Who are all these?" Edward asked. "Them orphans Mother told me about?"

Why did he have to be so blunt? I'd written my mother, several times, telling her all the things that were happening here. Maybe I shouldn't have. She and Edward weren't likely to understand. "They're our neighbor friends," I explained. "We've been to the Independence Day celebration in town."

"Good for you," Edward said, with something odd in his voice.

"We're not orphans," Rorey spoke up. "We got Pa over t' home."

"Rorey, shhh," Lizbeth scolded. "You all get back in the truck. We're going home."

"But I'm stayin'," Willy started to protest.

"No, you're not," Lizbeth insisted. "They got comp'ny, so it's not right. You can meet up with Robert in the mornin'. Mr. Wortham, is it all right that we take the truck on home?"

"I wanted to stay too," Rorey complained.

But I knew Lizbeth was right. I had to talk to Edward first, without the distraction of having them all sleep over. "That's fine, Lizbeth," I said quickly. "You all have a pleasant night."

"You want I take the truck to Mr. Post in the morning for you, then?" young Sam asked.

"Yes. Thank you."

Robert lifted Sarah down, but the rest of the kids got back in, much to the disappointment of some.

"Is it coffee you want?" Julia was asking my brother timidly. "Or would you rather have tea, or even milk? I'm afraid we haven't any lemonade. Or ice."

"Bye!" Harry called to us from the truck.

"Boys," I called quickly, "tell your father I'm still planning to help him work field tomorrow if I get the chance."

"Yes, sir," young Sam answered. And then they drove away.

"I don't like soured milk," Edward was telling Julia. "If you ain't got ice in this heat, how do you know it ain't soured?"

"I'm sure George milked fresh tonight," she answered. "And he'd have put it down the well for us."

"Who's George?"

"The father of all those children who just left," I told him.

"You got you a strange arrangement here, Sammy."

"It might look that way."

"I'll take the coffee."

It meant lighting the cookstove in this weather to heat the water, but Julia didn't seem to mind. Rather, she seemed to appreciate something quick at hand to do.

"Come with me, Sarah," she said. "We've got some cookies we can set out for our guest. You can help me."

"Go see that the cows have water, Robert," I added. "And the chickens too."

He did so without complaint, though George had probably taken care of it already. Robert knew so little about his uncle, and I knew he was curious. He'd have plenty of questions later.

"Quite a farm you got hold of, Sammy!" Edward exclaimed as his eyes followed Robert to the barn. "And animals to boot. How much you figure it's all worth?"

"Not much in today's market."

"You know what I mean!" he answered impatiently. "If you were to hold on here, you'd be worth a pretty penny, wouldn't you? Pretty slick, getting into an old lady's graces. Wish I could find me a deal like that."

Juli was more than halfway to the house, but she stopped. Nobody breathed a word for a moment. Feelings that were years old jumbled inside of me next to this new affront. How dare he speak of Emma that way? Of the way things were? There and then, I wanted to hit him.

"We've been blessed," Juli said gently. "It's not been easy, but God always makes a way."

"When did you get out?" I asked abruptly.

"March."

Mother hadn't told me. But unless I could reach her building in Albany by telephone, I never heard anything from her. She didn't answer my letters. It made me wonder sometimes why I bothered writing them at all.

"Looks like you found some kind of a deal yourself," I said. "How'd you get a car? And the money for the trip?" Jobs were so scarce, and he had come all the way to Illinois. Few men I knew could afford the gas.

"That's not especially your business, is it? What do you think, that I'm stealing again already?"

"I just asked."

He didn't say anything, and it was Julia who broke the moment's uncomfortable silence. "You might as well come on inside. Pleasant evening, but it's almost bedtime for the children."

Edward ignored her. "I never imagined you a farmer," he said with a touch of amusement in his voice. "How many cows you got?"

"Just two, and a calf. One's giving good milk. But Lula

Bell's getting old. We stand to lose her before winter, I have a feeling."

"Ought to shoot her and be done with it," he remarked. "Or is that too hard for you?"

I didn't answer. He hadn't said why he'd come, but if it was only to give me a hard time, I didn't need it and he could just go back where he'd come from. I started for the house.

Edward went to his car for a minute; I expected him to lift a big suitcase or something, but he just turned around again with nothing and followed me inside. Juli had the lamp lit and was lighting the stove.

"You need fresh water?" I asked her.

"If you don't mind."

Sarah sat at the table with her doll in hand and her wide eyes looking droopy. Edward stood in the doorway, looking the place over. Suddenly I hated to leave my family alone with him. "Come on with me," I told him. "We can talk while I draw the water."

"Nah." He shook his head. "I believe I'll sit. We can talk when you get back in."

I looked at Juli. She gave me a nod. Maybe I was just being foolish. It was only two minutes out to the well and back. And Edward wasn't violent. I picked up the bucket and went. But I could feel the deep uncomfortable churning inside me, so I took the time to pray.

Father in heaven, what's the matter with me? I don't want him here. I don't like that he's come. For so long, I've claimed I wanted my family to be closer, but here is my brother, and I don't want him. Not till he's changed.

I hurried to the well, praying for God's mercy. And for Edward, that if he had some ungodly scheme, it would fail and there would be some way to soften his heart. He'd been a burglar. An armed robber. *Lord, help him find you!*

I drew the water quickly and was about to march back to the house when I heard a sound I didn't recognize.

Robert was in the barn, but the sound wasn't coming from there. Or from the dog, who was prancing around at my side. It seemed to be coming from Edward's car. Teeny, whimpery noises.

At first I didn't see anything at all in the shadows. But then behind the driver's seat, a shape. A child. Huddled on the floorboards and curled up alone in the dark.

"Hello," I said softly. "I'm Mr. Wortham, Edward's brother. Who are you?" Edward didn't have a wife or children that I knew of. What was this about?

The child raised its head, just a little, and I could see the long, dark curls. A little girl. Why hadn't Edward said something? Why didn't he bring her inside?

"Are you hungry?" I asked her.

She just sat there watching me. I reached my hand toward her, and she drew back. Once again, I felt that churning inside me. I could have hit him, whatever he meant by this. Whoever this child was, how dare he just leave her in the car? And had he given her reason to be afraid?

I set the bucket down. "Why don't you come inside?" I suggested. "My wife would be happy to pour you some milk and get you a bite to eat."

She shook her head, just enough for me to see it in the darkness.

"Did he tell you to stay put?"

She was quiet for a moment. Then in a tiny, timid voice she answered me. "Yes, sir."

"Well. This is my home. Not his. And what I say goes here. You're coming in for a meal if you need one and a soft bed for the night. And if he doesn't like it, then he and I will have to settle matters and it won't be your fault. Do you understand?"

"Yes, sir."

"Come on. Okay? Don't be afraid."

Slowly she crawled toward me, never taking her eyes off

me as she moved. So small. Barely Sarah's size. Where in the world had he gotten a child? Why? A heat was growing inside me, fierce and awful. Scarcely was I ever angry. Not since long-gone days when I had been so much younger and Eddie had been such a torment. Now he was back.

"Samuel Wortham?" she whispered.

"Yes. That's right. Edward's brother. But I promise you we're not much alike."

She stood on the seat and took hold of my arms. She was a skinny thing; I could carry her easily, and the bucket too. She clung to my neck on the way to the house, resting her head against my shoulder. She sniffed once or twice, and I wanted to ask her name. I wanted to know plenty. But from Edward first.

I gave the door a push, walked straight for the table, and set the bucket down in front of Edward's face. I could feel the child's body tense against mine when she saw him. Juli gasped. I saw with relief that Sarah was gone. Juli must have sent her on up to bed. Thank God.

Edward rose to his feet before I could say a word. And he was laughing. "Well! You found her. That didn't take long! I was saving the surprise for later."

"You tell me what the devil you're doing with a scared child in your car!" I demanded. "Ed Wortham, where'd you get her? Where's her family—"

"Now, calm down." He was smiling, still laughing inside.

I might have set the girl down, but she was clinging to me.

"You're looking at my good deed for the year," he continued. "I met her mother back East. Told her I knew where the kid's father was and that I'd take her to him. Now isn't that a nice gesture on my part?"

"Where? Where's her mother?"

"I have no idea where she is now. She was in Albany.

On her way to Buffalo. But she'd be gone from there by now. A singer. Does a lot of traveling."

"Why would she leave her child with you?"

"Like I said, I know her father. Look at her, Sammy. She look like anybody you know?"

I didn't look. I didn't see much point.

"Trudy Vale, Samuel. That name mean anything to you?"

Not a thing. Julia walked up beside me and put her hand on the child's shoulder. "You want a cookie, sweetie? Or some bread and butter?"

The little girl didn't answer.

"Is that the child's name or the mother's?" I asked Edward.

"Oh, you're good." He shook his head. "You're good, Samuel. I wouldn't have expected it."

"Are you going to answer my question?"

"The mother's, of course." He looked at Julia and shook his head again. "The girl's name is Katie." He turned toward the child rather sternly. "Didn't I tell you to be quiet, kid? And I'd come and get you when I was good and ready?"

"How old is she, Edward? Do you even know?"

"I expect she could tell you that herself. Six or seven, I guess. Thereabouts. Little, though, isn't she? Kind of like her mom. Delicate. With those sweet eyes. Right?"

Whatever he meant by such words, it disgusted me. "Shut up. Did you feed her anything all this way?"

"Sure. A few times. What do you take me for? A heathen?"

I tried to set her down in a chair, but she still didn't want to let go. "I don't know, Edward. Right now, I really don't."

"Well, I can tell you I was glad to find you not so much the saint as you claim. Sly old devil, Samuel. Back in Pennsylvania. Trudy told me all about it."

"What are you talking about?"

He looked at Julia again, his smile barely hidden. "So sorry, Missus," he said. "But these things catch up to a man. Katie here is his. That's exactly what I'm told. And your little girl is almost this size, isn't she? You must have been sitting at home—"

"Shut up, Edward!" I handed the child into Julia's arms.

"What are you gonna do, Sammy?" he taunted. "Throw me out? Throw your girl out too? Huh?"

"She's not—" I saw the girl shiver. She was starting to cry. "Edward, we can discuss this outside. Let the poor kid—"

"You mean you don't want your wife to hear?"

"There's nothing I'd hide from Juli. Nothing. Our kids are the only ones I've got. But this is not something we need to fight over in front of a scared little girl!"

"Very good, Samuel." He sat down, smirking up at me. "We don't have to fight. Wouldn't mind a bite to eat, to tell you the truth. Got any bacon?"

THREE

Julia

We didn't have bacon, and I was glad. Samuel's brother or not, Edward was a skunk, and I didn't feel like giving him what he asked for. I couldn't imagine this poor child suddenly separated from her mother and carried across five states by this crude man. Was he even telling the truth about it? What kind of a mother would allow such a thing?

He wasn't telling the truth about Samuel, no matter what he wanted me to believe. He'd devised some sort of plan to make trouble, though I couldn't imagine why. Didn't he know Samuel would have welcomed him, just for a normal visit, if he'd only been decent?

I sliced what was left of the bread and went quietly to the basement for the butter in the cool pit. We had eggs left in there too. I could fry them up and serve some applesauce, home-canned from the pantry. The little girl was sure to like that. At least I hoped so.

By the time I got back upstairs, Robert had come in from the barn. Samuel sent him to bed too. He didn't seem to want the kids around Edward, and I couldn't blame him, the way that man talked.

"Julia, you are a sight to behold," Edward said when I was cracking the eggs. "Mother said you were something to look at, and she was right."

Samuel was sitting at the table now with the little girl beside him. I saw how he tensed hearing a remark like that, but I didn't say anything. And I wondered if Samuel would get any sleep tonight with his brother around.

I served the little girl first. But she looked from Edward to Samuel and then back again without touching her food.

"You can have all you want," Samuel told her. "I expect you're hungry from the trip, right?"

"Go ahead and eat," Edward added. "It's his house. You're not in my hands anymore."

Katie ate quickly, neatly, watching us all the while. I gave her more applesauce when she got the first of it done, and she ate that too. Edward had six eggs, three cups of coffee, and all the bread that was left. When he was done, he sat back, folded his arms, and stared at Samuel.

"So, brother—what do you want me to do? I appreciate the food. But if you don't want nothing more to do with me, I can head on. As for this girl, if you don't claim her, well, I guess I'll take her too."

"No. You're not taking her anywhere till I know more about this."

"You *are* claiming her, then?" he said with a smile.

"I didn't say that. But I'm not sending her anywhere with a jackal like you. I want you to tell me the truth."

I was surprised at Samuel's words, his tone. But even more surprised by Edward's answer.

"You can call me whatever you want, little brother. But you heard the truth, as sure as I'm alive. You can imagine what a shock it was when that beauty in the speakeasy got upset over me being a Wortham. Then she told me you were the father. I wouldn't have thought. But don't worry. I didn't tell Mother. She still thinks you're a saint."

"I don't know anyone named Trudy Vale," Samuel said sternly. "I don't know what this is about, but it's foolishness, and it won't gain you anything."

"Then I guess maybe we better go. I didn't expect you to own to it. Trouble is, what do I do with the kid, Samuel? She thinks she's yours. And I've got no way of finding her mama now, not that she'd want to be found. She said it was your turn. She couldn't keep her no more and travel. I was just doing her a favor, you understand?"

"No. I don't understand." Samuel looked truly hurt. "I don't know why you'd come all the way out here or where you got this innocent kid or why you're doing this. Is it that important to you to cause trouble now that you're out? You couldn't just settle down somewhere, look for work, and be a good citizen for a change?"

Edward rose to his feet. "Sammy, you're a devil of a liar. But you got some heart about you at least. You don't want me to take her. You want to know she's cared for, don't you?"

Quiet tears were spilling down the little girl's cheeks, and I felt sorry she'd had to hear all this. What had she already been through?

Samuel got up too, and he and his brother went outside. I was afraid, lest they might actually come to blows, though such a thing wouldn't be like Samuel at all. I didn't follow them out. Whatever else was said, I didn't want this little girl to hear.

"Have you had enough to eat?" I asked her.

She nodded, just a little, biting down on her lower lip. "Do you want me to go away?"

"No, honey. Not till we know where your family is or what's the best thing to do. You shouldn't go with Edward. You don't want to, do you?"

She shook her head, and I decided she was old enough to tell me at least some things.

"Was he mean?"

"A little."

"Is Trudy Vale really your mother's name?"

"Yes, ma'am."

"Do you know where she is?"

"I ain't seen her since Albany, like Mr. Eddie said." Two giant tears spilled down her cheeks. Big dark eyes. Narrow face. Dark hair. Edward's words stirred a chill in me. *"Look at her, Samuel. She look like anybody you know?"*

A stranger might have thought she was Samuel's. A stranger might have been willing to believe Edward's story. And I might have thought the girl was Edward's own child, if he hadn't been incarcerated back then. Of course, Edward's face and coloring was like their mother's. Except for his build, he didn't look much like Samuel at all. And, oh God, what were we to do with this child now?

I hugged her, and she cried in my arms.

"Are you tired, sweetie?"

She shook her head.

"You're welcome to stay the night, and as long as necessary to settle this. We can get some help maybe from the sheriff in town. He'll know what to do to find your family."

She shook her head, looking up at me with those deep eyes. "I want to stay here. With my daddy. Please?"

I couldn't answer her. I heard the sound of Edward's car starting and then driving away. Samuel came in and just stood for a moment in the doorway. Finally he sat in the chair beside me. "He just left. Maybe I should have tried to keep him."

"Why?"

"We'll need the truth, if we can get it out of him. Ben Law will have some questions."

Ben Law, the sheriff. An apt name. Samuel was thinking like I was. Somebody would have to find this child's family.

He took my hand. "What my brother said, Juli, it's not so."

"I know that."

He sighed. "I just thought it wouldn't hurt, to say it plain." He reached for Katie's hand too. "I'm sorry. For all that's happened. Are you all right?"

She nodded, staring up into his face. Lord, how she looked like him! Did Samuel see it too?

His dark eyes were stormy. "I need to know," he asked her softly. "Did he hurt you?"

"Not so much."

I could see Samuel tighten. "What do you mean?"

"Mostly he just talks and yells a lot. He didn't hit me but once."

Samuel hung his head. "Where'd he find you? Where's your family?"

"I don't know where Mama went. She told me to be good. And I been trying."

"You're being very brave." He stopped, turning his eyes to me. "What are we going to do now, Juli?"

I had to sigh. "It's too late to do anything more tonight. The kind thing would be to let her rest." I wanted to tell him that she believed Edward's lie. But I didn't.

"You're right." He looked at Katie again. "The kids are in the beds upstairs, but you can have ours. Okay? We can talk some more in the morning."

"I . . . I always sleep on the floor."

"You don't have to here."

She was quiet for a moment. "Is Mr. Eddie coming back?"

"I don't know."

Her eyes filled with tears. "Did he leave my bag?"

Samuel shook his head.

"My dollies—" She suddenly broke down in front of us.

"Oh, honey." I held her tight, trying to console her.

"There was . . . there was three of 'em . . . a mommy and a daddy and a little girl." She sniffed. "I cut a magazine . . ."

"Paper dolls? Those are special." I petted her hair a little, and she cuddled against me. And then I had an idea. "Would it help you feel better if I showed you something else that's special?"

She gave me a tearful little nod. Here she was among strangers, without anything familiar. Maybe my small gift could help just a little.

"Samuel, you know that box on the closet shelf?"

"The Christmas things?"

"Yes."

He got it for me, and I pulled out the little yarn dolls that our pastor's wife had made for us to hang on the tree. Rorey and Sarah still got them out to play with sometimes. I was hoping just having something to hold would help put this child at ease. "You can touch," I told her. "Pick out a few to sleep with, if you want."

"Really?" She looked frightened.

"Yes."

She picked out three. Two of the biggest and one of the smallest. "They're a real family," she said, looking at Samuel.

"Let's take them on to bed," I said before he had a chance to answer. I led her by the hand to our bed and turned down the covers. Samuel followed and lit the candle on the top of the dresser.

I helped her under the top sheet and rolled the blanket out of the way as Samuel opened the window to let in a little breeze. Katie lay her head back against the pillow with the yarn dolls clenched together in one fist. Still she was looking at Samuel.

Maybe he had relatives he didn't know about. Maybe one of them had fathered this child. What else could account for the resemblance?

"Katie—is that really your name?"

She nodded. I smoothed her hair and leaned and kissed her forehead. "Sleep well," I whispered.

She turned her eyes to me and gave just a little smile. "I thought you'd be mad. Mr. Eddie said you'd be real mad."

"He doesn't know me. This is the first time we've met."

Samuel went quietly out. And I stood up, about to go too, when little Katie called me. "Mrs. Wortham, I wish you was my mom. Then we could be a real family, right?"

I didn't know how to answer her. I wanted to say that she must have a real family somewhere waiting for her, wanting her. But what if it wasn't so? What would tomorrow hold for her?

"Mrs. Wortham . . ."

She looked so scared, lying there alone. I was certain that in her shoes I would have been scared too. "Would you like me to sing you a song?"

Her eyes opened wider. "Would you? Really? Mama doesn't sing to me. She's always too tired."

I hadn't thought. Her mother was a singer, so maybe singing to Katie was exactly the wrong thing to do. She shouldn't be thinking of me as a mother figure. She surely wouldn't be here very long. But I'd have to sing now, like it or not, because I'd offered. I took a deep breath. "Well, if you want me to sing for you, you have to close your eyes."

She did. And I sang the sleepy song, followed by a church hymn and then a lullaby that Grandma Pearl had taught me long ago. By that time, Katie was completely still, exhausted surely, and hopefully out for the rest of the night. I sat there for a moment on the edge of her bed, wondering where Samuel had gone so quietly. He was understandably troubled by his brother's sudden appearance. And the accusation.

I thought of the summer before we'd married, when we'd sat down to talk about our pasts and our future together. "I've only lied to you once," he'd confessed to me then. And I forgave him immediately, because the lie he'd told me was that he'd never known his father. "I didn't want you to know what I came from," he'd said. "I didn't want you to think I could ever be that way."

Violent. Irresponsible. Samuel's father had been that and much more. And his mother was a very difficult woman. Edward was like them, maybe. But not Samuel. Samuel was a tenderhearted, gentle, hardworking man. What must he be feeling about all this? Did he wonder if I would doubt him?

I rose up quietly, leaving the candle burning just a little while, in case the girl woke up and felt anxious in this strange place. I tiptoed upstairs to check on the children and found them sleeping quietly, Sarah sprawled sideways across her bed and Robert all curled up the way he'd slept since he was a baby. What would it be like in the morning when they came down to find this strange child here? How would Katie feel? Maybe having a little girl so close to her size to play with would make her want to stay that much more.

Going down the stairs, I sighed. Katie wouldn't want to leave anyway. If we were in a smelly old shack without another soul to play with, she would still want to stay. Because of Samuel most of all. What were we to do?

Dirty dishes were waiting in the kitchen, and ordinarily I would have done them just to have them out of the way before the morning's bustle. But this time I left them in the dishpan and stepped outside. Whiskers met me on the porch, and my eyes searched the dark yard for Samuel. Finally I saw him behind the apple tree, just standing. I went to him slowly, not wanting to interrupt if he were praying. But I needed a hug. Surely he would too. I put my hand on his shoulder, and he drew me into his arms.

"Is she sleeping?"

"Yes."

He held me for a moment in the quiet, struggling, it seemed, for the right words. "Juli, I'm sorry . . ."

I felt a sudden stir inside. What if it were true? But no, I would not entertain such a thought. Not about Samuel.

"I had no idea he was out. Or that he'd do something like this—"

"It's all right."

"No. It isn't. She's just a little girl. Can you imagine how scared she must have been, traveling for miles with a stranger? And Edward, as coarse as he is! How could he hit her? And what do we do? If it's true, that her mother didn't want to keep her—"

"We can't be sure of anything right now."

"I know. But she must have family somewhere." He grew quiet. "Juli, when he got in the car, he swore he was telling the truth. I don't know what to think. I've seen his lies plenty of times, but he's gotten better at it. I don't know what he's trying to do. Turn you away from me, maybe."

"Honey, maybe it's a different Wortham. Maybe a relative, even, that you didn't know about. He might just be mistaken—"

"Then why is he enjoying this so much?"

I had no answer.

"Sometimes I think you're the lucky one, Juli." He sighed. "All your family is dead. And they left you with fond memories—" His voice broke.

"Sammy . . ."

He sunk down to the grass, and I held him. I wasn't sure what was happening. I'd never seen him like this.

"It's been so long since I've seen him."

"Were you ever friends?"

"I tried."

I was quiet for a moment. "We should get some sleep. We have a lot to think about in the morning."

"Will you stay out here with me, Juli? Under the stars tonight?"

I didn't want to protest. But there was Katie inside, in a strange house. "Honey, what if that little girl wakes up?"

"You're right." He pulled himself to his feet. "How 'bout we stretch out a blanket in the sitting room?"

I didn't know why he'd wanted to sleep outside. He'd never before mentioned such an idea. "Are you all right?"

"Yeah."

I took his hand, and we walked to the house. He didn't speak again. I looked in on Katie and blew out the candle. When I came back to the sitting room, Samuel was unrolling Emma's big comforter quilt to give us something soft to lie on. We wouldn't need a cover, as warm as it was.

He sat there, looking up at me in the soft moonlight filtering through the nearest window. He looked so vulnerable. Like a child, almost. Like Katie, scared and alone.

"I've never known another woman, Juli. In all my life."

"Oh, honey, I know." I held him, kissed him, but I couldn't help but feel his tension. If Edward did this to him every time he came around, I hoped he never came back.

Finally Samuel lay still beside me, and I tried to sleep. Tomorrow he'd have to get to town. Maybe he could use Barrett Post's pickup again. Ben Law would know what should be done for Katie, whether she'd been abandoned, kidnapped, or whatever. Maybe he would want to talk to Edward. Almost surely he would. But I was still glad Edward hadn't stayed.

Late in the night, I woke to find Samuel shivering. It wasn't cold, not by any stretch of the word. Almost I waked him, thinking it was one of those dreams he used to have when we were first married. But I only kissed his forehead and let him sleep on, because if I woke him I thought he might not go back to sleep at all.

Slowly, quietly, I slipped to our bedroom to check on Katie again. She looked like an angel there on our bed, her dark curls spread out across the pillow. But then I noticed that her cheeks were wet. She was crying in her sleep. I gazed through the doorway toward Samuel on the sitting room floor. It seemed almost as if they were sharing something tonight. Some sadness that no one knew about but them.

I went back to my place on the quilt, thinking it might be better not to take this child to Ben Law. Who would care for her? It sounded as if her mother really did leave her, regardless of what Edward's role in that might have been. What if they couldn't find the woman? Or if she refused to take responsibility for her child, even if they did?

I lay down carefully, scooted up against Samuel, and eased my arm around him. He turned his head just a little. "Bear paws," he said. And then he was still.

"What was that?" I asked, sorry I'd waked him with my touch. But he didn't answer. He wasn't awake.

I lay there listening to his steady breaths. He knew everything about me. I'd told him what it had been like when I was a little girl, losing my mother and then my father. I'd told him about Grandpa Charlie, and especially about Grandma Pearl and all the things we used to do together. But I only knew Samuel's parents' names and that they hadn't exactly been pleasant most of the time. I'd met his mother and his cousin Dewey, the only relative he could halfway trust. But Samuel didn't tell me details. He just didn't talk about it, especially about his father or Edward.

Lord, you know. You make no mistakes, and I'm sure we've met Katie for a reason. But this is so hard for Samuel. Help him. And help us to help this little girl.

FOUR

Samuel

I woke with the dream still on me. My father. Holding me over the stair rail, shouting at my screaming mother.

Hurriedly I sat up. Juli was already started on her day, and the sun was rising outside. How could I have slept so late?

With a dull ache in my stomach, I went to the washstand and poured water from the pitcher to the basin. The water on my cheeks was cool; it felt good to wash away the night. But we still had the day to face. My brother's actions. And a scared little girl named Katie.

She was not in the bed when I peeked in. I found her and Juli together in the kitchen, stirring something in the batter bowl. I might have thought it was Sarah for size. But this girl's hair was darker, curlier. Sarah's was more like Julia's, lighter brown, straight, and beautiful.

"Robert's up already too," Juli told me. "I sent him to check the eggs."

"You should've waked me."

"It does you good to sleep in a little, Samuel. You're always up so early."

"This is not just any day."

Katie looked up at me, her sad eyes seeming filled with questions.

"Good morning," I told her.

But she didn't answer.

"I thought I'd let Sarah sleep as long as she wants," Juli continued. "But it won't be long. You know her."

"I better get the milking done."

Juli nodded. I took the milk pail and headed out to the barn. As I walked I thought on that child. She seemed to like Juli. Maybe her own mother hadn't been so warm and inviting. I certainly knew what that felt like.

Looking in on Lula Bell first, I noticed her bulging eyes, the slow breaths. "Not feeling the best anymore, are you?" I said aloud. "Hate to say it, but my brother might have been right. Might be better to end it for you than to let you go on and suffer. Guess I better ask George about it."

Lula Bell was a good cow, the first I'd ever milked. Emma's cow, Sarah still said. It wasn't a happy thought, to consider losing her. But some things are inevitable.

George would want to butcher. Save the meat. But Lula Bell might not wait till fall. I sighed, filling the feed trough, though the cow didn't show the slightest bit of interest. She didn't seem to want a drink either, or to go to pasture, though Sukey and her calf were eager. I milked as quickly as I could, but still Sukey was impatient. She didn't like standing still for me, not if she could go out and run and play like a kid.

Robert had long since taken the eggs in by the time I got done milking; he was back out at the well, filling a bucket of water for his mother.

"Can I still go fishin'?" he called to me.

"I think so. And I expect Willy to have a mind for it and probably meet you over there."

"Hope so," he said. "More fun with him there." He hurried to walk with me on the little path to the house, both of us with our buckets almost full.

Sarah stepped out on the back porch with Katie slowly following her and holding Sarah's doll. Maybe Juli had told them to play outside till breakfast. If so, I was glad. It might give me a chance to talk to Juli alone a minute. I would need to use Barrett's truck again, and now young Sam had it. I expected I'd have to walk over to Barrett's later and ask about it. I always offered him work in exchange for its use, since I couldn't fill his gas tank. And he was pretty understanding, knowing I wasn't the only one in these parts who couldn't afford an automobile.

"Dad, how come Uncle Edward didn't stay?" Robert asked.

"That's kind of a long story."

"I thought he was in prison."

"So did I."

He moved his bucket to the opposite hand and looked at me with some concern. "He didn't bust out, did he?"

"No. I suppose they let him out."

"Then he don't steal no more?"

"Let's hope not."

"Why'd he leave that girl? Is she my cousin?"

I looked to see where Sarah and Katie had gotten to. They were under the lilac bushes, safely out of earshot. "No. Robert, we don't know who she is. Or where she belongs. I'll have to take her to town today and see if I can get the sheriff to help me find out."

"Dad, that don't make no sense. Don't she know her name?"

"Yes. But we need to know where her mother is, or whatever family would be closest to her. We need to get her home, if she has a home."

"Well, why was she with Uncle Edward?"

"I don't know. I guess you'd say that what he told us didn't make any sense."

"Did he steal her?"

I'd wondered the same thing. But that didn't really fit with what Katie had said about her mother. "Probably not. I think he just happened upon someone who didn't want to take care of her anymore."

"Well, how do you know they'll want her back, then?"

"Robert." I shook my head, not wanting to think all this through. Or talk about it. "There'll be someone. Grandparents or something."

We were just approaching the porch steps when we heard the sound of Barrett Post's truck coming up the lane. I could always distinguish that tinny old Ford from what little other traffic came our way.

Young Sam pulled in quickly with Willy sitting in the front seat with him. Robert and I both set our buckets down and went to meet them.

"Still plannin' on fishin'?" Willy yelled. "I come just in case."

"It's all right," I told him. "You can go till noon."

"Get out then, Franky," Sam called.

I hadn't even seen the younger boy in the back. He climbed down and stood there silent.

"Let's get us some worms," Willy said.

"You can get started," I told Robert. "Take your mother the water first."

Robert and Willy both raced off, not waiting for Franky, and he didn't follow them.

"Pa said I ought to ride along, in case it was all right to fish," the boy said. "But if you don't mind, I'd rather be in the workshop. I got me an idea how to make a chair for Emmie Grace so she don't keep fallin' out a' the big ones."

"That sounds good," I told him. "And you're welcome to try it. But I can't promise any help. Especially not today."

"Don't want no help, if you don't mind. I'd like to see if I can do it myself."

I didn't doubt that he could. He'd helped me make two chairs and several other things. He was good with wood. Surprisingly good for his age. "Get some paper inside if you need it," I told him. "I like to draw a plan first."

"Thank you," he said. But he started straight for the workshop on the west end of the barn. I guessed he didn't need any paper.

"Your comp'ny gone so early?" Sam Hammond asked me.

"He left last night."

"Your brother?" he asked.

"Yes, he's my brother. Edward."

"Why'd he leave his girl?" he said, looking over toward the lilac bushes.

"She's not his girl."

"Oh."

Maybe I should have explained. But I didn't feel like getting into it, and he didn't ask. Sarah was climbing her doll up through the branches of the bush, and Katie just sat watching. For the first time I wondered what other people would think. That she was kin, probably. Why else would she be here?

"Sam, I'm glad you stopped by with the boys," I told him. "I need your father to come and look at Lula Bell."

"He said she weren't quite herself last night. I'll tell him."

"And if you'll wait a minute, I need to talk to Barrett Post. I'll ride along."

"Tell you what," he suggested. "You just take the truck, since you're goin' that way, and I'll walk back through the timber an' talk to Pa."

"You don't mind?"

"I figured I'd have to walk home from Post's anyhow. Not so far this way."

He got out of the truck. It almost surprised me that he didn't push for any details. His father would have asked where the girl came from. And why I had to talk to Barrett again when I was just there yesterday.

"Thanks," I told him. He only acknowledged the word with a wave and then started off toward their farm on the well-worn path our feet had made through the timber.

I went inside with the milk bucket and found Juli stirring cornmeal in a pot of water on the cookstove. Mush again. Not my favorite but passable with molasses. We had more cornmeal in the house than anything else.

She looked up at me with her tender green eyes. "Are you all right this morning?"

"Sure. And Katie seems all right. I'll need to go over to Barrett's now that I've got the truck. Maybe he won't need it today."

"That can wait till after breakfast, can't it?"

"I hate to put it off."

"Won't take me more than two minutes," she said, pulling a pan of muffins from the oven. She was baking something else, her soda bread, I guessed. There were at least two loaves in behind the muffin pan. I couldn't imagine my mother baking so early or so happily, especially if someone had just left off a child at her doorstep.

"Sammy," Julia asked suddenly, "what's 'bear paws'? I mean, other than the paws of a bear?"

I stared at her. To anyone but me or my cousin Dewey, that question would sound utterly ridiculous. How could Julia know about it?

"You were talking in your sleep," she told me, reaching for my hand. "But that's all you said."

"Just a password. Just a dumb thing."

"Tell me about it."

"Julia, it doesn't mean anything. Dewey and I, we used to run off to play alone sometimes. It was just a signal we used. I'd say 'bear paws,' and he'd know it was me coming, or he'd leave me a sign, and I'd know to meet him as soon as I could. We played Indian. It was part of the game."

She smiled. "I wish you'd talk about those things more."

"Not much point."

"Robby'd like to hear it."

I didn't reply, and she turned to face me. "I thought you might have been dreaming."

I nodded. But I didn't answer. I still remembered the dream. I was running for our secret spot. A temporary refuge.

"Sammy, I talk about Grandma Pearl all the time. All the things we used to do when I was little. I guess you know all there is to know about it. But you only mention Dewey once in a while. And you never talk about Edward. Or anybody else."

"I've got enough to think about with who's around here now."

"Yes. But—" She stopped, hearing Robert's footsteps on the porch.

He and Willy ran in the house. Surely they hadn't found enough worms yet.

"Mom, can we just go? We can dig around the pond for worms and catch grasshoppers and stuff."

"Wait two minutes and you can have some good breakfast first."

Willy took a strong whiff of Juli's muffins, even reached his hand for one, but they were still hot. "We can take some of these if you don't mind."

"All right," Juli relented. "I'll wrap a few in a towel for you. You'd better go get Franky."

"Ahhh . . ." Willy protested. "He won't catch nothin'."

Juli shook her head. "Willy, if he wants to go—"

"He doesn't," I told her. "He wants to stay in the workshop. I said he could put together an idea he has."

"Gee, thanks!" Willy exclaimed, as though I had done him a favor.

Juli wrapped some of the hot muffins in a dish towel and gave them to Willy. Robert grabbed his fishing pole from a hook in the back of the pantry, and they were out the door as fast as they could go. If eagerness counted for anything, maybe they'd catch aplenty.

"I need to go too," I told Juli again. "I'll just walk back if Barrett needs his truck. But if I can get to town this morning, I'll be back for Katie pretty soon."

"Sit down, and I'll feed you first. It's ready. You want eggs?"

"No. Give 'em to the kids."

She turned and looked at me. "The biggest eaters just left. It's just the little girls. And Franky, if he wants anything."

I always hated to eat the eggs. She might need them for baking. Or for somebody else. But she was trying to bless me, and I guessed I ought to let her. "I'll take a couple, then."

She leaned over and kissed me.

"What was that for?"

"Just because."

I reached for her hand. "Thank you. For being so good about this."

"I only wish you weren't so uncomfortable."

"I'm fine."

She turned toward the stove again and gave the mush another stir. "Was it a bad dream you had? Was it about Edward?"

For a moment, I closed my eyes. I would never have mentioned it. Not in a hundred years. And I really didn't want to talk about it. But she was asking, and I could hardly refuse to answer. "You really want to know?"

"Of course."

I stretched my hands out on the table in front of me, wishing I had something to busy them with while I sat. I looked away from her, out the window at the swaying branches of our old maple, thinking suddenly of the eagle tattoo my father'd been so proud of. It had always seemed to be looking at us when that arm was upraised.

"It wasn't Edward, Juli. It was my father. Hitting Mother. I got in the way, and he grabbed me. I thought he was going to throw me over the stair rail."

She turned away from the stove and put her spoon down, but I kept talking.

"When I got out of there, I ran to find Dewey. He was hiding, and I had to signal him. Then we disappeared until dark, when his parents started calling him. Mine were too drunk by then to care, and I just stayed outside."

She knelt in front of me. "Sammy—"

"I've got to get going, Juli. I better eat."

"It really happened, didn't it?"

"A lot of things happened."

"Where was Edward?"

I just shook my head. "I don't know. Lots of times I didn't know. You want me to call the kids in?"

"Yes. In a minute." She put her arms around me, and it felt so good that I pulled her onto my lap and just held on.

"What do we do, Juli, if it takes a while to find Katie's people, and Ben Law doesn't have a place to put her?"

She smiled at my change of subject. "She can stay here, Sammy, if you're comfortable with that. I'm sure she'd rather."

"Do you want to go into town with me, in case Edward comes back?"

She looked surprised that I would ask. "I'm not afraid of him. And there's a lot of work to do here. Besides, we don't want to be dragging kids into something like this."

"I guess you're right. And I don't really expect him. It's just with Edward, you never know."

"He was a thief. Right? He didn't hurt anyone?"

"Not that I know of. At least none that weren't trying to hurt him. He got in a lot of fights."

"We'll be fine, Samuel. Besides, if I came along, we'd have to take Franky back home and tell Robert and Willy to go that way for lunch in case we're not back. And then there's Sarah. I wouldn't want to leave them all on Lizbeth. She's got her hands full now."

She got up to serve the food, and I went out to call the kids. Franky wouldn't hear me clear in the workshop, so I started in that direction, calling to the girls at the same time. But Sarah didn't move. For a moment I didn't even see Katie, half-buried under the lilacs, her head in her hands.

"Daddy!" Sarah yelled. "Come here, Daddy!"

I went quickly. Katie raised her head to look at me with her teary, puffy eyes, but she didn't say a word. The poor child had been crying.

"This girl says you're her daddy," Sarah told me. "But I told her you're not *her* daddy. You're *my* daddy."

"Sarah. She's been told a lot of things. We can be considerate."

Katie stared up at me, her little lip quivering. I hadn't thought enough about how she might be handling things this morning. I hadn't taken the time. "Sarah, go on in the house. We'll be in in a minute."

"I wasn't tryin' to be mean," she explained. "I like her real good."

"I know, honey, and it's okay. But go on inside, all right? And get Franky from the workshop if he wants to eat anything."

She went, though she didn't want to. Katie kept looking at me, sitting on her knees with her hands clenched together in her lap.

"Would you mind coming out of the bush a little?" I asked her. "I won't fit under there as well as you do."

She didn't move.

"I didn't mean to hurt your feelings. Neither did Sarah. We're sorry."

She wiped at her eyes with one little fist and spoke very softly. "Why don't you want me?"

Lord! I sat down in the grass beside the bushes. "Come here. Come closer."

She eased out just a little, and I took a deep breath.

"It's not that I don't want you. If you were really mine, I'd be proud. You're a good girl, I can see that. But it's just not possible that you're my child. I never heard of your mother till last night. Robert and Sarah are the only children I've got."

She sniffed and came out a little farther. "Maybe you just didn't know."

"I would know, honey. A man knows these things."

"Do you want me to go away? You didn't want me to go with Mr. Eddie—"

"Eddie wasn't very good to you. And you're welcome to stay here as long as you need to. But we need to go to town today if we can, you and me, and talk to a man who can help us find your mother."

"I don't think Mama would want that. She said I wasn't gonna live with her no more."

I took her hand. "Maybe you won't, if she feels that way. Maybe you shouldn't. Do you have other relatives?"

Her eyes teared up all over again. "Mr. Eddie's my uncle. And you're . . . you're—"

"No. I'm sorry, honey, but I'm not your daddy. You're a very strong little girl, and I respect that. But I can't help what my brother told you. Ed Wortham isn't somebody you can trust all the time—"

"But he didn't say it! My mama said it!"

Her words shook me. I'd assumed that Edward must have just cooked up these "daddy" ideas.

"Mama told him, but first he didn't believe her. He said you wouldn't. But Mama told him my daddy is Samuel Wortham! And she's told me that before, lots a' times. But I never thought I'd see you—"

She stopped, shaking just a little. And I felt sorry for the child, despite the bizarre story she was telling.

"Come here."

She crawled into my arms. I held her, and she clung to me the way she had last night.

"My wife said it might be something like this," I whispered. "Unbelievable, I know. But there must be another Samuel Wortham out there somewhere. And he doesn't know what he's missing."

"But Eddie says I look like you."

It was strange to hear her calling him that. Edward had never liked being called Eddie. He'd hit me once when I'd dared to call him that after hearing another kid say it. But maybe he'd done some changing, after all. Maybe he was just part of a misunderstanding now, as Julia had suggested. But that didn't excuse him entirely.

"I'm sorry he was rough to you," I told her.

"He wasn't so bad as some a' Mama's boyfriends. George Call, he was the worstest."

"Your mother and you—did you have a house?"

"No, sir. We was travelin' too much. And that's why

Mama give me up. She said she could travel better without me, an' Eddie ought to bring me to find you."

"That's pretty much what he told me."

"He said you'd be mad."

"I was. At him."

"But it wasn't his fault."

"I guess not."

She leaned her head against my shoulder. "Can't I stay here? You're bein' nice. And . . . and maybe you just forgot me or somethin'. You sure look like that picture Mama showed me once."

"What picture?" I felt my heart jump in my chest.

"Mama had a picture of my daddy. In a park in Pennsa-vay-na."

I shook my head. This couldn't be real. At least I was sure I'd never been photographed in a park. Not know-ingly. "Did Edward see this picture?"

"I don't think so. I think it got lost when Mama's bag got stole one time in Newark."

"You've been very helpful," I told her. "You're a bright girl."

My insides were churning. How could this be? The only thing I could think of was my father. Another Samuel. He'd left us when I was very young, showing up from time to time and making trouble until I was about eight. Then we never saw him again. We never knew what he did, where he went, until he died when I was twelve. Maybe I had another brother somewhere. Maybe more than one. But would he give another child the same name?

"Let's eat," I suggested. "What do you say?"

She was looking up at me, her dark eyes still misty with tears. Juli was right. Edward was right. She looked like me. What was Ben Law going to think?

"I wished you knew about me," she whispered. "I wished you wanted me to be your little girl."

What could I do? She'd already heard me say it wasn't

so. She just didn't believe it. I held her for a minute, dried her eyes with my kerchief. It was too bad that picture had been lost. I would've liked to have seen it for myself.

Katie laid her head against my shoulder, holding tight to my shirt. She'd already lost her mother, maybe for good. But I wasn't her father. Someone, somewhere, knew the truth.

Carefully I stood up and set her down beside me. Breakfast was waiting. We had the day to face. I took her hand and started for the house.

FIVE

Julia

It scared me the way Samuel looked when he brought Katie into the kitchen. Not like the Samuel I knew. It was because of Edward. And Katie being here. Somehow it was stirring things in him I wasn't sure I understood.

He ate quickly and hardly said a word. Katie was just as solemn, glancing up at me from time to time, her eyes never losing their almost-tears. She wanted to stay. I knew she wanted to stay. Maybe she had good reason not to want to go back.

"Thanks for the milk and the muffin," Franky spoke up. "I wanna get back to that chair. I think it's gonna be real nice, but I'm only jus' gettin' started."

"Got everything you need?" Samuel asked.

"I think so. If you'll let me the nails."

"Don't have many small ones, but you can use what's there." Samuel shoveled a bite of eggs into his mouth and glanced at the cuckoo clock on the wall. "Be careful sawing," he told Franky. "Especially if anybody comes in the shop to look."

"Yes, sir."

Samuel took a last drink of coffee and got up from the table. "I'll be back before long, one way or another, Juli."

"Samuel . . ."

He barely glanced my way. "What?"

I didn't know what to say. Not in front of the children. "I love you."

He only stopped for a moment. "Thanks. That's quite a gift."

Then he was gone. And after looking at poor Katie's face, I found myself almost hoping Barrett couldn't part with the truck. It would be wrenching for her if Samuel had to just leave her in town, but the sheriff might suggest it. Maybe he knew a place for children in a situation like this. But would that be the right thing?

I sat for a moment, looking at the door.

"Where'd Mr. Wortham's brother go?" Franky asked out of the blue.

"I don't know. He just had to go."

"They don't seem much alike."

"No." I sighed. "They don't."

"Think me an' Willy's that differ'nt?"

"Oh, Franky, I don't know. It's not the same thing."

"We're born differ'nt," he said. "But then we choose differ'nt too."

I just looked at him. Thank God Samuel had chosen different. Thank God.

"Guess I better get started," Franky said cheerfully. "I wanna have somethin' to show by the time Mr. Wortham gets back." He stood up with a grin, reached his hat from a hook by the door, and then tipped it to Katie. "Was good t' meet ya," he said. "But I gotta get busy."

"Bye," she whispered, looking down at the dishes in front of her.

Sarah was picking hers up to carry to the dishpan. "Mommy, can we make ice cream today?"

"Oh, honey, we haven't the ice or near enough salt."

"Maybe Daddy could get some."

"No. Your daddy has too many other things to do." I never told her we couldn't afford such a luxury, even homemade. Robert would have understood that. But even he didn't know we were penniless.

"Blackberries is good too," she said. "Can we pick blackberries?"

"They're not quite ready yet, honey, but it'll be soon. There may be a few more raspberries, but I don't know if we'll get to them today. Let's get everything else done."

"Like what? What are we gonna do?"

"I've got plenty of garden work. And wash to do. Thank goodness I got the bread in the oven before the worst heat."

"I gotta play with this new girl," Sarah told me, as if it were a solemn duty.

"I understand that. But you can both help me. It'll be more fun that way."

"I like washin' in the summertime," she told Katie. "'Cause it's okay to get wet, an' you don't get cold."

Katie didn't answer her.

With Sarah's help, I cleared the rest of the dishes and washed them with some of the water I'd left on the stove to heat. The kitchen was already so warm I thought I'd let the fire go out and cook dinner and supper outside.

When the other dishes were done, I spread the leftover mush in a loaf pan to set. It would be good fried with the little bit of canned sausage we had left on the pantry shelf. For a moment, thoughts of those sparse shelves pinched my insides a little, but I shook away the worry. *The Lord will provide. He always has before. That's in his hands, and I've got other things to think about.*

I wasn't sure I should put Katie to working right along with us, but I knew no other way to do but just carry on with what was at hand. So I lugged the two big tubs out around the side of the house and got Franky to help me carry some of the water, because the buckets were too heavy for the little girls. I brought out warm water from the stove inside and let Franky draw from the well for the rinse. Then he went back to his woodwork, and I grated some of Alberta Mueller's lye soap and started dunking clothes in the tub.

Katie tried her best on the scrub board after watching Sarah and me. She seemed to like Emma's turn-crank ringer. We did all the dirty clothes I could find. Even Katie's. I put her in a jumper of Sarah's, since Edward had gotten off with her change of clothes as well as her dolls.

I let them run and play in the yard while I hung everything on the clothesline. It was a peaceful day, bright and sunny. I prayed that Samuel was peaceful too.

George came in his wagon before I had all the wash up. He had young Sam with him, and they went in the barn without a word to me. Samuel hadn't told me anything, but I surmised they were here to look at Lula Bell. I knew she'd been eating less. And hadn't given us milk for some time. Would George want to butcher? Surely not at this time of year. But she was already thinner, and by fall, there might be nothing left.

He came up from the barn with his slow steps. "She don't look good, that's sure," he said. "Samuel here?"

"He's not back yet from the Posts'."

"You tell him I was here and there ain't much we can do for that cow. May as well put her down, hot as it is. I'll ask Post if he can come one day next week to give us a hand. Lizbeth can help you do some cannin'. That way, there'll be some gain at least."

I hated the thought of losing Lula Bell. And using the meat was far from appealing, but George was practical about such things. We had to use what we could. His pantry was getting as bare as ours, and I knew he was right.

"I'll tell him."

"I'll be to the north field, if he gets time to work 'longside us today. But I'll unnerstand if he don't."

He was walking away toward the well, where Sarah had stopped to get a drink. Katie was standing there with her when he came up. He turned his eyes to her, and she backed up a step.

"What's your name, little girl?"

"Katie Wortham."

George glanced over at me for a second with a strange look on his face. "That so? Well, you're a purty little girl. Enjoy your visit."

He didn't say anything else, just turned back toward his team and wagon and went on his way.

I hadn't known Katie's last name was Wortham. I'd just assumed it would be Vale, like her mother. Was she just saying that now, because she was still trying to claim Samuel? Of course, people would think she was Edward's child, because of the name and because he'd brought her. And the poor girl might not really have a clue who she was.

I finished hanging what I could on our clothesline and draped one bedsheet over a bush. I wondered if Lizbeth had managed to get her washing done. The Hammonds always had so much, with ten kids and one of them a baby. Of course, I did some of theirs here, but there was still an awful lot on Lizbeth. I thought maybe I should walk over there later in the day and see if she could use some help.

Sarah and Katie agreed to help me pick the first green beans, so I got three bowls and we started in. Katie was so quiet as we worked. Maybe she didn't like the work but was too polite to say so. If she thought me hard, making her lend a hand, maybe she wouldn't want to stay here after all.

But what was keeping Samuel? He'd had more than enough time to walk back from Posts by now if he couldn't use the truck. Maybe Barrett had hired his help with something extra. I could hope. It had been months since that had happened.

Before we were done picking, though, Samuel came up the lane, truck and all. "He had hay for Joe Porter," he explained. "I helped him load and haul it to get the job done quicker."

Katie stood very still, trying hard not to cry.

I took her hand. "Samuel, this is going to be hard for her. Facing strangers again, for one thing."

He nodded. "Maybe I wouldn't go today, except she might have a grandma or somebody somewhere worried sick not knowing where she is. We've got to think about that too. Even if her mother's walked away, there might be someone else."

I knew he was right. But poor Katie. She must feel like both her mother and her father were rejecting her. She sat on the porch step quiet as a daisy while I packed the leftover muffins and a few fresh carrots in a brown paper sack for them to take along. Samuel was ready to go, to get this over with, but I made him wait a minute longer as I ran in our bedroom to get the three little yarn dolls Katie had left on our pillow.

When I came back out, she was still just sitting there. Sarah had come and put her arm around her shoulders.

I sat at Katie's other side and placed the little dolls in her hand. "You can keep these," I told her. "We have more."

She looked up at me and sniffed. "I don't wanna go."

"It'll be all right. All you have to do is talk to Mr. Law, answer his questions the best that you can, and then do what he says. You can do that, can't you?"

She nodded. "Will I see you again?"

"I don't know, sweetie. The Lord knows."

Samuel walked away from us to the truck. I knew he felt bad. But it wasn't his fault. He was right. She might have worried kin someplace. And if she did, we had to find a way to get them together.

"Maybe Daddy could decide to be her daddy too," Sarah whispered. "I wouldn't mind to have a sister."

I shouldn't have been surprised. Sarah liked everybody. But we couldn't just claim Katie. Something like that wouldn't be as easy as Sarah made it sound.

I took Katie's hand and gently led her away from the porch. "Right now, it's time to get to town and get business taken care of. Sarah, run and get Katie's clothes off the line. They'll dry quick enough in the truck if they're not already."

Katie was sitting on the truck seat, clutching those yarn dolls and staring back at me when they drove away. I felt cold and cruel inside. She'd come all the way from Albany, New York, thinking she had a new home. But now she had nothing at all except Sarah's jumper and the "real family" of yarn dolls she was holding in her hand. Maybe I should have told Samuel to bring her back if they couldn't find her someone like the grandma I'd had to make everything all right again.

SIX

Samuel

Katie didn't cry, didn't move at all. For the whole ride to town, she sat and stared straight ahead, not saying a word. A couple of times I tried to assure her that the sheriff was a nice man and she didn't need to be scared. But I knew that wasn't her worry. What would happen after we talked to the sheriff? Even I didn't know that.

In Dearing, we stopped in front of what had been the dry goods store a few months ago. Now it was boarded up like so many other businesses in town. Ben Law kept his office across the street, right next to the bank, which was also closed. On the rest of the block, only Blume's Milk Station and the Feed and Seed were still open.

Down the street I could see Herman Meyer's car in front of his aunt Hazel Sharpe's house. I hoped she was napping.

It had never been particularly pleasant to encounter her on a trip to town.

I helped Katie out of the truck. She was still holding those yarn dolls so tightly that her knuckles were white. But she didn't say anything. I held her other hand as we crossed the street.

Sheriff Law had a cowbell tied to his doorknob, but he didn't look up despite its clank. He was reading the Mt. Vernon newspaper, and after several minutes, he finally glanced our way over a headline saying something about candidate Roosevelt.

"Well, good morning," he smiled. "You're Wortham, aren't you?"

"Yes, sir," I answered, not surprised that he would know me. Hazel Sharpe had approached him when we first came here, telling him we were trying to trick Emma Graham out of her possessions. Emma herself had set all that straight.

"What can I do for you today?" He set the paper down, and before I could answer, he was asking another question. "This your little girl?"

"No, sir. That's why I've come."

I did my best to relate the whole story to him. Everything Edward had said, and everything Katie had told us. The sheriff just sat, eyeing the girl and nodding.

When I finished and asked him if there wasn't a way he could find her relatives, he leaned back in his chair and smiled. "I never heard you deny bein' from Pennsylvania."

"I am. At least we lived there a while. Harrisburg. But—"

He rocked forward. "Now, if your own brother was convinced, and the mother of the child—"

"Sheriff Law, if she was telling the truth, there has to be another Samuel Wortham."

He laughed. "And the spittin' image of ya, to boot."

"I don't know about that . . ." I could feel a surge of heat down my spine. He didn't believe me. How could I get him to understand?

He sighed. "Well, Wortham. I wouldn't a' thought faced with somethin' head on, you'd still be buckin', but some folks are like that."

I could feel my shoulders tighten, the heat rising in me. "I told you the truth, Sheriff. I never met the woman."

"No doubt you never met her kin, I'll grant you that." He shook his head. "You're in a spot, I know, already havin' kids to raise and this being sprung on you sudden. I'll do what I can to find a relative of the mother, but only 'cause I agree with you that they might not know what she's gone off and done. If it was my granddaughter hauled across the countryside, I'd want somebody to tell me."

He turned his face to Katie, who stood quietly beside me, watching him. "Tell me, sugar. This Mr. Wortham, here. He been treatin' you all right?"

Almost I said something, but I knew it wouldn't help my case any in his eyes.

Katie nodded her head and reached her little hand to mine again. "He's nice. And Mrs. Wortham is nice too. I like 'em plenty good."

"Well. I'm relieved to hear that. Right decent of the missus, especially. Wouldn't you say so, Samuel?"

It chafed me, what I saw in his eyes. Convinced of my guilt, he was taking me for a scoundrel. But I couldn't argue. If he truly searched the matter, he'd find out I was telling the truth, I was sure of it. "Julia's a wonderful woman, Sheriff Law," I agreed. "I'm blessed to have her."

"Well, then, I won't need to be concerned over leaving the child in your care. Your brother brung her to you, and the way I see it, she's your responsibility, 'less some other kin comes forward askin' for her."

"Sheriff Law—"

He held up his hand. "I don't see no reason to use the gas to get her to the orphanage, nor for them spending the upkeep when she's got a decent arrangement with kin." He turned to Katie. "You been told this man's kin, ain't that so?"

Katie nodded.

"See what I mean? These things happen, Samuel. Ain't an action in this world that don't bear consequences."

I took a deep breath. "I don't object to keeping her. She's already spent one night, and it might be easier for her not to spend the next one with a whole new set of strangers. If we can help for a while, that's fine. But let me describe my brother to you, in the chance you might see him. Maybe he could tell us something more. Maybe Miss Vale might have told him something about her family—"

"Didn't she tell you anything?"

I swallowed hard, careful to restrain the fire I was feeling. "No, sir. I've never spoken to her."

He smiled. "This is interesting."

He asked Katie some more questions—about me, my brother, her mother, and anyone else she could remember. There was a grandmother, we found out. Trudy Vale's mother. But Katie only recalled seeing her once when she was very little, and they'd been in so many towns since then that she didn't know where the woman lived.

Sheriff Law wrote a few things down. Then he lifted his eyes to me. "What about your mother?"

The question took me completely by surprise. "What do you mean?"

"I mean, is she still living? Would she take in this little girl if you and your wife decide that you . . . uh . . . just can't deal with it?"

I could feel a fiery rush of protest flooding my insides. How could he suggest such a thing? "She has nothing to do with this, and I wouldn't send a child to her home, anyway."

He raised one eyebrow. "Why not? What's the matter with her?"

I took a breath. I wished he hadn't asked. But I might as well tell him the truth. "The last I knew, Sheriff, she was drunk every chance she got. Her husband, my stepfather, owns a speakeasy in Albany. The liquor flowed through there like a river before the prohibition, and he bragged to me once that he knew sources the government didn't and his business would never be dry."

"You told the local officials about this?"

"No. I didn't have any proof, and the government was already watching him. Almost shut him down, but he was serving food and setting up entertainment and they couldn't find any liquor on the place. I don't know what he does with it." Quick as a jumping flame, it occurred to me that Edward might have met Trudy Vale right there in the speakeasy. Why hadn't I thought of it before? Maybe Mother and Jimmy knew her.

The sheriff was looking me over pretty straight. "Would've figured you to come from a Christian home, Wortham. But you're saying your mother's a drunk and your father's a cheat."

"My stepfather. My father's dead."

"Think I should have run you out of town when you first come?"

"You didn't have reason."

He smiled. "Well, you don't fly off the handle at me, anyway. Got to give you credit for that."

I told him where my stepfather's establishment was, and where he and my mother lived, in case they could tell us anything about Trudy Vale. But I wondered if it had done much good to come. The sheriff had almost nothing to go on in his search. And he thought me pretty ignorant and calloused, I'm sure, as though I were trying to lie my way out of an obligation.

Before we left, he promised Katie he'd try to find her

grandmother. But he didn't promise me anything at all. And he left me no choice but to take Katie back home with me. Of course, she was all right with that; but I wondered if it was really best for her. The closer she attached herself to me and to Julia, the harder it would be for her when the time came for her to go.

I crossed the street, holding Katie's hand again. It was getting sticky hot. Sweat had my shirt damp already, and I wished I had money in my pocket to buy the girl an ice cream and take something home to Julia and the rest.

At least Julia wouldn't be upset about me bringing the child back. She'd almost expected it. And I didn't know how to insist on anything different.

We were nearly to the truck when Hazel Sharpe and her nephew rounded the corner by the Feed and Seed, evidently on their way home from somewhere. I groaned inside, hoping they didn't see us. Or at least didn't pay us any attention.

But Hazel headed straight in my direction just as fast as she could walk. I didn't want to listen to her today. I didn't want her putting one word in on all this.

"Well, Mr. Wortham!" she was calling. "You with Barrett's truck again! I declare you drive it more'n he does. Is he gettin' rent?"

"I help him when he needs it, Miss Sharpe," I acknowledged with a sigh. "We have an agreement."

"Well, that's neither here nor there," she breezed on. "But I better tell you what Ella Cole says. Somewhere our pastor's wife got the cockamamy notion that your Juli can start up a church choir. And she didn't even come to me about it! Me, the piano player!"

"I'm sure she consulted her husband, Miss Hazel." I couldn't help smiling a little at her ridiculous conceit. As if no one was supposed to do anything without consulting her first.

She crossed her arms impatiently. "I want you to tell that wife a' yours that our church ain't had a choir for forty years, and if it ever has one again, they'll have to have my help! There's no sense her even startin' otherwise. Loretta Crenshaw lef' me in charge a' the music when she was on her deathbed, and I'm the only one knows how to go about such a thing, anyhow."

"As far as I know, Juli knows nothing about this yet."

"That's why I'm tellin' you! Ain't you listenin'? You tell her that when Juanita Jones comes around, she needs to come and talk to me. How they gonna have a choir without the piano player? I never heard a' such a thing!"

I smiled at her. "Are Pastor and Mrs. Jones at home? Maybe you need to discuss this with them yourself."

"If she don't have the courtesy to come to me, I ain't gonna darken their door!" Miss Hazel huffed. "It's not my job to go runnin' over there every time they don't think somethin' through! You just tell Juli to tell her she can't be goin' around steppin' on toes like this. There's got to be order in a church! When you got music already put in place, you don't go shovin' it aside to start up somethin' else with somebody who don't know what they're doin'. An' Juli don't know what she's doin'! She's never led no choir, has she?"

"No, ma'am. She hasn't," I said, trying to step past her toward the truck.

"See what I mean? It's the confoundest thing I ever heard! What is that Juanita thinkin', anyhow?"

I tipped my hat. "Miss Hazel, I really must be going. But I'll tell my wife what you said." I wondered what Juli would think. I could imagine a shrug of her shoulders, her quiet smile. She knew Miss Hazel better than I did, and handled her better than anybody I knew. Since Emma Graham, at least.

"I hope you tell her. Don't be forgettin'." She stopped, suddenly staring down at Katie. "Now, look here. This ain't George Hammond's girl."

I winced inside. "No, ma'am—"

"It ain't your Sarah neither. I'd know her 'cause she looks like her mama. So who are you, child? Speak up! What's your name?"

Taken by surprise, Katie backed up a step, squeezing my hand. I didn't blame her for being scared. This bent old lady was formidable, even for grown-ups. But the child managed to get her head together enough to whisper her name. "Katie. Katie Wortham."

"Wortham, you say?" Hazel's head shot up. "What kin is she?" she demanded. "I never heard tell of this!"

I wanted to tell her Katie was my brother's, or just make something up and tell her anything. But I couldn't lie. And just to say he brought her wouldn't be enough. I sighed, thinking on how many people would hear about this now and the kind of twist Hazel Sharpe might put on my words. "Miss Hazel, I'm not sure if she's kin. We're hoping to find out."

"What kind of riddle is that? Wouldn't you know if somebody's kin? Normal folks would!"

I could only sigh again. "We need to go."

But Hazel wouldn't let me by so easily. "You're hidin' something! Sure as I'm alive!" She grabbed Katie's arm, making the poor girl jump. "Who's your daddy, girl? You can tell me. You must know who your people is. Who's your daddy, girl?"

Little Katie shook, and tears welled up in her eyes. She looked at me, and the tears started to fall. "I don't know."

"You don't know!" Miss Hazel exclaimed. "My, oh my! What do you mean—"

"That's enough!" I surprised myself, being that abrupt. But Miss Hazel had no business talking to a child that way.

No matter what she'd think of me, I wouldn't have it. I picked Katie up, out of Hazel's grasp. "She's staying with us for a while, until we find her family," I explained. "That's all there is to it. I'll give my wife your message."

I set Katie in the truck, and Miss Hazel stood there and watched as I climbed in too. Herman gave me a sheepish sort of nod. I always wondered what he thought of his aunt's ravings.

"There's something mighty strange about this," Hazel declared.

"Maybe so," I told her. "But if a child came your way, you'd have to help her, wouldn't you? That's what we're doing, and we'll do our best." I started the truck.

"You're a strange one, Sam Wortham."

I tipped my hat. "Have a good day." Then I backed away from the curb and drove off. Julia always said the best way to handle Miss Hazel was to be as sweet as possible. I didn't figure I'd been that, but at least she wouldn't be able to say I wasn't civil.

I called my mother's building from the telephone at Charlie Hunter's service station. I didn't know what to say about all this, only that I needed to ask her myself if she or Jimmy knew anything about Trudy Vale, and to let them know our sheriff might be asking too. I had to wait a long time while the gentleman downstairs went up to see if she was in. And when my mother finally came, she sounded awful. She said she didn't know who I was talking about and it wasn't right for me to give the sheriff their names. We didn't talk long. We never did.

Charlie didn't charge me for the telephone call. The sun was getting high, but Katie wasn't hungry and neither was I, so I traded Juli's muffins with Charlie for a little gas. Maybe someday Barrett would tell Miss Hazel that I hadn't brought his truck home empty.

SEVEN

Julia

Sarah and I were snapping the beans for dinner when we heard the roar of an automobile coming up the road. Samuel, I hoped. I wasn't expecting anybody else. But I looked up to see Edward's roofless old car coming up our lane and nearly dropped the bean bowl. I should've listened to Samuel's concerns. Now what was I to do?

I stood as he parked his car across Emma's golden irises. He jumped out, waving his hand as if I'd be thrilled to see him.

"Samuel at home?"

"No. But he'll be home pretty soon."

He started in my direction. "I didn't mean to cause you no trouble last night."

I didn't answer. I couldn't figure out why he'd come back. I would've thought he'd be glad just to move on once he'd gotten Katie to us and had a chance to make Samuel uncomfortable.

"Can you spare me something to drink? Gettin' mighty parched on this dusty road."

I handed Sarah my bowl of green beans and told her to take them inside and stay. "I hope water from the well's all right," I said to him, heading toward the bucket and dipper.

"Still don't have no lemonade?" he asked with a smile.

"No. Nor anything else, unless you want some strawberry leaf tea. Or coffee again, but we're almost to the last of that."

"I never heard of strawberry leaf tea," he said, coming closer. "That something you make yourself?"

"Yes. You want some?" I didn't want to refuse anyone a drink. It wouldn't be right. But he was making me more and more uncomfortable, just looking at me, just walking in my direction. I wished Samuel were home, or even Robert or one of George's big boys.

"I'll take the water, thanks," he said. "Don't know about that leaf stuff." He laughed. "I ain't used to such potions."

I hurried to the well, drew a bucket of fresh, cool water. He was at my side by the time I was done, and I handed him the brimming dipper.

He drank the water down quickly and filled the dipper twice more. "Boy! That sure is good!" He poured one dipperful over his head, shook like a wet dog, and then laughed when I stepped back from his splatters. "You don't know what to make of me, do you? Ah, Mrs. Wortham, I don't know what Sammy told you, but I just love the simple things, sort of like yourself."

"Why did you come back?"

"I needed a drink, just like I said. Don't know anybody else around here."

"Anybody would give you a drink. That's common decency. You could ask anywhere."

"Yeah, but I'll have to admit—we're family, you know. Never got a chance to know you before."

I started walking to the garden, thinking it best to show him I was busy.

"How's Katie getting along? Didn't see her when I pulled in. Sammy didn't go and give her up to no county people, did he?"

I started pulling turnips, every other one to give the rest more growing space.

"Must be hard for you, finding out the kind of thing your Sammy was up to."

That did it. I could abide his presence if I needed to. I could put up with a lot. But not his ugly accusations. "Samuel was up to nothing except being a good father! You're wasting your breath talking otherwise, because I'll not believe it."

He just laughed again. "That's pretty naïve, now, don't you think?" He squatted down in the turnip row in front of me.

I scooped up all the turnips I'd pulled and turned away from him toward the well.

"I heard tell you were friendly," he said to my back. "But you're not being too friendly at the moment."

I stopped and turned to face him. "What do you expect me to be? You come back with nothing but ill words about my husband. What do you want? He's caused you no trouble. A brotherly visit is one thing, but this is something else!"

"But it is a brotherly visit. First chance I've had." He shook his head. "You know, I didn't want to believe it either, but what else are we gonna do? How would some singer woman get his name? Answer me that! How would she be able to tell me the state he was living in at the time, if he never met her?"

I looked down at the turnips. "It's just someone else."

"With the same name? And he happens to look like Sammy too, huh? She described him to me, and you can see him for yourself in that little girl's face!"

I remembered what Samuel had asked me—why is Edward enjoying this so much? I didn't know. But it was making my head swim and my heart hurt. "Why did you come here? Just to see what he'd say? Or how I'd react? Why are you so glad to be bringing such a claim? Why are you laughing about it?"

For a moment his eyes were cold, and I wished I hadn't asked. I didn't know this man. He wasn't like Samuel. There was no way I could predict him from one moment to the next.

Finally he answered, looking somehow distant. And his words came out with bitterness. "Sammy's a good boy. I used to hear that, you know, all the time. But he was a scared little nothing who ran and hid every time Mother got drunk. I took care of him. I went and stole stuff so there'd be something in the house for him to eat. But I'm the bad one. I'm sure you've heard that. I'm trouble. But he's the Christian, isn't he? Maybe I came just to teach you a lesson. He's not so good after all. We're just alike, him and me. Except he's livin' a lie."

My heart was pounding at my insides. "If you really knew him, you couldn't say that."

"I know him better than anybody."

"No. You haven't seen him in—"

"Fifteen years, Missus."

"Then you must know a lot has happened in that time."

He took a step toward me. "Yeah, you happened."

Quick as anything, he reached and put his hand on my arm. At first I didn't know what to do. But then without another thought, I pulled away, plopped the turnips at the base of the well, and grasped the dipper in my hand.

"Am I making you nervous, Missus?"

"You should have a seat under a shade tree," I told him. "Sit and wait. Samuel will be along before you know it."

"You hope so, you mean."

"Of course I hope so! His brother's here, needing to be taught a thing or two about how to conduct himself!"

He laughed. "You're pretty. Even prettier when you're upset. Sammy's lucky. You wouldn't think to attach yourself to anyone else, now would you?"

For a moment I just stared at him. How dare he say such things! Usually I could be just as pleasant as you please. But Edward Wortham had crossed the line. Without a word, I dunked the dipper full and flung the cold spray in his face.

He stepped back in surprise and then shook his shaggy head the way he'd done before. Out of the corner of my eye, I saw movement by the barn. Little Franky coming out with a hammer in his hand. Thank God for him.

"Mrs. Wortham!" the little boy called. "Wanna come see the chair I'm workin' on? Shapin' up to be somethin'!" He stopped short and looked at the tall, wet stranger. I'm sure he remembered Samuel's brother. But I could see the distrust in his eyes just the same.

"Yes, Franky, I'll be glad to see it," I told him. "I'll come right now."

I didn't know if Edward would follow me or leave. Or maybe even wait under a shade tree like I'd suggested. But he did none of those things. When I turned toward the barn, he started for the house. Franky noticed as soon as I did.

"Where are you goin'?" he asked.

"Thought I'd help myself to—"

"Nope," Franky interrupted. "If you want somethin', you should ask polite. Otherwise, you hadn't ought to be comin' 'round, 'specially goin' in the house nor botherin' Mrs. Wortham, 'less Mr. Wortham's here."

Edward looked at me. "So who's this spunky kid?"

"Franky." I put my hand on the boy's shoulder.

And Edward stared him in the eye. "I never seen the like for unfriendliness. All I wanted was a bite to eat."

"Did you ask?" Franky looked up at me, as though he might not trust Edward's answer.

"No, I didn't ask," Edward said impatiently. "Ain't it your place to offer?"

Franky crossed his skinny arms, hammer and all. "I don't know. Mrs. Wortham, ought we give him anything?"

I didn't want to. But Emma had fed even the tramps who came around. And somehow or another, this character was my husband's brother.

So I let him sit at our table again. I didn't have anything ready, or my fire lit yet for cooking. But I opened the last jar of peaches, and he ate them all with a chunk of fresh bread and a strip of George Hammond's rabbit jerky.

"You serve a strange meal, Mrs. Wortham. I figured country folks to cook up something bigger."

"Not at this time of day." I wasn't anxious for him staying.

Sarah played upstairs, but Franky sat and watched the whole time Edward ate. And I kept expecting Samuel to pull in. It was almost dinnertime. I knew I should start my fire in the ring of creek rocks Samuel had brought up for outside cooking. I should put the green beans and the baby turnips in a covered pan over the coals. But I didn't want this man to take that as an invitation. How would Samuel react when he found out how his brother had talked to me? Maybe I shouldn't tell him.

Finally Edward stood up from the table and stretched. Franky stood up too, and Edward shook his head at him. "Ought to leave your hammer in the barn when you come out to greet folks, boy. Liable to be scarin' people away."

"Some folks needs scared, I figure," Franky replied with a solemn face.

Edward only laughed. "What'd you think I was gonna do? Take off with Mrs. Wortham here? And you were gonna stop me?" He kept chuckling. "Stupid brave kid."

"You needn't talk to him like that," I said. "Franky's a sensible child and I appreciate him."

Edward looked long at me, his dark eyes so different from Samuel's, and yet, strangely, suddenly the same. "If I was really wanting to make trouble, Missus, I could. I'm not so bad as you think. I sure ain't gonna hurt you, whether you want to believe me or not."

He walked outside, and I watched from the doorway as he crossed the yard to his car. He got in and started the motor and looked up at me. "Almost forgot!" he yelled. And then he threw a little blue bag out onto the grass and sped away.

Katie's things. I wondered at him. I wondered if that wasn't why he'd really come. He was a puzzle. Why he acted the way he did was beyond me to understand. But maybe somehow he was trying to do the right thing, on Katie's part at least.

By the time Samuel drove back up, Edward's visit was all a jumble in my brain. *Maybe I shouldn't speak a word of it. Samuel has been so upset already. Maybe he doesn't need to know.* But of course, I couldn't explain how Katie's bag got back.

He kissed my cheek when he got out of the truck. Katie sat there looking at me, like she was fearful of what I might say. *"You can see him in her face,"* Edward had said. I shook the thought away.

"I'm glad you brought her back," I told Samuel. "I didn't know what they'd do, and I've heard that some children's homes are not very pleasant."

"The sheriff didn't leave me much choice. I guess he

believed Edward's words better than mine. That's what can happen when you judge on appearances."

He was studying me so close, almost as though he could read my thoughts, and I felt pricked to the heart. *Oh, Samuel! God help me not to doubt you!*

"Are you all right?"

Franky was coming up from the barn. He'd tell all. I knew he would. At least all he'd seen. "Sammy, Edward came back. He . . . he left Katie's bag."

"Is that all? What's the matter?"

Samuel was upset already. I didn't want to make it worse. "I fed him. He wasn't here long."

"Where *is* my bag?" Katie asked.

"In the kitchen, honey."

"Can I get it?" She hadn't moved. Not an inch.

"Of course. I'm sure Sarah would love to see your paper dolls."

She climbed down from the truck seat and headed for the house. But Samuel just stood there, watching me.

"I don't think your brother was very nice," Franky suddenly spoke up. "Looked like he was arguin' or somethin' with Mrs. Wortham over by the well, and he grabbed her. She throwed water right in his face. I was proud."

I saw the color drain from Samuel's face. "Juli . . ."

"Now, it wasn't really that bad. He didn't really grab me. Just touched my arm."

"I shouldn't have left you here."

"How were we to know? He didn't do any harm. You can't just stop what you're doing or do something different just because he might come around again. He might and he might not. I'm not going to let it affect me one way or another."

He reached his hand out. The warmth of it touched me just below the shoulder. I should have let him hug me. I should have been glad for his waiting arms just then, but I turned away. I marched myself into the barn, just to have another place to go. I'd check on Lula Bell. Poor old cow. She'd been so good to us.

I heard Samuel before he got to me, first the creak of the barn door and then the rhythmic sound of his boots on the straw-strewn floor. He came up behind me. He didn't touch me this time, just stood there, waiting.

"I think you're right," I managed to tell him. "Lula Bell's just getting worse." She turned her head to look at me, and I leaned over the rail to put my hand on her side.

"Honey . . ." he said.

"Sammy, I told you already, he didn't do any harm."

"What did he do?"

"Insulted you. Laughed at me for believing you. Ridiculed Franky for standing there with a hammer in his hand." I smiled. "You should've seen him. Edward didn't know what to think, this bold little boy . . ."

Gently, slowly, Samuel pulled me away from Lula Bell's stall to face him. "I'm so sorry. I should've known he might—"

"You did." Those two words just hung in the air, and I was immediately sorry I'd said them. I wasn't trying to blame him for anything. The encounter with Edward was my own fault. I could've listened. I could've gone to town like Samuel had suggested.

Samuel encircled me in his arms, and I felt strangely cold. What was wrong with me? He was the same warm, tender man.

"I'm not sure I know him anymore," Samuel said. "I don't know what to expect from him." He was looking at me so closely, trying to read what I wasn't saying. "Did he threaten you, Juli? I need to know what happened."

"It wasn't really a threat. More like he was testing me, just to see what sort of reaction he'd get. Telling me that Katie's mother had described you, and that you were living a lie."

Samuel didn't say anything at first, only looked down

at my hands still straight at my sides. Why wasn't I hugging him back the way I usually did? Oh, why was I being this way?

"What do you think, Juli? Is it too much to believe me?" He took my hand in his for just a moment. "You might as well know that Katie knew my name before she met Edward. I don't know how it's possible, but she says her mother told her, well before that, and even showed her a picture."

I could feel my hands shaking. "How?"

"Juli, I don't know. I just don't know." He turned away. "There's a lot to think about. But I thought . . . you said you thought there must be some other man, with my name." He turned his face to me again, hopeful, wanting me to affirm my stand.

"Maybe so," I told him. "It's possible."

But he knew my words were different. I saw the change in him; his eyes grew stormy, his face drawn. He looked more like Edward. Lost. And alone.

"Samuel—"

"Please just tell me why he touched you. If he meant you any harm, I'll tell the sheriff—"

"No. I—I don't think he did. He—he doesn't know us either. He doesn't know how a God-fearing person acts. Maybe he thought I would scorn you. I don't know."

"It won't happen again. I won't leave you alone."

"You can't let him dictate—"

But he was turning away. "I have to watch for my family."

I wanted to stop him. I wanted to tell him it was all okay, that I didn't doubt him for a second. I should have. But he was walking away, back toward the house, with his shoulders bowed.

We tried to have a normal rest of the day, as much as possible. Lunch first. Turnips and green beans without the fish Robert had hoped to bring home. Afterward, Samuel went to work field with George because he'd promised, and maybe because he didn't know what else to do. But he left Robert home and told me to send Franky running to the field if Edward showed up again. I didn't expect him, maybe ever. He didn't have anything to return this time.

I let the girls play most of the afternoon. Sarah loved Katie's paper dolls, just like I'd thought. Of course, she'd seen some before, but these were torn from a magazine and it made her want to get some the same way.

"Don't we have a magazine, Mommy?" she asked.

"No, honey. I might could find you a catalog—"

"But, Mommy, they needs to be in color."

"Then I can't help you. Maybe Louise Post would have a magazine. I've seen them over there before." I shouldn't have said even that much.

"Can we go ask her?"

"Not now. Why don't you get your Crayolas and make your own?"

Sarah wasn't too enthused with that idea, but Katie was, and it occupied them for quite a while as I weeded the lettuce, thinned the beets, and then started looking around the yard for something to put with the beet tops for supper. I was picking yellow dock and lamb's-quarter when Franky came out of the barn.

"I got it done. You wanna see?"

"The chair? Already?"

"Yeah, it's just a little one."

Robert stopped chopping kindling and went with me to look. It was a little chair, very little, but just about right for a fourteen-month-old baby sister. It even had arms and a curved top in back.

"That's very nice, Franky," I said.

"Yeah," Robert agreed. "Good job."

I was so glad for Robert's compliment. It was a rare thing for Franky to get much but ridicule from other boys. And he was fairly beaming. "You think Mr. Wortham'll like it?"

"'Course he'll like it," Robert said immediately. "Why wouldn't he like it?"

But Franky's question bothered me a little. Was he also wondering what his father would think? He didn't ask that. "I think your pa will be proud," I told him, hoping he'd believe me.

Franky only shrugged. "Won't give him cause to complain, at least. 'Long as I sand the edges smooth. Wouldn't want Emmie gettin' no slivers."

Did George really complain so much? Not at everybody, I guessed, but unfortunately more with Franky. "He's painful clumsy," George had told me once. "Sometimes it's better not t' have him underfoot."

Lizbeth had told me nearly the same once, that if any of them tipped a bucket or spilled a dish of something, it was likely to be Franky. Yet he never seemed to be that way here.

"You think this design'd work for big chairs too?" Franky was asking Robert with all seriousness.

"I don't know. You try any weight on it?"

"Not yet."

Robert put his foot in the seat of Franky's chair, and I held my breath, not wanting to see the careful project smashed to pieces. But the little chair held up under the weight Robert gave it, and both boys smiled. "I think it'd work," Robert said.

"Good. I still think me'n Mr. Wortham oughta make more stuff and set by the road to sell. Or in Dearing someplace, if somebody'd let us. We could make money at it."

"I don't know about that," Robert said. "If other people buy like us, we wouldn't sell nothin'."

"I wanna make some more, anyhow," Franky announced. "Wanna help?"

Even though Robert was older, he wasn't adverse to the suggestion. He seemed caught in the middle sometimes. Best friends with the often thoughtless Willy, and yet in the right moments, he could relate to Franky better than all the rest.

I left them alone and went back out to gather greens. They cooked down so much that I'd need three times more than it looked like I should. All the family was used to them by now too, we'd had them so much.

George let Franky stay the night, I guess because he was already here. But he sent Rorey over too, because when she heard there was another girl about her age, she just couldn't be contained. But Samuel came home quiet, sweaty and tired and not saying much. After supper he sat and played checkers with Robert, but more than once I saw him watching the girls playing in the corner. I knew he was concerned for Katie in this strange situation, and it was no more than right. None of this was her fault, after all.

Franky helped me with the supper dishes, and just about the time we got done, thunder was rumbling outside. We'd have a storm, like as not, and I was glad. Maybe it would cure the heat a little. And we could use the rain.

When it was bedtime, Sarah didn't want to go upstairs. She was always like that in a storm. She wanted to stay as close to her parents as possible. And Katie was just as nervous, maybe more. So Samuel said they could all camp downstairs if they wanted to, and he helped me spread the blankets and pillows.

I knew the storm didn't bother either of the boys, or Rorey either, so far as I could tell, but they all liked the idea of being in the sitting room. Robert and Franky plopped right down, but the little girls took the time to carefully position all the yarn dolls and paper dolls and Rorey and Sarah's cloth dolls beside their pillows. I hoped they felt rich.

"Where's your folks?" Rorey asked Katie, much to my dismay.

"I don't know," the little girl answered quickly. "Do you got a real family?"

"Sure," Rorey declared. "We got Pa at home. We're missin' Mama, though, 'cause she died."

"Oh. That's partly a real family."

"We just visits over here," Rorey said. "All the time."

"We're kinda like two families smacked together in one," Sarah explained. "I like it that way."

"It's time to lie down, girls," I told them, hoping they'd go to sleep quickly, despite the threat of storm. I wanted some time with Samuel. He hadn't said much to me since he got back home.

It wasn't raining, but the wind was picking up; there were dancing flashes of light in the sky, and the thunder was rumbling louder than before. The girls did as they were told and lay very still. But even in the dim light, I knew their eyes were open. Katie was staring up at the ceiling, the tiny glint of a tear just glazing her cheek. She wiped it away, but I knew Samuel must have seen it too.

"Would you like a story?" he asked them.

"Yeah!" Sarah answered with enthusiasm.

"You go on if you want," he whispered to me. "Get some sleep." Then he sat cross-legged on the floor next to an outspread blanket.

I sat down too, wanting to hear. It was so like Samuel to ease the children into sleep in a new place or whenever there was something different to think about. He'd done it for our two, for the Hammonds, and now for Katie.

"What about you?" Samuel was gently asking the girl. "Want to hear a story?"

She turned her head just a little, and I thought of her tears last night. *May there be peace this night,* I prayed. *For Samuel too.*

"Once there was a princess," Samuel began.

"A princess?" Rorey asked abruptly. "I thought all your stories had animals."

"Shush," Sarah whispered. "I like princesses."

"You don't know if it's an animal or not," Franky added from across the room. "He didn't say what kind of princess."

"It should be a princess bee," Katie whispered. "Because they have queens."

I took a breath, wondering how Samuel could tell this story at all, with so much help. But it didn't seem to bother him.

"Okay. A princess bee." He glanced in my direction, but I couldn't be sure what I was seeing in his expression. "One day the princess bee went flying around her hive on a very lovely day, and she wasn't sure how it happened, but she got very, very lost."

"Do bees get lost?" Rorey interrupted again.

"This one did," Samuel maintained. "She was pretty little, and she went a very long way."

"Well, the queen should have gone with her, then," Rorey declared.

"Queens don't leave the hive," Franky told her. "Except to swarm, and that ain't what the story's about."

"Right," Samuel went on. "Anyway, the little princess bee was all alone and far from home, and she didn't know what to do."

"Did she cry?" Sarah asked.

"A little bit. But she was very brave. She flew right down

into a perfect patch of flowers and sat on the very prettiest little daisy, because she knew that some other bees would come sometime and find those flowers too."

I wondered if this was the story Samuel'd had in mind at first, or if he'd started with any idea at all. Maybe he just let a story happen, the way Grandma Pearl had made vegetable soup with whatever came up at the moment.

"She waited there a long time," Samuel went on. "It started to rain, but the princess bee didn't move very far. She just slid under the daisy petals and waited some more, all alone."

I heard Katie sniff. Maybe she knew how that felt.

"Finally, after a long time, the sun came out again, and some other bees were flying around, looking for the best flowers they could find to make honey with. And they found the little princess, sitting on a daisy petal and drying out in the sun."

"Were they her bees?" Sarah asked. "From her own hive?"

"No. But they were very friendly. They took her home and fed her honeycomb, and she took a nice long nap cuddled up in one of the little bee rooms."

"How'd she get home?" Rorey asked.

"Just a minute," Samuel told her. "I'm getting to that. It got to be night, and all the other bees were buzzing around, trying to figure out where the little princess came from. But when she woke up, she couldn't tell them. She didn't even know which direction she'd flown, because she'd turned so many times and gone so far."

He glanced at me again, and I heard him sigh. Dear Samuel. He had so much on his shoulders.

"Every day for many days, the queen of that hive sent her workers out in all directions, looking for the hive that the princess had come from. And every day the princess's own hive sent out workers too, just to look for her. Finally one day, at the top of a giant sunflower, two little bees bumped into each other and asked what the other one was doing there. 'I'm up here high looking for the princess's beehive,' said the first one. 'Well, I'm looking for the princess,' said the other. 'Because she hasn't come home.' And then they both knew that they'd found what they were looking for. They flew all the way to the hive where the princess was playing with other little bees just her size. And the bee that was looking for her took her all the way home."

He glanced at Franky, who was up on his elbows, and at Katie, who was staring at the ceiling again. "But they didn't go alone," he went on. "Half the bees from the new hive went with them, just to visit. And every summer after that, bees from both hives went back and forth, because they stayed friends forever. So much that the littlest bees weren't always sure which bees belonged to which hive. And when the princess bee became a queen, she swarmed right over to the pretty flower patch so she could see those daisies right outside."

"Why'd she want to see the daisies?" Rorey wanted to know.

"Because she met her first new friend there. When she'd been really alone, God sent bees that she didn't even know about before, and she ended up with twice as many friends that really cared about her."

"That's kind of like our families," Sarah said. "Only we wasn't alone in the flowers."

I could see Franky looking at Katie, and I knew he was thinking. Katie'd been pretty misplaced, like the bee. I was surprised at Samuel for making such a direct reference to it.

"I bet the queen bee was glad to see the princess," Rorey said.

Oh, this was awkward. How would Katie feel? What if she thought of her own mother, who might not be so glad to see her?

Katie didn't look at any of us. She just kept staring up at the ceiling, not moving at all. "Do bees have daddies?" she finally asked.

Samuel sat silent for a moment. Looking at the floor and then at the little girl in front of him. "I guess they must."

"They don't know 'em, though," Franky added. "They only know the queen. There's boys that's the fathers, but they don't know which ones. We learned that at school."

"Well," Rorey said. "Next time I see her, I'm gonna tell Teacher you ain't dumb, 'least about bees!"

Samuel wasn't paying a bit of attention to Franky or Rorey. Little Katie's hand had crept toward him, and he took it in his.

"I wish you was really my daddy," she whispered. "Maybe you could be."

"I'm sorry," he whispered back. "But I can be your friend. Just like those bees."

Samuel stayed in the sitting room until they were all asleep and then eased up quietly and went in to our bed. I followed and sat beside him, hoping he'd want to talk.

"I love you," I whispered.

"Thank you." He sounded so far away.

I knew he was hurt that I might not believe him. No matter what, I should believe him. What was wrong with my thinking?

"I forgot to tell you," he said suddenly. "I saw Miss Hazel in town. She said Pastor's wife would be talking to you about starting a church choir. She's pretty upset about it."

"I guess she always needs to be upset about something."

He lay there with his shirt off in the heat of our house as the wind tossed cooler air through the still-open window. Staring up at the ceiling, maybe deep in thought, he didn't answer me.

I'd shared so much with Samuel. The wonders of two children. The grief of losing Emma. But especially love like I'd never known before. I should've apologized to him. I should've told him his word meant more to me than all the evidence in the world, more than pictures or names or what anyone else could say. But just as I was about to speak, I thought I heard a sound from the sitting room again. A sob and then movement.

Samuel started to get up, but I stopped him. "Stay and rest. I'll go."

I went quickly, knowing it would be Katie who I found up. She was leaning her head against the wall in the corner closest to Sarah, crying so quietly now I could barely hear her. The others were still asleep, and I wondered if Katie might really be too. But when I came near, she grasped hold of me, breathing hard. The poor child was scared, just scared in the thunderous dark, here in our house that still seemed so strange to her. I held her, and she clung to me, crying softly into my blouse.

After a while I could hear it start to drip rain. And then I heard Samuel rise up and shut our bedroom window, then move through the house, shutting other windows. Finally he stood in the doorway, looking in at us, but he didn't say anything before going back to our room.

I just stayed where I was until Katie finally dropped back to sleep. Then I scooted a pillow close and eased her carefully down onto the blanket beside Sarah. I tiptoed back to bed, hoping to find Samuel still awake. I needed the talk we should've had before, the strong and gentle arms I should've taken advantage of earlier in the barn. But Samuel lay with one arm across his face, still in his work denims, sound asleep.

EIGHT

Samuel

Mother's liquor bottles were strewn over her dresser top, most empty, some on their sides, some with a bit of their poison remaining. She lay on the floor by the bed, where she'd fallen on her face the night before.

My father was on the couch in the living room, an uninvited guest after an absence of nearly a year. Edward was gone again. I wasn't sure if he'd even been home last night.

I got my books from the corner table, my sweater from a pile of clothes on the floor. I could get to school. If I managed to get out the door without waking anyone.

Asleep on the couch, our father didn't look much older than Edward. Mother called him a "young buck," but she despised him as much as he despised her.

I thought about breakfast, about lunch at school, but I didn't even bother to check our kitchen cupboards. I knew what I'd find. Endless bottles. I often wondered why my mother valued them so much that she never threw any away. Edward did. Edward would collect them in gunnysacks and throw them at the school building or the streetlights or the front window of Calding's Corner Store.

I almost made it out. I was only three feet from the door when Dad sat up and stopped me cold with his yell. "Samuel!"

His face was white. Chalky white. His dark eyes were big and frightening. He grabbed me, threw my books across the room . . .

I opened my eyes in the darkness. Dreaming again. An irritating habit I'd somehow fallen back into.

It was hot. Too hot to stay in bed next to Julia's warmth, at least until I found a way to cool off a bit. I walked to the kitchen and then outside, wondering what time it could be. Buckley the rooster hadn't crowed. And there was no sign of the sun.

I went to the well and doused my head with water. The storm was over, but it had rained little and left no cooling influence. This would be a steamy day if it was this hot even before daylight.

I sat on the edge of the well's hard wood platform, letting the cool water drip down over my shoulders and back. I thought of Mother actually reading me a book once and another time kissing my cheek as she tucked the covers tight around me on a snowy night. Such moments were rare, but they happened, and they made me want to pray for her all the more. She had a goodness about her, hidden under all the garbage that enslaved her. Maybe Father had too, but his was even more buried. I only saw it once.

"Samuel's a strong name," he told me when I was eight. "I always did like it. I gave you a decent, strong name so you'd have that even if I couldn't give you nothing else."

That was the last time I saw him. For so long he'd been dropping in unexpected, with months or even years between visits. But he never came back after that. And then when I was Robert's size, Mother said he was dead. Drowned in some river somewhere.

Whiskers sauntered up and pushed his nose under my hand. I petted him, feeling obligated, I guess. It wasn't often he was so insistent. "Silly dog," I scolded. "What are you doing awake at this hour?"

Over in the timber I could hear the frogs singing. A howl swept in with the breeze coming from the other way. Coyote, maybe. Whiskers heard it too. His hair bristled a bit, and he looked out over the field.

"Relax," I told him. "They're not going to bother you. You're bigger than they are."

But he whined a little, prancing back and forth. Maybe he'd been dreaming too.

I stood up and stretched, thinking I could catch a little more sleep before the day started. But Sukey started lowing in the barn. I don't know if she heard me or not, but she usually didn't make a sound. I went to the house for a lantern so I could check on her and Lula Bell, just to make sure there was no disturbance.

Sukey was bawling when I got to the barn. Her calf was asleep in the hay. The howling I'd heard was sounding closer, but such a thing had never bothered her before. I patted her nose and told her everything was all right. Then I went to check on Lula Bell, two stalls down.

I was used to finding her standing up. She stayed on her feet nearly all the time now, whether she was awake or not. But this time she was down. I thought she was asleep.

I petted her neck, expecting to feel the steady rhythm of her life flowing beneath the soft, warm fur. But she was stone cold and still.

At first my mind whirled. She must have gone some time after supper last night, after I'd milked Sukey and come to check on her. She'd been standing up then, seeming just the same. But it must not have been long after, for her to be so far gone. Stiff. I couldn't use the meat now. In this heat, I couldn't trust it.

Flies were already buzzing around her. I took the lantern and left the barn just as Buckley let loose with his first morning song. The rooster crowed twice, and I just stood there, staring out over the yard. George had lost a cow last year and three pigs in the winter. Maybe it was the way of things. The pigs had been babies, born when it was still too cold. But the cow had been younger than Lula Bell, just suddenly sick.

It made me worry for Sukey and for the rest of George's cows. Maybe it was the same sickness with Lula Bell, and not her age at all. Only three days ago, she'd seemed strong enough not only to make it to fall but longer than that. Two weeks ago, we'd talked of breeding her, trying to get her milk flowing again. Sure, she was getting old for a cow, but this was too fast.

My gut ached, thinking about disposing of the carcass, and the loss of the meat. I knew I should tell Juli and then head on over to George's. I was going to need his help. Lula Bell was too big for me to handle, even with Robert and Juli's help.

Quietly I went in the house, taking the lantern with me into our room, where Juli was just stirring on the bed. For a moment I watched her, thinking of yesterday in the barn when she'd offered her consoling touch to Lula Bell at the same time she was refusing mine. I never dreamed Juli would look at me the way she looked at me then. I never wanted to see it again.

"Samuel?" She turned her eyes to me and then reached out her hand.

I didn't take it. I just stood there with the lantern in my hand, feeling cold and wasted. "Lula Bell's dead, Juli. I'll have to go get George."

She sat up. "Oh no." She was quiet, but then she tried reaching for me again. "Samuel, please sit with me a minute."

"No. Better not to wait on these things. I'll be back as soon as I can."

She got out of bed. But I didn't linger. I set the lantern on the kitchen table as I went through, knowing I wouldn't need it outside much longer. And sure enough, as I started through the timber, the first pink light was showing itself in the east. Buckley was crowing again, and I heard some dog besides Whiskers barking somewhere to the north.

I walked fast, putting distance between me and Juli as much as I was going to find George. Maybe the day would be full. Maybe she'd be so busy with Katie and Sarah and our world of things to do that she wouldn't have time to talk. Maybe I'd be so busy looking at everything else that I wouldn't have to see the doubt staring out of her eyes.

NINE

Julia

I felt sick. Because of Lula Bell, but even more because Samuel had gotten up and gone before I'd had a chance to tell him how sorry I was. He looked so tired this morning.

But I scarcely had time to think about it. Robert was up with the dawn, and I told him to milk Sukey and put her and the calf out to graze but to leave Lula Bell's stall alone. He knew what I meant, and I saw the worry cloud his face. "Mom, I was prayin' she'd get better. I was thinkin' if she had milk again, we could be selling some and still have enough to make butter and cheese."

"I know, Robert. But Sukey's healthy and giving good milk. We'll be all right."

"We been makin' it, Mom. But we're not gettin' ahead."

"The same as everybody we know," I told him. "We can be grateful for food on the table."

But he frowned. "Last winter there wasn't enough. We come short a few times, I know, but you pretended we was just fine and that you didn't want much anyway. Dad prob'ly lost ten pounds. It kinda scares me, thinkin' about this winter. What if we don't have enough again?"

"Oh, Robert. You're too young to worry."

"Hammonds is the same way. They're gonna have to butcher a lot to have enough, and then what do they do for next year?"

"The Lord will provide."

He picked up the milk pail. "Yesterday he only give us two little fish and another mouth to feed. I guess we're s'posed to do a miracle."

He marched outside before I could say anything else. And I felt like crying.

Franky was up next and volunteered to get the eggs. Then Sarah, Katie, and Rorey came in the kitchen, all holding hands.

"Can we get us a magazine from Mrs. Post today?" Sarah asked first thing.

"No. At least not till we get other things taken care of."

"What things?"

"Never you mind. We always have plenty to do."

"Well, maybe sometime soon," she said agreeably. "That's okay."

She was easy to please. Often easy to delight, with no worries at all. I sometimes wondered why Robert was not so. God said we should be like little children. Trusting, I thought that meant. But Robert had been prone to worry even at Sarah's age. I began to consider how Sarah would react when she learned her favorite cow had died. I should probably distract her or maybe even take her to pick what was left of the wild raspberries, just to make sure she wouldn't be standing there watching them deal with the body.

It was sultry already. I had the girls pick up sticks for me, and I lit a fire in our outside ring of rocks and put a pot of water on to boil. With the old rooster following at his heels, Franky brought me nine eggs. All but one went in the water pot, and I used the last in a batch of cornbread.

Robert wasn't very hungry. Neither were Franky and the girls. I had plenty left for Samuel when he came back. But he wasn't in the mood for eating.

He had George and Joe with him in their wagon, and Robert and Franky followed them to the barn. I cut a handful of rhubarb and took the girls in the house to help me mix a bowl of batter for a quick cake. I decided to put the last of our old potatoes in the coals too, so we'd have something for lunch already done.

Maybe Robert was right to worry. The new potatoes weren't ready to dig yet. So many things in the garden needed more time and weren't bearing as well as I'd hoped. We had so little left in the cupboards. And no way to shop. I knew George would be discussing whether or not we could use that meat.

Finally Samuel came up to the house looking pretty solemn, and I sent the girls into the next room to make sure the bedding was all folded and stacked.

"We'll take her to the edge of the field and dig a hole," Samuel told me. "Not much else we can do. Can't take a chance on the meat. Can't be sure what she died of."

I nodded to him, knowing we were left with no meat of our own to put up for winter. Except the chickens. Or Sukey's calf, which we were hoping to raise bigger.

He turned around, but his weary shoulders grieved me. "Samuel—can we talk just a minute?"

"I can't leave George waiting."

"Why not? You've waited for him plenty of times."

He turned to me only for a second. "I'm not going to leave him waiting. I want to get this over with. Keep the little girls away, all right?"

I hardly knew how to respond to him, he was so abrupt. "I'll take them to the timber," I said quickly. "We need to get what's left of the raspberries and check the blackberries too. We'll be needing all we can find."

"Good."

That was all he said. He went back to George and the boys, where they'd left the horses hitched and were tying a length of rope at the back of the wagon. They were going to pull the carcass, I realized. Much easier moving it that way. I grabbed four little pails, my foraging bag, and a knife.

"Sarah! Katie! Rorey!"

They poked their little heads in from the sitting room, where they'd been pretending the paper dolls were dancing at a ball.

"Let's go picking. We'll get berries if there are any, or whatever else we can find."

I took them out the front door, which we almost never used, because I wanted to avoid what the men were doing in the back. Sarah thought it was funny, going out that way. We'd have to make a curve toward the path, but I didn't mind. I'd just be looking for whatever we could use.

"Mom, what's Daddy doing today?" Sarah asked me. "He ain't gonna take Katie to town again, is he?"

"No. Not today."

Katie looked up at me, and I tried to smile. I didn't know how long she'd be here. Until Sheriff Law came out to bring us some word, I supposed. However long that might be. *"He believed Edward's words better than mine,"* Samuel had said. I hadn't expected that. I hadn't expected anyone to believe Edward or to doubt Samuel. Especially not myself.

I tried to put it all out of my mind. I stopped and cut a bunch of wood sorrel because its leaves and flowers could be eaten raw or steamed like spinach. I tried not to think about Katie. But she was right here with me, watching me, quiet as a new lamb.

She'd heard Samuel's name before she met Edward. She'd seen a picture. *Oh, Lord, let it stop. Let it all have some reasonable, credible explanation.* What would people think? What did I think? I didn't know. I didn't want to know. I just wanted it all to go away.

We walked on, each with a pail in hand and me with the bag I used every time I went walking through this timber to harvest what I could find. All across the countryside women were probably doing the same thing. Lots of folks would be taking to the timber before long, looking for blackberries, due to ripen in a couple of weeks, maybe less. The raspberries were an extra blessing, and not as plentiful. Emma had told me about them, that they were planted by her husband Willard's grandmother and long since gone wild. We'd already gotten a few. There wouldn't be many this year. But I was hoping for better from the blackberries. Today it seemed almost a matter of survival.

"Mommy, I hope there's eight hundred tons of berries!" Sarah exclaimed, as though she could hear my thoughts.

"Goodness, that would be a lot."

"We'd eat 'em. We could make jelly like last year!"

We needed plenty, but I knew that picking berries would turn my thoughts to Emma. She'd been with us last summer, and it had been a joy working beside her, making what jelly we could. There hadn't been enough to last the winter through, and it would be good to have more. But it wouldn't be the same without Emma's wise words and willing hands working beside me. I thought of how hard it must be for Lizbeth this summer, trying to do all the things that her mother was here for last year. We'd done well, after a fashion, making it this far. But it still hurt, being without them.

Thinking of Emma made me wonder how she would have reacted to Katie being here. Oh, she'd have loved the girl, I had no doubt about that. But what would she have done about Edward? And what would she say to Samuel?

I could imagine her having us kill a chicken to fix Edward the finest meal she possibly could, whether he was a bit of a skunk or not. He was Samuel's brother, so she would have been as gracious and generous as ever. And she would probably have gone somewhere with Samuel, him pushing her in that wheelchair he'd made, just so they could talk away from the kids and the problems. If she were here, Emma would tell him God knows the truth. God loves him and everybody else despite the mistakes we all make. God forgives us when we sin and rewards us when we patiently endure false accusation. And whichever one this is, God is still in control.

I didn't realize my eyes were filling up until Sarah asked me what kind of tree was ahead and I couldn't tell.

"What's the matter, Mommy?"

"Oh, honey, I'm all right. Just thinking too much."

"I never heard a' that," she said, tipping her head sideways. "In school, Teacher used to tell us most every day it was time to think. Right before 'rithmetic first thing in the morning."

"She was right."

"But you're prob'ly not thinking 'bout 'rithmetic. Right, Mommy? What was you thinking about?"

I couldn't possibly tell her. Nothing about this whole

situation was bothering Sarah in the slightest, and I wanted to keep it that way. "Never mind," I said. "I just need to be thinking about berries and greens and such."

She nodded. "Too bad there's no more mushrooms."

"The eating kind that grows out here is a spring food. But there's plenty of summer food too."

Katie had been walking along so quietly that I was surprised when she spoke. "Aren't there any grocers where you live?"

Her question made me smile. "Yes, honey. There are grocers, but they're miles away, and we grow and gather all we can."

I would not say we were poor. I would not tell her we had no money, even for the smallest things. I didn't want these girls burdened the way Robert was. I would've preferred all the children to see us the way Emma always had—rich in grace, rich in potential.

"I guess there aren't so many things to grow and pick in cities," Katie went on.

"I expect not," I agreed. "Though folks could do pretty well if they have a yard."

"We never had one," she said sadly. "Especially one so big it has a whole forest in it."

Our little timber must've seemed like a forest to her, if she'd never lived in the country. "I think I see a sassafras tree," I told the girls.

"Goody!" Rorey declared.

"What's sassyfass?" Katie asked.

"A tea tree. We can cut a chunk of root and some leaves to make a nice big pitcher of sassafras tea. The big boys would love that on a hot day." *Especially if we had ice,* I thought to myself. But we could cool it a little in the well or the pit in the basement. It would still taste good.

I pulled a branch down and had the girls help me pull some leaves and twigs. The root was better, but I didn't cut very much. I knew George would be harvesting some one of these days, and I didn't want us being too hard on the trees.

When we came to the creek, Rorey ran right in, followed a little more gingerly by Sarah. But Katie stood there in her scuffed-up buckle shoes and looked at me with a frown. "Do the rocks hurt your feet?"

"There's not that many rocks in this creek," I told her. "Have you ever been wading?"

She shook her head.

"I'll hold your shoes. You can try it out. All the children I know love it."

"Are you going to wade?"

"Yes. Because it's the quickest way to the old smokehouse, where the raspberries are. And I like it."

She took off her shoes and handed them to me, then followed me into the water slowly, easing her feet in like she was afraid the little creek might bite. I watched her face, waiting for the smile I knew would come. And it did, pretty quickly.

"Nice and cool," she said.

She stayed close to me as Sarah and Rorey ventured ahead. I turned my attention to the brambles on the east bank of the creek. Blackberries, scads of them, spreading east and north in tangled and thorny bushes. They'd been a pretty sight earlier in the season when little white blooms decorated the branches. And even prettier now that a few here and there were beginning to turn. Last time I was here, they'd all been green as grass and hard as little stones. If every one of them ripened, we'd have plenty. I would make sure Lizbeth got her share. I thought maybe I should even walk over there and tell her how they were coming along. She would have her hands so full with Harry, Berty, and little Emmie Grace that I doubted she'd checked.

"You're right, Mom," Sarah spoke up. "They're not ripe yet."

"Maybe tomorrow," Rorey said, suddenly splashing Sarah.

"Quit that!"

"Why? Don't it feel good?"

"Rorey, don't splash people unless they want you to. Some people don't like it."

"Don't see why not. It don't do nothin' but cool you off."

"If I want cooled off, I'll cool my own self off," Sarah said rather indignantly, reaching her hand to the water and spreading the wetness across one arm.

"Let's not argue, girls. We've come to pick what we can."

It wasn't long before we got to the spot where Willard's grandfather's smokehouse had stood. I'd never asked Emma why they'd built it so far into the timber and not closer to the house. Maybe they'd had a house or cabin over here back then. I only knew what she'd told me about it, that high winds had collapsed the structure when she was a little girl, without doing a bit of damage to the raspberries growing behind it.

"There they are," I said, stepping out of the creek and pointing toward the little spots of purple dotting the green.

"Ohhh!" Katie exclaimed. "Real berries. Can I pick?"

"Sure. Just watch out for the thorns."

She followed me onto the bank, not saying a word about her shoes. Sarah lingered a little while longer and then came behind us, but Rorey stayed in the water. Katie was proceeding very cautiously, checking every weed and branch for thorns. Finally she was in reach of the few scattered raspberries, just to my left. She smiled up at me.

"They come right off, like they're wanting to be picked," she declared.

"I suppose they are. Once they're ripe, they could want nothing better than to be carried off someplace and leave seeds. When they're not ripe, though, they hold on to the branch real tight, knowing it's not time to leave it."

She tugged at a green berry and chuckled. "You're right. It won't let go."

Sarah had started picking on the opposite side of her. "Can we eat some, Mom?"

"I suppose so. The Bible says not to muzzle an ox that's treading out corn. So whoever's doing the work gets to eat their share. But you'll have to leave some if you want any later."

Sarah smiled and popped three berries in her mouth immediately. Katie tasted one too, but more cautiously. I waited for her comment, but she didn't say a word.

"We sugar them a bit at home sometimes," I told her. "If they need it."

She nodded and went back to picking without complaint. But there were not many in reach of little hands; it wasn't long before neither girl could get to the berries very easily, and Rorey was yelling for them to join her.

"Is it okay if we wade again?" Sarah asked me.

I nodded my consent. I could get the rest by stretching through the brambles. And there would be more picking to do when the blackberries came on. For now I didn't mind them playing.

"Can we get some creek clay?" Sarah asked. "I could show Katie how to make a dish."

Sarah's clay dishes were rather lopsided, and I wasn't a potter to teach her much better. Still, I appreciated her love for the blue-gray stuff, so cool and smooth. The clay was a natural treasure I'm sure the Indians probably used to advantage long years ago. It lay hidden beneath the sandy pebbles and slate rock along the west bank of the creek around a bend and a little farther down. We'd discovered it one day by accident. And now Sarah brought some home every time she got the chance.

"I'll tell you what," I told the girls. "It's not far. Why don't you take one of the pails and get some clay while I stay here and pick the rest."

"Yea!" Sarah shouted as she dumped her few berries into Katie's pail. "Come on, Katie! Let's get lots. We can make people and dogs and stuff, if you want to."

"Clay?" Katie asked, looking at me oddly.

Maybe she'd never seen clay. That wouldn't be so strange. But it made me wonder about her background. Had she been to school? Did her mother cook, sew, and do all the other normal things that most little girls her age were beginning to learn? She hadn't known much about washing. Or which green beans were big enough to pick. She would need help, I was beginning to think, just learning the normal things of life.

"Go along with Sarah," I told her. "Leave your pail here. She'll show you where to find the clay. You can help her scoop it out of the bank. Then wash your hands in the creek and come back."

"Rorey! Come on!" Sarah yelled. "We're gonna get clay!"

"Okay! Goody!" Rorey splashed her way back from wherever she was going in the other direction, apparently now as enthused as Sarah.

"We're gonna wade again?" Katie asked them.

"'Course," I heard Rorey answer. "That's how you get there."

I watched them go. Three little girls almost the same size. Rorey ran ahead, but Sarah and Katie stayed side by side, hand in hand again. *Oh, Samuel,* I lamented. *They're becoming so close! But what's next?*

I went back to picking alone, trying to keep my mind on the berries. There wouldn't be many, barely enough for a mess, but they'd sure taste good. And soon enough, the blackberries. Thank God for them. We'd need every one.

I could hear the girls, just out of sight around the curve in the creek. Sarah and Rorey knew where to find the clay, and I wouldn't have sent them alone if it were far. I could hear their little voices as they filled the pail, though most of what they were saying I couldn't make out. Then I heard them splashing back through the water. The creek didn't get any deeper than my shins, so it didn't worry me in the slightest. I guessed that Katie had gotten comfortable with wading already, because they were laughing together. Despite my concerns, I was glad they were having a good time.

But then the voices stopped abruptly. I almost called to them, thinking that maybe they had sat down along the bank to fashion something or other out of their newly dug clay. But before I opened my mouth, a piercing shriek ripped through the woods. I dropped my berry pail.

"Mom! Mom!"

"Sarah?" I went running in their direction, hardly noticing if I was in the creek or out of it. But then Rorey was laughing. I figured it must have been Katie who screamed.

"Mom! Look!" Sarah kept calling.

I got to them in time to see Katie back up a few steps and fall with a splash. She got up with a cry and ran in my direction as soon as she saw me. Rorey was still laughing, at Katie obviously, though the poor girl was nearly white with fright. And Sarah was pointing at something on the creek bank, barely three feet from where Katie had been. At first I didn't see it. But then when I did, I smiled. They'd given me quite a start, and I was very glad to let out a sigh of relief.

"What is it? What is it?" Katie asked me in sobs.

"Honey, it's a snapping turtle. Don't worry. He won't hurt you."

"You should've seen that girl jump!" Rorey squealed. "I thought she was gonna land in a tree!"

"Rorey, you'd have been startled too, to come upon something like that if you'd never seen one. And maybe she hasn't."

"It's big, Mom," Sarah declared. "I didn't know turtles got that big."

"Some kinds get even bigger," I told them. "But he is big for a snapper. The biggest I've seen in a while."

I started to go closer, but Katie grabbed my arm. "Do they bite?"

"He would, if someone stuck a finger or toe right in front of his face. Otherwise, there's no way he could get you. You're ten times faster than he is."

She clung to me, still uncertain. But I was thinking, a bit to my surprise, that here was the making of quite a meal. I'd never cooked turtle, but Grandma Pearl had. The Hammonds had too. I'd heard them talk about it.

Thank you, Lord, I prayed. *Coming to the woods on a sunshiny day ought to be a profitable experience. And you've made it so. You've given us meat.*

There would be plenty to make turtle soup. I thought turtles usually stayed closer to the pond. But maybe this one was here because we were meant to find him.

"Get me a big sturdy stick," I told the girls.

"Why?" Rorey asked.

"To carry him with. I'd rather not touch him, if I don't have to."

Her eyes lit up. "Are we gonna catch him? Are we gonna be real hunters? Boy, Pa's gonna be proud!"

I had to smile at that. It didn't take much hunting to catch a turtle out of the water.

Sarah brought a stick, nice and thick and still a little green. I knelt down close to that big old turtle and stuck the middle of the stick in front of him. He didn't do a thing, just looked at me with those beady, mud-colored eyes, so I gave him a gentle tap with the stick, right in the face. He latched on like I was hoping he would, like Grandma Pearl had told me about once. He bit down and wouldn't let go.

I lifted the stick and had to use both hands, one on each side of that turtle. He was terribly heavy. "Well, girls. We about had all the berries anyway. Let's see if we can get our prize over to Lizbeth. I think she'll be able to tell me what to do with it. Can you girls manage the pails and my bag?"

Sarah ran and got the berry pails and the bag of sassafras and sorrel. Katie stood looking at me like she wasn't sure what to do. I must have been a sight. Maybe she wondered what sort of strange people she'd come to.

"Can I carry him?" Rorey wanted to know.

"I don't think you could by yourself. But he's so heavy, I could use your help, if you think you can hold one end on your shoulder." She was delighted to try. And I knew she was strong and wiry. Of these three, she was probably the only one who could manage it.

"Where's the clay, Katie?" I asked. "Do you think you can carry that? It would be easier to bring it along than to have to come back and search."

"Yes, ma'am." She walked to the middle of the creek, where they'd left the pail on a rock. She lifted it carefully as Sarah came running back to us with her hands full.

And then we were on our way, with Rorey and me straining with the weight of that turtle, Sarah beside me looking pleased as punch, and Katie trailing along, not wanting to get too close.

We were as near to Hammonds' now as home, so it just made sense to go and ask Lizbeth how she'd cut and cook one of these.

"Are we going to eat that?" Katie asked as we made our way through the brush.

"Not us," Sarah had decided. "Rorey's pa will. All their family."

"Whoever wants to, I suppose," I told them. "We always share around here."

Katie looked a little green, but she didn't say anything else. I wondered who had taught her to be so polite about something like this. Most children, my own included, would come right out and tell you what they thought when it came to food. Even Sarah, generally the most mannerly of the bunch, wasn't about to eat any turtle.

We walked rapidly, with the turtle stubbornly holding tight to the stick. I wondered what he thought he was accomplishing dangling in midair like this when he could easily drop to the ground. But maybe the fall would hurt him. Maybe that's why he just kept on biting down hard. I didn't know if all turtles were as stubborn as him, but I was glad he hadn't gotten somebody's toe.

My arms were pretty tired by the time we got to George Hammond's farmyard, and I knew Rorey must be tired too, though I'd been trying to carry most of the weight. She was proud and wanted everybody to see what we'd brought, but her father and two brothers were at our house, and the rest of the big boys were in the field, I guessed.

"Hey! Look!" she called anyway.

Harry was up a tree, throwing twigs down at little Bert, who got hit in the head with one when he stopped wiggling to turn and stare at us.

"Turta!" he said, without seeming to notice the attack from above.

"Harry, don't throw any more sticks!" I called. "You could hurt somebody."

"Ohh! What you got? Is we gonna keep him?" He started sliding down out of the tree.

"I thought I'd ask your sister if she thinks turtle would make a decent meal."

"Can I have the shell?" he asked immediately. "We could make me a real soldier helmet."

"It might be your brother who needs the helmet."

"Why?" Harry asked innocently. "He don't even like playin' soldier."

Lizbeth was coming around the side of the house with a basket of clothes to hang on the line, and little Emmie toddled at her heels. With one still in diapers and nine others to think about, she always had a lot of wash to do. But she looked my way with a smile.

"Mrs. Wortham! I didn't know you to be out huntin' up dinner. Pa'll be real happy to see that."

Sarah had been right. George and his family would take to a turtle meal just fine. I was thinking maybe I should leave the whole thing here with them.

Harry and Berty came running up close, and Rorey grabbed her chance to show off our catch. "Touch him!" she told them. "Feel how funny he is. He's even hard on the bottom. An' we caught him all by ourself! I could keep him, jus' to play with, if he wasn't good for food."

Strange to hear a girl carrying on about such a thing. Usually it was one of the boys proud to show me turtles, snakes, stinkbugs, a dead possum, or what have you. But Rorey was all tomboy, which sometimes put a gap between her and Sarah.

I lowered our turtle to the ground, and the stubborn thing drew his head inside the shell as far as he could without letting go of the stick. Some people were that stubborn. Good thing Sarah had brought me a fat stick.

Rorey touched the turtle's back first, then the tips of its feet, which made Katie squirm.

Not to be outdone, Harry tried his best to find the hidden tail and, that failing, sat down and pushed against one side.

"Big!" Berty declared, much to Rorey's satisfaction.

"Grab him, Sarah!" Harry challenged.

"I like lookin' at him okay," Sarah told him. "But I don't wanna touch him. Mommy didn't neither."

"I'll help you hang your wash," I told Lizbeth. "But where do you want this fellow for now, out of the way of these kids?"

"In the corncrib, I guess. He won't get outta there. We'll cut him up this mornin' so he can soak some hours afore supper. Be best that way."

Katie looked even greener than she had before, the poor child.

"Look out!" Harry teased her. "He could chomp your whole big toe clear off!"

Rorey laughed.

"Leave her alone, you two," I warned and quietly took Katie's hand.

"You know how to cook it?" Lizbeth asked me.

"No. My grandmother told me about it, but I've never done one myself."

"I know enough. I helped Mama more'n once at it. You want me to teach you?"

She looked pleased with the notion, so I said yes. Extra knowledge of anything was a good thing, I figured, especially in times like these. The one time I'd eaten turtle before, when I was a child, I hadn't especially liked it, but just like Samuel and my cornmeal mush, you learn to eat what's available.

"We'll be wantin' onions to go with it," Lizbeth told me. "You want I pull some from the garden, or should we find us some wild?"

"We'd better let what's left in our gardens get bigger. I'll get the wild."

"Berries!" Berty hollered, peeking into my pail and snitching two or three.

"Are there any more?" Lizbeth asked. "I was thinkin' to check 'em sometime today or tomorrow."

"No. This is almost all of the raspberries. But there should be quite a few blackberries. More than last year. Maybe we could all go picking together when the time comes."

She happily agreed. I knew she loved it when I came over. For the change of pace and the help.

Carefully I pulled our turtle to the corncrib and shut him in, stick and all. I was glad to get him away from Harry and glad to be done with moving him, at least for now. He was heavier than he looked.

Then I helped Lizbeth get her wash on the line. Memories flooded back as I hung up the yellow bib that Emma had made for baby Emma Grace when she was born. Of course, it'd been too big then, but here it was, still being used now. And the vest Wilametta had made in the fall to give to George, thinking ahead of a Christmas she didn't live to see. He still wore it, and Lizbeth washed it carefully as if it was something sacred.

Hanging up towels, I thought of Emma over here struggling to help Wilametta bring her tenth child into the world breech. How scared I was, called on to help in such a task as that! But the baby'd been fine, and strong and healthy ever since. Far worse was the night, months later, when Emma and Wila both went to be with the Lord and there was nothing I could do to help either one of them.

Emmie Grace started pulling at my dress, and I smelled something most definitely stinky. "Is she telling you now?" I asked Lizbeth.

She looked at me and her baby sister from behind a sheet and smiled. "Sometimes. After the fact. You want I change her?"

"I will." I picked up the little tike, and she played with my hair all the way to the house. I knew where the diapers were. I knew where everything was here, almost as well as my own house. And all the Hammond kids knew where our things were too, we were back and forth so much.

I could've changed Emmie in the sitting room, but I went and laid her on the bed where she was born, where her father and probably several kids slept at night even still. Sometimes it was strange being in that room. As though Wilametta could still talk to me there. But I felt more connected to Emma at home, outside. Especially in the garden, which she'd loved.

Little Emmie giggled when I pinned her diaper, which neither of my children had ever done. She had stick-up-straight hair, still short and fine. Strawberry blonde, like her mother. I smiled to think of her being so happy. Lizbeth had done well, filling her mother's shoes. Maybe we'd all done well.

I stepped out on the porch in time to see Berty running past the house chasing a goat.

"Harry!" Lizbeth was yelling. "You shut that gate and don't you open it again, you hear me!"

"Harry let a goat out," Sarah ran up to tell me.

"I noticed."

Katie stood beside the new porch pillar that Samuel had made when he spent some time this past spring helping George with some vital repairs. She looked a little lost. And frightened by everything going on around her.

"I promise you we're not always this wild," I told her. "Would you and Sarah like to keep Emmie here on the porch for me? And I'll help round that goat in."

Both girls were pleased to have the baby left in their charge. I called to Berty and told him to sit down and quit chasing the goat. Then I reached up and pulled a little branch from the nearest maple tree and led that silly goat back to his pen with the branch just out of his reach. He thought I had quite a prize, I guess, and I threw the branch in once I had the gate shut. He had to shove past two other goats for his leafy share.

Harry watched the whole thing and thought it was hilarious. So Lizbeth made him sit on a stump and stay there. She was done hanging out the laundry by then, and she turned her attention back to me.

"Mama let turtle soak overnight sometimes. But she said if you get 'em in the morning an' let 'em soak all day, they're all right by supper too. You wanna do that?"

"Whatever you think."

"I didn't know what we were having for supper," she confessed. "This is such a blessin'."

I was glad I'd brought the turtle, because I knew what she meant. Their garden couldn't keep up with their need, and their pantry might be barer than mine. We had our work cut out for us this summer, gathering in everything we could. Lord help.

Lizbeth salted down a washbowl of water to have ready, and then she brought the doomed old turtle from the corncrib and whacked off its head. She started cutting immediately, looking up at me with a smile.

"Some folks stick 'em in boilin' water, shell an' all. But we won't have to do that if we leave him soak in the salt water and then stew him good with some milk after a while. Be some fine soup, an' it'll go further than fryin' him. That's good too, though."

She cut off the bottom plate first, then cut the rest of the turtle loose from shell, gutted it, and started cutting the meat in pieces to plop right away into the water. She saved all she could, even off the legs, but set the bones aside.

"I won't boil 'em like you'd do a chicken's bones," she said. "Mama didn't think turtle made good broth. That's why you gotta soak it, then cook it in milk. The bones is the dog's food for today, if that's all right with you."

I couldn't remember whether Grandma Pearl had said anything at all about boiling turtle bones, so I didn't say a word. Whiskers would appreciate the carcass. He'd been rather sparsely fed recently.

"So who's the girl you got with you?" Lizbeth suddenly asked me.

I guess I'd thought we might just be here a while, with Lizbeth never even noticing the extra child. She hadn't looked Katie's way or seemed to pay the slightest bit of attention. For some reason it had never occurred to me that she might ask. And now that she had, I was unsure what to say. "Um, she's Katie. Kin of Samuel's. Maybe."

"Maybe?"

My cheeks burned, realizing I should never have said such a thing. How foolish of me! Now I was stuck giving some kind of explanation. "His brother brought her," I said quickly. "He says she's kin, but we don't know for sure her family."

Lizbeth was looking at me sideways. "That's plenty peculiar, Mrs. Wortham."

"I know."

"So where was she the other night when we saw him there?"

"In the car."

She shook her head. "Well, how come he knows her well enough to bring her to visit, but he still don't know her people?"

"Oh, Lizbeth, I don't know. He's difficult. And he just left her without answering all the questions, and to tell the truth, we're not sure what to do."

My words came out in a rush, and for a moment she was quiet. I knew I shouldn't be talking so much, confiding in her like she was an adult friend. What was the matter with me? The poor child had enough to think about.

"You want to sit a spell?" she asked me. "This whole thing's got you all wore out, I can tell."

"No. We should just go back and do a little more picking on the way home. You can have the turtle. I'm glad to bring it."

"We thank you for it. But are you sure you're not wantin' to sit? The berries an' whatever else can wait, you know."

"No. We should go."

I glanced over to the porch, where Rorey had joined Katie and Sarah. The three of them were happily occupying Emma Grace with one of the cloth balls I'd made for the little boys last Christmas.

Knowing Harry couldn't sit still for long, I would have expected him to be up off that stump and clamoring for the turtle shell to play with. But he didn't come. I took a look around the farmyard, and he was off the stump, all right, but I didn't see him anywhere. Or Berty either.

"Lizbeth, where are the little boys?"

"Oh, prob'ly in the barn," she said without a trace of worry. "They're always playin' 'round there. They don't get into too much, most times."

"I'm going to check," I told her. "Sarah!" I hollered toward the porch. "Did you see where Harry and Berty went?"

"No!" she called back.

"They's 'round here somewhere," Rorey yelled. "They was just here a minute ago."

I had a funny feeling in my stomach then, kind of like the first time I was over here and noticed what precious little attention Wilametta was paying to those little boys. And now Lizbeth got so busy she just took for granted that her brothers would stay in their boundaries while she was working. I should have checked sooner. Because with Harry, you never knew for sure.

I checked the barn and hayloft. No little boys. I checked the goat pen, the outhouse, even the chicken coop, and found nothing. They weren't up a tree or in the garden. So even though Harry and Berty weren't ones to play in the house when they could be outside, I headed there, not knowing what else to do.

"Harry! Bert!" Lizbeth called, sounding more aggravated than worried. But I was glad she was looking now. Those boys were only four and almost six years old. Somebody should know where they were.

Surely if they'd gone in the front door, the girls would have seen them. So I went toward the back door, thinking, *I don't need this, none of us need this. Lord, help us find those boys.*

I was almost to the back steps when the little hooligans scurried out from under the porch at me like wildcats, screeching and carrying on just to see me jump.

Sarah darted around from the front porch to see what the commotion was about and only smiled when she saw them. "Oh, good. You found them." And she went back the way she came.

"Harry! Berty!" I scolded when I had my breath. "Don't you ever do such a thing again! If you want to play hiding, you tell somebody first. Do you understand?"

Little Berty nodded right away. But Harry had started snickering and turned his head to yell at Lizbeth. "I scared Mrs. Wortham! Made her jump clean outta her skin!"

Lizbeth wasn't impressed. "Oughta whup you good for pullin' somethin' like that! Didn't you hear us callin'?"

"Yes, but—"

"I don't wanna hear no but. Next time we're callin', you answer, or Pa's gonna hear about it! You unnerstand?"

He nodded, still snickering to himself. I knew that the threat of George hearing about it was not much of a deterrent.

"Go get the goats some water. An' don't you let one outta the pen again!"

The boys ran off, hopefully in obedience, and Lizbeth shook her head. "I swear, those two make me wonder if I'm thinkin' straight wantin' to be a teacher one day."

"You'll do fine as a teacher," I assured her. "And they're normal boys, for the most part. It just worries me a little that something could happen if they were to wander off alone."

Lizbeth nodded. "Franky caught 'em one mornin' on the way to the pond, figurin' to go swimmin' all by themselves. Harry might a' been all right. But Berty can't handle water a'tall without somebody there. We had to tell 'em if they ever tried that again we'd switch 'em good. An' I think they learned their lesson."

"I hope so."

I started walking around to the front of the house, thinking to tell Sarah and Katie it was time to go.

"Thank you again for the turtle," Lizbeth told me. "God uses you, Mrs. Wortham. Pa said we were gonna have to kill a kid of the goats before long to make it through the summer if things don't get better. That or chickens, an' I don't want to do neither for thinkin' on the winter's need. Joe an' Sam've been tryin' to hunt, but they haven't had no better luck than Willy at fishin'. And here you bring in somethin' with no more than a stick."

"Tell them to keep hunting. Keep trying. And we'll do what we have to do."

"Sorry to hear 'bout your cow."

"So am I."

"You got what you need for supper over there?"

Her eyes were filled with gentle concern. It was so like her to think down the road a little. Asking about supper when we hadn't had lunch. Considering winter in the heat of July. "Yes, Lizbeth, we'll have the leftover cornbread with fresh milk over it. And I'll be gathering what I can in the timber on the way back."

Suddenly I thought of those berries in my pail. Not many. But they would be such a treat for this teenage girl who'd been too busy with responsibilities to go and pick. "Lizbeth, I'd like you to have those raspberries."

"Oh, Mrs. Wortham, I couldn't do that. You already gave us the turtle, and that was . . . that was a godsend."

"I want you to have them. Mix a little batter for a cobbler, maybe. That way they'll go further."

She hugged me. And it wasn't till she let go that I saw her tears.

"I think I'd go crazy if it wasn't for you," she said. "I know I shouldn't be worryin', but I can't seem to help it. We're eatin' ever'thin' the garden can bear, an' I'm afraid there won't be nothin' left to can. The fields aren't lookin' so good, it's been so hot an' full a' grasshoppers, an' I know that bothers Pa. What are we gonna do when the flour runs out? If we have to start killin' the stock, we won't have no livin' left for next year."

"There'll be a way," I told her, hoping my words didn't sound hollow. "We've gotten this far. We'll make it. The good Lord will take care of it."

"I wish I had your faith."

I didn't know what to tell her. Seemed like it was Emma's faith speaking out of me, or God's own, seeking to give her comfort. I didn't feel very big in faith myself.

"You s'pose you'll be keepin' that girl for long?" she asked me rather timidly.

"I don't know. As long as she needs us, I guess."

"Emma picked the right folks," Lizbeth said. "You're

a saint, same as her, Mrs. Wortham. I b'lieve you'd help everybody in the country if you could."

I turned away from her, suddenly tight inside. She just didn't see. She didn't see all the doubt and turmoil swirling around in me. It was a wicked heart, not a saintly one, that had me doubting my husband and speaking words of faith I didn't feel.

"Sarah! We should start back now!"

Rorey came running around the house almost smack into me. "I wanna go with you! Can I go back to your house?"

"Rorey Jeanine, you've already been there," Lizbeth scolded.

"But . . . but if I don't go back," the girl protested, "I won't be able to make clay stuff with Sarah an' Katie! That's what they're gonna do, an' I wanna do it too!"

"I should take the little boys along," I told Lizbeth. "Or Emma Grace, and let you have a break." I said the words, sounding saintly again, I suppose. But I only felt tired of it all and didn't really want even one more child to see to today.

Maybe she knew. Or maybe she was just being kind. "No. You got enough to think on without the littlest ones. If you don't mind Rorey, she can go an' make a clay pot or somethin', but I want her to come back by supper."

"Ahh—" Rorey began to protest.

"Don't you want to brag on the turtle you helped catch?" Lizbeth asked her. "An' eat some?"

"All right," the girl relented.

"You can all come if you want," Lizbeth told me. "I can stretch a soup pot. Ask Mr. Wortham an' see what he says."

Sarah was walking Emmie down the stairs in Lizbeth's direction. "We gotta go?" She let go of the baby's hands when they got to the shaggy grass and turned to get the waiting bucket of clay. But Katie just stood at the base of the porch steps looking at me. I hadn't called her, I realized. Only Sarah.

"Come on, Katie," I said quickly. "Time to go home." A poor choice of words, maybe. It wasn't Katie's home. At least not for long, surely.

I grabbed my picking bag and the two empty pails, leaving the berries behind for Lizbeth's cobbler. Maybe we *would* come tonight. It was as much my meal as the Hammonds'.

TEN

Samuel

George was about keeled over from exhaustion, with sweat rolling down his cheeks by the time we got Lula Bell in the ground. Despite the little bit of rain, the ground was hard as rock and already almost dry.

I sent George to sit in the shade with Robert and Franky. Joe was still shoveling valiantly beside me.

"You oughta rest a while too, Samuel," George called to me. "It's awful hot. Even fer July."

"This dirt won't jump in the hole by itself."

"We'll get it," he persisted. "No use killin' yerself."

I stopped long enough to pull the kerchief from my pocket and wipe my brow. Odd as it may sound, I thought of Juli always taking the time to press and fold my handkerchiefs so neatly. She even stuffed them in the pockets for me. Every clean pair of pants I put on already had one in it, just in case I'd need it. Summer and winter. Springtime and harvest. That's the way she'd always been. A kerchief in the pocket. And a smile for me in her eyes.

"Somethin's differ'nt 'bout you today," George said. "What's botherin' ya?"

"I just lost my cow. What do you think is bothering me?"

"Dunno. Somethin' more'n ol' Lula Bell, I'd wager. Has to do with that little girl your brother left you, don't it? Wonderin' how you'll feed her?"

"I might be wondering how to feed everybody, the same as you, George."

He pulled his hat off his head and slapped it against his knee, sending tiny sweat droplets scattering across Franky's back. "Well, we got that to think about, you're right." He looked at each of the boys for a minute. "Say, Joe, you're looking tired too. Why don't you go on t' the well and fetch yerself a drink?"

"I'm all right for a while, Pa." Joe barely looked up. He liked to finish what he started.

"No use overdoin' yerself," George persisted, standing to his feet. "You boys all go on. Make sure the critters is got water too. Gotta check 'em more often in this weather. Me an' Samuel'll finish. Hard part's done."

"You sure, Pa?" Joe asked.

Robert was on his feet, looking at me.

"'Course I'm sure. Go on."

I didn't say anything. Robert accepted that well enough as agreement, and he and Franky and Joe put their shovels in George's wagon and started for the well.

"Julia's seemin' differ'nt too," George said as soon as they were gone.

I shoved my spade in the pile of dirt just as hard as I could.

"You can tell me 'bout it, you know. Ain't no reason you can't."

"There's nothing to tell."

"Sure, there is. I'm knowin' that, jus' from what Sam told me. Mighty strange, your brother coming to visit so late at night an' not even stayin' over."

"That would be *his* business."

"An' yours. Whose girl did he bring, anyhow? I unnerstand she ain't his."

I said nothing, hoping he'd shut up and work. I dumped another shovel load of dirt into Lula Bell's shallow grave. And he was just standing there watching me.

"Is she yours?"

My shovel stopped, and I looked up at him. "No," I said simply, not figuring I owed him any explanation.

"'Scuse me for askin', but there's some resemblance, you know. An' she told me herself she was a Wortham. That, an' seein' you all uptight. I couldn't figger why—"

"It's not your job to figure," I blurted out. "I already told you no."

George cocked his head a bit. "I didn't mean t' offend you. I know you pretty good by now, Samuel, that you're too much a Christian t' be steppin' out on your wife, but that's now. We all done things in the past we ain't proud of."

I could feel a stinging sort of heat crawling up my spine again. "I've done things. But not that."

"I'm jus' sayin' if it was so, you could tell me, even if you couldn't tell ever'body else. I'd unnerstand. We all make mistakes. Mine was drink. You know 'bout that. Everybody's got somethin'."

I only stood there, fiery anger working in my bones. How could he so quickly accuse me, when he hadn't even heard the half? It should've been no surprise with Ben Law, especially after I told him what Edward and Katie had to say. But George? I wouldn't have expected this from him. From snooty Miss Hazel, maybe, but not him.

George was working his hat around in his hand, looking a little sheepish. "Can't see why he left her with you, you know—"

"Because times are hard!" I said too sternly, too loudly. "Because her mama didn't want to feed her anymore or take her along while she goes skipping around singing at one disreputable place after another! And my brother was fool enough to think that she could be mine without looking for facts. Because of the name. Because somebody said so. And that's where we're at, George. Keeping her till somebody else will, because somebody has to! And if you think Juli and I are acting different, just consider how you'd feel if someone came and left you another child!"

"Well, yeah. I see what you mean. Another young'un'd be a little taxin', considerin' the ten I already got. An' you been bearin' 'bout half my burden there, so I can see how you're already shoulderin' enough—"

I was scooping again, impatient with his talk. "You gonna help me level this ground?"

"Got you a burr under the saddle today, don't ya?" He reached the crumpled and dirty kerchief from his own back pocket and swiped it across his forehead, leaving a long, gray smudge.

I didn't want to be angry at him. He was just curious. He'd ask anybody anything. He wasn't spiteful about it. I took a deep breath, shoveled some more, and reminded myself how he'd struggled over losing his wife. We'd become like brothers. He just wanted to know what was going on with us, that was all. Maybe if I were in his place, I'd be asking questions too.

I thought of Juli again, her clear green eyes clouded with cares. How could I help her be sure of me?

"So the little girl's some kinda kin, then?" George persisted.

"I don't know." I sighed. "Probably. Sheriff Law is trying to help me find her people. We'll know for sure before long, I guess."

"What about your brother? Don't he know?"

I wondered if half the countryside would be asking me this before it was all over with. "No. He just jumped to conclusions. Like everybody else so far."

George looked at me long and straight. "He thought she was yours?"

"So did you."

He shook his head. "But he must a' knowed somethin' where she come from, to have her with him such a long trip—"

"He met her mother. In Albany."

Something different, something strange was working in George's eyes now. And I knew immediately what it was. A mother would know who her child's father was. Of course she would know. And Edward should know because he'd talked to her. So why would anybody believe me?

I sunk the spade one more time into the pile of dirt, feeling almost numb on my feet. "Think what you want, George," I said. "I told you the truth."

"Now, I never been one t' accuse you a' lyin'," he said quickly. "Just mighty strange, that's all. Where'd your brother go? He say?"

"No. He might be on his way back to New York by now."

"Long trip for such a short visit."

"Visiting wasn't the priority."

George scratched his head and put his hat back on. "He come, didn't he?"

"Yes." I took another deep breath. "He came."

"Such a long way. That's some kinda priority."

We finished filling the hole and leveled the ground pretty quickly after that. George didn't speak again until I was about to throw my spade into the wagon.

"Your brother live in Albany, then?"

"I guess so."

"You ain't sure?"

"He just got out of the penitentiary in March. I don't know if he's really settled anywhere yet."

"Oh." George was quiet again, putting his own shovel in the back of the wagon and gazing long at the sky.

"Well," he said finally, not looking at me. "I come t' wonder why you never talk on yer fam'ly. Not perticularly heartwarmin', I wager?"

"Not particularly."

I started walking back toward the house, toward the well. We had a lot more work to do. We should clean out Lula Bell's stall. And Sukey's too, to be on the safe side. We should shovel out all the manure and old straw and hay and sop it out good with buckets of water before Sukey and her calf came back in. That way, if it was a sickness, maybe we could stop the spread.

I was at the well, drinking another brimming dipper of water when I heard the motor car down the lane. I knew its sound immediately, but I tried to tell myself it was somebody else. Sheriff Law maybe, with good news.

But I wasn't surprised, turning to see my brother's beat-up Model T. For the first time, for just a moment, I felt a new and bitter question rising in me. *He's trouble, Lord. Always has been. Never tried to work an honest day. Why does he have a car? Why have you blessed him that way?*

And then something else took over. Another anger. Why was he here? Why would he come back? Looking for Juli, to harass her some more? I wished George and his boys would leave. Robert too. Because I wasn't sure what Edward was up to. Or what I would do about it.

He gave us all a big wave like he was a long-lost son.

"That's him, ain't it?" George asked me.

"Yeah. That's him."

"Well. I'll be right pleased to meet him."

I didn't reply to that. I just headed for Edward's car as he came driving in; I wanted to be the first to hear whatever he would have to say. All three boys came out of the barn and stood watching. Company wasn't an everyday occurrence around here, that was for sure. But still, it would've been nice if they had known not to stop everything for Edward's sake. Maybe that was what Edward wanted. Just to disrupt our lives again and again, showing up and claiming everybody's attention when we had plenty enough to do already.

"Found you home today!" he called in greeting. "Glad of that. Spare me some fresh water?"

"You could've gotten that at any well in the state," I said, knowing I sounded unfriendly but not caring. George looked at me funny, but I didn't care about that either.

"Sure," Edward said with a smile. "But not every well is guarded by my little brother and his fierce little wife. Nice to see you again. Can I get that drink?" He stepped out of the car.

"Help yourself."

He walked to George and quickly extended his hand. "Edward Wortham, sir. Pleased to meet you."

George looked at me. He glanced over toward the boys by the barn, standing all stair steps for height, Robert in the middle.

"Can sure tell which one's the Wortham," Edward said. "Built like his father." He glanced at George. "So the other two must be yours. Fine-looking boys."

George smiled. "George Hammond. Closest neighbor. Nice to meet ya too." He started walking with Edward toward the well. "You thinkin' to stick around these parts?"

"Don't know yet what I'll do. Haven't got a place to stay over yet. Been sleeping in my car."

"Samuel ain't asked you?"

They both looked over at me.

"Nope." Edward smiled carefully in my direction. "I think he's a little sore. On account of Katie."

George gave a knowing nod. "Strange thing to bring on a fella, if you don't mind me sayin'. Some little girl he ain't never see'd before."

"He might've had some idea. In the back of his mind." Edward defended himself. "And what was I to do? Leave the kid alongside the road?"

I stared at the both of them, talking like they'd known each other a lot longer than two minutes. Maybe George was curious. Maybe he just didn't care. But Edward was enjoying himself again, I knew that much.

"You two can jaw all you want," I told them. "There's work to do around here, and somebody's got to do it. I told you both the truth. Make what you want of me. I'm going to go clean that stall."

George started in. "Well, now, your brother just got here—"

"He never said he needed me for anything. Only my water."

George shook his head at me. And Edward laughed. "Don't expect him to be too friendly," he said. "I told you he was sore. And I did nothing but try to help."

"Help?" The fire of anger wrenched through me like a storm, and I found it hard to contain myself. "She said you hit her, Edward. A scared little girl. Six years old. What kind of help is that?"

His smile at me was bigger than ever. "Don't you sound like a father?"

I almost hit him. Honestly, I'm not sure why I didn't. George standing there, maybe. Or the boys. "It doesn't matter what I sound like. Why'd you hit her? What kind of excuse do you have for that?"

He averted his eyes for a minute, looking out over the timber's treetops. "I won't give you one. I know it wasn't right. But you know, it was an awful long ride. And after a while she wouldn't keep her mouth shut. Fussing one minute and talking up a storm the next. I 'bout lost my mind." He looked at George. "Know what I mean?"

"Well . . ." George drawled. "There's times a little quiet's harder t' find than a penny under the new moon, I can unnerstand that. But I wouldn't hit no kid that weren't my own and then only a lick or two to the backside to learn 'em a lesson. You unnerstand?"

"Yes, sir," Edward said. "You s'pose I ought to apologize?"

His question bothered me immediately, like he was just looking for an excuse to stick around.

"Yeah," George answered before I got a word out. "Thing to do is make things right."

"That's what I'm trying to do," he said, suddenly looking at me again. "Ever since I got out. Whether folks want to believe me or not."

"Well, you made a good start," George was continuing. "Just by admittin' you was wrong. Don't you think so, Samuel?"

"If that's what he did."

George eyed me again. "How long's it been since you brothers seen each other?"

"Fifteen years," Edward said right away.

"You been writin'?"

We both shook our heads.

"Well, it don't seem you got much of an unnerstandin' goin'. Shame to leave it that way, case you end up with miles between you again. I reckon the best thing is you sit down an' talk. I'll clean the stall an' get the boys to help me." He looked at both of us. "Think you can do that?"

I didn't answer.

Edward was looking at me too. "I don't think he can. It's not me hitting Katie but bringing her here that's got him the most worked up. Being found out for the cheat he is."

"That's all you want, isn't it?" I questioned. "To spread your lie and see what trouble it can bring. You came all this way savoring the thought, didn't you? But why? What did I ever do to you?"

He laughed. Long.

I turned my back.

"He can't do it," Edward said. "He can't sit down with me. I knew when I come he couldn't."

I walked to the barn, leaving him and George behind me. I knew that perhaps I was behaving badly. Maybe George and the boys would all think less of me. But if I stayed, it might just be that much worse. Edward wasn't wanting to reconcile. He seemed to be wanting to drive me to distraction. Maybe get me to fight him. I didn't know.

I grabbed the biggest shovel and headed for Lula Bell's stall. This was hot, hard work today, and I was in no mood for Edward's mockery. I found myself hoping that Juli and the girls would go over and eat the noon meal with Lizbeth, and that Edward would be gone before they ever got back.

Robert came in to help me, followed closely by Franky.

"Why does he have to be like that?" Robert asked me.

"I don't know. Maybe he thinks he's funny."

"He wants to stay till that girl Katie comes back," Franky said. "Pa told him she went berry pickin' with Mrs. Wortham, so he decided to stay right here till they get back so's he can say he's sorry."

"I need the wheelbarrow. Think you can get it for me, Franky? It's over in the middle, where the hay hooks are hanging up."

"I'll get it," he said quickly and disappeared.

"Robert, I want you to watch for your mother. When you see her coming, you come and get me right away. Edward was a bother to her yesterday, and I don't mean for it to happen again."

"Why don't you run him off? All he does is laugh at you."

I looked at my son and could have hugged him then and there. He, and maybe he alone, seemed to understand. "What do you think? What's he saying?"

"That he's thinking to apologize. And maybe work on his car while he's waiting. But I don't know, Dad. If I talked to you like he does, I figure I'd pay for it."

"Do you know what it means about something being personal?"

"Yeah. Like it's your business and not anybody else's."

"Yes, but with Edward talking to me the way he does, it's a different kind of personal. He's got something against me that makes him want to hurt me some way, that's the only way I know to explain it."

"But what? You never picked at him or nothin' when you was a kid, did you?"

"No. I knew better than that."

He was looking at me so solemnly. Then Franky came carefully back in, balancing the heavy wooden wheelbarrow as well as he could.

Why didn't I run my brother off? It was an honest question. And I wasn't sure of the answer. I wouldn't ask him to stay, despite George's feelings on that. But I guessed I'd let him work on his car in my yard if that was what he wanted. And maybe let him apologize, if he really meant it. After all, he seemed to think he was telling the truth, and Katie did too. I *would* look like a cheat to him, then, if he really believed it all. That wasn't his fault. Maybe there'd be a way to part with some understanding. Or at least in some measure of peace.

I put down the shovel, thinking I'd better try again. "Will you boys shovel for me a few minutes?" I asked.

They both looked at me in question, but then Joe came in, shovel in hand.

"Yeah," Franky said. "You do what you have to."

"Pa said we oughta stay an' help," Joe told me. "But it's gettin' on toward noon an' he's fixin' to head over to home in a little while to see what Sam and Kirk and the rest is got done."

I nodded and stepped outside. Edward had the top open over his engine, and George was standing there still talking to him. I would have gone and offered to help with whatever the problem was, so we could talk things through and come to some kind of conclusion. But I could hear tiny voices of singing coming through the timber. It sounded like Sarah and somebody else. All the little girls, surely, with Julia on their way back. George looked up, and Edward with him, in time to see them breaking through the trees.

Juli! I should have been more prepared. I didn't know what to tell her about why Edward was here or how long he'd stay. It seemed like a betrayal to have him standing here so peacefully.

Even at the distance I could see her slow down. She would have questions in her eyes, I knew she would. She would look at him, and at me, in a way I wasn't used to seeing. Distrust. Dismay. Why was he back? Why was I having it so?

It was all to Edward's pleasure, apparently. He was smiling again.

ELEVEN

Julia

"Look," Sarah whispered. "Is that Uncle Edward over there?"

"Yes." I didn't say anything else, only took her hand in silence and gave it a careful little squeeze.

Katie sought my other hand of her own accord. "Did he come back to take me away?"

"No," I assured her. "He's not taking you anywhere."

Rorey ran on ahead like the wild little thing she was sometimes, shrieking to her father about the turtle we'd caught. A stranger's presence didn't faze her in the slightest. I shouldn't let it bother me, either, I decided, but I went to our yard slowly, glad it was Samuel taking the first steps to meet us.

"He's not been here long," he told me when he was near enough. "He says he wants to tell Katie he's sorry."

I couldn't help it. I stopped and stared at him. "You're speaking for him, now?"

He lowered his eyes. "No. I just wanted you both . . . to be prepared, I guess. You don't have to talk to him at all if you don't want to."

"I don't want to," Katie said right away. "He said if you wouldn't own me, he might just take me away and we'd join the circus."

"That's not up to him."

She turned her big dark eyes to Samuel. "Is it up to you?"

"Only partly. So long as Ben Law has you with me."

The little girl tightened her grip on my hand, and I felt so sorry for her. Samuel wasn't making her future sound very secure. Of course, he couldn't help it. He was only being honest. But it left her looking rather crestfallen. And I realized she was still hoping that Samuel would indeed "own" her. I looked down at the child who was clinging so tightly to me. She hadn't given up. She still wanted her father. And there seemed to be nothing I could say.

"Mommy," Sarah whispered, "I'm hungry."

"Yes," I answered her. That was, of course, why we'd hurried back. Nobody'd had much breakfast, so I'd figured on an early dinner.

I looked over at the tall man at George's side, who was wiping his hands on a grease rag. Maybe he would just keep showing up. Expecting a cool drink and a plate of food. I thought of the sorrel in my bag, of mixing it with our seedy garden lettuce and some lamb's-quarter, and serving that with those few potatoes and the rhubarb cake I'd forgotten and left in the coals. If he thought yesterday's meal was strange, maybe he'd find this one strange too.

I wondered why he didn't just buy his meals in town. If he had money for the gas to keep driving that car out here, surely he'd have some to spare for a bite or two.

I almost felt like telling him we couldn't afford to feed anyone else. Katie was enough.

But then I remembered what I'd been thinking in the woods about Emma. She would have fed him with a smile. She would have killed a chicken, plucked it, and cooked it in nothing flat. And she would have been telling him how much God loved him, even while she was working. Tears came to my eyes. I couldn't hold a candle to her. I just couldn't.

"Juli . . ." Samuel reached his hand to me, but I didn't let go of either girl.

"I'm fine," I told him quickly, before he could say anything else.

"Don't worry about dinner. We can wait. It's plenty early."

"I'm going to kill a chicken," I said so quietly that I barely even heard it. My own words had taken me by surprise. Kill a chicken? One of our precious egg-laying hens? For Edward? Oh, Emma. Oh, Jesus. Must I?

"What?" Samuel asked me.

"I'm going to kill a chicken," I repeated, steeling myself to the idea.

"We get to eat it?" Sarah asked. The shock was plainly evident on her face. Killing a chicken ought to be undertaken only with careful consideration, I'd told both my children many times. Because we mustn't rob tomorrow, thinking about today.

"Are you sure?" Samuel asked. "We can make do with whatever else."

"No," I told him. "We have a guest, and we haven't yet treated him like one. Maybe it'll make some difference. We can hope."

He looked at me like I'd lost my mind. "I thought you wanted to keep them for winter—"

"Things change," I said quickly. "Things come up."

I started for the house in a hurry, wanting to get this

over with before I changed my mind. There were only six potatoes, not enough if the Hammond children stayed. I could devil the eggs that were left, but there weren't many. I'd have to get creative rather quickly if we were to have a feast. We'd had the green beans yesterday, so I knew there weren't enough ready yet. And the tomatoes weren't ready either.

"Sarah, you and Katie take one of the empty pails down by the road and pick me all the unopened daylily buds you can find."

"We gonna eat that too?" Sarah asked. It wasn't entirely new to her. We'd done it once or twice last summer.

"Yes. And we'll need quite a few with company here."

The girls hurried off together.

Samuel grabbed my hand. "Julia—"

"Now don't even try to talk me out of this. He's your brother. What would Emma do? She'd serve him the very finest meal—"

He leaned and kissed me. Right on the lips while I was trying to talk. Not caring that all the world could see. "I love you," he said. "You've got a bigger heart than I do."

I could feel the tears welling up, and I tried my best to deny them. "No. I'm bitter and mean and I'm just doing this because it's the thing to do. I didn't say I liked it."

He smiled. "I love you anyway. I don't think you've ever been mean."

"You watch," I said. "It might happen." I hurried the rest of the way to the house, knowing it wasn't only Samuel's eyes watching me. Inside I got a soup pot and came charging back out. Samuel was waiting on the porch.

"Fill this with water," I told him. "I'm going to stir the fire back up."

Samuel kept a pile of wood next to the ring of rocks, right there handy for summer cooking. I pulled my cake pan out of the coals, stirred the embers, and added little sticks to get a flame again. By the time Samuel came with the pot of water, the fire was blazing. He set the pan over the fire for me, and I took a peek at the cake. Too done on one side, not quite enough on the other. That's what happens when you just leave something without checking. I set it on a rock with the underdone side toward the heat and marched right on to the chicken coop. Emma's chicken catcher was just like Grandma Pearl's. Wooden handle on a long, stiff wire with a crook at the end. I grabbed it from its nail on the wall.

"You want me to do that?" Samuel asked.

I hadn't even realized he'd followed me. "No," I said quickly. I knew I needed to do it. I needed to be able to, not so much for Edward as for Emma and our merciful God.

"Just guard the gate, if you don't mind," I told him. "Make sure none of them get out."

I took that chicken catcher by the wooden end and stepped inside the coop with it. Right away, those hens knew exactly what was on my mind. Every one of them lit out the back flap into their yard, squawking up a fuss. I tried hard to get the last of them, Lazy Susan, we called her. But even she was too fast for me.

I came back out of the coop, pushing the hair away from my face. All the chickens were gathered in the corner opposite Sam at the gate, probably figuring him to be in on this little attack. I knew it wouldn't do a bit of good to sneak up. I just ran at them as they started to scatter, and I swung the hook end of the catcher right into the middle of those fluttering feathers. I hit one of them and gave it a yank.

Wingy. That was Sarah's name for the hen. She'd given all of them names. At least this one wasn't my best layer. I pulled the hen close. The hook of the catcher had got her by the leg. I struggled to reach past her flapping wings to grab her by both legs and hold her upside down.

"That's a pretty piece of work," Edward declared from

beside the fence. I hadn't even seen him come up so close. "No wonder Samuel married you. I bet you take care of him real fine."

I'd never admitted to hating anyone. Maybe I never would. But I sure hated his words, his attitude. Here he was, disparaging my husband right in front of him. Samuel didn't say a word, but I couldn't be so meek about it.

"He's a good provider," I said. "*He* takes care of *me*."

The rest of the hens had run for cover back in the coop again, and the old rooster was pacing back and forth, looking at me with suspicion.

"Uh-huh," Edward scoffed. "I don't suppose he's worked a job since he lost the one in Pennsylvania. Have you, Samuel?"

My quiet husband opened the gate for me, ignoring his brother completely. "Hatchet's sharp already," he said. "Let me kill it for you."

For a moment our eyes met, and I saw something I hadn't expected to see. He was angry. Sad and angry and trying just as hard as I was to maintain control. I handed him the chicken. *It's a sacrifice,* I suddenly thought. *Lord, receive it from us.*

I hadn't noticed George Hammond. But suddenly he was standing beside us, telling us he had to get home.

"You got yer comp'ny," he said. "An' I got me a' plenty to do. Don't worry 'bout gettin' to the field this afternoon, Samuel. I know you got your hands full." He looked sideways at Edward. "Maybe some folks don't know that farmin's all work. Long hours, purty near ever' day. Don't have to be in no fact'ry to work your tail off, that's for sure."

I smiled.

"I'll leave Joe an' Frank to finish them stalls, if you don't mind feedin' 'em, Mrs. Wortham."

"No," I said, thinking about the food I'd have to muster up. "I don't mind. Thank you."

"Yes," Samuel echoed. "Thank you." He started walking to the shed with the chicken. I thought of how strong he'd had to be, facing the sheriff and his brother and even little Katie, telling them all the same thing. The truth. Why couldn't I have just believed him without question when he needed me to? And now he was facing a day like this, having to bury our cow and then stand and take Edward's ridicule. What was he thinking inside?

I glanced at Edward, who was still gawking at us with his cocky kind of smile. How could two brothers be so different?

I followed Samuel, and Edward spoke to me quickly, before I could get out of earshot. "You'd be loyal, no matter what. Rather that than do any thinking, I guess."

Samuel was reaching for the hatchet, an old one, longer than most, which he kept good and sharp and clean. He was good about that, like he was good about so much.

There was a stump to one side of the shed. We'd killed chickens there last year when Emma was still living, and once in the early days of spring when we'd had to have the meat. Holding Wingy upside down, Samuel took her there, laid her across the flat old stump, and with one quick whack, took off her head.

Suddenly killing this chicken seemed awful, when Lula Bell had died and we'd killed a fine, healthy turtle earlier in the day. That was farm living, I knew. That was survival, even. But at that moment, I didn't like it one bit, because it just spoke of our need. *Oh, Lord, help us.*

"So you pluck it now?" Edward asked us.

I was still watching Samuel holding the headless hen with its wings flapping and the blood oozing down onto the ground. "You want to do it?" I asked Edward right back.

"I don't have the slightest idea how."

"Maybe you should learn," I told him. "It's a useful skill. Someday you might want to settle down somewhere and provide for yourself."

Samuel looked at me rather oddly. Edward didn't reply, but he was looking at me differently too. And I knew I was wrong to let bitterness do the talking. I knew what Emma would do. I swallowed hard, mustering my courage.

"God loves you, Edward Wortham," I said. "He may not like the way you behave, but he loves you just the same."

Edward stared at me in silence, glanced over at Samuel, and then back at me with some distant thing churning in his eyes. But whatever it was vanished away quickly, and he laughed again, loud and ugly.

"Mother told me about you! She said you and Samuel can't hardly take two breaths anymore without getting all religious! You gonna take up preaching? Huh? You gonna build you a church out here somewhere? Next to the outhouse, maybe, and preach to the chickens and the neighbor kids and anybody that'll come and listen?"

"We go to church in Dearing," Samuel said. "That's good enough."

"You think you're better, that's what it is," Edward continued, addressing Samuel directly this time. "That's what I've been talking about. You act like you're better, but you're not."

"Better than what?" Samuel asked, his deep eyes looking soft.

Edward didn't hesitate. "Me."

I wished to goodness Edward had kept his mouth shut long enough for Samuel to answer that. It might've changed things for both of them. But Edward rushed headlong into another tirade, not giving Samuel a chance for even a word.

"You'd be nothing without your woman here, and you know it! You don't know what to do out here on no farm. You're a city boy. Couldn't even make it in that factory! And now you think you're Mr. Christian Do-Good all of a sudden! Don't you think you owe her an apology—"

"No," I cut in. "He owes me no apology at all. But you do, for coming in here and tearing him down. I don't want to listen to it."

Samuel started walking toward the fire and the water that hopefully had gotten hot enough.

I followed, and Edward followed me, shaking his head. "Gads, woman. You must be in love."

"Of course I'm in love!" I replied. "And I always will be."

Samuel dunked the dead chicken in the bubbling water pot and back out again. I looked up at him, glad he'd heard me. Maybe I could redeem myself in his eyes.

"I know Samuel well," I addressed Edward again. "Better than you do. So I don't believe what you say about him. Not any of it. About Trudy Vale or anything else. And he was doing fine in that factory. He'd been promoted three times. It wasn't his fault the place closed down. Everybody lost their jobs the same day. It had nothing to do with him."

Samuel laid the chicken across a rock and started plucking feathers. I picked up a stick and poked the well-done potatoes farther to the side than they already were, and then started helping.

"You're being mighty generous," Edward remarked with another shake of his head. "Julia Wortham. Quite a wonder."

"It's Samuel Wortham who's the wonder," I argued. "If you were in his shoes and he came railing on you in your own home, do you think you'd be quietly plucking him a chicken? Or running him clear out of the countryside?"

He laughed. "Well, at least the hospitality here has improved a bit."

"That's because God loves you," I said again and took a deep breath. "We do too, and we're trying to show it, despite what you think."

"You're incurable," he said. But he got real quiet. He looked at us both and then past us to the road where the girls were still picking daylily bulbs.

"I think I'll work on my car while you're fixing," he said. "It was sounding funny on the way out here this time."

"Not bad," Samuel ventured. "Just a bit of a knock."

"What do *you* know?" Edward asked him, but without the malice his words had had before.

"Will you let me help you?" Samuel asked. "Just to take a look?"

Edward didn't answer. He just turned around and walked to the car.

I took the chicken from Samuel's hands, and he leaned and kissed me again. "Thank you," he whispered and then headed over to Edward's side.

It was strange seeing them together, with their heads bent over that automobile. From the back, they truly looked like brothers. And working together that way, they almost looked like friends.

I had to run in the house for my knife, fry pan, and lard pail. Then I cut the chicken quickly while my pan was getting hot. Sarah came running up with the pail of daylily buds and a fistful of flowers.

"For you, Mommy."

Maybe she knew I needed such a gesture then. I hugged

her and thanked her and then sent her inside for a vase and a bowl of flour for the chicken.

"Do we get chicken too?" she asked when she came back.

"You get some too. I cut a few more pieces than usual. That means they'll be small, but they'll go around to everybody before Edward digs in and finishes it off."

"We don't get seconds?"

"Not this time, sweetheart. At least not till Edward finishes. After everyone has their piece, I want you to let him have all the rest that he wants, and that goes for everything we make, even if he eats it all. Okay?"

"Okay," she said. "But why?"

"Because I'm making him a feast. Or at least the best that I can. We're going to celebrate your father's brother being here and pray that he comes to know the Lord, honey."

"Oh. He don't know about Jesus?"

"Well, not much, I daresay."

"Want me to tell him? Or Franky could. Only he's in the barn right now."

"Either of you could, and it might be fine. Only wait a while, all right? Until we're eating, maybe."

I glanced over at the men tinkering so quietly on that car. As far as I could tell, there'd been scarcely two words between them. Why didn't they talk? Why couldn't Edward just listen to reason? There must be some sort of a logical answer about Katie. Maybe they could think of it together. Maybe their mother had mentioned some relative or something. If Edward would only listen to reason, maybe he would go and leave us in peace.

And maybe Sheriff Law would put Katie on a train to her family and we'd be all back to normal. I looked across the farmyard to where Rorey and Katie were playing with Whiskers. We could write to her. It would be good for Sarah to have a pen pal.

"Can I flour the chicken, Mommy?"

"You can help me. We have plenty to do."

Once the chicken was frying, I sent Sarah to rinse her pail of buds at the well, and I went to the garden and lopped off the tops of half a row of turnips. I used the big old soup pot for them and then pulled up a few carrots and onions, both smaller than I liked. Too bad the sweet corn wasn't ripe. And too bad what few peas we'd had were already burned up in the summer sun.

I cut the carrots and onions together with the daylily buds. I'd cream them along with some salt and the sorrel from my picking bag. I didn't know if Edward would like it or even try it, but my family had learned to eat pretty much whatever there was. I opened one of the ash-covered potatoes and found the outside crispy but the inside white and soft. They'd be fine, despite my neglect. I was surely flustered this morning, not to think about them or the cake. It wasn't like me to just stick them in the coals and leave without even asking Samuel or Robert to check them. Oh well. They'd come out all right.

After turning the chicken, I hurried to the house again for sugar and vanilla extract to make a glaze on the cake. We would let Edward eat the better side. I wondered if he'd ever had rhubarb. Samuel hadn't when I'd first met him.

Then I remembered the eggs. There were five boiled ones left from our breakfast, down in the cool pit, with what was left of the morning milk. By the time I came up from the basement, Katie and Sarah had both come in the house. They helped me peel and halve the eggs. Then I let them mash the yolks while I opened the second-to-last jar of pickles. We stirred a little cream, a cut-up pickle, and a dash of sugar and paprika into the yolks, and stuffed the halves as neatly as we could.

Katie said she'd never seen deviled eggs before, which surprised me. But maybe she just meant she'd never seen any like those. Of course, we made do with what we had. Grandma Pearl had hardly ever had mayonnaise, and neither did I anymore.

After we finished, we marched outside with the plate of eggs, the rest of the jar of pickles, and a blanket big enough to spread on the ground and seat everyone. I realized I hadn't done anything with the sassafras, so I filled the coffeepot with water, dumped the sassafras in, and set it on the fire. But I'd forgotten bread too, so I had to run back inside for a loaf of the soda bread I'd baked that morning. Then we were ready to eat.

I called the boys from the barn—they were a filthy sight, but it didn't take them long to clean up. They'd been working so hard, I was glad to give them a good meal and a break.

Whiskers was getting excited about the chicken smell. Poor dog. I'd forgotten the turtle bones. But he'd have chicken bones soon enough. Robert shut him in the barn to keep him away from our plates.

Samuel and Edward came from the car in silence as I was setting the last of the food down in the middle of the blanket.

"Something smells good," Edward said, picking up a plate. He was about to help himself when Sarah spoke up.

"We need to say grace."

I could see Edward's stormy eyes turn to Samuel. But Samuel only waited a second for all the children to be still, and then he prayed.

"Heavenly Father, we thank you for the food you have provided. We thank you for the families you've given us, to love and to honor. Guide us in your will, Lord, that we may be pleasing in your eyes."

As soon as he'd closed his prayer, the boys were ready to grab what they could. Especially the chicken. And they were entitled to it, I figured.

"We have a new tradition," I said quickly. "The children get to choose their pieces first."

Samuel glanced my way, but I only smiled and passed the chicken carefully to Sarah and Katie. Once every child had a piece, I let Edward take what he wanted. Samuel had a wing. Edward ate the rest.

Of course, there weren't enough potatoes to go around, but I split one between Rorey and Katie and gave the rest to the men and boys. Sarah wasn't very fond of them cooked that way, so she and I did without. I filled my plate with turnip greens and the lily mixture and sat back and watched everybody eat.

"This is mighty good," Joe remarked. "Ain't had this kinda meal since Easter."

"Good chicken," Edward agreed, in the middle of a bite. "Good pickles."

My eyes met Samuel's as he was passing around the eggs. He didn't say a word, but his look was enough. I knew I'd done the right thing.

"Want some daylily buds?" Sarah asked her uncle sweetly. "I helped pick 'em."

"What is it?" he asked, a little uncertain.

"Daylily. If they don't get picked, they open into a big orange flower."

"Oh. We're eatin' flowers."

Sarah smiled so innocently. "Flowers is good. I like the little violets that grow in the yard, and the sorrel ones too, that's yellow as the sun an' taste like pickle."

Edward looked around at our faces. "You always eat like this?"

"No, sir," Robert answered. "This is the biggest, fanciest we've had in a long time. An' it ain't even a holiday."

For a moment I thought Edward was going to stop eating; he looked a little surprised and solemn. Maybe he'd thought we bought more food, I don't know. Maybe he thought he could never live like this, never in a million years.

Sarah suddenly smiled wider. "It's a Jesus holiday," she declared. "It's a holiday for Daddy's brother and Jesus."

Edward furrowed his brow and bit into his chicken. But Sarah was not to be stopped. "Did you know Jesus loves you? He got killed a long time ago, and then he came alive again and we get to be forgiven."

"That don't make much sense," he told her. "Even comin' from you, sweetheart."

"You have to know why he died," Franky added. "He was bein' punished instead a' us. That's why we're forgiven. We're not guilty no more if the price is already paid. Wipes it all away, you know?"

Edward stared over at him, chewing furiously in silence. Finally he spoke. "What's done is done. You can't make it undone."

And he wouldn't hear another word.

With the meal behind us, I cleaned up the dishes. Robert and Joe had gone back to the barn, and the little girls helped me for a little while and then went to play beneath the lilac bush. Samuel and Edward were back at the car, still not saying very much. Franky stood beside me, thinking, I knew. Finally he spoke.

"He just don't unnerstand. Why don't he let us tell him some more about Jesus? I think he knows he's sinned. He oughta want to be forgiven."

"We can't make him open his heart," I told the boy.

"Yeah. But ain't there somethin' we can do to get him thinkin'?"

"The only thing I know is to show him as much of the love of God as we can. Pastor Jones said once that it's the goodness of God that draws men to him."

Franky was quiet again, and then he seemed to brighten.

"What if I washed off his car for him? It sure does need it. It's just full a' dust."

"Are you sure you want to do that?"

"Yes, ma'am. If he asks me how come, I'll tell him 'cause Jesus loves him. Can I use a bucket a' water?"

"I suppose so," I answered, too surprised to know what else to say. Franky had his bucket filled quickly and was soon started on the job. I watched to see Edward's reaction. Franky said something I couldn't hear, and Edward shook his head, turning his attention back to his motor.

The next time I looked up, Samuel was talking and Edward was looking angry. They were having words. I should've called Franky back, but I didn't think of it in time.

"You can fool the whole blame countryside if you want!" Edward yelled. "But it ain't fooling me! You're a dirty liar, and that's all I have to say about it!"

It happened so fast. He started his car in less than two shakes, and almost at the same time Samuel yelled, fierce and loud enough to make me jump. The car jerked backward several feet. Franky screamed. And I dropped the fry pan and went running.

Samuel fell to his knees beside Edward's car. Franky was lying so still. I could feel my heart pounding. How could this happen? How could Edward hit the boy? When Franky was only doing him a good turn, how could he back up and run right into him?

I rushed forward, and Samuel looked up at me. Edward didn't even get out of the car.

The boy's legs were halfway under the car, bent. He held his eyes squeezed shut. I could see the pain in his face.

"D-did the wheel go over him?" I gasped. Behind me I heard one of the girls crying, but I didn't turn to look.

Samuel nodded, looking absolutely broken. He was

holding Franky's head, calling his name, and the boy's eyes popped open.

"Can you move?" Samuel asked him.

Franky jerked his head from side to side. "It hurts. It hurts." Then he shut his eyes again. His hands were already shaped into tight little fists.

"We'll have to get him to a hospital," Samuel told me. "Can you get something to wrap him and help hold him still?"

"Joe!" Rorey was screaming. "Joe! Get Pa!"

My first thought was George's wagon. Or Barrett Post's truck. And maybe that was Edward's first thought too. "Move him out a ways," he told Samuel. "I'll go get somebody."

"No," Samuel said coolly. "You're taking us."

I only stayed long enough to catch a glimpse of Edward's pale, ugly expression.

The skunk! The horrid, no-good skunk!

I ran for the house. What could I use to keep Franky still? He wasn't moving now, but in a bouncy car on bumpy roads . . . Oh, it would hurt so bad! I grabbed every pillow and blanket I could carry.

I wanted to go with him in the car. I wanted to hold that little boy I'd come to know so well, kiss him and tell him this would pass, that he'd be okay. But I already knew that I would have to stay home with the other children.

Joe was beside them when I got back. I'd not seen him look so upset, since his mother died last December.

"He'll be okay," I said as soon as I was close enough. But the words haunted me. I'd said the same about Wilametta, and she hadn't lasted even one more night. But this was different. It was just his legs. So far as I could tell.

"We can stop for your father," Samuel was saying, and Joe gave his solemn nod. "But you ride along. If he's in the field, we won't be able to wait for him. We'll take

Lizbeth, and you can send him after us and stay with the little ones."

"Yes, sir."

"Can I come?" Rorey asked.

Samuel glanced at her, but I answered for him quickly. "No. You stay with me."

I dropped everything I was carrying at Franky's side. He winced when we moved him. He squeezed his skinny arms tight to his chest and bit his lip to keep from crying, but he cried out anyway.

I wrapped a blanket around his legs as firmly as I dared, wondering how they'd manage him in the car.

"Help me with him, Joe," Samuel said. "It'll be easier if I get in the back and just hold him. Then you can pad all around us, Juli. As much as you can."

It was Sarah crying, I realized. But I didn't see her. Or Katie. I wondered where they'd gone. Robert was suddenly beside us, holding the car door and helping his father maneuver. I put one blanket down beneath where Franky would be. Edward still hadn't moved. *Like a stubborn, stinking old billy goat,* I thought. *And it's all his fault.*

I stuffed the pillows around Franky as carefully as I could, then kissed his forehead and clasped his hand as Joe squeezed his long and lanky frame between his little brother and the back of the front seat.

"Do exactly what I say," Samuel ordered Edward. "Drive not too fast, not too slow."

"I didn't see him," Edward whined. "I didn't know he was still up so close. Fool kid—"

At that moment my anger at Edward seethed raw, but it was Samuel who yelled. "Shut up! I don't care what you didn't know! Shut up and drive!"

With Samuel sitting and holding Franky's chest and head and Joe leaning into the pillows to keep his legs from bouncing, they started away. I could see the tears on Franky's cheeks. But he was being so quiet. So brave. Managing to take it better than I could have.

Edward, on the other hand, was mumbling as he turned the car around right over top of Emma's irises. Something about Samuel. And something about Katie.

I would have kicked him if I could.

TWELVE

Samuel

As we drove up, George was in the yard rounding up goats. Joe started yelling, and George and Lizbeth both came running, leaving Willy chasing a goat out of the garden.

"Lordy!" George said when we told him what happened. "Lordy be! I shouldn't a' left him with you. He gets to daydreamin'—"

"It wasn't his fault," I said quickly, incensed at George for daring to blame his son. "We need to go. Are you coming?"

"Yeah. Yeah, I'm comin'."

"You want me to stay?" Joe asked his father. "Or come along?"

"You better stay. Lizbeth is gonna need more help gettin' them goats in, or we'll lose the veg'table patch. The rest a' the big boys is in the field."

"Pa," Lizbeth said, reaching her hand to Franky's hair.

Franky looked up at her, crying just a little. The poor kid. I could feel him all tense in my arms. Shaking. I knew at least one of those legs was broken.

"You gotta stay, Lizbeth," George said. "Won't be nothin' you can do there yet, anyhow." He climbed in the front seat as Joe got out of the back.

"Pa—" Lizbeth protested again.

"We can get the goats in without her, Pa," Joe said quickly. "I can watch the little ones too. Where's Emmie Grace?"

"Nappin'," Lizbeth answered.

"Let her go, Pa," Joe begged. "He might need her there, since he ain't got Mama."

George didn't say anything more. He only nodded, rather reluctantly, and Lizbeth hurried in the back where Joe had been, looking scared but relieved to be going.

"Go to Mcleansboro," George ordered. "It's a sight closer'n Mt. Vernon."

"I didn't see him," Edward started in right away as soon as we were moving again. "Didn't know he was so close."

"Just a accident," George replied, looking tense.

"Turn east at the next road," I told Edward, knowing he wasn't used to these parts. He did as I said, and kept quiet.

I wondered at both of them. At George, who had climbed in front without leaning close to his son for even a second, without even speaking to him. And at Edward, who kept excusing himself and had never once asked how bad it might be. I guessed Edward was just too hard and detached to care. But George . . . George would have reacted differently if it had been his oldest son. Or his youngest. Maybe any of the others but Franky.

With Franky, George's first thought was of it being the boy's own fault. He worked Franky along with the rest, but he didn't trust him to work alone; he didn't seem to see the boy's accomplishments. He only wagged his head at Franky's failures in school.

"Can't figger how he come to be stupid," he'd told me once. "He don't appear stupid, to look at him."

Nothing I could say made any difference. George didn't seem to hear Lizbeth or Julia about it, either. Only the teacher's words: "He's not learning. I don't know if he *can* learn."

Franky hollered once when we went over a bump, and I held him tighter. Lizbeth held him too, with tears in her eyes. He started crying, trying hard to be so still, and I knew he was hurting badly. He was one tough little kid.

George was the only one of us who'd ever been to Mcleansboro, and that was before the hospital had opened in 1929. But it wasn't hard to find someone who could direct us. We found Market Street pretty quickly, and Edward pulled up in front of the hospital with a lurch that almost made me yell at him again.

The place looked like a house. Had been once, I could tell. "One of you go in and see if they have a cart," I said.

But Franky shook his head. "Carry me."

So I carried him. Nine years old and barely heavier than Sarah. He rested his head against my shoulder, took a deep breath, and whispered the name of Jesus.

"He's with you," Lizbeth assured him, hurrying along at my side. George was following, I knew he was. But Edward didn't get out of the car.

THIRTEEN

Julia

"Is he gonna be okay?" Sarah asked me for the tenth time as we dragged rugs out of the house.

Busy work. Something to tax my muscles but not my brain. "Of course, he'll be okay. He may have to stay in bed a while, but he'll be okay."

I shook out every rug as the girls watched. Then I sent them to go and make whatever they wanted with that clay before it dried out entirely. I threw the rugs over the clothesline and retrieved Emma's rug beater. It was new in 1911, she'd told me once. It didn't look new now.

I wondered if Emma had ever beat her rugs just to have an excuse for beating at something. Grandma Pearl had told me once about making beaten biscuits, where you pound the dough with a wooden paddle till you're nigh exhausted. I couldn't do that. I'd lost the recipe clear back in Pennsylvania. But I could get the dust out of these rugs if it killed me.

I beat and I beat, tears streaming down my cheeks. I was so mad I scared myself. I could scarcely imagine Emma or my grandma or any other woman feeling so mad as I was. It wasn't like me. Not even with all we'd been through.

I knew it was different because it was Edward, shaking Samuel in ways I didn't understand. Making me doubt my own love and trust in him. And now hurting an innocent little boy without even the decency to admit his mistake or say he was sorry. I could have whacked him as easily as one of those rugs.

It took me a minute to realize I wasn't alone. I'd thought Robert was back in the barn and all three girls under the apple tree with that clay. But I turned, feeling eyes on me. And I found Katie, her face full of question.

"Why are you doing that?" she asked, looking fearful.

"To get the dust out." I whacked at the nearest rug again, but not so viciously.

"Seems like you'd tear 'em all to pieces." She was looking at me with her eyes wide, but she had to turn her head to cough for a minute, I was stirring up so much dust.

"Rugs are sturdy," I told her. "Or they wouldn't bear walking on. They can take a beating. Best way to get the dirt out."

"Mama only shook hers," she said after a pause. "She only had one, an' we took it with us every place, rolled up in the bottom of Mama's bag. But it was stole in Newark 'long with the other stuff, and Mama cried."

I stopped and looked at her. "Why would your mother travel with a rug?"

"'Cause her grandmama made it. She said it was a keepsake."

I couldn't help wondering how a woman who would abandon her daughter could get sentimental over a throw rug. "Your mother's grandmother?" I asked. "Did you ever meet her?"

"Don't think so. Only my own grandma. Not Mama's."

"Do you know her name?"

Katie smiled. "Pearly. Just like pearly gates in the sky."

I almost dropped the rug beater. Katie's mother had a Grandma Pearly? *Lord, this is too much!* Doing things with my Grandma Pearl had been the dearest part of my childhood. Where had this girl come from? Finding such a coincidence startled me.

"Lacey Pearly," Katie continued. "Mama told me once she should have named me after her. 'Cause it sounds so much like a wedding dress. Lacey Pearly. Ain't it pretty? But she's dead now. That's why I didn't tell that sheriff her name. He won't find her, unless he goes to the pearly gates."

The name wasn't the same after all. Pearl had been my grandmother's first name. Pearl Evan Carlton. But I wondered why this grandmother had been so special to a woman like Trudy Vale. Why did Katie even know about her when she knew so little about her mother's mother, who, hopefully, was still living? "Katie, did your mother talk about her grandma a lot?"

"Sometimes. 'Specially when she was sad."

"Well, the sheriff ought to know. You might have some other relatives named Pearly. Wouldn't it be nice to find them?"

"No."

"Why not?"

"'Cause Mama said none of 'em care about her." She glanced up at me and then quickly down at her shoes. "An' I wanna stay here."

I leaned the rug beater against the clothesline pole. "But we don't know yet how long—"

"I—I mean all the time." She took a deep breath and let the words roll out. "I promise I'll be good every single day.

I'll help you with everything all the time, just tell me what to do. I can be quiet too, I promise, only . . . only . . ."

"Katie—"

She was looking at me with pleading in her eyes. "I'm sorry what happened to that little boy, Mrs. Wortham. I—I'll do his chores. I'll help you, I promise. You don't have to be mad. Not at me or Mr. Wortham, 'cause I'll be good. I promise."

I stared at her, stunned for a moment. "Honey, that accident was not your fault."

"I know," she said as a tear slid to her cheek only to be wiped away furiously.

"I'm not mad at you. It's just that you're bound to have family somewhere else who cares for you—"

"I don't think so. I think Sarah's daddy is the only daddy I got. It's just like Mama said—he's got two other kids. And I promise I won't be no extra trouble."

For a moment I was speechless. "Edward told you we had two children?"

"I dunno. Mama said my daddy told her, before he left the last time, because she asked him if he had family someplace else."

Suddenly my heart was racing. "How old are you?"

"Six. Didn't I tell you?"

"Yes. But . . . but when is your birthday?"

"I was six in winter. In January."

Sarah'd been six in August. She was less than a year old when Katie'd been born. But we'd had two children.

Suddenly I thought of the picture. Stolen with the rug and who knew what all else. But a picture. My eyes filled with tears. "He really does look like your daddy?"

She nodded, and I reached my hand to the clothesline above me, just to steady myself.

"Please don't be mad."

"I'm not." I managed to choke out the words. "I'm not . . . mad."

FOURTEEN

Samuel

Only one leg was broken. The other was bruised and sore, but they didn't find a break. The right leg was broken just below the knee. Painful. More than one nurse told us how brave Franky had been not to scream when they had to touch it and try to set it.

He was clinging tight to Lizbeth and me both. They thought I was his father at first, until we told them different. George just stood looking on.

"Be strong, now, boy," he said once or twice. "Don't fuss no more'n you have to."

I knew it touched George to see his child in pain. I could see it in his eyes. But he didn't move to touch him, even when I tried to get him to Franky's side.

"We'll have to keep him here awhile," Doctor Hall told us. "I believe we have it set right, but I'll want to check him, and he shouldn't be moving it."

George clenched his hat in both hands. "How long's a while?"

"Weeks. Three at least. Maybe he could go home then. If you can get him there easily enough and he can stay in bed."

The doctor left us, and George shook his head and paced the floor a while. "I don't like doctors," he finally told me. "Don't like hospitals. Can't pay 'em. You know that."

"I don't think you have any choice right now," I said. "And they haven't asked for money, but we'll find a way."

"You're still sayin' we, Samuel. Still claimin' us all?"

"Why wouldn't I? I guess you claim us too."

"We's more trouble than you ever been."

It was strange to hear George admit something like that. Finally he went to Franky's bedside and touched the boy's hand. But by that time, the medicine they'd given Franky for the pain had put him to sleep. He looked peaceful, and more like George than I'd ever noticed.

"He's a good boy, George. Way smarter than you know."

"You always did think that. He oughta been your boy. At least you unnerstand him."

"You could. If you talked to him more."

"Nah. Tried that. He'll say stuff like he's a grain a' wheat or he's wonderin' what'd happen if some storybook character was to show up in our backyard."

"All children have a strong imagination."

"But he's differ'nt! You know that! He's clumsy an' awkward. He ain't normal, staring off into space and thinkin' 'bout how come the sky's blue an' dirt ain't. It don't make a lick a' sense to me. He asked me the other day what the world'd be like if there weren't no trees an' the cows weren't no bigger'n m' arm! He can't milk without tippin' the bucket. He can't read a lick. Only thing he can do right is whittle wood an' hammer an' saw with you when you got the time. An' now this! I dunno what'll come of him, Samuel, don't you see? What if he's cripple on top a' ever'thin' else?"

At Franky's bedside, Lizbeth was watching us and listening but not saying a word.

"I see he's a thinker, George. And he *is* good with wood. But he knows what he's talking about with a lot more than that. He'll be all right, one way or another."

George was shaking his head, and it bothered me.

"I happen to know that you don't read, either," I said quietly.

"Well, it weren't 'cuz I failed at tryin'!" George snapped. "I didn't go to school like Franky goes! Never went but one day, so it ain't the same a'tall!"

Maybe he was a little too loud. Maybe we both were. A nurse came in, looking at us rather sternly, and asked again which one of us was the boy's father.

"That'd be me," George said, suddenly looking timid.

The nurse told us I'd have to leave in a little while. Only Franky's parents could stay with him after visiting time.

"He don't have a mama livin'," Lizbeth told the woman. "So can I stay an' take her place?"

"You're the sister?"

"Yes, ma'am."

The nurse agreed. And I wondered how any of us would manage to get back home. Me tonight. But then Lizbeth and George and eventually Franky. Barrett Post would come in after them, if I could get to his house to tell him about it. But if Edward hadn't stayed, how was I going to get across the miles back home? A long walk, I guessed. Or hitchhiking, the way my family had done to get out here from Pennsylvania.

Juli would be wondering about Franky, I knew. And she wouldn't be the only one. So when the time came to leave, I made my way to the door. George wanted to go too, but I told him he ought to stay. Franky needed him more than the kids at home did right now.

"Most of 'em is fine, sure," he said. "But Emmie Grace'll be fit to be tied without Lizbeth there. An' it ain't just that. There's the milkin' to do—"

"Your boys are well capable. But I'll check on them. They'll be wanting to know about Franky, anyway."

I knew Lizbeth was glad to stay. And glad her father was staying too.

I walked outside in the evening sun, expecting to start looking for a stranger headed to Dearing. But Edward was still there, in the same place we'd left him, only he was sitting on the front of his car with a bottle of something and a cigarette. He stood up when he saw me coming.

"I thought you'd left," I told him.

"You didn't need me in there. But I thought I better stay long enough to see how he's doing."

It was a surprise, a pleasant one, to find that maybe he cared. "The one leg's broke pretty badly, but he should be all right. He'll be here a while. On bed rest a while."

He threw his cigarette down in the street. "Was hoping you'd be bringing him right back out."

"Things don't always work the way we hope."

"You can say that again, little brother."

For a moment he looked younger, softer, like the boy who'd shared pickle loaf with me once in the middle of the woods on the edge of Albany.

"What do you think we'd have been like if Mother wasn't a drinker?" he suddenly asked.

"I don't know, Edward. Seems like our choices are our own, regardless of Mother."

"Yeah. I might expect you to say something like that."

"What are you drinking now?" I asked him, knowing I was risking his anger.

But he didn't seem upset. "It ain't alcohol, if that's what you mean. I ain't stupid enough to pull out any of that out here in the open. It's Pepsi-Cola. You ever have one?"

"No."

"It ain't bad." He took a long swig.

"I need a ride," I told him. "I can't pay you, but if it's not too much bother, could you take me home? They'll be wanting to hear about Franky."

Edward was looking down at his boots. "Just you? The rest are staying?"

"Franky can't go. And they'll let immediate family stay with him. That's all. I'll have to tell our pastor and friends about this so they can check in on them."

He lifted his eyes and gave me an uncomfortable look.

"I know it was an accident," I told him. "You weren't watching, but I know you didn't mean to."

"Well," he said with a sigh. "Good of you to say it. Thought maybe you'd think I did it for spite. The little hammer boy was trying to run me off yesterday. Brave little cuss."

For a moment his words rankled me, as I thought about him laying his hand on Juli and Franky having to rush to her defense. Why had he come back again today? He'd never even bothered to explain. *Lord,* I prayed just to calm myself, *maybe he's trying to be different. Maybe. At least he's not being so hateful right now.*

"I didn't hurt him on purpose, Sammy," he said. "If there was anybody out there I'd want to hit, it'd be you."

There was no great malice in his eyes. No laughter.

I wasn't sure the reason for such a confession, or how to respond to it. "Well," I finally said, "I guess I'll walk downtown. There's bound to be somebody over there heading back to Dearing."

"Get in the car, you fool," he told me. "I'll take your sorry hide home. And you don't have to pay me a cent."

I got in. But I knew we were in for a face-off. I knew that whatever was eating at him was bound to come out when we were alone.

It took a while—most of the ride we sat in stony silence. But as we passed close to Delafield, he finally started talking.

"Sammy, your wife knows what you did," he said with a smirk. "She's just being such a sweet little Christian that she doesn't want to look at it."

I didn't want to hear this. I didn't want to talk. But here it was. "She knows everything I do. I tell her everything."

"Sure. Maybe now. But not before, I'd bet. And the poor thing's trying to tell herself how wonderful you are—"

"Will you shut up?"

"This is my car, little brother! I don't shut up unless I feel like it. What do you think, huh, about her callin' you a good provider?"

I looked over the rolling fields beyond the road. Edward was driving slow now. Maybe he liked that I was stuck having to listen.

"Don't feel like talking, huh? That's all right. I'll just tell you what I think." He glanced my way, and I could feel my stomach tighten. "That little old lady was the good provider. You got yourself a real farm. All that land. I never stole anything that big in all my life! Never could talk as smooth as you, I guess."

He was egging me on, I knew he was, trying to get me upset. But why? I didn't plan on saying much of anything in response. What would be the use? He'd only believe what he wanted to. And God knew I hadn't stolen a single thing from Emma Graham. God knew how hard it had been for me to receive the gift when she offered it. I hadn't even been able to, not completely. Not until she died.

"You're really something, that's all," he continued. "Never seen a better liar. Not in all my life."

"I haven't lied, Edward."

"Oh, yeah. I forgot."

"Your turn's up ahead."

He glanced at me and laughed. "Too much a coward to belt me, aren't you, Sammy? You need the ride and you're not knowing if I might pound you into the ground if you try anything."

"What are you talking about?"

He turned the corner, suddenly looking more like my father than I ever remembered. Something about the set of his jaw. "I s'pose you're mad about yesterday," he said. "Hard telling what your wife and that little boy told you. Guess I'm some awful villain."

I hadn't expected him to want to talk about it, or to push me for a reaction. But he was right. I *was* mad. "You could try telling your side."

"Why bother?" His words came out hard. "You wouldn't listen. Wouldn't matter what I said."

"Yes, it would. At least Julia told me you didn't hurt her."

"What do you think? Do you think I would?"

"I haven't seen you in a long time. We haven't talked. I don't know what's motivating you right now."

"That's pretty! Oh, Sammy, that's rich! You know good and well I came here telling the truth, don't you? You know all about it."

"No. I don't."

He stole one glance at me and stopped the car so suddenly that I was thrown forward and had to catch myself against the dash. "What are you doing?"

"Just you and me," he said real slow. "I figured we could quit the games. There's nobody else to hear. It's not going to hurt you to tell me the truth."

"I have."

"Hogwash! There's no way Trudy was lying. How could she tell me your name?"

"I don't know, Edward." I felt like getting out of the car and walking away, but I had to at least answer the charge and let him know I was trying to give him the benefit of the doubt. "It does look like you're telling the truth, so far as you know it. But so am I."

"You expect me to believe that?"

"No," I sighed. "I'm not sure if anybody would."

He looked at me pretty straight. "Then why bother? Admit it, Sammy. Would it hurt you that much?"

"It didn't happen. That's all I can say. Except that I wish you'd hear me. I don't know her at all, and now I have to figure something out for that little girl. You could help, if the woman said anything else about Katie's father or any of their relatives."

I saw the fire in his eyes. So much like our father's. Quick and destructive. Except that with Edward, the anger was a bit easier for me to understand.

"You want to know what she said? That's easy! She said you were thin, dark haired, almost as tall as me. Pretty smooth to talk to and not bad looking. But ugly as homemade sin when you found out she was pregnant. You roughed her up over it, then didn't come around no more till a couple of times after the kid was born, just to make trouble. And I was mad, Samuel, 'cause I used to think you were different than that! I guess I was fooled as much as everybody else."

I took a deep breath. I couldn't answer it all. I could only hope for a way to show that it wasn't me. "Did she say what town?"

"Harrisburg, you idiot! You called me a jackal, but at least I know a good thing when I see it. I'd have kept Trudy if I could have! But she wouldn't trust no other Wortham 'cause of you. And you already had a good woman! Get out of my car!"

"What?"

"Get out!"

I got out, thinking he would roar off down the road without me. And maybe it would be for the better. There was no way to convince him, and he was too hot. I'd seen it before. He was too mad at me to stay in control. Just like Dad.

But he didn't drive off. He jumped out of the car without even opening the door on his side. He walked around the front to face me. "You're a fool, Sammy! You don't deserve either one of 'em! Do you beat Julia the way you did Trudy?"

I backed up a step, seeing his doubled fists and cold, hard eyes. I wasn't sure how to answer him, but I opened my mouth and had plenty to say. "No. I don't beat her. I never have. And I've never cheated. Maybe you think I'm like our father, or you wish you could prove me to be. But it's not true. I swore when I was a kid that I'd never be like him. Or like you, either."

"What was so bad about me?"

"The fighting. The stealing. Only looking out for yourself."

Without warning, he hit me hard in the face, sending me reeling. I had to struggle to catch my balance against his car.

"Only looking out for myself!" he raged. "I was stealing for you, you lying little weasel! You never cared the trouble I got in, but I was stealing for you!"

I didn't believe it. And suddenly I knew the fire was burning in me too. "Wilford Brink's Model A, Edward? Was that for me? Liquor and tobacco from the store on the corner? Money, jewelry, who knows what else from how many houses, Edward? Ten? Twenty?"

He came at me swinging again, and I tried to block him this time. But I was never the fighter he was. He hit me with his left, in the gut, and I doubled over.

"I wasn't talking about those times," he insisted.

He stood over me, and I found myself looking at his right arm, in the place where Father's bird tattoo had been. There was no such mark on Edward. *Lord, help us,* I prayed. *Us. Yes. Lord, help Edward.*

"I meant before," he snapped at me. "When you were little. I used to get bread all the time. Those little bottles of milk sometimes too. I'd hide 'em in my shirt and sneak 'em home. Don't you remember? Did you think the groceries just showed up for you like some kind of magic? Or maybe Mother went and bought them with what was left after she paid for her booze? But she was drunk, wasn't she? Stretched out on her bed, if she got that far."

I tried to breathe deep but could scarcely manage it. He was strong. He'd socked me good.

"Ain't got nothing else to say?" he demanded. "You want to hate me so much you can't tell me thank you, can you? How do you think I got started? Everybody knew I was stealing! Everybody knew I was no good! By the time I got big enough, there wasn't nobody gonna hire me! What else could I do? I wasn't good at nothing but stealing, anyway." He shook his head. "But it started with food, Sammy. Your food. 'Cause you were a pathetic little whelp, and I couldn't stand to see you cry."

I looked up at him. I figured, as mad as he was, he'd hit me again, no matter what I said. I didn't care. I was used to him lying like a dog. But I knew he wasn't lying about this.

"Thank you," I managed to tell him.

My words didn't change the anger in his eyes. "Now you say it! Now you say it, after I come all this way and beat it out of you. You're just trying to get me off your back!"

I swallowed hard, but it did nothing to relieve the awful taste in my mouth. "I'm sorry, Edward. I guess there were things I didn't see—"

"You didn't want to see!

"Maybe not. And I'm sorry."

I tried to straighten myself, but it hurt. Suddenly I thought of him hitting Katie. Lord, have mercy. Did he even know how strong he was?

"You're pathetic," he said. "Do you know that?"

I took a deep breath. "What about the pickle loaf, Edward?"

"What?"

"Did you steal pickle loaf once?"

"Yeah, you runt. And I gave it to you."

"Most of it," I acknowledged. "I think you had a little."

He shook his head. "You were sitting in your stupid little campsite, playing you were somebody else. Some stupid little Injun named Gray Bear."

I nodded. "Thank you, Edward."

He just stared. Then he laughed. "You're really thanking me?"

"Yeah. I am. Thank you."

"You already said that."

"Some things bear repeating." I pushed myself away from the car and started walking in the direction of the farm.

"Sammy," he called after me.

"What?"

"Where're you going?"

"Home."

"You really didn't remember?"

"No. But I'm glad you told me." I kept walking, aching pretty fiercely.

He followed.

"I don't blame you for the way you went," I said, knowing he was close enough to hear. "You probably didn't know how to do anything else. I'm sorry I didn't understand it."

He came alongside me, talking more calmly, but the

anger was still in his eyes. "It might've been worse, Sammy. It's a good thing our daddy died when he did, 'cause I was gonna kill him. I'd made up my mind. He done us wrong. He done our mother wrong. He was the one started her drinking, did you know that? I was gonna find him and kill him, but then Mother came and told us he was already dead. I was pretty mad about that. Kind of felt like he cheated me. Probably for the best, though. If I'd started killing, maybe I wouldn't have stopped. Once the door's open, you know. That's what happened with the stealing."

I glanced up at him, wondering if he'd ever really come close to such a thing as murder. I could almost believe him. I'd seen his temper when he was a teen, and it was far worse than what had happened today. He'd only been sixteen when Mom gave us the news that our father had died. I'd felt relief more than anything, just to know he wouldn't be showing up anymore, wreaking havoc on my life. But Edward had raged, throwing things and stomping off. And I'd never understood why.

"We can be thankful for God's timing," I told him. "He surely knew what you were thinking."

"Listen to us," he laughed. "Talking decent. While we're at it, you might as well go ahead and level with me, Sammy. I won't think less of you."

"I am leveling with you."

"No. I'm talking about Trudy now. I haven't lied about the things I've done or the things I've wanted to do. I think you ought to talk to me just as straight. I want you to admit it, and I'll understand. She's real pretty. Enough to tempt anybody, married or not. You're just human, Sammy, and that's all I need to hear. I won't say nothing else to nobody."

"I'm human. And I've made plenty of mistakes, Edward. But not that one."

He got in front of me, stopping my progress. "What's

the matter with you? Don't you know your stupid wife's gonna love you no matter what? I'm not gonna tell her what you say! Just own up! Don't you owe me that?"

I could feel every muscle in my body tighten. "I'm telling you the truth."

He shook his head, kicked at the dust. "At least I can admit what I done. You always were a coward, running from every little thing. But what good is it gonna do you running from this? It's already caught you, can't you see that?"

He got quiet, but I knew he wasn't finished. And I just waited, knowing it wouldn't solve anything to say something else or to try to walk away now.

"You're supposed to be a Christian," he finally said, talking quiet and slow. "What do you think your God's gonna say one day about you lying when you don't even have to? And what are you gonna do about Katie, huh? Can't you find the decency to claim her?"

"I'll take her in," I told him. "I'll raise her as my own if we don't find her family. But she's not mine. Not like you think."

I knew what was coming, and I didn't fight it. I just stood there as he took another swing, hard and fast, this time landing me in the dirt.

"Why ain't you fighting back?" he yelled. "You ain't the runt you used to be. Get up and let me see what you got."

"No."

"You're weak," he taunted. "That's all you are. You're a spineless cheat and a coward."

Part of me wanted to grab him by the legs, knock him to the ground, and show him I had some fight in me. But I knew it wouldn't be right. My brother was just mistaken about something. He was just thinking something that wasn't so. He didn't know any better. *Lord, touch him. Help him see.*

"You don't deserve none of what you've got, Sammy! I would've left you alone! I'd have been your friend, if you wanted one. But now I'm gonna see that folks know what a lying skunk you are! People 'round here ought to know what's living in their midst! Julia ain't the only one. They should know you for the thieving cheat you are."

"Edward—"

"I'll be doing a community service, Sammy. The kind of thing you oughta be proud of."

He turned to his car, and I struggled to my feet. *Oh, God. What can I do?*

"You wanted to walk. Go ahead and walk. I got work to do. I been decent enough not to lie to you, Sammy. You should've been straight with me when you had the chance. I'll make you sorry you weren't."

He drove away in a flurry of dust, faster than anybody should drive. *Lord, help him,* I prayed. *Help me.*

What would he do now? Maybe he was right, maybe we could have been friends somehow. But all this about Trudy Vale was a cruel hoax, or the unkindest of coincidences. He would tell people, I had no doubt. And they would believe him, in spite of themselves. How could anyone take my side, against even Katie's word? She was only an innocent child. I couldn't expect a grown soul to believe me. Except maybe Juli. Maybe.

I started walking again, thinking about the doubt I'd seen in her eyes. She had come out of that for a while, standing up for me right to Edward's face, but would it last? When she had the time to think on it all, would I see the questions in her eyes again?

My head was pounding and my gut burned like fire. But I didn't care about the pain. Franky was still in the hospital, and I'd have to let people know. I'd have to see Barrett Post about going back to Mcleansboro. There were too many other things to think about to let myself be very concerned over what Edward did or said. Let him tell the world whatever he wanted. I would stand or fall before God alone, and there was nobody else that really mattered.

Except Juli. And my kids.

FIFTEEN

Julia

It might sound terrible, but I took the chicken bones and boiled them for broth before I gave them to Whiskers. "Get two meals off a chicken if you can," Grandma Pearl used to tell me. "No use being extravagant."

I had the girls helping me cut noodles I'd mixed and rolled out across our tabletop. It was so hot that we were all drenched in sweat, so I stopped every few minutes and wet a washcloth to touch to the backs of our necks. Willy had come by, bringing me Emma Grace, who wouldn't stop fussing for Lizbeth. I'd gotten the baby down for a nap, and now Willy was helping Robert finish cleaning the barn stalls.

Nobody was saying much about Franky. I guess because we didn't know what to say. It made me hurt inside, thinking of the pain on his face. But I was glad Lizbeth was with him. She was always quicker to comfort the little ones than her father was.

I prayed as I rolled noodles and let the girls cut any shape and length they wanted. Noodles would be such a treat that nobody would care what they looked like. I wondered why I was taking the time, except that the noodles would go well with the chicken broth and keep the girls happily occupied, now that they'd used up every bit of the clay making bowls and lopsided whatnots.

"Why'd he run over Franky?" Sarah asked.

And Rorey's question was even worse. "Is he gonna die like Mama?"

I didn't want to talk about it, because I knew I'd cry, so I just kept on keeping them busy.

Katie was the quietest. But just her presence made me feel worse than ever. She'd known Samuel's name, what he looked like, where we used to live. She'd known we had two children. It gave me an ache inside that wouldn't stop. What if it were all true and this little girl was my Samuel's child? Or what if it wasn't, and here I was doubting him again? What kind of wife was I?

He would be hurt if he knew the questions that were roaming around in my brain. What would he say to me when he got the chance? I knew I shouldn't doubt, not for a second. I should be strong enough to shake it all off like it was nothing. Maybe he wouldn't want to say anything to me at all if he knew the way I was thinking. And I couldn't blame him, not the least little bit.

Robert and Willy came up to the house, looking dirty and tired. "We're done, Mom," Robert said. "I'm hungry."

"You deserve to be hungry after all that. Did you wash up?"

"Our hands. Got any more a' that cake?"

"Only the one edge that got too done, and it's hard as rock. I thought I'd set it out for Whiskers."

"Well, give him a chunk, but I'll soak some in milk. Okay?"

I'd whacked two pieces apart and had the milk up from the basement when Whiskers started barking.

"Can we go fishin'?" Willy asked, ignoring the sound.

I looked out the window but didn't see anything.

"Maybe squirrels, Mom," Robert said. "I didn't hear no car."

"You wanna go fishin', Robert?" Willy persisted.

"I dunno. Seems like my dad's been gone an awful long time. They oughta be comin' back. Don't you think?"

"Maybe they're stayin' the night," Willy suggested.

"No, 'cause that's bad," Rorey said immediately. "If they's stayin', it means Franky's hurt bad."

I wished they wouldn't talk about it. But I knew to expect it. Of course they'd be wondering. "He's probably just needing plenty of rest," I tried to assure Rorey. "And it's quite a ways. If they stay, I'm sure we'll hear something in the morning."

"Dad wouldn't stay, would he?" Robert asked. "I know Edward wouldn't."

"Why not?" Sarah asked innocently.

"Because he wouldn't care enough."

"Well, Daddy would," Sarah protested, her eyes suddenly wide with concern.

"Of course, he cares," Robert told her. "That's different. But he'll be coming back home to see about us."

I should've been thinking about that. I should've sent Robert over to Barrett Post's a long time ago to tell him what happened. Because sure as anything, Samuel would get home if he could, and bring George and Lizbeth and Franky, if Franky were well enough to leave the hospital. But they'd gone with Edward. I should've been thinking! I should've sent one of the boys to ask Barrett Post to go after them. Because Robert was more than likely right. Edward might just up and leave them stranded in Mcleansboro. Who could tell what he might do?

"Robert, maybe you and Willy should go over to Barrett Post—"

The dog started barking again.

"Coons," Sarah said.

"Not before dark," Robert corrected her. This time he looked out. His face grew even more sober than it already was. "Mom."

I looked, and at first I didn't see anything. But then Whiskers went running out to the road, just as far east as we could see from the window. He wasn't barking anymore.

There was a man coming our way. Walking. Limping. Samuel?

I went running outside. Every one of the kids followed me. What in the world could have happened? Had I been right to think of Edward just leaving them? Surely Samuel couldn't have walked all that way back. Not this soon. Did they even get that far?

Whiskers was prancing around him in greeting now. Samuel had stopped to lean over against a fence post, and I knew he was hurt. But he saw us coming and straightened back up, trying to walk as normal as ever.

Thoughts went flying through my head. Had there been another accident? Had Edward done something else just as careless, just as foolish?

"Daddy!" Sarah yelled in delight. But then she stopped, suddenly scared. "Where's Franky?"

I stopped too, when I saw Samuel's face. It was swelling, turning red and purple. Suddenly it wasn't the day's heat making me feel so awful hot. Whatever had happened, Edward had done it. After hurting Franky so badly, now he had hurt Samuel too.

"What happened?" Robert asked, something hard in his voice.

Samuel tried to smile. "Don't any of you worry, all right? They wanted to keep Franky in the hospital a while. His leg's broke, but he'll be all right. George and Lizbeth are staying with him."

"Samuel, sit down," I said. "Robert, bring me the water bucket and a cloth."

"I can make it to the well, Juli." Samuel looked strange. Strong and broken all at the same time.

"You don't have to. Sit here in the shade. Please." I touched his side, and he winced. "Sammy, what's happened?"

"Looks like somebody beat him up," Willy said.

I could've screamed at his insensitivity, for saying something like that in front of the little girls!

Sarah was grabbing for her father's hand. "Are you okay, Daddy? Are you okay?"

Katie was standing beside me speechless.

"I'm fine," Samuel told us all and started walking past us toward the well.

I knew he wasn't. I knew by the way he moved that he was bruised even more than we could see. But he moved quickly to the well, took a long drink of water, and then poured a dipperful over his head.

I thought of Edward doing that, pouring water on himself. Only he shook like a dog, and Samuel didn't shake. He just stood there for moment, letting the wetness drip over him. How far had he walked in this heat? He sat down, and I knew he was pretty spent.

I dunked a cloth in the water and tried to touch it to his swelling cheek, but he pushed my hand away.

"Leave me alone a minute. I'm all right."

"No. Honey, you're not. I know you don't like to talk about it in front of the kids, but they've already seen. Please let me help you."

"Juli, it's nothing. Have the kids eaten?" He pushed me away again.

"Did he hit you, Dad?" Robert questioned.

Samuel didn't answer. He just pulled himself to his feet and started to the house.

"Why would Uncle Edward hit you?" Robert called after him. Sarah stood looking at me, biting her lower lip. Katie slipped away to the lilac bush and hid beneath its branches. Rorey followed her halfway and then just stood there, hands on her hips.

"Are any of you children hungry?" I asked them, feeling like lead inside.

"Not anymore," Robert answered. None of the others said a word.

I told them to stay there, and I followed Samuel. He looked so tossed. And that was scaring me more than the bruises. "Sammy?"

He ignored me as he went up the porch steps stiffly. Without a word, he pulled his shirt off and dropped it beside the washbasin on the porch. Then he poured water from the pitcher to the basin and washed his face and neck. I could see the red on his stomach, and I knew the boys were right. They'd fought. Or at least Edward had.

"Let me help you," I begged him.

"I don't need help. I just need to get over to Barrett's. Send Willy home, all right? So he can tell them about Franky, that they're staying."

"Sammy, what happened?"

"Don't call me Sammy. Just . . . just leave me alone."

Tears clouded my eyes. It didn't sound like Samuel talking. For a moment I didn't even know him. I didn't know what was going on in his mind, his heart. God help us!

He turned to me slowly; he must have seen my tears. At first he just bowed his head, looking so defeated. But then he took me in his arms.

"Juli, I'm sorry. None of this is your fault."

I didn't know what to do. I didn't know what to say.

"I'm sorry," he said again.

I should've said he didn't need to be. I should've told him he couldn't help the cruel behavior of his awful older brother. I should've just held him and told him how much I loved him, but he beat me to it.

"I love you," he whispered so softly. "With all my heart."

For a long time he held me tight. I was surprised to find myself not sure what to think. *Sammy! Love of my life! I would give anything, do anything for you! Why am I feeling confused?*

He started to pull away, and I quickly found my tongue. "Are you sure you're all right? Honey, let me at least put a cold cloth on your eye. I'm afraid you might have some awful color."

"Wonderful." He shook his head. "Just in time for church tomorrow."

"Why did he hit you?"

"Because he thinks I'm lying. Miss Vale described me, I guess, and he can't understand why I don't just admit everything." He looked into my eyes and then solemnly kissed my forehead. His lips felt hot. "Thank you, Juli, for not coming right out and saying what you think."

My heart caught in my throat. "I don't know what to think."

He nodded and turned away from me. "I know."

"Oh, Samuel! I didn't mean that how it sounded. I didn't mean—"

"Yes, you did."

He walked into the house looking so heavy. I followed him in. I hurried, hoping to find some way he'd let me help. But he went in our room and shut the door.

I remembered one night when we first came here, when we were without food, without a home. Samuel had been so depressed; it had troubled him so badly not to be able to give us more. But he let me come to him that night and tell him I knew it wasn't his fault and that we would all be all right.

I tried again. I opened the door and went to his side. I was going to tell him I didn't care what anybody said, that I would stand by him no matter what.

But before I could get the words out, he was shaking his head at me again. "You don't have to follow me. I just had to get a shirt. And maybe I need some time."

He walked away, out of the room, out of the house, and into the swaying cornfield in the direction of the Posts'. With my heart feeling raw, I could only stand on the porch and watch him go.

Why were we so far apart? I felt as if some huge canyon had been dug right between us, and I didn't know how to bridge across. Why was he acting like this? Why did he shut me out? I couldn't help the things that were churning inside me! Could I? What else could I do?

At that moment I imagined Edward as an instrument of the devil, sitting somewhere laughing because he'd done so well tearing apart our peace. I couldn't even hold my husband without wondering about him. He couldn't even let me comfort him after an assault.

I knew the children were watching, worrying. They couldn't possibly understand all this. I didn't understand it myself. But we had always weathered everything together. We would weather this too. We would come out better for it in the end. I had to believe that. And surely Samuel would too.

I prayed for him. I prayed that he wasn't hurt too badly. I prayed that he wouldn't let Edward shake him from all that he'd come to know. But most of all, I prayed that he'd let me feel close to him again, that he'd give me another chance. And I cried. Because I knew that I'd failed him.

"Mommy?" Sarah stepped up quietly and tugged on my sleeve. "Where is Daddy going?"

I dried my eyes. "Over to Barrett and Louise's house, honey. They need to know about Franky. Maybe they'll have to go get him when it's time to come home."

"Is Daddy mad at Uncle Edward?"

"Maybe. And he probably has reason to be."

"Is he mad at us?"

I leaned over and took our little angel in my arms. "No, honey. He's just upset over whatever's happened."

"Robert said Uncle Edward must've beat him up. Why would he do that?"

"Honey, I don't know. I guess some people have so many problems inside that they take them out on other people."

"But Daddy's nice. And strong. I don't see how anybody could hurt him or why they'd try."

Wickedness, I wanted to say. *Your Uncle Edward is an awful, horrible man.* But instead I took a deep breath. I couldn't say such things to my daughter, no matter how I felt. "Edward is a difficult person. Because he's sick, maybe, inside his heart."

"Because he doesn't know Jesus?"

"Yes. We need to pray for him, don't we?"

She nodded, but her eyes were clouded with uncertainty. "Robert said he ought to bust him up if he comes back."

"That wouldn't solve a thing."

"Would it make Daddy feel better?"

"No. It wouldn't."

Rorey had come up beside us, but I wondered about Katie. She'd been so quiet. "Is Katie still by the lilacs?"

"Yes, Mommy," Sarah answered, but my question didn't turn the direction of her thoughts at all. "Do you think Daddy hit Uncle Edward back?"

I had to think about that a moment. "No. Probably not."

She frowned. "I don't know if I would have."

I patted her head and sighed. "I would have wanted to. But your father's stronger than we are."

"'Cause he could have beat him up?"

"Because he probably didn't."

She stared into the cornfield for a while. "I wanted to follow him, Mommy. But Robert said I couldn't and he'd be back pretty soon okay."

"Robert's right. Don't worry."

She looked up at me. "Then why was you crying?"

I pushed away from the porch's column and headed down the steps. "It's just hard." I couldn't say anything else. I knew I'd better find Katie, the poor child. What must she be thinking after a day like today?

Sarah followed me across the yard. It was the boys we found first. Willy was standing under the walnut tree, looking like he was waiting for me. I told him to go, to tell Joe and the others that Franky would be all right. And to come back if they needed anything.

"You gonna keep Emmie Grace here?" he asked.

"Yes, we'll keep her."

He turned and started for home through the timber; I wondered if I should have sent Rorey with him. But no. Without Lizbeth and George over there, Harry and Berty were more than enough to watch out for.

Robert was pacing beside what was left of the fire. I knew he was mad, but I didn't know what I could do about it.

"Are you hungry?" I called to him.

"No. I don't wanna eat nothin' when Franky's in the hospital and Dad's walkin' around all busted up. I think

Uncle Edward's a horse's hind end and he ought to be put back in jail where he belongs!"

"Robert—that's no way to talk."

"Well, don't you think so?"

For a moment I stammered, trying to answer that question the way it should be answered. "It doesn't matter what I think. We can't let anybody, no matter how distasteful they act, shake us from behaving the way we should."

"I don't think there'd be nothin' wrong with him gettin' what he's got comin'."

"But that's not up to you. That's in God's hands."

"Well, why doesn't God do something about him, then? Why'd he even get out?"

I put my arm around my son, temporarily stopping his pacing. "I don't believe he really meant to hurt Franky. He was just careless. About your daddy, I don't know. That's between them—"

"He don't even talk nice. I couldn't get by with that."

"He wasn't raised like you're being raised—"

"Dad wasn't either, an' he knows better."

How could I argue? "I know. They're different. Thank God your father made the choices he did."

"We oughta pray for Uncle Edward," Sarah said quickly.

"I don't feel like it."

"Well," I admitted, "I don't either. But maybe doing it anyway would help us as much as him. If we let ourselves get all bitter, Edward might not care, but we'd be miserable. Better, I think, not to let him get us down."

"I'm not down. I'm mad."

"It looks almost the same. Feels almost the same too, doesn't it?"

He just looked at me.

"I'll pray for Uncle Edward," Sarah said. "And Franky. And Daddy."

"I'm gonna split some kindling," Robert said as he marched away from us. I had never realized before that he was so much like me. But there he was, wanting something to whack at. Just like me and the rug beater.

From the house I could hear the wail of Emmie Grace waking up, but Katie was still under the lilacs and I knew she shouldn't be ignored.

"Sarah, Rorey, will you please go and play with little Emmie for a few minutes? That's probably all she needs right now—just a little company."

"I don't wanna," Rorey said immediately, but she changed her mind when she saw that Sarah was going.

I turned toward the little girl hiding in the bushes. She must be seeking some sort of refuge away from all the crazy things around her, to keep running to the lilacs over and over. And I'd been so swept up thinking about everything else that I'd given her far too little attention. She must be feeling awfully alone.

"Katie?"

She was all curled up just as far into the center of that clump of bushes as she could go. She peeked out at me when I said her name, and I could see that her cheeks were wet with tears. Again. What a horrible place this must seem to her!

I tried crawling in to her, but of course I couldn't fit as well as she could. "You know," I said, "when I was little, I used to hide up in a tree sometimes. I'd climb up and just stay there until they came looking for me or I got so hungry I had to come down."

"Why?"

"I was lonely. Missing my mama."

"Like me?"

"Kind of like you. Except that my mother died, so I knew I wouldn't see her again in this world. You might, some day, especially if she stops traveling so much." I didn't know if those words would help or hurt, but they'd come out anyway. I prayed that the Lord would help me comfort this child and help her be happy, at least while she was here.

"Is it because of me?"

"That she travels, honey? Oh no. I think that's what she wants to do. And right or wrong, she must think it's more important than anything else."

She came crawling out a little ways. "She said she loves me."

"I'm sure she does."

"Do you love me too?"

Her big brown eyes stared up at me, pleading. "Yes. But it's not the same. I haven't gotten time to really know you."

She came closer, enough for me to draw her onto my lap. She leaned into me, laid her head against my shoulder for just a second, and then looked up at me again. "Does Mr. Wortham love me?"

I had to choke down the bitter gall in my throat. "I—I expect he feels the same way I do."

"He got hurt."

"Yes. But not badly, honey. He's all right."

"It was because of me."

"No. I don't think so. I think it was because of Edward and maybe things that happened when they were boys, before either of us ever met them. You certainly can't blame yourself."

"Lots of bad stuff keeps happening . . ."

"But it's not your fault."

She reached her little hand down and started fumbling with a stick. "Maybe if I went away, it would stop."

"Franky's leg would still have to heal. Edward would be just the same. You going away wouldn't change much, Katie, except we'd wonder where you were and if you were all right."

"Really?"

"Yes."

"But I'm not yours."

"Rorey isn't either. Or the baby, or the children in my Sunday school class at church. But I still care about all of you."

Her eyes filled with tears all over again, and I thought sure I'd said something wrong. She clung to me, sobbing. My back and my neck were getting stiff from being bent over, but I didn't try to move.

"Why doesn't . . . why doesn't Mommy care?"

I could have argued it with her, but the truth was that I didn't know. Maybe her mother did care. Maybe she didn't. I didn't know what to say, so I said nothing at all, only held her until Rorey came charging out of the house looking for me.

"Emmie Grace is stinky!" she declared. "You gotta leave that girl an' change my baby sister."

"No," I said quietly. "You can ask politely, Rorey Jeanine. And I don't think I have to leave Katie at all." I looked down to find Katie looking at me. "You'd like to help, wouldn't you?" I asked her. "Want to help me change the baby?"

She nodded, wiped her face with the back of her fist, and slowly got up. But she took my hand in an unexpected gesture, trying to help me up off the ground.

"Thank you," I told her as I got to my feet. "That was very kind."

"You're welcome."

Rorey just stood and looked at us. By now, she was used to being Sarah's only close friend and the only other little girl around, excepting the baby. She'd been fine to Katie before, but now she was giving her a scowl.

"If that man takes you away, maybe he wouldn't come back no more then! He's too mean. He hurt my brother. If you just go away, maybe he won't come back."

"Rorey!"

"If they both go away, things'll be back like they was."

"Rorey! That's an awful thing to say, blaming Katie for a grown man's actions. Edward has his own problems that have nothing to do with her."

"He's a horse's hind end," she said, echoing Robert's words.

"He's a lot of things, but that doesn't make it Katie's fault. I want you to tell her you're sorry. This minute."

"Sorry." Rorey stared out over the garden to where Whiskers was napping in the shade of the toolshed, then turned her eyes back to me. "Is that mean man her pa?"

What an easy solution that would be. It would solve so much just to care for Katie as our niece. But Edward had been in the penitentiary far too long. There was no way it could be so.

"No," Katie answered before I got a chance. "I don't need a pa. Just friends. Like you and Sarah and Mrs. Wortham."

I was surprised at the bravery of her answer. And the kindness, considering Rorey's words.

"We all need friends," I agreed quickly. "Now let's hurry up before Emmie gets to protesting that messy diaper."

Katie took my hand. Rorey ran on ahead. And I knew I really would think of Katie if she had to go away. She felt like family, whether it was really so or not. And seeing her bouncy curls, her sweet face, her gentle eyes, it wouldn't take much to convince me. *Samuel must have another brother,* I thought. *That must be what it is. Someone not raised by Samuel's mother or his father. Someone more like Samuel than Edward could ever be.*

SIXTEEN

Samuel

Barrett Post brought me home that night promising he'd go into Mcleansboro after church the next day. He didn't ask about the way I looked. He stared some. But he didn't ask.

I walked up the front steps, feeling stiff. Edward had really walloped me, and I guessed I'd be feeling it for a few days. Maybe the whole thing was my fault somehow, though I wasn't even sure why I was thinking that.

"It started with food," Edward had said. *"Your food."* I could see that now. The petty theft kept getting worse and worse until it was no longer petty, no longer child's play. Certainly no longer just food. But he was putting the blame on me. And the community's distrust of him. If I'd stolen my own food or didn't need any, if somebody had hired him or at least hadn't shooed him out of their stores, maybe his life would be different.

I'd wondered plenty of times what the world would have been like for us if Mom had always been sober and my father had been patient enough to hold a job and not be so hard on us. I'd been angry once. I'd thrown bottles like Edward. Busted a streetlight. Even tried the drink that plagued my parents so deeply. But I never went so far down that path. I was too afraid of what the drink was doing to my mother. And what the stealing was doing to Edward. So I quit drinking. I didn't steal.

And I met Juli. And Jesus. The same year.

Anyone who knew how I felt about both of them would understand how I could never consort with Trudy Vale or anyone else. I hoped Juli knew. Obviously, Edward didn't. I'd tried to tell him about the lightness I'd felt since I found God, but he would never listen. Called me crazy. Swore up and down that I'd better leave him alone. So I did.

And maybe that was wrong. Maybe I shouldn't have given up. Even though Edward had wearied me then the way he wearied me now. Always hard. Always bitter. Never wanting to listen. I was only the stupid little brother who ran off into the woods. Like that neighbor boy who'd called me "Worthless" instead of "Wortham," Edward seemed to like knocking me down.

I stood for a moment on the porch, not really wanting to go in. I hadn't explained much to Juli. I was sure to get more questions. And the questions would be hardest coming from the kids. I didn't want to tell them anything. But I couldn't just stay away.

They hadn't heard me. Rorey and Sarah were singing in the house.

The singing stopped when I opened the door. Sarah spun around and squealed, "Daddy!"

Her hair was combed long and wet down her back,

and she was already in her nightgown. Saturday was bath night. I could see Juli's feet below the sheet draped in the corner. She peeked over its edge at me. "I'm glad you're home. There's noodles in the covered pan on the stove if you're hungry. I'm rinsing Rorey's hair, but we'll be right out."

"I'm sorry," I told her right away. "I should've been here to help you lug the water."

"Robert helped me. I'd rather you rest, anyway. Are you all right?"

"Yes." I could hear the baby in the next room. With Robert, I assumed. Katie was sitting at the table, solemnly looking at me the way she had the first night. For a moment I wondered how everyone would react if I just declared myself her father. Katie would be delighted. Juli, I supposed, would find it in her heart to forgive me. And Edward would treat me like something more than a schlop. Maybe.

"Katie's next," Sarah told me. "'Less you want to." She came close to my side, reaching her hand up to my face but not touching me. "Does that hurt?"

"Only when I laugh."

"Then you must be okay," she said with uncertainty in her voice. "'Cause you're not laughing."

I hugged her. "I'm fine, pumpkin."

"I'm glad Mr. Eddie didn't hit *me* that hard," Katie suddenly said.

"I'm glad too." She was so sad eyed; almost I wished I could hold her and Sarah at the same time. Maybe I could, but I didn't try.

"Can I get you a wet cloth?" Juli asked. "You've got a bit of swelling."

I knew that. I could feel the pressure, the soreness around my eye. It was probably purple too. Maybe a good reason to stay home from church. I could imagine all the attention I would get.

I guess I didn't even answer Juli's question, but she brought me a wet cloth anyway when she ushered Rorey out of her bath.

"Katie's turn," Rorey said, looking at me. "She didn't wanna be first."

Juli was touching the cloth to my eye so gently. Of course, any swelling it was going to do was already done by now. I hoped she didn't know he'd busted me in the stomach too.

"Can I get you some noodles?" Juli asked. "Or did Louise feed you?"

"She offered. I turned her down."

"Was Franky feeling all right, and George?"

I saw the worry in her eyes, and I knew she would fix everything for us if she could. I took her hand. "George hates being there. But he can stand it tonight. Franky was still hurting quite a bit, so they gave him some medicine and it pretty much put him to sleep. If you want to go, Barrett and Louise will be heading that way tomorrow."

She looked around at the girls. "I don't know, honey. We'll see." She swished the cloth across my forehead and then touched it to my eye again before leaning and kissing my cheek.

Robert came in from the sitting room, holding Emma Grace's hand. He looked so tall suddenly. Somber. He didn't say a word.

"Do we have to go to church tomorrow?" Rorey asked.

"No," Julia answered quickly. "But we're going anyway. It's a privilege."

"I never been to church," Katie told us.

"Never?" Sarah asked, quite amazed.

"You'll like it," Julia assured her.

I hoped that was true. I remembered my first experience at Dearing's little church. Everybody knew everybody, so there'd been gawking eyes at the newcomers, even a bit of hard feeling from those who thought, thanks to Hazel Sharpe, that we were trying to swindle Emma Graham. But Katie was just a child. She'd have none of that kind of problem. And besides, everybody knew us now. There'd be only my shiny black eye to create a stir.

"Is Kirk an' Willy and them goin' to church?" Rorey persisted.

"I don't know," I told her. "They may start out early in the wagon the way your father does when he goes. Charlie Hunter'll be by for us."

"I bet they don't go," she said with a pout. "'Cause Pa an' Lizbeth ain't there to make 'em."

"Sam'll get there," Juli said. "If he can find a way."

Her words made me remember Thelma Pratt catching young Sam Hammond off guard at the Fourth of July celebration, asking if she would see him at church. It seemed so long ago now.

"Well, we better get the baths done so we can get to bed at a decent hour," Juli was saying. "Are you ready, Katie?"

"Do I have to?"

"I should think it would feel nice on a hot day like this," Juli told her. "Don't worry. I'll be real gentle with your hair."

"Can I do it myself?"

"Well." Juli was surprised. "The other girls your age like help. But if you can do it, that's just fine."

Katie said she could do it. She went to her bag and got out her nightdress and ducked behind the sheet quick as a wink. She didn't take very long at it, but she came out with her hair wet. Juli didn't question her, didn't even check behind her ears.

"Your turn, Robert."

Sarah and Rorey ran in the sitting room with their dolls, and I held Emma Grace while Julia carefully combed the tangles out of Katie's hair.

"You always take care of bathing by yourself?" she asked.

"Yes, ma'am," Katie answered.

"Well, you're very grown up. And very polite too. I appreciate that."

"Thank you."

Katie sat so quietly. And I began to wonder about Trudy Vale. Why would she send her little girl to a man who had beaten her? Why not one of her own relatives instead, particularly her mother?

Maybe she knew. Maybe it was no misunderstanding at all, and she knew that Edward's brother was not really the man she'd known. But that would be taking even more of a chance with her child. Wouldn't it? And it seemed only God could arrange the kind of coincidences she'd been able to take advantage of. Same town. Same name.

Once again I entertained the notion that Trudy Vale could be lying. That maybe she had duped Edward and coached Katie with all the right words to say. Maybe there was no Wortham involved at all. But that didn't explain the details they knew. Or Katie looking like me.

"Katie, was there anything else your mother said about your father?" I asked suddenly.

I could see Julia tense. "Samuel . . ."

"It doesn't hurt to ask. She might remember something. Or about any relatives."

"I don't know," Katie said with a sigh. "I wish we still had your picture. You look more tired-er in it."

"It's time for bed," Juli said, laying down the brush with a suddenly shaking hand.

But Katie was thinking on something. "Mama was surprised," she said abruptly. "When Edward said you was younger than him, she was surprised."

"She thought I was older?" I thought that was good news. Finally, something that didn't fit. Maybe the man, whoever he was, really *was* older than Edward. But Juli was looking at me as if it pained her. And then I realized why. I should have said *Katie's father* was older. Not *I*. But correcting myself now might only make things worse.

"Edward's immature," Julia said quietly. "Robert acts older than he does." She stood up. "Sarah! Rorey! Let's go say your prayers." She turned her eyes to me. "Do you mind keeping Emma Grace while I settle them down? She had a late nap and it'll take me longer to get her to sleep."

"Juli . . ." I wanted to find the right words to say, but Rorey and Sarah came bouncing back into the kitchen and I knew it would have to wait. "That's fine," I told her. "She's no problem."

Katie wanted to stay with me, but Juli called her in to bed with the other girls. I could hear her singing softly to them while Emma Grace pulled on my ear and giggled.

Robert emerged from behind the draped sheet and came up close, looking at my eye. "That's pretty awful, Dad."

"It'll heal."

"Why'd he bust you?"

"That's a long story."

"Did you bust him back?"

"No, Robert—"

"Why not? I would have."

I didn't doubt it to be true. Robert was more hotheaded than I was.

"You ought to tell the sheriff. About what he done to Franky too. He shouldn't just get by—"

"It's in God's hands."

Robert shook his head. "That's kind of what Mom said. But what if God doesn't do anything?"

"He will," I answered, not sure why I could feel so confident about it.

Sarah and Rorey had been asleep a while, and Robert had gone upstairs when I started polishing shoes for Sunday morning. Juli was rocking Emma Grace in the sitting room, so I was surprised to hear little feet padding my way. I looked up to see Katie coming in the kitchen, her eyes round and sleepy, both hands holding tight to yarn dolls.

"Can I watch?" she asked.

"You're supposed to be sleeping. Didn't Julia see you?"

"She had her eyes closed. She's singing to the baby."

I nodded. I hadn't noticed singing. Lost in my thoughts, I guess.

She watched closely as I wiped some of Juli's homemade walnut stain across the fronts of my church shoes. The stuff worked well enough in the stead of brown shoe polish.

"Why are you doing that?" she asked me.

"Because the shoes are old, and I want them to look their best. I buff them a little and they'll be all right. You want me to do yours too?"

"Mama only fixed up shoes before a show. She said everything was supposed to look good for a show."

"Well, this isn't for a show. But God's house is important. We want to look our best."

"Your wife sings pretty."

"I know."

"Mama sings pretty too."

"I figured she must. But don't you think you ought to be sleeping? We've got to get up and around in the morning."

She sat on the floor next to Sarah's little shoes. "I know." She rested her chin on her hands and looked up at me. "But I can't sleep too good."

"Why not?"

"I guess because I don't know about church. An' I'm kind of . . . kind of . . ."

"Scared?"

"Yeah."

I set my cloth down. "I can understand that. The first time I ever went to this church, I was pretty nervous too. I didn't know anybody except the people I was going there with. And it's okay to be nervous. But there's nothing to be afraid of."

"What do you do?"

"First you greet a few folks. Find a seat. Sing a hymn or two and go to Sunday school."

"I've never been to any kind of school. Mama says I'll have to go in the fall."

"Yeah. I expect so. But Sunday school's not the same. It's all year and only on Sunday. You learn about Jesus and the things God wrote in the Bible."

"Does Sarah like it?"

"Yes. And Sarah's mommy is the teacher for your age, so you don't even have to have somebody you don't know."

She smiled. "Is Sarah going to school in the fall?"

"She's already been. For the first time last year. But she'll go back. And she likes that too."

"I hope I can go where she goes."

I wasn't sure how to answer that. Katie would probably be going back East. To her grandmother, if we could find her. "Right now you need to go back to bed. Morning comes pretty early around here."

She got up, and I thought she was going to do what I told her, but instead of going in the other room, she came right up and gave me a giant hug the way Sarah did sometimes.

I held her for a minute, praying for her and hoping she'd go on to bed without me prompting her again.

But she didn't move. For a long time she clung to me, and I wasn't sure what to do. She'd been this way the very first night, like I was a lifeline of some kind.

"Katie?" I finally said. "Are you feeling okay?"

"I wish you'd rock me like the baby. Mama used to, but it's been a long, long time."

She wasn't crying. But I knew she was close to it. "You're a little nervous about more than church, aren't you?"

She squeezed me tighter. One of the yarn dolls dropped to the floor. "I know you're gonna send me away. An' I don't wanna go."

"I have to be honest," I told her. "If we find family, I'd have to send you away. I wouldn't have much choice about it. And I know that's scary, especially if you haven't met them. But you'd get used to them, and it probably wouldn't take long."

"I thought I'd be scared of you. And I was, but only for a minute."

"See?" I tried to look into her eyes. "It'll likely be the same way with your family, wherever they are."

"What if it's not? Mama said her relatives don't like us."

"I'm sure God's got someone willing to like you and take very good care of you."

"Mama said *you* should."

"But your mama never really met me. She only thought I was someone that . . . that she really did meet once."

She looked at me with a little shake of her head. "I only think one thing about that."

"What?"

She took a breath. "If she did meet you, then you both got kind of mixed up, 'cause *you* forgot, and *she* said I'd have to be really good 'cause you were kind of mean sometimes. But you're not."

"Thank you. I appreciate hearing that."

"But maybe the others is mean! Maybe you're the one God got willing!"

"Katie—"

She wasn't listening to me. She was crying now. "I like Sarah! I even like Rorey and the boys! I like Mrs. Wortham lots, even though I never did see anybody cook like her. She sings to me an' tells me about stuff like beating up rugs and walking in a creek. I don't wanna go anywhere else. I never liked any other place this much! Even with Mr. Eddie bein' so bad, because I think he'll go away pretty soon and leave us alone."

"He may. Eventually. But I can't promise you can stay here. We just don't know yet what we're going to find out."

She kept crying, and my heart went out to her, but I knew of nothing else I could say. Ben Law could show up tomorrow to tell us about that grandma or someone else willing to take her in. And she'd have to go. But she needed something, some kind of an assurance. My heart was heavy, thinking of the hurt of a child with no certain tomorrow. I had to tell her something.

"Katie . . ."

She shook a little, trying to push the tears away.

"I don't know what's going to happen. I don't know if you'll have to go, or when. But I'll make you a promise. If Sheriff Law can't find a place for you with a relative where you'll be safe and happy, then I'll keep you. You'll be my little girl, just like Sarah is. Whether we're blood or not."

You'd think I'd promised her the world. She jumped at my neck so quick that it hurt. She was squeezing me and crying, and I was hoping I'd done the right thing. But then I saw a shape, and I looked up and saw Juli standing in the doorway. I wished I knew how much she'd heard. I hoped she wasn't upset with me for making such a rash promise without even talking to her about it first.

"Time for bed, Katie," I said.

"Yes," Julia agreed. "Come here, sweetie. I'll take you."

She went. They both went. And I didn't know what to do but go back to shining my shoes. I didn't really know if what I'd said was bothering Julia or not. She was much too kind to say anything about it in front of Katie. But she was so good-hearted, especially with kids, that I guess I shouldn't have worried.

"You did the right thing," she said when she came back in the kitchen. "She's claimed us like family already. If they don't find her a home, it wouldn't be right just to put her with strangers in an orphanage or something."

"You're an incredible woman. We've only known her a few days."

"She's seen a lot in that time. Franky getting hurt. And the results of the first fight I've ever known you to have." She reached and touched my cheek.

"It wasn't much of a fight."

"Pretty one-sided?"

I looked down at the shoes in my hand. "Yeah."

She sat down beside me. "What possesses him to keep after you? Can't he see you're trying to be peaceable?"

"I don't know, Juli. I guess he's always been kind of blind."

"Then we need to ask Pastor Jones to pray for him tomorrow, along with Franky."

I sat quiet, considering. "Do you really think I should go?"

"Of course you should! You mean because you're going to have quite a black eye for tomorrow? Is that why you're wondering?"

"Yeah, I guess. I'm not anxious to have everybody looking me over."

"They might think any number of things. But you have nothing to be ashamed of. You didn't provoke him or even hit him back, did you? You can't help it if someone flies off the handle, any more than I could."

Those words churned my blood. "If he lays a hand on you again, I'll do more than hit him."

She put her hand on my shoulder. "You know what I think?"

I looked over at her. "No."

"I think I'm blessed. You don't seem mad at me. But you could be."

"Why would I be mad at you?"

"I think you know why. Don't you?" She put her arm around me and kissed me on my bruised cheek. It hurt. But I wasn't about to tell her.

"I can't blame you, Juli. If I didn't know better, I wouldn't believe myself."

"But I know you. I've seen your heart. That should be good enough."

"It's hard to argue with what looks like evidence. But at least we know now that the guy might be older and rougher than I am."

She smiled, relief apparent in her eyes even by the light of the oil lamp. "You're right. That's wonderful!"

She hadn't been sure. She'd been acting so sweet and wonderful to me even when she wasn't sure. For a minute that bothered me. But then I thought, that's love. "I love you, Juli. For being willing to hug me even if I was a lying bum."

"Oh, honey, I never meant anything like that."

"But if it were true, you'd stay with me, wouldn't you?"

She squeezed my hand. "It isn't true. You told me it isn't. But if it were, I couldn't throw my whole life away. I need you. And I always will."

"I don't know about that sometimes. Seems like you could handle anything whether you had a man here or not."

She looked a little upset suddenly. "Well, I guess I could if I had to! If you're talking about just any man.

But I'm not! I mean it when I say that I need you! And I believe you too. Katie's father is some mean old ruffian that happens to share your name. That's all. And you're good enough to take in his little girl and love her already! I see that you do."

I took her hand. "I think you do too."

Julia was quiet for a moment. "More than that, she loves us."

SEVENTEEN

Julia

Sunday morning was just as hurried as ever. Maybe more so, because every time I about got something done, little Emma Grace started spreading pans across the kitchen or trying to undress herself one piece at a time. We ended up eating nothing more than yesterday's leftover corn bread with milk over it. And Emmie threw hers on the floor.

"My shoes is too tight," Sarah complained.

"They weren't so bad last week," I tried to coax her. She had to wear shoes for church, even if she never wore them at home in the summer. And we had no others for her.

"Maybe she'd fit mine," Katie said suddenly.

"But you'll need them."

"I can try hers. Mine is too big for me anyway."

"They are?"

"Yeah. Mama got 'em from a big box, an' they never did fit right, but she said I'd grow."

"A big box?" Sarah asked. "I thought new shoes come in little boxes."

"They're not new. They came from a big box outside the Wyatt Hotel where folks throws away stuff. Only I don't know why anybody'd throw away shoes. They must be real rich or not very smart."

"Well, girls, you can swap and try them if you want to. It can't hurt."

Rorey looked on while Sarah and Katie eagerly tried on each other's shoes. To my great surprise, they were both satisfied.

"They fit real good, Mommy!" Sarah declared. "I gotta thank God for shoes now!"

"Are you sure those are all right on you, Katie?" I asked, not wanting her to be obliging at her own expense.

"They're nice. Better than the others."

But just in case, I leaned down to feel the toes, and sure enough, they seemed to fit her fine, with even a little growing room. "Well, all right. If you're both sure."

"We're sure," Sarah said for both of them. "I think that means we fit together perfect."

Rorey scowled. "Well, both pairs is kinda ugly."

"That's okay," Sarah answered back, not the least upset. "Until school starts, we don't have to wear them except Sunday, anyway."

I put bows in the girls' hair while Robert tied the tie that Emma had made for him, and Samuel pulled Emmie Grace out of the empty potato bin she'd managed to crawl into.

"Look, Daddy! New shoes!" Sarah proclaimed proudly.

"And see mine!" Katie added, training her eyes on him.

I knew she was still looking for the acceptance she'd felt last night. And Samuel smiled at both of them.

"I see. Who would have thought? Smart thinking, Katie."

She beamed like she'd been called a queen.

"I wish I had new shoes," Rorey complained.

"At least yours will do for now," I assured her. "I'm afraid you aren't the only one needing new shoes this year."

"Even Pa does," Rorey agreed. "He patched his boots for the 'leventy-hundredth time, an' they's started to fall apart."

"We'll have to be praying on all that," I told her. "You'll help me, won't you?"

"All right. I guess so," she said, seeming to feel better about it already.

Charlie Hunter was right on time, but he seemed earlier than usual, because I was in the middle of changing Emmie Grace for the third time. I knew we really should start training this child, but neither Lizbeth nor I had gotten around to trying. When Charlie pulled up and honked, I was in such a hurry that I poked the baby with one of the pins by mistake. She cried, and I felt terrible.

"So sorry, sweetie." I tried to comfort her, lifting her up to my shoulder. She started tugging my hair down, and I made her quit, which upset her all the more.

Samuel offered to take her, but she didn't want to go to him this time. So she stayed with me, fussing and carrying on until we were outside and Sarah said, "Look, Emmie! Bunny rabbits!"

Emmie looked and got real quiet. I looked too. Three big rabbits, helping themselves to the green beans and cabbage we would need so much. I handed Emmie to Samuel whether she wanted to go or not and ran at the garden with a shout.

Charlie just waited, and all the kids watched, probably thinking me a sight, running across the yard in my Sunday clothes.

"We can't keep them out while we're gone," Samuel said.

"Well, I can sure try while I'm here." I watched the furry thieves go hopping away from me toward the cornfield. "Where is Whiskers? This is his job."

Robert whistled long and shrill, and Whiskers came loping out of the barn, stopping in front of me to stretch.

"I wish you'd nap out here," I told the dog. "Maybe the rabbits would stay away."

"Least it ain't deer," Charlie Hunter put in. "Over by Belle Rive, they're having a terrible time keepin' the deer out."

"They've been in the corn around here too," I told him, suddenly very weary. We struggled constantly, against weather and animals and prices and the whole economy around us. And I was tired of it. More tired than I'd even realized.

"Ready to go?" Samuel seemed to be asking everybody.

I hurried to crowd myself into Charlie's car along with the rest. But for the first time in so long, I wasn't feeling real about going to church. I was going because we always went, but I didn't feel like it. I would have rather stayed home all by myself and talked to God in the vegetable garden, keeping the rabbits away at the same time. I would ask him why times were hard, even for praying people. I would ask him why he'd taken Emma and Wilametta last winter when we were so unprepared. I would ask what we were supposed to do about Katie and Edward. And why Franky had to get hurt. And what we were to do now.

"We're not supposed to have all the answers," Franky had said. Well, maybe that was just fine. But I didn't see why we couldn't at least have some.

What if Edward came back again? After all he'd done! What then?

Seventy times seven. The words popped into my head before I could begin to think what they could mean. *Seventy times seven.* I knew I'd heard them before, I'd read them before, but I didn't remember when. And I didn't want to think about it.

Little Emmie snuggled up to me, and Charlie took to driving as fast as always, faster than anybody else I knew, but I'd come to like it. I guessed he was in a hurry to get back to his new wife, whom he always left in town when he came to get us. She walked the few blocks to church, and he drove seven miles to pick us up. I'd told him over and over he didn't have to come, that we'd find another way, but he wouldn't quit. He said he'd pledged to God and Emma Graham to make sure we got there as long as we wanted to go.

He was a marvel, I guessed. One of those friends that if you thank God for him every day, it still isn't enough. Pastor and Juanita Jones were the same way. Precious and kind. I loved to see them, to get the chance to sit and talk to Juanita. She'd been wonderful last Christmas and was still just as wonderful to us. If it hadn't been for her, I wasn't sure how I could have handled it all. I shuddered even now, just remembering.

I saw Samuel looking back at me and knew he was wondering if I was all right this morning, but he didn't ask. He was a jewel, even more than Juanita. There he sat with his puffy black eye and bruises, but he didn't seem the least bit concerned over himself. Maybe nobody would say much of anything about how he looked. I hoped not. But just as I was thinking that, Charlie Hunter turned his head slightly in Samuel's direction and started with the questions.

"What happened to you? Walk into the barn door?"

"No. It's a long story."

"We got a while to church," Charlie maintained. "You mind tellin' it?"

"I'd rather not."

Charlie gave him an odd look. "Okay." He was only quiet for minute, turning a corner and then glancing at Samuel again. "I see your company's still here. Bet that's been fun for Sarah. Best times I remember when I was a kid was when cousins came to visit."

"She's not our cousin," Robert replied. "We don't know what she is."

"Robert!" I exclaimed in dismay. Why in the world would he say something like that, right in front of her?

"We claim her as kin," Samuel said quickly. "My family's kind of mixed up and distant."

"Not sure what that means," Charlie admitted. "But I knew you were family when I saw you in town the other day."

Charlie always had an innocent way of looking at things. He didn't ask for more details and didn't seem bothered at all that Samuel didn't supply any. He would have taken Katie for a cousin and left it at that if Robert hadn't said anything. And Samuel's bruises! Walking into the barn door was a perfectly reasonable explanation to Charlie. Unfortunately, that wouldn't be what most people would think of first.

I was considering Hazel Sharpe and her abrasive tongue as we parked along the street in front of the church. Too bad everybody couldn't be like Charlie and his bride, Millie. She was waiting for us under a tree in front of the church, looking like she would swoon with delight when he got out of the car.

"What's church going to be like?" Katie asked again nervously.

"Sometimes it's dull as old nails," Robert volunteered. "But other times it's good as radio."

"Robert John—" I started.

But Charlie was laughing. "Dear ol' Emma taught him to speak his mind, Mrs. Wortham! You can tell he remembers his lessons. Besides, that was quite a compliment to the pastor. Good as radio even once in a while's doing mighty fine, I'd say."

I let it go. If I was going to talk to Robert about "speaking his mind," now was not the time.

I walked toward the church, carrying Emmie Grace, who'd amazingly gone to sleep over my shoulder. Katie reached her little hand into Samuel's as Charlie left us to join his wife. Through the open church window, I saw Hazel Sharpe and wondered if I could dare sit with her the way I usually did once Sunday school got over. She tolerated it, sometimes without speaking to us at all. But today I knew I couldn't trust her to hold her tongue. Of course, maybe it would be worse if I didn't sit with her. Maybe she would think we had something to hide, something to be ashamed of.

Sarah and Rorey ran on ahead of us, looking for their Sunday school friends. Robert lagged behind me the way he usually did. But Samuel walked up the church steps boldly with Katie at his side. *He could never be that much of a liar,* I thought. *If it were really true, what Edward says, he'd be ashamed to show his face here.*

I thought Samuel very brave, like Daniel must have been, knowing he was facing a den of lions. Sure, this was our church family, but there were a few members who could bite and claw with the best of them. I took a deep breath and followed my husband, knowing we were already drawing glances.

"I heard about him," Ella Cole was whispering to Magnolia Burns as we walked past. "Can you believe it?"

I nearly tripped on the stair. Emma Grace opened her

eyes with a start, and I eased her little head back down to my shoulder. Why should I think they were talking about us? So what if they were? God knew the truth.

For a moment, Samuel turned his eyes to look at me. *God knows the truth,* I thought again. *And maybe he's the only one who needs to. Who cares what anybody else thinks or says?*

I watched my husband take another step toward that church door, even as Harold and Bernice Walker were starting in our direction and looking at us so strangely.

At least Samuel was here, presenting himself to God—bruises, accusations, and all. That was what mattered.

I smiled, feeling ready to conquer the world at my husband's side. I didn't think I could be shaken. I didn't think one soul here could upset me, not even Hazel Sharpe, no matter what they'd heard or what they said.

"Mr. Wortham!" Harold Walker was calling. He didn't say Samuel, the way he usually did. I wondered if he and Bernice had been waiting for us. They lived next to the church and were usually among the first inside.

"Mr. Wortham!" he called again, even though Samuel had already stopped on the stair and turned around.

"The Bible teaches us to be frank with one another," Harold started out, all in a rush. "You know, if we have somethin' again' a brother to go to him an' all . . ."

Samuel nodded, not saying a word. I had a feeling he knew exactly what was coming. And I wasn't nearly as prepared as he was.

"Some fella come up here yesterday lookin' for the pastor. I tol' him where to find him, but when he found out I was church folks with you, he tol' me some of his business, so I could pray on it, you know. An' it's just about kept us up all night, being concerned about you and all."

Bernice was standing beside him, nodding her head and looking at me like I was some poor lost child.

"Now, we understand that your personal business is

your own," he went on, "but when it comes to the family of God—"

Samuel cut him off impatiently. "Just tell me what he said."

Harold stopped, looked at both of us and then down at Katie. "Well . . . he said quite a lot. That you were befriending us all for gain, that was one thing."

"I haven't asked for anything," Samuel said simply. "I haven't taken anything either."

"You've taken quite a lot, seems to me," Harold argued. "Ever since Christmas, folks has been givin' you all kinds a' things. Scarves for the kids, peach preserves . . ."

Samuel bowed his head.

"We've appreciated every bit," I said quickly. "It would've been a hard winter for us and especially the Hammonds without the church's kindness."

Harold's eyes narrowed. "Kindness is one thing, but when it comes to takin' advantage—"

"I haven't asked for anything," Samuel repeated, starting up the stairs again. "And my brother just likes to make trouble."

"He said *you* was the trouble," Harold pressed, following Samuel up a step. "Having us all hoodwinked 'bout what you done to Emma."

Samuel turned around, and I saw the fire in his eyes. He could have said plenty. He could have done a thousand things. But he only sighed and turned away again. "Believe what you want to believe."

"He also said you had you an illegitimate child!" Bernice Walker burst out in a shriekish voice. "And here you are bringing her into God's house!"

"Where else would I bring her?" Samuel said wearily and walked on inside.

Bernice stood there in shock. "He didn't deny it! Oh, dear Lord, Julia! He didn't deny it!"

She reached her large arms toward me, and I wasn't

sure whether to receive her awkward hug or step away. He didn't deny it? So what? He was just tired of hearing it! Tired of the accusations. Why should he have to defend himself in the house of God?

"You stink!" Robert suddenly exclaimed, and I whirled in surprise.

"Robert!"

"It ain't right, them marching up and saying stuff like that about my dad! You stink, that's all!" he told the Walkers again. "Just 'cause some stupid criminal comes and says a bunch of stuff doesn't mean you have to believe it!"

Harold and Bernice stared at him, shaking their heads, clucking their tongues.

"Robert, that's no way to talk, no matter how you feel."

"Why don't you tell them that? My dad's the best person in this place! He don't believe lies about everybody else! He don't march up saying ugly stuff—"

"Children should be taught to hold their tongues," Bernice said sanctimoniously. And oh, how I wished she would just go away! Robert was right. Why should I have to correct *him*?

"Robert, dear, you might as well go on to your Sunday school room," I said quietly. "Sit with your friends. We'll talk about this later."

"It ain't right, Mom. He didn't do nothing! An' Katie might be illegitimate, who knows? But she ain't Dad's. That don't make no sense at all."

I hadn't been aware that he understood what that word meant. But he did, obviously. "I know. But go on. Please."

He walked away; Harold and Bernice were still shaking their heads at me. Like I was doing wrong for not reproving my son for standing up for his father.

Let them shake their heads. I was glad for Robert. Maybe I'd thank him later. But Samuel was right too. Let them believe what they want to believe. I marched up the steps and into the church, hugging Emma Grace tight.

"Julia?" Bernice called.

I ignored her.

"Julia?"

I could hear other scattered voices behind me, people gathering from the churchyard, but I didn't stop.

Bernice sighed, her disapproving voice floating over all the other chatter.

"Well, I'll be . . . that Juli Wortham . . . don't she know the kind of man she's married to?"

EIGHTEEN

Samuel

As soon as I was in the church, Hazel Sharpe made a beeline in my direction. "What happened to you? Your eye's true purple. You've been fightin'! A grown man!"

Beside me, Katie squeezed my hand, surely remembering this sharp-tongued woman from our previous encounter.

"I heard tell from the Posts about one a' those Hammond boys gettin' hurt at your place. And now look at you! What kind of foolishness have you had goin' on out there, anyway?"

"Barrett told you about Franky?" It surprised me, it truly did, that he would come and talk to Miss Hazel.

"Well, a' course he knew folks from church oughta know. I seen his truck over at the pastor's last night, and I went right over there to see if there was anything I could do."

It must have been quite an evening for Pastor Jones. With Barrett bringing such news, Hazel dropping in, and apparently Edward showing up at some point to tear me down.

"Lot more to you than meets the eye, Samuel Wortham," Miss Hazel was saying. "You been hidin' things."

I was looking toward the front, where Pastor Jones was kneeling in front of the cross as he did before nearly every service.

"I know you was in to see Ben Law the other day," Hazel continued. "I seen you comin' from there. I went an' talked to him, I'll have you know! Law-abiding citizens got an obligation to the community. If there's trouble, we got every right to know! He told me about you, so you don't have to stand here so bold-faced. I know the shameful sort a' things you been up to—"

"Excuse me, Miss Hazel." I tried to edge around her, toward the pastor. But she didn't let me by.

"Sin is sin, Samuel Wortham, whether it's yesterday or six years old!"

Pastor lifted his head and looked over at us with a frown. He'd told me once what a trial it was, having Hazel in his congregation. Of course, it wasn't only her today. He stood to his feet quickly and came in our direction, reaching his hand to me.

"Good morning," he said, looking from me to Katie and back again.

"Disgraceful, ain't it?" Miss Hazel asked him.

"Are you all right?" Pastor asked me.

"Yes, sir."

"He's been fightin'!" Hazel proclaimed. "An' he calls himself a Christian! You'll have to set him straight, Pastor! That little boy hurt on account a' him, and now him bringing this girl right in front of us like he ain't got the sense to be ashamed! We can't be havin' it! Not in God's own church!"

There was a heaviness in the pastor's face unlike anything I'd seen in him before. "I *would* like to talk to you, Samuel," he said. "And your wife. After the service."

"Yes," I told him, suddenly feeling a heaviness of my own. "That would be fine."

"This is a pretty young lady you have with you today," he continued, taking Katie's hand.

For the first time I noticed the tears in Katie's eyes. Scary Miss Hazel. I should have known better. Even though Katie had wanted to be with me, I should have sent her straight on with Sarah so we wouldn't run the risk of such an encounter. But it was too late now.

"What's your name, child?" Pastor was asking.

She looked up at me, her little lip quivering.

"It's okay," I told her. "The pastor is my friend."

She sniffed. She glanced at Miss Hazel and quickly turned her eyes away. "Katie," she said, barely a whisper.

"A lovely name," Pastor told her. "And we're very glad to have you today. I hope you enjoy the service."

"Pastor Jones!" Hazel exclaimed. The hat on her head was quivering, though she looked to be standing still.

"Do you see that picture over there?" the pastor asked Katie, pointing to a framed portrait of Christ. She nodded. "That's Jesus," he told her. "A long time ago he told his disciples to allow the children to come to him so that he could bless them. And that's exactly the way he feels about you now."

Hazel scowled, and I wondered if she didn't understand the pastor's words as the gentle rebuke they were surely meant to be. Regardless of any guilt of mine or her parents, Katie should be welcomed by all the church folks, smiled upon, loved, and blessed. I was grateful to the pastor for having that understanding.

"We can't condone sin in the church," Hazel declared bluntly. "We'd have the whole town runnin' wild. You can plain tell he ain't one bit sorry."

For the first time, Pastor turned his attention to the stooped old lady.

"I already said I would meet with him after the service—"

"I sure would like to hear what he has to say for himself—"

"Privately, sister. This is no more concern of yours. Let us be thankful that in a difficult time, Samuel has come to the house of God for comfort."

"He oughta have come for repentance," Hazel huffed.

"And we are not to judge unless we're prepared to be judged," he added gently.

Suddenly Julia was placing her hand on my arm. I hadn't even seen her walk up to us. Pastor saw her gesture and gave her a nod.

"The thought of bein' judged don't scare me at all," Hazel insisted.

"Perhaps it should," Julia said quietly.

You'd have thought the old woman had been hit by a club. She staggered back a step and was suddenly breathing hard. "Pastor Jones, did you hear that?"

"Yes. I did. I think Julia means all have sinned and fallen short of the glory of God. We have to acknowledge that we need repentance of our own in order to safely stand before his judgment."

Hazel shook her head at him. "You ain't speakin' to no heathen here. I've heard that all my life."

"It always serves us well to reflect on our hearts and the extent of God's grace."

"Yes. Of course," she told him impatiently. "But the prophets an' Jesus hisself made plain that we can't just nod our head at sin. We're s'posed to rebuke it. Put it 'way from ourselves—"

"And love one another," the pastor added.

I smiled.

"The Hammond boys are here," Pastor Jones suddenly

said brightly. "Dedicated young men. I didn't know we could expect them without their father."

He started for the door, and Juli and I followed him, leaving Miss Hazel to stand and stew by herself. Young Sam and Joe were just coming in with the little boys. It didn't look like Willy and Kirk were with them. If they'd come in George's wagon, they must have started out well before we did.

Thelma Pratt hurried to Sam, asking about Franky and taking hold of Harry before he crawled under a pew.

"Good morning, Mrs. Wortham," she said quickly. "Are you going straight to your Sunday school room? I can hold Emmie for you if you'd like."

"Thank you, Thelma," Juli said. "That's very kind."

Juli took Harry's hand, and Thelma took Emma Grace. Thelma stared for a moment at my black eye. I guess everybody was wondering, but it was Joe who asked.

"What happened, Mr. Wortham? Pa wasn't mad at you, was he? Surely he wouldn't bust ya—"

"No. It had nothing to do with him."

"Must a' been your brother, then," Joe decided. "Hope you cleaned his clock. I sure wouldn't blame you. I felt like bustin' him myself. They hadn't oughta let people drive who don't watch. Franky was just tryin' to be nice, cleanin' off his car for him."

"I know. He's a good kid. I feel bad that he got hurt."

"Weren't your fault."

Hearing those words, Pastor turned to me again. "Barrett said he'd take me up to see Franky this afternoon. Would you like to come along, Samuel?"

"Yes. Thank you."

Thelma took Emmie to a seat next to Delores Pratt, her mother. Julia took Harry, Berty, and Katie with her to a Sunday school room. Joe went to find Robert and the older class. And I found a seat with Sam Hammond, behind Thelma Pratt. Sometimes Julia sat with Hazel and stayed in the sanctuary for the opening hymn before taking the little ones to class. But not today.

For adult Sunday school, Clarence Cole got up at the sound of a bell and talked on and on about sin and repentance, looking most of the time at me. I was glad Katie wasn't in here. I was glad Juli taught the Sunday school for her age. At least the child wouldn't have to be uncomfortable in her classroom.

I was feeling more and more uneasy. Sore. And closed in, as if the sanctuary were full of nothing but stagnant, dead air, though the windows and door were wide open. I bowed my head, feeling awfully heavy. But then, before Hazel Sharpe got up to play more hymns on the piano, Ralph Gray moved from his usual place to sit beside me. He didn't say anything. He didn't even look at me. He just sat there. And the world seemed better for it.

By the time the kids came back in, most of the heaviness was gone. Ralph's wife, the other Sunday school teacher, was ahead of Julia and sat down next to her husband. Their daughter, Rachel, my son, Robert, and Joe Hammond filled the rest of the pew. And just as Hazel Sharpe was sitting back down, Julia, with Sarah, Katie, Rorey, Harry, and Bert, moved quickly to join her. Most Sundays, Hazel tolerated Juli's presence, ignoring her for the most part. I would sit with them sometimes, and we would get a sideways glance or two and a pat on the back and a chuckle from some of the other church family who thought the whole thing funny. Worthams sitting with Hazel Sharpe. And nothing she could do about it! After all, she wouldn't get up and move. It was *her* pew.

But today, Hazel was particularly incensed. She tried to scoot over so there'd be less room for all the kids, but that didn't bother Harry at all. He only clambered around to the other side of her. She plunked her shawl down on the seat, but he promptly sat on top of it. Juli didn't even seem to notice. She was sitting between Sarah and Katie, with Berty trying hard to climb up on her lap.

"Let us turn to the book of Luke," Pastor was saying.

Hazel pulled her shawl out from under the boy, sliding him noiselessly on to the hard seat. He stared up at the feather in her hat, and she turned her eyes to the front, looking sour indeed.

"Judge not, and ye shall not be judged: condemn not, and ye shall not be condemned. Forgive, and ye shall be forgiven . . ."

Harry's hand was slipping up, while he watched Hazel's face to see if she was noticing. I was too far away to stop him. Juli didn't see. And Vivian Day, sitting directly behind them, didn't pay the slightest bit of attention.

"Harry, no," I whispered. But of course he didn't hear me. I was hoping someone closer to him would. Maybe they would stop him. But quick as a wink, Harry's little hand shot the rest of the way up, yanked that bright yellow feather from its place, and then jerked back down again. And he sat up straight, looking at the preacher as if nothing had happened.

Hazel's hat fell off her head. I could see her turning crimson, whether from embarrassment or rage, I wasn't sure. And Harry, the little rascal, just sat there snickering.

". . . with the same measure that ye mete withal it shall be measured to you again . . ."

I saw the pastor smile, turn his eyes toward Harry, and gently shake his head. Only then did I see that Harry was waving the feather in circles, down low where he wouldn't create too much of a scene. Hazel reached and grabbed the feather away from him. Juli finally noticed, but there was little she could do about Harry now.

Harry fidgeted, raced his fingers across the back of the pew in front of him, and otherwise gave poor Hazel fits until Pastor's wife reached back and handed him a piece of paper. He spent the rest of the service carefully tearing it in shreds. When Hazel got up to play for the closing hymn, tiny bits of paper were clinging to her skirt and falling piece by piece to the floor.

She played loud and fast—the bounciest version of "The Lily of the Valley" I'd ever heard. And I kind of liked it.

NINETEEN

Julia

"Don't *ever* allow that little heathen to sit beside me again, Juli Wortham!" Miss Hazel puffed just as soon as Pastor dismissed the service. "What in the world is his father teaching him? What are *you* teaching him?"

"Well, not to be heathen, surely," I said. "I'm sorry. I was so busy watching for Bert and Katie that I didn't notice him slipping ahead."

"I'd hate to see what your classroom is like! We shouldn't have teachers who can't control the children, I say!" Hazel looked scornfully down at Harry. "Apologize, young man. Right this minute!"

Harry just gazed up with a coy little smile. "I 'pologize. I like your hat."

Hazel looked like she could burst. I thought she might yell, but she didn't. "You are not to touch a lady's hat again! Do you understand? Nor any piece of it."

"Yes, ma'am." He smiled all the more brightly. "Purty feather. Nicerer than our chickens' feathers, I'll say."

Miss Sharpe held it out like it was some distasteful thing and dropped it in his direction. "You might just as well keep it then, since you bent it all up. But if your father were here, I'd insist he take you to the woodshed! Juli, I expect you to inform George Hammond of his son's outrageous behavior."

She started brushing the remaining bits of paper off of her skirt, and I tried to help her, but she only gave me a scowl. "Better tend to your own," she warned. "Keep an eye on that husband of yours."

I knew what she meant. And it was a cruel taunt, inferring that Samuel was untrustworthy.

Maybe I was feeling as ornery as Harry, but I just couldn't resist turning it around. "Why, thank you, Hazel. Some folks assume that a mother and Sunday school teacher has her place just with the children. It's nice of you to understand how much a blessing it is to train my attention on my own dear husband."

I gave her a hug. A huge hug, right in front of everybody milling about. She looked at me like I'd completely taken leave of my senses. Shaking her head, she couldn't seem to utter a word.

"Have a wonderful day," I told her. "Won't you come out and have dinner with us sometime? Have Herman bring you, and he can stay too."

I hardly knew what I was saying. I could scarcely imagine being able to put anything on the table good enough to suit Hazel Sharpe, we had so little of everything. But Emma would have approved. Even if Hazel never came, I was glad I'd offered. After all, she had gotten Bibles for every one of the kids at Christmastime. In memory of Emma Graham. A stunningly generous act that had shocked everyone who had heard about it.

I hugged her again. "Thank you," I whispered. "Thank you again so much."

"Just . . . just what do you think you're doing, Juli Wortham?" she stammered. "I never seen the like!"

"I just appreciate you so. Those Bibles that you gave the children—"

She frowned. "Did they even bring 'em to church today?"

"Robert and Sarah did. I think the Hammonds forgot without Lizbeth home to remind them."

"Without Lizbeth!" Hazel rolled her eyes. "George couldn't no more raise his kids than the man in the moon! Why, if it weren't for you an' Lizbeth, they'd all be naked and starved by now."

"Well, women have an important role, that's sure, but George is doing his best."

"That ain't my point! Lizbeth ain't a woman yet! An' your husband an' George Hammond are the poorest excuses for fathers in this whole church. I declare, Juli, why you put up with it all is beyond me. Havin' a liar and a cheat! But then maybe you don't know what else to do but follow 'long on his coattails."

It was like being slapped, and I guess she meant it that way—even after I'd tried to pay her a compliment. I just sighed. "I can't say I understand you, Miss Hazel. Or why you say the things you do. But I'll love you anyway. Nothing will change that. Not even the way you feel about my husband, the dearest soul in the world to me."

"He's got you blind, Juli-girl."

I was surprised at her calling me that. Nobody had but Emma. I shook my head. "It's everyone else who's blind," I said with a confidence I hadn't known I had. "Everyone else who thinks he could do anything at all to hurt his family."

I started to turn away. Behind me I heard her muttering something about Samuel's fighting getting Franky hurt and teaching the children who knows what. *She's just ignorant, that's all,* I told myself. *God have mercy on poor, ignorant Hazel.*

I smiled down at Sarah and Katie. And Berty, who was tugging on my skirt. Rorey and Harry had already darted outside.

Before the rest of us could go out, Juanita Jones came up and put her arm around my shoulder. I was glad. The pastor's wife was such a dear friend, and I always liked the chance to talk to her. But this time, there was pain in her eyes. "Let me take the children for you. Paxton would like to see you and Samuel."

It made me a little anxious to think of the pastor asking special to speak to us. It just wasn't right, the lies that were spreading like wildfire. But Pastor was amiable as always as he sat beside us in the front pew and began to explain his concerns about what he'd heard.

"Your brother was very angry," he told Samuel. "But I found it difficult to believe what he was telling me. Nothing sounded like the Sam Wortham I know."

"It isn't," Samuel said solemnly.

"Do you know who Katie's father is?"

"No. That's the problem. We need your prayers. We're not sure what's next for the little girl, whether we'll have to send her somewhere to family, if we can find any, or keep her here."

"Her own mother doesn't want her?"

"Not as far as we know, from Edward and from the girl herself."

"Why do they say you're the father?"

"I don't know."

"Well, how did the woman know your name?"

"I don't know that either. We've been thinking there must be someone else with the same name."

"But not anyone you know?"

Samuel was quiet. "No," he said finally. "Not since my father died when I was twelve."

Pastor shook his head. "The child's not old enough to be your sister."

"I know."

"But she does look like you."

"Everyone has noticed. That's why Ben Law didn't believe me. Too much to look past, I guess."

"It was your brother who hit you?"

"Yes."

"Why?"

"He's angry, like you said. That I wouldn't admit it. He really believes I'm guilty. In a way, I'm glad. At least he's not lying to me."

"But the rest of what he said, about you tricking Mrs. Graham and trying to fool all of us—"

"His anger talking, I guess."

"Is he dangerous? To anyone else?"

"I don't think so. Not on purpose. It was an accident with Franky. A stupid and careless thing because we were arguing. He just wouldn't let it drop and got in my face again on the way home. I tried, Pastor, not to lose my temper, but it wasn't easy."

Pastor didn't have much more to say. He'd only wanted confirmation, I guess, of where Samuel's heart stood. And he told me he believed there should be no secrets between a husband and his wife. That's why he'd wanted me there.

"Your mild spirit is something to be admired in all of this, Julia," he said.

I wondered what he would think if he knew what my real thoughts had been.

I was expecting Charlie Hunter to take us back home, but much to my surprise, Pastor asked us all to their house for dinner so we'd still be in town when Barrett came in to take the pastor to Mcleansboro. Barrett was helping move his sister, Pastor said, and should be there in the early afternoon.

"You should both come along," Pastor told me. "I'm sure Franky, and George too, would appreciate seeing you."

I wanted to go. But I was still thinking the same as I was before. "What about all the children?"

"They can stay with Juanita. It'll be fun for them. How often do they get to have a time out visiting?"

"What about Katie?" I worried. "She doesn't even know Juanita yet."

"Sounds like you've both taken that girl to heart."

I nodded my head but didn't answer about going to see Franky.

"Relax. She'll be fine with my wife for an afternoon. She'll have them playing tag and hopscotch. Who knows, maybe she'll pull out the paper dolls she used to play with when she was a girl."

"Katie loves paper dolls."

"Then see?" Pastor smiled at us. "It's a good fit."

He made me smile too; he was so generous to accept the things Samuel had to say and make a way for us to see Franky. I was so glad that no matter what anybody else said or did, Pastor was willing to give Samuel the benefit of the doubt.

He prayed with us, and then we all walked outside together. Juanita was playing ring-around-the-rosy with Berty and the little girls. Sam Hammond and Thelma Pratt were sitting under a tree with Harry and Emma Grace climbing all over them. Joe and Robert were standing talking to Thelma's younger brother, Elmer.

They were all rather pleased about going over to Pastor's house and having ham and beans and cherry pie. But when Barrett and Louise finally got there, most of the children wanted to go with us into Mcleansboro.

"I think I'd better stay here and help you with them," I told Juanita. "Just the baby's a handful. And then there's Harry and Bert and—"

"You ought to go," Louise told me. "That Franky thinks an awful lot of you. He'd be glad seein' you, I'm sure. I'll stay here with Juanita. Won't hurt me none to chase after little ones a while. My grandkids keep me broke in, you know."

"Are you sure?"

"Yes, I'm sure, or I wouldn't say it."

Barrett, Pastor, and Samuel walked outside talking while I admonished the children to be on their best behavior. Sam Hammond decided he'd go on home and maybe take some of the others with him. "Tell Pa I'll come in the wagon tomorrow after the milkin's done," he said. "I wanna see Franky too."

Samuel and I rode in the back of Barrett's truck. It was the first time we'd been without kids in a long while. Barrett and the pastor sat in front without saying much the whole trip, and we got bounced quite a bit in the back, but I didn't care.

Samuel was so quiet. Thinking about Franky, maybe, and how unfortunate this whole situation was. It was hard for Samuel, I knew. And I felt like I should have been watching. I should never have told Franky it was all right to go over by that car. I should have known better. But I knew Samuel was probably blaming himself too.

What about Edward? Did it plague him at all? How could he not have looked behind him? How could he forget the little kid rinsing the road dust off his back bumper? It made me angry all over again. It hardly mattered to Edward who he hurt. He didn't care much for Katie or for Samuel, that was clear by the way he treated them. Maybe he didn't really care for anybody at all.

I could scarcely imagine anybody that hard-hearted. But I guessed the world held quite a few of them. At least Hazel Sharpe with her cruel tongue and mean spirit didn't go around putting people in the hospital. She only wounded their spirits and slashed at the heart.

I sighed, looking up at Samuel. He'd taken both kinds of wounding so well. Better than me. Suddenly I had the bizarre thought of introducing Edward to Miss Hazel. Then we'd see which way the fur would fly. They could give each other a taste of their own medicine.

Seventy times seven.

The words hit me again, sudden, like a seed dropped from above right into my lap. I knew it was Jesus' answer when Peter asked how often we should forgive.

But I tried to toss the thought away. *I do forgive,* I told the Lord and myself. *I've already forgiven. Everybody knows I don't hold any grudges with Hazel. I sit with her nearly every week. Who else does that? And Edward—well, we didn't call for Ben Law. We could have had him arrested—he hit Katie, he hit Samuel, he broke Franky's leg!*

Seventy times seven.

God was being insistent. With three strong words dropped into my heart. How many times do we forgive, Lord? When our brother does us wrong?

My head was arguing over that one. *He's not* my *brother. He's not even a Christian brother. Surely this is different. And Hazel—Hazel's already forgiven. I pray for her every night just like Emma used to do.*

Seventy times seven.

I sat back against the rough rail and searched out Samuel's hand. *I've already forgiven, Lord. At least, I thought I had. And I'm not trying to hold anything against Edward. It's just that he makes trouble—he brings it on himself. And he wouldn't care anyway, what I thought of him.*

Clear as a bell, I knew the Lord's response. It's not for Edward. It's for Samuel.

Samuel? I don't blame Samuel. He didn't ask for any of this any more than I did.

I looked up and found my husband's eyes closed, his head back and bouncing with the bouncy road. He looked so peaceful. And he'd handled everything so well. He didn't even seem angry, when he had every right . . .

Suddenly I noticed Samuel's free hand clenched into a fist. I thought of the dream he'd told me about, of his father's violence, his mother's drunkenness. And Edward. I hoped there wasn't something festering inside, some part of Samuel I didn't know about to be unleashed by the sheer strain of Edward's animosity. So I prayed. For Samuel. For the forgiveness that I needed in my heart and that I knew Samuel would need too. Even for Edward, that God would touch him somehow. For Samuel's sake.

I could forgive all the horrible things that Edward had said. The calloused touch. The laughing eyes. The bruises on my husband's face, and even the carelessly broken leg of an innocent child. I could forgive it all. Not for Edward's sake but Samuel's. Because God told me to. We'd need to. Samuel would need me to. I didn't know when or why. But I had to accept that it was so.

TWENTY

Samuel

As we pulled into the hospital parking lot, I half expected to see Edward's car sitting there again. I don't know why. He had no reason to come back. It'd been surprise enough that he'd hung around as long as he did yesterday, when it would have been easier just to leave us and go. Maybe he'd wanted to know how it was with Franky. Or maybe he'd just been waiting for his chance to knock me in the dirt.

He wasn't there this time, and I was glad. Maybe he was already on his way back to Albany. I couldn't imagine anything that would hold him here. And he'd done enough damage, surely.

Juli took my hand as we walked toward the hospital. None of us said much of anything. I wondered if the pastor and Barrett blamed me at all for what had happened to Franky. I certainly couldn't blame them if they did. I should have been watching for him better. I should have been watching Edward better. Why hadn't I known to warn the kids away?

Poor Franky was just trying to do good to a man who needed an example. "Because Jesus loves you," he'd said when Edward asked why he was washing his car.

Franky was looking pale when we came in his room. His leg was all set in heavy plaster. Too heavy, it looked like, for such a little guy to move. And I knew it was still hurting him. I could see it in his eyes.

"How you doing, buddy?" I asked him.

"Okay," he said with a sigh.

Barrett waited in the hallway. Pastor greeted Franky and then prayed with him and George and Lizbeth. Juli hugged Franky as soon as he was done. Then I hugged him too, and he didn't seem to want to let go of my shirt.

"You wasn't fightin', was you?" he asked. "On account of me?"

"I wasn't fighting," I told him. "I was being fought at."

"That's good." He smiled. "The Lord says that's good."

I didn't know how he meant that, if he remembered hearing something like that from Scripture, or what.

"Sure glad all of you come," he said. "I wasn't expecting nobody today."

"You should have been," I told him. "Of course we'd want to come. You're a special boy."

"They's all special," George said from his chair by the wall. "And this'un 'specially needs to be more careful."

"Pa," Lizbeth protested. "It wasn't his fault."

"Not like he planned it or anything," George acknowledged. "But any a' the others'd known to watch around movin' vehicles."

Franky didn't say anything, but I saw the weight of his father's words on his small shoulders. How dare George Hammond blame him for what happened!

"There was no way he could've moved in time," I said

quickly. "It was my fault as much as anything. I should've been paying better attention. I should've known not to let him by that car. But none of us knew Edward would be hightailing it in such a stupid hurry."

George looked at me with a frown. "It's done. Ain't nothin' for it now but to see it through."

"Has the doctor been in?" Juli asked.

"Yeah, but he don't say much, just that they want him stayin' right here. He'll hafta be near six weeks off it, can you imagine that?"

"Not very well," Juli said softly.

"Neither can I," George continued. "It's already costin' me time an' money sittin' here like this. And I ain't got the money, that's sure."

"George," the pastor admonished. "Do you really think your son needs to hear such talk?"

"Don't know why not. He's involved, like it or not."

I could tell Pastor was put out by his attitude; I was relieved I wasn't the only one.

"God works all things, don't he, Pastor?" Franky asked. "I heard you say it one time. He works good outta ever'thin' if we love him. Even this."

George shook his head. "How's good come from a broke leg?"

"We'll eventually see," Pastor assured him. "Your boy has a strong faith. The Lord is pleased and will bless him, I'm sure."

"The Lord don't seem to be blessin' Hammonds right now. Not by much, I mean," George said with a frown.

"I suppose most of the country might say that," Pastor told him. "Times look hard, and hard things happen to everybody. But God brings us through."

"Yeah," George said, still frowning.

"Least we got a hope," Franky said. "A lively hope by the resurrection of Jesus."

Pastor turned and looked at the boy in surprise. Maybe

he didn't know how Franky's mind worked, how deeply the boy memorized the things he heard. "You heard that in a sermon, didn't you?"

"Yes, sir. Four weeks ago. You read Peter's letter that said we was in heaviness 'cause of temptations, but the trial of our faith is better than gold. I don't unnerstand what the temptations is, but I sure hope this comes 'round to praise an' glory for Jesus like you said. 'Cause I love him, even when I ain't seen him, jus' like them people Peter was writin' to."

For a moment, Pastor sat in stunned silence.

"'Scuse him," George said. "He rambles like this—"

"Often?" Pastor asked in amazement.

"Fairly often," Julia said with a smile.

"Well, bless his heart," the pastor said. "Franky, I'm glad you love him when you can't see him. I'm very glad you've been listening so well."

"I try to listen," the boy said with a serious face. "My mind wanders an awful lot, though, all kinds a' ways, an' I'm sorry 'bout that."

Pastor smiled. "You do very well. Even compared to the grown-ups." He didn't look at George, but George frowned anyway. "I'm sure this situation will come around for the glory of the Lord," Pastor continued. "Especially when he finds your heart so eager to please him. Do you want to know what 'temptations' mean?"

"I know what it means," Franky said. "That's when you feel drawed to what you hadn't oughta be messin' with. I jus' don't unnerstand what temptations I got about this, 'less it's to bellyache and fuss 'bout not feelin' good. But I'm tryin' not to."

There were tears in his eyes. I moved closer and put my hand on his shoulder. George got up and said he had to find himself a drink of water.

"It's okay to say you hurt, isn't it, Pastor?" Lizbeth questioned. "Isn't it okay for him to cry if he feels like it? I been cryin', an' I'd cry even more if it was my leg broke."

"Of course it's okay," Pastor assured them both. "Franky, it's all right to complain about what's troubling you. You're not expected to keep it to yourself."

"Ain't it a sin to complain?"

"There's a difference between stating the problem and getting swept up in a spiteful attitude about it."

"I ain't never hurt so bad," Franky said quickly. "An' I'm scared it won't quit." There were tears traveling his cheeks now, and Juli moved to hug him.

"Oh, Franky," she cried. "Who told you you had to be so brave?"

"Pa said big boys don't cry."

"Even Jesus wept," the pastor said solemnly.

Once he was given the permission, Franky wept most of the rest of the time we were there. Twice the nurse came in, just checking on him. She told us there was very little more they could do. Even for the pain. He'd just have to keep still, that was all. And it would eventually feel better.

We hated to leave. Especially with George so unsympathetic. But we had to see to the rest of the children and take care of things at home.

George insisted we take Lizbeth with us. "Emmie an' Bert's gonna be needin' her by now," he said. "No use both a' us sittin' here. The nurses takes care a' most things."

Lizbeth wasn't happy to be sent away, but she didn't argue. I'd often wished that George would spend more time with Franky, try to understand him, try to appreciate him a little better. But I had my doubts that this was the time and place. Franky needed more than his father was willing to give at the moment. Pastor must have thought so too.

"Why don't I stay?" he suggested. "Your oldest boy's

coming with the wagon in the morning. I could ride home with him. I'd like to be here with you."

Franky looked relieved, and I wondered what kind of a night it had been for them last night.

Pastor stayed. Lizbeth hugged her father and brother both, planting a kiss on Franky's cheek. "Don't you worry about nothin'," she said. "You just rest and get better and don't worry so much about temptations an' stuff. You're just a little boy."

He nodded. "Okay."

She thanked the pastor, and then we all said good-bye. And Barrett took us back to the pastor's house for the kids. I was glad he'd stayed with George. I just couldn't fathom why George had taken it into his head to blame Franky when he ought to be mad at Edward or me.

Sarah was so excited to see us that she came running out of the pastor's house and climbed right up in the truck to jump on Julia before we had a chance to get out.

"Goodness!" Juli exclaimed. "What's got you all bouncy like this?"

"Pastor's wife, she taught us how to make a funny baby cradle with a bunch a' string, an' she's got the neatest dolls, Mommy! They's paper but not cut outta magazines like Katie's! They's real dolls outta paper like Helen Jorgenson used to have back in Pennsavaney! Can we get some? Please? Are we gonna stay at their house a while longer? I'd like to really sleep over!"

"Slow down, Sarah. One thing at a time. I'm glad you had fun."

Rorey came out of the house, followed slowly by Katie. I could see the tears in Katie's eyes. Harry and Bert rushed past her to greet Lizbeth, but Katie stood and stared at us timidly.

"Katie was the only one scared," Sarah whispered. "She thought you might not come back. Least not for her."

I hadn't even thought how she would feel with Juli and me both gone. I got out of the truck, intending to talk to her a minute, to put her at ease. But to my surprise she turned and ran the other way, straight out to the pastor's backyard, just as far as she could go without crossing the neighbor's fence. She started up a gnarled old tree with low side limbs and kept climbing till she was hidden in all the green leaves.

For a minute I just stood there. What had come over her to make her run? Maybe I hadn't ought to follow her. Who knew how she'd react?

But Juanita Jones came out of the house, holding Emma Grace and looking back at that tree with concern. "You ought to talk to her, Samuel," she said gently. "Something's been troubling her the last hour or so and she sure won't tell me."

I took a deep breath. *How had this responsibility come to me? Why, Lord? Won't you please show us who this child is?*

Reluctantly I went to the backyard. I knew Barrett was waiting. He'd wanted to pick up the kids and hurry home. He had things to do. But he'd have to wait.

"Katie, how about coming down from the tree and telling me how your afternoon's been? Did you like visiting?"

No answer. I got to the base of the tree and looked up. She was staring down at me, the tears still filling her dark eyes. But she didn't let them overflow, kind of like Julia sometimes, trying to choke down the sad stuff.

"What's the matter?"

She still didn't answer. Just looked out over the yard toward the rest of our bunch gathering at Barrett and Louise's truck.

"Will you come down? Please? If something's upset you, we can talk about it."

She shook her head.

"We need to get going."

She didn't move, didn't speak. In the shadow of the tree, she looked like she did the first night I found her in Edward's car. So small and alone. With a sigh, I stepped on to a tree limb and started climbing, half expecting her to panic or go higher. She didn't. She just watched me, looking worried and confused by something.

"If you won't come down, I'll come to you," I said. "At least for a minute. It's been a while since I climbed a tree, though. If I need help, will you help me?"

She shook her head. "I couldn't help somebody as big as you. If you get stuck, we'll have to call the policeman."

I smiled. "I'll try not to get stuck." I managed to get myself to a sturdy branch not far from her perch, where I could sit and see her face-to-face. "Katie, I'm sorry things have been tough. But I don't know what to do to make it easier."

Her eyes filled up with tears again, and I was almost sorry I'd spoken. But there was no backing down now. Might as well talk straight, even if she didn't want to talk to me. "You know, I wish I could tell you all that's going to happen from here on. But Sheriff Law's not brought one word, and I just don't know what to expect. I'd keep you, you know I would. But there still might be somebody else, and I just don't know what would be best for you. Don't know if you've noticed or not, but we don't have much of anything right now, except people to play with."

"But they all belong here," she said, looking toward the truck again with a deep and solemn expression.

"Well, yes."

"Do I?"

I had to sigh. "I wish I knew. But right now I can't even tell if you want to."

She looked at me for a moment with something different in her eyes. "Do you ever get mad? Real mad?"

I thought of Edward's taunting words, Julia's encounter with him at the well, and my aching bruises. "I guess everybody gets mad. One time or another. But I try not to."

"Was you ever mad at my mama?"

We'd been through this before. "No, honey. How could I when I never met her?"

"But you did!" She shook, some of the tears escaping. "I didn't remember before, but you did! You was there one time when I was little! I dreamed about it! You was there, but I didn't even remember until today, because Mrs. Pastor has a kewpie doll just like the one you broke—"

I reached my hand to her. "Katie, you said you dreamed it. If it even happened, it wasn't really me—"

She scooted back. "Yes, it was! Yes, it was! It was really dark, and you was looking all tired and mean, and Mama kept saying, 'Samuel, don't! Samuel, don't!' Over and over!"

I just stared, thinking of my mother crying those same words. "No," I said, afraid of what I was seeing in this girl's eyes.

"I was hiding in the dream," she said. "I think I was really, really little, because I forgot all about it. Till I saw that dolly and I knew I used to have one like it." She stopped, looking at me with a sharp uncertainty. "You . . . you threw it," she said and started shaking so much that I was afraid she was going to fall out of the tree. Just to be sure she wouldn't, I reached for her again and pulled her into my arms. She didn't resist. She only cried. A long time.

I felt like crying too. She didn't know my father, but maybe she thought I was like him. Edward thought I was like him. And somewhere, somebody really was—some cruel bum who had my name.

Finally, she started to settle down a little, and I felt like I could breathe again. "Why did you grab me?" she asked between sniffs.

"I was afraid you were going to fall."

"Don't you . . . don't you remember being there one time? When I was little?"

"No. If it happened, it was somebody else, honey."

"That was a long time ago. I was really little. But I wasn't as little when the picture got stolen, so I remember it better. Then you were wearing a vest and leaning on a tree. Only I guess you washed off the birdie."

"The birdie?" My stomach dropped like a stone, and I felt suddenly cold. "What birdie?" I could only think of my father with his hand upraised, that dreaded, ugly eagle tattoo staring down at me from his threatening arm.

"There used to be a birdie. In the picture. On your arm."

I felt like I could heave, right there. It couldn't be possible. "Let's climb down," I said, suddenly not sure I could stay upright. The leaves and branches seemed to be weaving.

"You look kind of sick," she said. "Are you mad I remember that stuff? I won't tell anybody if you don't want me to."

"It's not that," I told her, having trouble even getting the words out.

"I guess I was supposed to be a secret," she said in a rush. "But I didn't know that when I came here, and that's why I said stuff before. But if you only want me to be a secret, I won't say nothing else, I promise. Can I be your girl if I be secret?"

Tears fell to her cheeks again, and I could barely stand looking into her face. She looked like me. I looked like my father, Samuel Edward Wortham. Married too young. Too cruel. Too reckless for anybody's good.

According to my mother, he was long dead. But was he?

TWENTY-ONE

Julia

I didn't know what had taken place between Samuel and Katie in that tree, but when they climbed in the truck, they were both still drying their eyes. Samuel looked like he'd been run over by a truck. I guessed he was still awful sore from the bruises, and having a lot on his heart to deal with, what with Franky in the hospital and Katie still here needing us.

He sat beside me, not looking at me very much. Something was different, I knew. He looked lost somehow, utterly confused, and I couldn't picture how that could be possible from just talking a child down out of a tree.

"Are you all right?" I asked him, but he didn't get a chance to say anything before Harry climbed on top of him, whooping about catching a bear.

"Be careful," I told Harry. "He's still sore. Don't be jumping now."

Samuel didn't say a word. Katie sat still as a little stone, just looking over at the paper dolls Juanita had sent along for the girls to play with. When Sarah tried to hand her one, she only looked at it.

Barrett had the truck moving in no time. He and Louise were up front, with all the rest of us piled in the back. Sam Hammond had gone home already, taking Joe and our Robert with him, but they'd left the little girls and Harry and Bert. Just like George had predicted, Emma Grace and Berty were both snuggled up to Lizbeth like they hadn't seen her in months. She started singing to them. The song was nice, but my own heart was feeling a little too heavy for singing. I reached for Samuel's hand, and he took mine in his and held it tight, but he didn't look at me. He was looking off in the distance, somewhere far away. Miles away. Years away. Katie looked up at him a time or two and then finally turned her attention to the dolls.

"Is there a daddy one?" she said. "There ought to be a whole, real family."

Poor child with her unending dream. A real family. Father, mother, and all. It couldn't happen. Not with her actual father. Maybe not even with her mother, not anymore. But maybe it would, somehow. Lord willing.

Samuel was quiet that night. He said all the Hammonds could stay over if they wanted to, the way we did sometimes on Sunday nights, but he didn't seem like himself. I read from our *Illustrated Bible Stories*, thinking of Franky, who always loved for me to read out loud. Maybe Samuel was thinking of Franky too. After a while he got up and went outside.

I would have handed Lizbeth the book to finish for me, but Emma Grace was getting tired and fussy, and Lizbeth was trying to get her settled down. All of the older Hammond boys could read, but I knew they didn't like to. So, with my heart yearning after Samuel, I handed the big book to Robert and asked him to read one more story.

It was dusky gray outside with a lot of clouds moving in. I hoped it would rain overnight for the sake of the crops. The little we'd had wasn't enough. I brushed a pesky insect away from my face and walked to the apple tree, where Samuel stood still as a statue, staring up at the sky.

"Franky'll be all right," I told him softly. "He's in good spirits. Very good, considering it all. I hope you're not blaming yourself."

"I should. I should've shooed the kids inside when we saw Edward coming."

"There was no way you could have known."

"I know." He looked down for a moment, then out across the field.

"It was an accident," I said. "Even as coldhearted as he seems, I'm sure Edward didn't mean to do what he did."

"Yeah. I know."

"Samuel, what's wrong?"

He turned his eyes toward me. "Did you ever lie to the kids?"

"No," I said instantly, surprised he would ask such a question. "There are things I don't tell them. But . . . but I don't lie."

"I know. You're a good mother, Julia. You're a blessing."

"Samuel—"

"No. Don't say anything right now." He took me in his arms. He held me tight, and I could feel the tension in his shoulders, in his back. I wanted to ask him what in the world was going on, why would he question me about something like that. But even more, I wanted to respect his simple request, so I didn't say a word, only held him and prayed that the storm in his heart would soon be past.

Finally he stepped away, just a little, looking like a

weight was dragging him down. "Juli, what if she's my sister?"

I stood for a moment, speechless. Sister? It couldn't be. She was only six years old.

I didn't have time to say what I was thinking. Rorey and Harry came running out of the house, yelling that Robert was done reading and could we catch fireflies or play "Twelve O'Clock the Ghosts Come Out"?

"No," Samuel said, more quickly than I expected. "No ghosts around here."

"No ghosts at all," Rorey laughed. "Mama tol' me long time ago that's make believe, but it's still a fun game."

The other kids were coming out, and Samuel looked toward the porch, where Katie was standing, looking our way. It seemed that tonight they shared the same haunted eyes. It made me remember Katie's first night here, with both of them dreaming unsettling dreams.

"Samuel, your father's dead, isn't he?" I had to ask, though he'd plainly told me so, after finally admitting he'd known his father.

"I don't know," he said.

I didn't know what to think. He'd lied once, telling me his daddy left when he was an infant and never came back. But he'd made that right, telling me the truth later. Hadn't he?

"Samuel, you said—"

"My mother said," he corrected, and I could see the pain working in his eyes. "But, honey, I don't know. Katie told me she remembers some ruffian named Samuel. And hiding from him—maybe. If it wasn't all some crazy dream. She thought it was me. But he had the same tattoo. A bird. Like my father had. How could she know about that?"

"Oh, Sammy . . ." I held him again, though the children were watching us now. Strangely, he didn't seem to care.

"What if he's alive?" he asked me. "What if my mother

lied? What if he's out there somewhere, still wreaking havoc? Why didn't he ever come back?"

"Shhh," I said gently. "Too many questions for one night. Maybe there's a way. Maybe we can find out something tomorrow—"

"I don't know if I can call her again. What is she going to think, after all this time, if I ask her—"

"Who cares what she thinks? You have a right to know."

He looked at me strangely, as if he'd expected me to say he should spare his mother the shock of being doubted. "We can go into Dearing and use Charlie's phone," I told him. "We should go to town anyway, to see if Ben Law has found out anything more."

"We?"

"If you want it to be we."

"You don't think this is ridiculous?"

"You don't. And you know what that little girl told you."

He looked over at Katie, who was still waiting on the porch steps.

"Hey! Will you play with us?" Harry was yelling.

Samuel looked at me, and much to my surprise he smiled. "Let's play."

"Are you sure? You look so tired."

"Not tired. Weighed down. Maybe I need a good game." He went straight for the porch, took Katie's hand, and explained to her the silly game the Hammonds had taught us sometime last summer. All the kids gathered around him. It wasn't every night that they got the grown-ups to play along. It was enough to convince even the older ones to join in too. All except Lizbeth, who had just laid Emmie down and was inside rocking Bert. I didn't want her feeling alone, so I pulled a rocker onto the porch for her and, when she came out, sat down beside her to watch most of the kids disappear behind bushes, trees, wherever they could find a place. Samuel and Katie were "it" together the first time and went walking out from the house.

"One o'clock the ghosts come out." A giant step.

"Two o'clock the ghosts come out." Another step. And on, one giant step at a time, toward the middle of the yard, counting out an hour with every step. When Samuel and Katie got to twelve o'clock, all the kids jumped from their hiding places with a yell and ran like mad for the porch steps. Samuel and Katie, once she got over the start, had to tag as many as they could before the kids got home.

They played over and over, with all of the children agreeing that Samuel was the scariest to have leaping out from behind a bush in the dark.

Soon they were running around catching fireflies and letting them go. Lizbeth leaned her head back in the old rocker, looking like a skinnier version of her mother in the moonlight.

"I may not have so many kids," she told me. "Except in a classroom. Did you know the Porters are making a special fund for people who want to be teachers? Ben told me about it. College money. Only you have to pass a test."

I hadn't realized she'd had time to talk to the Porter boy while getting her little brothers some lemonade on the Fourth. But I was glad for what was surely a God-given opportunity.

"You're going to try for it, aren't you?"

"Ben said I should."

"I agree with him."

She smiled. "I knew you would. But I didn't tell Pa yet. Don't think he'd want me gone."

"He'd get used to it," I assured her. "Everybody'd manage just fine. Don't let that stop you."

"It'll be hard. But the test's not till next spring. I have time." She looked out over the wide yard, her smile getting bigger. "Mrs. Wortham, it's like having a sweet little dream all to myself."

I smiled too, glad for the ambition that would surely move Lizbeth to good things in her life. She looked up at the sky and out over the yard, quiet for a few moments. The clouds had left, and it was getting really dark now.

"Guess we'd better get the kids to bed," she told me with a sigh.

I nodded, thinking that she sounded more grown up than ever. "Bedtime!" I called, knowing it was late and eyelids would be getting droopy.

Sitting on the porch was so peaceful that I wondered why in the world Samuel had decided to run himself all over the yard with the kids. But they loved it, every last one of them. It was hard, rounding them up for bed. We'd have the whole bunch sleeping on the sitting room floor again, and I wondered if Katie felt overwhelmed, having such a crew here.

I hoped Franky was doing all right. I missed him, because out of all of the kids, he would be the most likely to sit on the porch with Lizbeth and me and say something unexpected or profound about dreams of his own. And I thought about George. Maybe he just didn't know how to take Franky. Maybe that was his problem. His son was the only nine-year-old we knew who couldn't read. And the only person under twenty to understand half of what the preacher talked about. No wonder George was confused.

Lizbeth's thoughts right then must have been similar. "I hope Pa's keepin' quiet," she said. "And I hope Franky's doin' okay. I'm sure glad Pastor got a chance to talk to him like that. He oughta know what goes on inside Franky's head. Do you reckon he'll be a preacher one day?"

"I don't know, Lizbeth. Seems to me he could be."

Little Harry had run up to us on the porch. "Does we have to go to bed so soon?" he complained.

"It isn't soon," I told him. "It's already late. And we have plenty to do in the morning."

"Like what?" he questioned, his eyes shining bright in the moonlight.

"Same chores we do every day, silly," Lizbeth told him. "You don't have enough of 'em, that's your problem."

"I wanna catch me a turtle," the little boy said. "Joe finished cookin' that one, an' it was yummy."

"Well, I wish you would. We could stand another one. But we got to finish the regular stuff first."

"You mean I can go?" Harry asked with enthusiasm.

"Not tonight," Lizbeth said with a sigh. "Sometime. But you gotta take somebody with you."

Harry smiled, nodded his head, and marched in the house. I was just thinking how easy this was compared to the struggle he usually put up, when I heard Sarah yelling, "No! No! Mommy don't like you doing that!"

I rushed in to find Harry standing on the kitchen table, about to take a flying leap into the middle of the room. Before I could say anything, Samuel whisked him off and plopped him onto the floor.

"We don't do that," he said sternly. "Not any time, for any reason. Jump off the stump in the yard tomorrow if you want to."

"Okay," Harry laughed.

"How come you didn't play with us, Mommy?" Sarah asked.

"I was enjoying just watching this time, honey. Sometimes I like to look at all of you having fun together. That was fun for me."

"It's not hard if you want to learn it next time," Katie told me. "I'd help you."

I smiled. "Thank you. That's very kind."

"She already knows how!" Rorey burst out. "Me an' Willy teached her a long time ago!"

Katie kept looking at me. "You're not scared, are you?"

"'Course she's not!" Rorey roared. "There ain't no real ghosts."

But I had a feeling Katie was talking about something else considerably more than a childish game. I wasn't sure what it was, but I knew what I should say. "No, honey, I'm not. And you don't need to be either."

She looked over at Samuel and smiled.

Could she be his sister? That would certainly explain the resemblance. But could it be?

"How long's this girl gonna stay with you, anyway?" Rorey asked, just as rude as could be.

"I don't know," I answered her. "But she'll always be welcome. Time to hush and get yourself ready for bed now."

We spread covers all over the sitting room for the kids to lie on top of. Berty and Emma Grace were already asleep. Katie got her paper dolls to set by her pillow, and Sarah snuggled in beside her.

"I wanna be by the window," Rorey complained. "Come on, Sarah, let's go by the window."

But Sarah and her dolly were already settled next to Katie's paper family. "No, I want to stay here."

"Humph," Rorey answered and plopped herself just as close to the window as she could go.

"I'll be by you," Harry said. "Let's pertend we's wolves. See the big ol' moon out there?"

Rorey and Harry both took to howling like mad, and I had to shush them quick for fear they'd wake the baby.

"You two be still," Lizbeth scolded. "If you be real nice, maybe Mr. Wortham'll tell you a story."

"Okay!" Harry exclaimed immediately. I could tell that Willy and Kirk were less than thrilled, but they didn't say anything.

"Will you tell us a story, Daddy?" Sarah begged. "Please?" Turning to Katie, she whispered, "Don't you want Daddy to tell us a story?"

I winced just a little, wondering how the girl would react. She sniffed just a little, her eyes on the little paper figures. "I would like a story," she said quietly. "If it's a real *good* story."

"All Daddy's stories are good stories," Sarah bragged. "He has the bestest stories of anybody. An' I know, 'cause our teacher told us one and it wasn't near as good. An' she's the *teacher*."

"They're just made up things," Samuel said. "Not much of anything. But if you all lie down and get quiet, I'll tell another one."

All the younger Hammonds lay down obediently, along with Robert and Sarah, even though I knew Robert and the boys his age or older didn't feel the same about bedtime stories as the littler ones did. Sam and Lizbeth, the oldest Hammond kids, walked back into the kitchen together, and I could tell they were discussing their day tomorrow, just what needed done by whom with their pa and Franky gone. And whether anybody ought to go along when young Sam rode into Mcleansboro. I sure hoped Franky would be well enough to come home soon. Three weeks they'd said he ought to be in that hospital bed, and then more time in bed at home.

"Tell a scary story this time," Harry was begging Samuel.

"Well," he said, sitting down in the middle of the floor. "I don't know if I know any scary stories."

"I bet you do too!" Harry argued. "Ain't nothin' scary ever happened to you?"

Almost my heart skipped a beat when Samuel didn't answer right away. I wished I knew more about his relationship with his father. I wished he'd talked about it all a little more.

"Tell you what," he suddenly said. "I think I just might be able to tell a story like that. Just a little bit scary, at least. Not too bad."

"Good!" Harry proclaimed.

Katie was dead silent.

"Once upon a time there was a rabbit who—"

"A rabbit!" Rorey immediately interrupted. "Rabbits aren't scary."

"Sshh!" Sarah scolded. "Maybe the rabbit got scared." By the light of the oil lamp I could see her reach over and grasp Katie's hand.

Samuel waited a minute, just to make sure they all were quiet. "This rabbit got scared a lot. Almost every day, in fact. And especially at night. So much that everybody thought that he was scared of everything. The poor little rabbit couldn't even go outside without being afraid of a bird flying by, or a branch swinging in the breeze, or even of his own shadow."

"That's a silly rabbit," Sarah whispered.

"Yeah!" Harry proclaimed. "There's nothin' scary 'bout those things!"

"But one day a very big bear came to town," Samuel told them. "Very, very big. Tall as eighteen or twenty rabbits, with the biggest teeth they'd ever seen. And every night he went prowling around, marking trees with his giant bear paws and growling really loud."

"Did he eat rabbits?" Rorey asked.

"Well, the rabbits weren't sure," Samuel continued. "But they were all very scared. And nobody could sleep because the bear made such an awful lot of noise going around scratching on tree trunks and growling all night. So they had a meeting and decided that somebody had better ask that bear to be quiet or move a little farther away."

"I bet he got real mad about that," Harry said.

"Shhh," Sarah warned.

Kirk snickered. "Kids," he whispered to Joe.

"Did the bear get mad?" Rorey asked.

"Maybe he ate 'em all up," Harry suggested.

"How's he gonna finish the story if you don't hush up?" Robert asked them.

"It's all right," Samuel said. "I don't mind a few comments. The problem those rabbits had was that none of them wanted to be the one to go and tell that bear. So they cut a whole pile of straws, all the same length. Except one. And they decided that every single rabbit had to take one, and whoever got the short one would have to go and ask that bear to be quiet or move."

Samuel stopped for a second and looked over at me. I wasn't sure what I was seeing in his eyes. I couldn't help thinking about his words: *"What if he's out there somewhere, still wreaking havoc?"*

"Bear paws," I whispered.

Samuel looked at the floor for a moment. "Yes. This bear had big paws." He glanced over at me and shook his head. "It had the biggest footprints any of them had ever seen. Nobody wanted to go talk to that bear. But they all drew a straw. And guess who got the short one?"

"The most scared rabbit?" Sarah asked.

"That's right. He thought he was going to fall over right there, just faint dead away. He thought there was just no way he could do it, he was so scared. But all of his friends were counting on him. They were all so tired and so sad and scared—"

"Did the bear eat him?" Harry asked quickly.

It was Joe that answered. "No, Harry. Just listen."

"He thought the bear would eat him," Samuel said, his voice a little slower. "But he went hopping away anyway, to do what he had to do. He hopped and he hopped, looking for that bear, and he was still looking when it began to get dark."

None of the children said a word. Samuel paused, looking around at all of them and at me for just a second.

"What happened?" Sarah said, sounding a little nervous.

"At first he didn't find anything at all. And then he began to hear, way off in the distance, that big bear growl, sounding really mad and mean. He wanted to just turn around and run. He thought he should, but he couldn't get his little hopping legs to move. So he just stayed right there, saying, 'Please be quiet, please be quiet,' over and over again."

"And then what?" Rorey asked.

"The bear came closer and closer. Closer and closer. The little rabbit could hear those awfully sharp big bear claws tearing at the trees. And that growl sounded so awful fierce, he could just scream with fright. The bear came closer and closer and closer, and the rabbit got more and more scared. He couldn't even twitch his nose, he was so scared, and just when the bear came bursting through the trees near him and he thought he just couldn't stand it anymore, he opened his little mouth and he screamed—"

Samuel stopped. Nobody breathed a word; nobody moved. "Do you know what he screamed?" he asked.

"Nope," Sarah said timidly.

"*'Please be quiet!'*" Samuel said, making a whisper sound huge. "He said it so loud that he startled himself. He fell over backward, and he was just about to run away when he heard something very strange."

"What?" Harry asked.

"Yeah, what?" Rorey echoed.

"It was the bear. At least he thought it was. On the other side of a big tree. The rabbit went just a little closer, and he could hardly believe that he saw that great big bear sitting there shaking and crying his eyes out. The rabbit was so stunned he almost forgot to say anything, but then he remembered his tongue and said, 'Why are you crying?' The big bear nearly jumped clear out of his skin. 'Don't hurt me,' the bear said. 'Don't hurt me.'"

Harry laughed. "What a dummy bear!"

"Why was the big bear scared?" Sarah asked.

"That's what the rabbit wondered. He even asked him. He sat down beside him and promised not to hurt him and told him all about the rabbits and the straws and how scared he'd been. And that bear admitted something that he'd never told anybody else. He was afraid of the dark. He went roaring through the woods every night making all kinds of noise because he was really afraid that if he just lay down and went to sleep in the dark, somebody would sneak up on him and scare him awake. So he kept everybody else too scared to come close. Until the rabbit startled him so much it made him cry."

The room was quiet for a moment. "How do you think of stuff like that?" Joe finally asked.

"It's not hard," Samuel said. "I don't even really try."

"It's kinda dumb for a bear to be so scared," Harry observed. "A bear could beat up anythin'."

"But that bear didn't think so. He didn't feel strong at all. But the rabbits helped him. They let him sleep every night with a circle of rabbits around him so he would feel safer. And then all the rabbits could sleep too."

"That might be your strangest story ever, Dad," Robert said.

"Maybe so," Samuel admitted. "But it might also be the truest."

"What do you mean?"

"People can be like that. Some people act the roughest and toughest when they're really scared inside and don't want anybody to know. And some people who think they're too scared to do anything are the bravest and most daring of all when a real problem happens."

"Really?" Sarah asked.

"Sounds strange. But it's true."

"Are bullies really scared inside?" she asked.

"Probably. And sad and mixed-up too."

"You mean like Uncle Edward?" Robert asked.

Samuel got quiet. "Yeah. I guess."

"So maybe I'm brave," Katie said in a tiny voice.

And at that moment, I wanted to keep her. Whoever she was, whatever the truth came out to be, she belonged with us. She fit. With Sarah. With the whole bunch of kids. But especially with Samuel, no matter what anybody said. There was something more alike about them than the dark hair and dark eyes. They were family. They had to be. They'd survived the cruel legacy of Samuel's past, lived through Edward's assaults, and understood human nature better because of it.

"Time to sleep," I said quietly, not sure anyone even heard.

"Time to sleep," Samuel echoed. "No bears here, scared or otherwise. Close your eyes. Thank the Lord for this home, and his peace—"

"We oughta pray for Franky," Sarah said. "I think he's very brave. Even if he don't act scared."

I had to smile. Samuel prayed for Franky. And Sarah, Robert, and Joe said amen.

Soon they were all asleep, and Lizbeth and young Sam were done talking and ready to lie down too.

"We think Pa'll want to come home tomorrow," Lizbeth told us. "But I prob'ly oughta stay with the little ones like he said, so if he comes back, Sam's gonna stay. We don't want Franky to be up there alone."

"Thank you," I told them. "That's good of you both."

The house got very quiet after that. Samuel and I lay down together in the bedroom, and at first neither of us said anything. He was so still beside me. I wondered what he was thinking. When I laid my head down on his shoulder, he didn't even move.

"Can I call you Sammy again?" I whispered.

He took me in his arms and kissed the top of my head. "I was just upset. You can call me anything you want. But it sounds different, coming from Edward."

"Everything sounds different from him. Like it gets dipped in spite before it comes out of his mouth."

"Probably does. I should've been writing to him. I should've been better—"

"None of them wanted anything from you," I told him. "Your mother doesn't even answer your letters. It's nothing to beat yourself up over."

He sighed. "I don't know how Edward's going to react, you know. About Katie's daddy having a bird on his arm. I guess Trudy Vale never told him that."

"Maybe he'll never know about it. He might not come back."

"He will. I don't know why. But I think he will."

"Do you want to go to Dearing tomorrow?"

"I don't know. I hate to go asking Barrett for the truck again. And they're using the wagon. Sometimes it seems like I ought to stay home till I can make a better way for myself."

"Samuel . . ."

He rolled slightly, taking me with him.

"I don't know what I want. I'm not sure what to think. I don't even know for sure about what Katie was telling me, how much is real and how much is a dream."

"Or maybe both?"

He was quiet.

"I think it's both with you, Samuel. I don't understand all of it. But I'd like to. Tell me more about bear paws."

"There's nothing more to tell."

"There must be. Why would you say it in your sleep?"

"Who knows? I could say all manner of gibberish—"

"But it isn't gibberish. It meant something to you."

He sighed again. "I guess it's like my dumb story. Dewey

and I were pretending to be tough. Acting like we were a couple of braves from the bear clan, but when it came right down to it, we were always scared. Both of us. That's why we ran off in the first place."

"There's nothing wrong with that."

"Maybe not. But maybe I'm still running and hiding. I don't want to talk to my mother. I don't think I want to know."

"You never had proof of his death?"

"What kind of proof would there be? We never went to a funeral. Mother's word was good enough. I don't even know where the funeral was supposed to be. She didn't go. But who could expect her to? He broke her nose twice."

"Oh, Samuel."

"Shhh. Okay? I don't want to hear any 'Oh, Samuel.' I want you to treat me like always and talk to me like always. I'm no different than I ever was."

"Except that you have Katie here."

"That doesn't have to change anything."

"It already has." I kissed him, tender on the lips, hoping he'd know I didn't mean that in any bad way.

"I don't understand you, Juli," he whispered. "Why aren't you kicking me out of bed?"

For a minute my breath froze. "Why would I kick you out? What do you mean?"

"Any other woman might think I'd have to be guilty. That I'm making up some harebrained thing to get myself off the hook. And not owning up, like Edward says. He'll probably be ready to belt me again."

"If he does it around here, he'll have to watch out for me and Robert. We're liable to hog-tie him and throw him in the shed."

I thought he'd laugh. I thought he'd be glad somebody felt that way, even though we'd never actually do it.

But he sat up. "No, Juli. Don't talk like that."

"Sammy, why?"

"Our father did that once." He looked out over the darkened room, toward the blowing curtains in the window. "It was the only time I ever saw Edward cry."

Samuel slept like a log, but I tossed and turned that night. I kept waking up and thinking about Samuel's mother, Joanna. I'd met her several times, but she was a strange person to me. Since my own mother had died so young, Grandma Pearl was the mothering image I thought of first. She was thrifty, clean, always busy at something, maybe several somethings all at once. She never cursed, never touched a drop of anything alcoholic. In comparison, Samuel's mother seemed almost as unreal as the man in the moon. How could a mother be like that? It was almost unfathomable. And I supposed I wouldn't be able to understand Trudy Vale any better.

I got up a couple of times, checking on kids and just walking about, since I couldn't seem to settle down very well anyway. Once Sarah was laughing out loud in her sleep. Robert used to do that all the time when he was smaller. But he was getting so big now. They both were. Thank God they could grow up happy. Even though we had little, they would never have to doubt their parents' love.

Thank God for Grandma Pearl raising me up right. Thank God especially for Samuel, a miracle of a man living wise choices when he could have turned out like his brother. Or even worse.

Katie rolled over and opened her eyes. "Mama?"

"Honey, you're here," I whispered. "It's Mrs. Wortham. Go back to sleep. It isn't morning."

She looked up at me groggily. "Do you like me?"

"Of course I like you, but it's not time to be up talking."

"I'm glad you like me. I like you too." She smiled. "I never been in a house with so many kids. I dreamed I got to stay for always. I dreamed I got to be a big kid and I was milking the cow and everything."

"Sounds like a happy dream." I couldn't pledge its reality. Not yet.

"It was happy," she said. "Sarah was my new sister, and we wore matching dresses and went to school."

"Well. You'll definitely have to go to school. Eventually. But right now you'd better try to get back to sleep."

"Mama never cared too much what time I went to sleep."

"Things are different now. I expect there'll be a lot to get used to." I leaned and kissed her forehead. To my surprise, she reached her little hand up to touch my cheek.

"You're pretty."

"Thank you. Now close your eyes. Long time yet till morning."

"Am I pretty too?"

"Yes. Very pretty."

"Mama said I wasn't because I look too much like my mean old dad."

"There are a lot of things she doesn't understand very well, I'd say."

"I figured something out. I think your husband and Mr. Eddie must have another brother. That's what it must be, right? Because this daddy doesn't lie."

"That could be it. Maybe. You're right about one thing. My husband doesn't lie."

"I wished he did. Kind of. I wished he was mine. 'Cause I don't want to go away."

"I know, sweetie."

"Will you please sing me a song again? Please?"

I was a little afraid of waking the other children, but I hated to tell her no. So I sang as softly as I could, an old lullaby Grandma Pearl had sung to me. And before I was even halfway through, Katie was asleep again. I patted her little hand, smoothed the wavy dark locks away from her face, and then looked around at all the other sleeping children. I prayed for each and every one of them, that they would grow up wise and gentle hearted. And then I said an extra prayer for Franky. Already wiser than his years, already gentle, he seemed to have different challenges to face.

TWENTY-TWO

Samuel

The next day started out hot. Sukey was lowing, not too anxious to get out to pasture. That worried me considerably after what had happened to Lula Bell, but the calf seemed fine, and after a while Sukey got to seeming like herself too. All the heat, maybe. I'd have to keep checking her drinking trough and make sure it stayed full.

About half of the Hammond kids went over to their house early. I let Robert go fishing with Willy and Kirk till noon again and started working on what had once been Emma's husband's tractor. George and I were going to need it for harvest soon enough. We still had hay to get in too, but I knew that I'd have to wait until George or one of his older boys was ready to help me. I had last season's experience only, and that wasn't enough for me to start in on something like that by myself. But I knew what the tractor needed, and I spent the better part of the morning getting greasy and fixing it back into running shape.

I dug some little new potatoes, and Juli fixed some kind of greens with them for lunch, along with the fish Robert caught—two decent-sized bluegill. I knew Juli was wondering about me going into town, but I felt like I'd been spending too much time already just running around. That could wait.

I didn't want to go at all, truth be told. I didn't want to know what Mother would say. If my father was alive somewhere, I preferred to be ignorant of it, foolish as that might seem.

Clouds came and went in the sky, and I took to praying that it would break loose and rain. Robert and I sickle cut a small stand of hay to the east of the barn. That much we could do without help, even storing it unbaled in the barn after it cured, without having to use any machines. We were both dripping with sweat when I heard a vehicle not far in the distance. Maybe I shouldn't have, but I prayed it wasn't Edward. I just wanted to put in a full day's work without having to stop everything and contend with his foolishness. I wanted us to be back to what was normal around here. Katie didn't interrupt that. She was a good kid, over there helping Julia pull weeds out of the beets.

As the car got closer, I could tell by the sound it wasn't Edward. It wasn't Barrett, either. Or Charlie Hunter. I looked up when it got close. Not too many people came by here, most days.

A dusty black Chevrolet with a star on its door pulled into our drive. The sheriff.

"Better stop and get a drink," I told Robert. "Check Sukey's trough for me and make sure it's full."

Robert was looking over at the sheriff's car too. "Yes, sir," he said without argument. Juli came from the garden as Ben Law was getting out of his car. We both stood there waiting for what he had to say. I glanced to see that Juli had sent the girls to the porch to play. Whatever the sheriff said, we should hear it first, before any of the children.

"Afternoon, Mr. Wortham, Mrs. Wortham."

I returned his greeting, feeling impatient. "Good afternoon."

"Still got the child here, I see."

"Yes, sir."

He was looking at me very straight. "How old are you?"

I wasn't sure what that had to do with anything, but he must have a reason. "I'm thirty-two."

"That true?" he asked my wife.

"Of course it is," Juli said, giving him a funny look.

"Well, I found the grandmother," he finally told us. "She lives in Hershey, Pennsylvania, and she doesn't happen to know where her daughter is. Says she's been near impossible to keep track of for years now, she does so much moving around."

I nodded. None of that was much of a surprise.

"How do you suppose a Pennsylvania girl come to meet up with your brother, clear over to Albany, New York?"

"I don't know," I told him. "She must meet a lot of people traveling so much."

"Uh-huh," the sheriff said. "Miss Vale's mother tells me she come home to have that baby and tried to leave it there, but when they wouldn't have it, she ain't been home much since."

"That's too bad," Julia said. "Katie might have benefited from knowing her grandparents better." She was looking a little pale as she squeezed at the corner of her apron, and I understood that she deeply cared about what would happen to Katie from here on out. I wasn't sure the law would agree, but maybe it would be better for us to keep her than for her go to a place she wasn't wanted.

"What about now?" I asked. "If you can't find her mother, would they rather Katie be with them?"

He looked at me pretty straight. "I told 'em why she was here, that we figured you was the father, and they said that suited them fine. It oughta be on your hands. Only thing is, Miss Vale's mother claims her daughter'd been cavortin' about with an older man. And you seem to be three years younger'n her."

Juli smiled, but I'm not sure he noticed, because he was still looking at me.

"I need to tell you something Katie told me yesterday," I said. "She remembers that picture her mother had, of the man who was her father. She says the man had a bird on his arm—"

"You mean like a parrot sitting there?" the sheriff questioned.

"No. A picture. Probably a tattoo. I don't know what else that could be."

"You got any tattoos?"

"No, sir. But my father—"

"I wanna talk to that girl. Hey! Katie child! Katie Wortham!"

She looked up and then stood reluctantly. Her steps toward us were slow ones, and by the time she got all the way over, she was biting down on her lip and squelching back tears.

"Tell me about the picture again," Sheriff Law commanded her, not giving Juli or me time to tell her anything of comfort. "The one your mama had and said it was your father."

She sniffed and took a quick glance up at me. "He was outside by a tree, kind of leaning on it. He was wearing a vest. He looked like this Mr. Wortham, only not quite, because that one was tireder or something and he had a bird on his arm."

"What kind a' bird?"

"I don't know. Sort of like an eagle or something."

She hadn't said it was an eagle before. And I hadn't

told her about my father's tattoo. "Was the bird right side up?" I asked her.

"I think so," Katie said, looking afraid.

I knelt beside her and took her hand. "Don't be scared. We just have to know. Was the man's arm raised up?"

"Yeah. Because he was leaning against the tree with it. I remember."

The sheriff was staring at me pretty sternly. "Let me see your arm."

I rolled up both my sleeves, proud to show him I hadn't followed my father's example of marking himself.

He looked and then shook his head and stared me in the eye. "I can't be sure you didn't coach her to say that. You've had plenty time enough. And that poor grandma might be mistaken, especially if her daughter's took up with more than one gent in her goings-about. But suppose you tell me what the devil difference it makes to you whether the bird was upside down?"

I had to take a deep breath before I could answer. "My father had a tattoo of an eagle on his forearm. It was only right side up when he lifted that arm."

"And I suppose you're gonna tell me you look an awful lot like your pappy?"

"That's what I'm told."

"Then why didn't your own brother think a' this?"

"He thinks our father's dead."

"And you didn't tell him different?"

"I thought so too."

Sheriff Law took a step back. He shook his head, stared at me. It was a long time before he spoke. "A man can't father children if he's dead. What's your mother say about it?"

"She told us years ago that he drowned. I don't know what she'd say today."

"You're calling your own mother a liar?"

"I don't know. I don't know what to think. I just knew I needed to tell you."

Ben Law sat back against the front of his car and thought a moment. Eventually he turned his eyes to Katie, who was standing there silent, gripping my hand. "Are you sure you're telling me the truth, child?" he asked her. "They didn't tell you to tell me none of that?"

"No, sir. I mean, yes, sir, it's true. But I wish it weren't." She shook just a little and ducked her head, fighting tears again.

"Speak up, child!" the sheriff pressed. "How come you wish it weren't true? Huh? Why's it matter?"

"Because . . . because if I'm not *this* Mr. Wortham's, you're prob'ly gonna . . . you're prob'ly gonna take me an' . . ."

She couldn't finish. Julia leaned over and took the girl in her arms.

"Go easy on her, will you?" I said. "She's so young—"

"And what do you think I'm gonna do?" the sheriff demanded. "Haul her off to the jail?"

I held my ground. "You're talking awful stern, and she's scared."

"I don't know what of. I ain't takin' her home with me."

Katie looked up at him.

"I understand you claim she ain't yours," he continued. "I can't even swear to it myself, now, though I ain't convinced either way. If your pappy's dead, we ought to be able to find that out fast enough. In the meantime, seems like she's still kin. Are you willing to keep the care of her?"

Juli and Katie both looked at me. "Yes," I said. "I am."

Katie spun around and hugged at me so fast I nearly toppled over.

"Guess the explainin's easier if you're a big brother," Sheriff Law said, but I caught his bare hint of a smile.

"I don't know how to explain it at all," I told him. "Hard to imagine he could be alive. But with the same name—"

"So your father was a Samuel too?"

"Yes. He was."

"It is mighty strange, I'll grant you that. But I'll tell you what. The mother's family's been notified. I told 'em where you was. If they're wantin' contact, they can sure contact you. The rest ain't the business of the law unless you especially want it to be. I'm settled on the matter."

"Does that mean you intend for her to stay here?" Julia asked.

"Don't see we got much choice in the matter. Other side of the family ain't pressin' no claim, Mrs. Wortham. An' if your husband says this is his sister, there ain't nobody here to argue. He's happy to take her in, she's happy to stay. Nothing I need do 'bout any of that, 'less you're wantin' to know for sure 'bout Samuel Wortham Sr., an' I'd expect a small payment for that sort of an investigation, since it ain't necessary in the eyes of the law."

I wasn't sure how he'd arrived at what was "necessary," but I let it go. We had nothing to pay, and maybe before long I'd get around to asking my mother for myself. At least we'd learned the important thing. There was no place for Katie with her mother's family. She needed us. And that was what we needed to know.

With a feeling of relief, we said good-bye to the sheriff. He never asked me how I'd come to get a black eye. Maybe he'd heard something around town.

I picked up Katie and swung her around. "Sarah!" I called. "Robert!" They both came running, along with Rorey, who was staring at us with her arms folded.

"Katie's staying," I told them. "She's going to live with us."

"Yea!" Sarah squealed. "She can be my sister!"

"She's really kin, Dad?" Robert asked, looking far too serious.

"Yes," I told him. "But let me explain it to you later, okay?"

I looked at him and at Juli and Katie's smiling eyes, and I wondered how we'd ever manage. Sure, it had to be done. What else could I do? *Lord, you'll have to help me. There's so much we're going to need.*

I wasn't expecting anything else that day except a report from young Sam Hammond when he got back, telling us how Franky was doing today. Or maybe George stopping and telling us he'd left his biggest boy there and come home to see to things himself. So it came as a surprise to Juli and me when Joe came pulling up with the wagon in the late afternoon. Not until it had almost stopped did we see young Sam in the back, leaning way over. Juli went running up to them, and I did too, thinking something was wrong.

Sam was holding on to Franky. The little kid was lying in the back of that wagon on a pile of blankets, hugging on his brother for dear life. He was hurting awfully bad. You could tell it in his face. And no wonder, after a bumpy wagon ride with a broken leg.

"Why did you bring him?" Juli gasped. "Why didn't you stay at the hospital?"

"Pa insisted." Sam spit out the words like they were bitter on his tongue. "He argued up an' down with the nurses that we couldn't pay, an' that Franky could sit just as well in bed at home. I tried to tell him it'd be awful hard, but he wouldn't listen—"

"Well, where is he?" Juli asked, understandably confused. "He didn't come with you?"

"He stopped at the house," young Sam explained, looking mad enough to chew nails. "Joe helped me from there, 'cause I didn't want Franky back here alone."

I climbed in the bed of the wagon, and Franky latched hold of my neck. "I'm okay," he told me. "I'm okay."

But I didn't believe him.

"Did George tell you to bring him here?" I asked the boys.

"Yes, sir," Sam answered. "He said Mrs. Wortham'd know doctorin' better'n him or Lizbeth, 'cause a' learnin' it from Emma an' all. Lizbeth was sure upset. She'll prob'ly be by here later, but Emmie was wet an' Berty was screamin' at her from the outhouse an' Pa said for us to go on. I ain't never seen her so mad. An' I don't blame her. Not one lick. Franky oughta been able to stay in hospital a while longer, 'least till he was fit for travelin'. It weren't right. Look at him."

"I'm okay," Franky told us again.

"Put him on our bed," Juli told me. "I'll draw fresh water for some cold cloths."

Gently as I could, I lifted the little boy from the wagon. He seemed even lighter than he had before, despite the plaster cast on his leg. What was George thinking? We could have found some way to pay. However long it took.

"Where was the pastor?" I asked. "What did he say about this?"

"He wasn't there," Sam said gravely. "Pa said Herman Meyer come this morning to fetch him. Miss Hazel was mighty bad sick, the way he tol' it."

Juli turned to me in shock, her face going pale. But she hurried away from us anyway, to the well after that fresh water.

I set Franky on our bed, and he lay over on his side, still trying hard not to cry.

"I had a broken arm once," I told him. "Feels awful for a while. But it'll heal up in time. Good as new."

"I don't wanna go back to the hospital," he said. "Pa didn't want me there."

"I know. And I don't want to move you again. But I'm going to send your brothers after the doctor."

"Pa won't like that."

"This is not his house. That's a decision he made, whatever his reason."

"You ain't mad at him, are you?" He looked up at me with his silver-gray eyes tainted with pain.

"I'm not sure what to think."

"He asked me if I wanted to go home."

"That's not the kind of decision for a child to make."

Juli rushed in with a bowl of water and two or three clean cloths. She put one on Franky's head and plumped his pillow. Then she turned her attention cautiously to his leg. Sarah, Rorey, and Katie snuck behind her into the doorway.

"Is he okay?" Sarah asked.

"He's still hurt bad," Rorey surmised.

Katie didn't say anything at all, just stood there looking solemn.

"Girls, go on out," Juli told them. "I'm going to have to sit with Franky a while."

"I'm okay," Franky valiantly told us again.

"Yes," Juli told him. "You are. At least you're going to be. It's your father I wonder about, what's gotten into his fool head—"

"Juli—"

She turned to me with a gentle fire in her eyes. "You would never do this, Samuel. You would never leave your child for a second, or put him through such an agonizing trip. Where is he now? What's the matter with him?"

I didn't have any answer.

"We should pray for Miss Hazel," Franky said, seeming to have trouble getting the words out. "They said she might not live the night."

"Did they say what was wrong?" Juli asked tensely.

"No, ma'am," young Sam offered from behind me. "I'm not for sure that they know."

Juli sent me for an herb she'd seen growing just outside the cow pasture and soon had water going to steep it in. She was sweating as bad as I was, and Franky maybe worse. I prayed for a cool breeze or something, and not long after that some clouds blew in. Sam and Joe left to fetch the one old doctor who lived closer than the hospital. He'd come if he could, though he was trying to get most folks to go into Mcleansboro or Marion or Mt. Vernon for their care if they could. He wasn't well himself most of the time now.

It took a while, but eventually Juli got Franky settled down to sleep. She said that was the best thing for him. I wanted to go over and talk to George, ask him why he didn't come along if he wanted us nursing his son over here. It wasn't right that he just expect it from us without a doctor's approval or without consulting us at all. What was so pressing at home that he couldn't at least come and bring Franky himself?

Lizbeth showed up well before the doctor, hurrying through the timber with Emma Grace on her hip. She was still mad. It was clear from the way she stood, before she ever said a word. She gave the baby to Juli and leaned and kissed her brother, being careful not to wake him up.

"Think it'll hurt him?" she asked. "Bein' moved like that?"

"It hurt, no doubt," Juli said. "But his leg ought to be

all right, set the way it is. The doctor should be able to tell us for sure."

I went and sat outside. The day's work had definitely been interrupted, and I didn't feel like getting back to it. Sarah came and sat beside me, and then Katie sat beside her. Robert approached me too, but he didn't sit.

"Franky's gonna stay too, isn't he, Dad?" he asked.

"I don't know. At least for a while. We have to see what the doctor says. And what his pa is thinking."

"Why'd Mr. Hammond send Franky over here when it hurt him so bad?"

"I guess he thought he knew best. Wanting Franky home, and not being able to pay for him to stay in the hospital."

"But Franky ain't home, Dad. He's here."

"I know."

"His pa don't like him."

"That's pretty harsh, Robert."

"I don't think so. Willy told me one time that Mr. Hammond said Franky oughta quit actin' so all-fired smart if he's gonna play stupid at school. He can't have it both ways, an' it ain't right, you and Mom likin' him more than the rest."

"That's not so."

"Well, Willy thinks it's so. You spend more time with him than the rest."

"That's because he's usually the only one who wants to work in my woodshop. Except you."

"I know, Dad. I'm just tellin' you what they said." He sighed. "I'll do the milkin' tonight. You got other stuff to see to."

"Thank you, Robert. That's thoughtful."

He only nodded as he walked away. I almost went with him, thinking I owed him the explanation about Katie that I'd promised.

But Sarah took my hand with a worried look in her

eyes. "Katie said she might be your real sister. But that means she's Uncle Edward's sister too. Do you think he could come and take her away?"

"No."

"Are you sure?"

"I'm very sure."

She perked up immediately. "Okay." She turned sparkling eyes to Katie. "Let's go pick flowers. We can give some to Mom and Lizbeth, and Franky too, when he wakes up."

I watched them skip away across the yard, holding hands like they were meant to be together. Rorey joined them reluctantly at the apple tree, Sarah grabbing for her hand too. They danced around a while and then started picking the dayflowers springing up along the fence. I sighed, looking out over this farm of ours. I'd taken on an awful lot, and it seemed like I kept taking on more. But I had a good feeling inside about it, not a bad one. Even about Franky. Maybe it was for the best, him being over here for a while, even if his father and at least one brother felt the way they did. At least there was peace for Franky here.

Then I wondered about Hazel for a minute. She was so old. And cantankerous. She was a feature in that church for so many years, but was she truly saved? She was so prickly to be around that it was hard to know about something like that. But Pastor would know. If he was with her right now, he would try to make sure.

I thought of Edward when he was a kid, when he was throwing bottles at the brick walls of a church, and I wondered if he'd ever find it in his heart to call on God. It was what he needed, surely. I was glad Juli had told him God loved him. I wasn't sure I could have right then. Even now, if I saw him coming up the lane again, I wasn't sure how I'd react. It would depend an awful lot on what he did next.

I sat and I prayed, feeling like it was the most important

thing I could do. I prayed for Miss Hazel, for Edward and my mother, Franky, Juli, and Katie. I prayed for all of us, that God would provide, and for myself, that he would grant me the wisdom I needed.

This had not been a normal day after all, and I had a feeling it wasn't near done. If Hazel Sharpe really was dying, I knew Juli would want to say good-bye, regardless of the way Hazel had treated us. And I'd have Edward to face again, I knew, somehow. He hadn't gone back East. Not yet.

And there was Franky to care for, Katie to raise and love. Thank heaven Robert and Sarah were willing to understand.

There was so much work to be done here before the winter came again. But Emma had known we'd belong. *God bless her generosity. God grant me the faith and the goodness she had.*

I thought of something she'd told me once, that George and I were called to be like brothers. That being the case, I was going to have to face George, for Franky's sake. It wasn't right, like young Sam had said. And if I seemed to like Franky more, maybe it was because all along I'd been able to see the need in him. That little boy longed for his pa, reached for him every time he got the chance, but I'd never seen George hug him or hold him the way he did the youngest boys or speak to him with the respect he'd started showing the older ones. Franky had gotten caught in the middle. Pushed away and left out. So he came to me because he was hungry, pure and simple. I'd have to make George see.

A jay called in the tree nearest the house. Sarah and Katie snuck past some bushes in my direction. I rose to my feet just as they darted the rest of the distance between us. Together they presented me with a most delicate little bundle of dayflowers and violets.

"I thought these were for Mom and Franky," I told them.

"We'll get them some," Sarah promised.

"But these are for you," Katie finished, both of them smiling broadly.

They flitted away like butterflies. And I smiled too, standing there with flowers in my hand.

TWENTY-THREE

Julia

The doctor got there before we expected him to. His son drove him, and I thanked God for that small favor, because I'd started to worry, Franky was feeling so warm. But Doctor Howell assured me the fever wasn't large and that I should keep him uncovered and keep bathing him with the cool water.

The doctor was fairly confident about the leg too. "If Emory Hall says it's set, then it's set," he told me of the Mcleansboro doctor. "He wouldn't a' plastered it otherwise. Just keep him off it. And don't let nobody be jostlin' him till he's feeling stronger."

I promised we wouldn't. I promised to do everything just exactly the way he said. And even though Lizbeth was sitting right there, he told me plain out that it was good Franky was with us because he had no confidence his instructions would be followed "over at the house."

Then he wrote out for me some suggestions and approved of my doctoring herbs. He promised he'd look in on us again in a few days if he could. Franky woke up just a little to talk to him, and the doctor seemed encouraged that he was sounding as good as he was.

"I was just over to see Hazel Sharpe," he said as he was closing his bag. "My wife sent those Hammond boys over there to find me. I'll be going back, and Herman and his wife asked if I could do them the favor of bringing you along."

"Bringing me?"

"Seems Miss Hazel was asking for you before I got there. Wasn't much of what she said I could make out."

"How is she? What's wrong?"

"Well, she fell. But I fear it's the apoplexy, and there's nothing much I can do for that. I told them that, but she won't go to the hospital. She shook her head plain enough. I'll check in on her, but she's in the Lord's hands."

My heart was pounding just thinking about it. I didn't really want to go. "But, Doctor, with Franky here . . ."

"Only for a little while. I'm sure Herman will bring you home tonight. Lizbeth and Samuel oughta be able to manage. Herman pretty well begged me, taking it as a blessing almost that I was called out to your place. Miss Hazel's not got long for this world. You ought to come."

I didn't want to leave Franky and Katie and the rest. But Samuel insisted that I should go, and Lizbeth assured me she had heard every word the doctor said. They would manage just fine while I was gone.

So I went. With butterflies scurrying around in my stomach and a thousand memories of snippety Hazel whirling in my head. Not long for this world. And calling for me? I tried to pray but wasn't sure how.

Herman must have loved his aunt. Bless him for that. God bless him for all his patience. There ought to be some kind of prize.

Herman and his wife and one of his brothers all met the doctor and me at the door.

"Auntie's right this way," Herman said, ushering me straight for her bedroom. I'd never been inside her house before, but it was just like I might have imagined. I would be afraid to let any of the kids inside for fear they'd move something out of place.

Herman slowed his pace to her bed. And the rest, even the doctor, stayed behind me.

She seemed so different. Shriveled, almost. Pastor was sitting in a chair, looking exhausted. God bless him too.

"I brung Mrs. Wortham," Herman was saying.

Hazel's eyes opened slowly and started shifting to and fro, searching the room. I came closer and took her hand. Finally, her eyes rested on me; I almost expected to see the same scorn I'd seen there so often. But it wasn't there. Instead I saw fear. Dark and deep. Something I'd never expected to find in Miss Hazel.

"So sorry you're ailing," I told her, not sure how else to begin.

She opened her mouth. At first I couldn't tell what she was saying, but then I made out the one word, *pray*.

"Pastor," I said quickly. "She wants—"

Hazel shook her head, frowning. "You," she said with obvious effort.

"You want *me* to pray for you?" My hands started shaking. My knees felt weak. Why in the world? Why would she want my prayers?

I obliged her as best I could, praying for the Lord to touch her body and give her heart and mind peace.

She stared up at me for the longest time. A tiny tear slid down one of the deep crevices by her eye and slowly traced a path to her ear. She said something, but it was so low I couldn't make out the words.

"Thank you again, Miss Hazel," I said. "For all you've done." I began to think what our church would be like without her presence. She was fading just as the doctor had said. I could see it. I already knew we would be without our piano player next Sunday, without her fussy hats and snippety tongue.

She was shaking her head at me, frowning, and I wondered what on earth I'd done to upset her now. She tried to lift one hand, and when she couldn't, she just squeezed at my hand weakly with the other one.

"N-no," she managed to say. "All . . . *you've* . . . done . . ."

Tears filled my eyes.

"Hats," she said.

I didn't understand.

"What about hats?" Herman asked. "What do you mean, Aunt Hazel?"

"Hats," she said again, pulling her hand away just enough to point at my chest.

"You want her to have your hats?" Herman asked, every bit as surprised as I was.

Hazel nodded, just a tiny bit, and said another word we could hardly make out. *Hammonds,* I thought. Herman thought so too.

"What about the Hammonds?" Herman asked. But we couldn't make out the rest of her words, and soon Hazel closed her eyes. She grasped at my hand again and held it, but I could feel her grip going weak. Herman's wife, Viola, hurried the doctor up to the bedside, but he shook his head, said she was sleeping and there was nothing he could do. Pastor stood and led us in prayer.

Hazel didn't open her eyes again. She didn't wake up. Less than an hour later, she was gone to meet the Lord.

I scarcely knew how to react.

Coming home that night was strange, and I couldn't help thinking of the way Emma died. In Wilametta's rocking chair, waiting for a psalm and a cup of apple mint tea.

The house was dark and silent. I expected everyone to be asleep on the floor again, probably, though maybe some had gone upstairs. In the kitchen I lit a candle and was just turning around when Samuel came out of the shadows of the sitting room.

"How is she?" he asked.

"Gone, Sammy."

He put his arms around me. "Are you all right?"

"Yes. Of course." I pulled away, just a little. "How about Franky?"

"He's sleeping. He's pretty peaceful. He said he liked it better here than the hospital. Do you want to sit down a minute?"

"No. No, I thought I'd check on him—"

"Lizbeth stayed right in the room with him, and I was just there. He's doing all right—"

"What about Katie?"

"You know she's happy."

"Still scared?"

He tried taking me in his arms again. "Who wouldn't be, with this crew? Harry snuck a frog in and put it on her pillow. Berty was dancing around her like she was a maypole. But she seems fine. Better us than facing the unknown."

"Oh, Sammy."

He was pulling up a chair before I knew it. I hadn't realized how weak and spent I felt until he lowered me to the seat, still holding me all the while.

"Are you sure you're all right?" he asked again, and this time I didn't know what to say.

I kept thinking of poor Franky and how he'd been when his mother died. And all the kids, and George, without Wila. And us, without dear Emma Graham. Somehow I was shaking, feeling cold and hollow, like the night they left us. But this was different. This was Hazel! Stuffy, condescending Hazel!

"It don't appear she lets nobody near her heart," Emma had told me once. "She don't want 'em walkin' over the sore spots, that's all."

But Hazel had let me in tonight. Just a little. And I couldn't help myself. I sat right there and cried.

TWENTY-FOUR

Samuel

Katie was up with the sun, and the first thing she did was take a bucket and try her hand at filling it from the well. She could only carry it half full, but she was mighty proud to have found a way to help. Julia thanked her hugely for making the effort.

Franky was cheerful. He wanted to go outside and try sitting on the grass, and I promised him we would try that, only not today. The doctor had said he shouldn't be moved at all just yet, and it was better to obey, so he'd have to put up with the four walls a while. But I opened the window wide, and Juli took down the curtains so he could see out unhindered.

Just like Emma Graham, I thought. She'd liked her windows without curtains, so it would seem as if she were living outside.

Samuel

Sukey seemed fine when I went to milk her, which made me wonder what I'd been worried about yesterday. She gave good milk; at least we had that. And we had eggs, though not enough to sell. That and the garden vegetables and yard greens and such that Juli found would keep us through the summer. Winter was in the Lord's hands. There'd be a way.

After breakfast, it started bothering me again that George hadn't come over. All of last evening and now this morning. Lizbeth had fed the little boys a bite and took them with her back over to their farm, saying she had too much work waiting just to leave it. She'd be back, I knew it. Sometime before the day was out.

But what about George? Morning chores were done. He could've found the time to come over here and check on his son.

I fretted on it while I bandaged the calf where he'd scraped his leg on the gate. Nothing serious. Just needed a little bag balm and a wrap.

I set Robert to raking in some of the hay we'd cut. I wanted to work again, and spent a fair part of the morning in what we still called Emma's cornfield, where the ground was right, she'd told us, for the sweetest of the sweet corn for selling. This year the crop wasn't looking good because of the heat and the wildlife traipsing through it. But I was praying for more rain and stringing wire around the field, hoping to discourage at least some of the critters before the ears were ripe.

We needed to harvest the wheat field and get more hay in. What George was working on this morning, I didn't know, but I expected he'd come for my help if he was starting on any of that. By late morning, he still hadn't shown up, so I decided it was time I got myself over there to have a talk with him. He needed to take a father's part with Franky. I'd told him that long ago.

Juli wasn't keen on me going. Afraid we'd argue, I guess. But I told her I had no intention of arguing with George; I just wanted to tell him my concerns and leave it at that.

I trudged through the timber under a clear blue sky. Gnats were darting around in my path, and the sweat went rolling down the back of my neck. This hot already. What would the afternoon be like?

I didn't expect to find George at home. I figured he'd be in the fields somewhere working and that I could find out which way from Willy or Kirk. Or Lizbeth, at least, if he'd taken all the big boys with him. Coming out of the trees, toward their farmyard, I never expected to see his wagon in the yard, horses still hitched to it and standing stock-still. And on the other side of the house, mostly hidden from view, was a parked vehicle. All I could see was one wheel and the dusty black bumper. But it was enough.

Edward. Here. What he had in mind, I had no idea. But George was a friend. A brother, like Emma'd said. Edward had no business making trouble for the Hammonds. He'd done enough of that already.

I was walking faster, hurrying past a rooster and a couple of scratching hens till I could get around the back of the house and see what my headstrong brother might be up to. Why would he come here? He hadn't stopped in to see us this morning. Maybe he couldn't face me now, after landing me in the dirt. But he'd have to. Like it or not, he'd have to.

They were together in back of the house, Edward leaning against the side of his car, George sitting on the splitting stump. I was already getting angry, thinking my brother was doing something underhanded again, telling his lies, the way he'd done with the other church folks.

But then I saw the jug in his hand. There was no question what it was. He was taking a hefty swig and passing it to George. And I hardly knew what I did next.

"What the devil!" I yelled, remembering George heaving into a bucket last Christmas morning, barely able to manage the holiday with his brokenhearted children. He couldn't drink again! It made him crazy. It made him forget far too much. He should know better!

I ran at them, the fire in my bones too deep to be denied. "What do you think you're doing?"

They both stood up. I grabbed the jug from my brother's hands and hurled it as far as I could into the goat fence. The sound of breaking glass only fueled my fury. "What are you doing?"

I shoved Edward. Knowing he was bigger, knowing he was stronger, I shoved him anyway—away from his car and clear to the ground. But he grabbed at my shirt at the same time, taking me with him.

"Didn't have but one sip," I could hear George saying behind me. "Was jus' calmin' my nerves a little—"

Edward took a wild swing, punching me in the side. And I punched him back.

"Samuel, come on, now. Get up," George was pleading. "We wasn't meanin' no harm."

I couldn't get up with Edward holding on to me. But I didn't even want to. I wanted to beat the living tar out of him and then start in on George. Never mind that the liquor was illegal under prohibition. That was bad enough, but Edward knew what drink had done to our family. George knew what it could do to his.

I hardly felt Edward hitting me, trying to push me off. I was madder than I'd ever been, hitting him with all the strength I could, ignoring George, ignoring somebody else now coming from the other side.

Strong hands had hold of my shoulder and one arm. Somewhere off a ways I could hear little Harry yelling. "They's fightin'! They's fightin'!"

"Go get in the house!" I heard Lizbeth command, somewhere to my right.

"Mr. Wortham, come on an' get up." Joe's voice, along with his hands, were pulling me up and back.

George was pulling me too. Pretty soon they had me off, but Edward didn't let it rest. With them holding my arms, he lit into me, and Joe had to let go and try his best to push Edward back.

"Stop it!" George yelled at us. "Stop it! Both of ya!"

I wanted to turn on him, acting the innocent peacemaker. But I saw Joe's face, all worried and confused, and I knew this wasn't the way to handle things. *Lord, help me. I have never been so close to losing control.*

"You think you own the whole countryside!" Edward glowered at me. "You got no business in something going on over here. Get your fool self back home before I—"

"What?" I answered right back. "Just hit me again? I don't care! This is my business 'cause he's got a boy right now over in my bed, laid up with a broken leg. And my wife caring for him and more besides! You think it's not my business if he decides to drown himself in your stinking bottle—"

"No." Joe was struck. "Pa, you wasn't drinkin'?"

George shook his head, staring at me. "Just a sip or two was all it was gonna be, Samuel. With Joe in the barn, none a' the kids lookin', now what could it hurt? Just to be neighborly, to show no hard feelin's. He done said he was sorry over what happened. He was tryin' to make things right—"

"He doesn't make things right," I said bitterly. "He piles one wrong on top of another and anoth—"

Edward broke away from Joe and lunged at me. We

were back in the dirt again before I knew it, this time with me on the bottom.

"Stop it!" George was yelling again. Once more they struggled at pulling us apart, and Lizbeth had to whack Edward with the handle of a hoe before they could get the job done.

"I'd shut you both in the corncrib an' let you settle it," George complained. "Only I fear you'd kill each other. Jus' sit, both a' you. Calm down a minute."

I wouldn't sit. I got back on my feet, and Edward did the same. "I paid for that jug fair and square," he told me. "You owe me for it."

"You owe me for getting rid of it before it could eat at your insides," I countered. "And for not heading into town right now for the sheriff. He wouldn't have you distributing liquor in his county."

"I wasn't distributing—"

"Close enough."

George shook his head. "Now, don't you think you're taking this too far, Samuel? Weren't no harm done."

"Shut up, Pa," Joe said, his voice low and angry.

"Plenty of harm!" I argued. "Franky's leg's broke! You got him all the way out here against the doctor's orders and then just left him. What are you thinking? How is a drink going to help you, George? Tell me that. How is it going to help him?"

"Shut up, Mr. Holy Man!" Edward shouted. "Gotta preach to everybody! Playin' like you're Mr. Perfect! I should've tore you open when I first got to your place, knowing how you'd be."

The rage in his face stopped me for a moment. And made me remember our father. "Edward," I said, suddenly calmer. "Katie told me the man in the picture had a bird on his arm. A tattoo."

"What picture? What the devil are you saying?"

"The picture Trudy Vale had. Of Katie's father. She said

she saw it before it got stolen, and he had a bird on his arm."

He was glaring at me; he was so mad I knew better than to think he couldn't be dangerous.

"She's going to stay with us," I told him. "Trudy's mother couldn't take her. The sheriff . . ." I hesitated, knowing Edward wasn't willing to believe anything I said. "The sheriff agreed she couldn't be mine. Because of the tattoo, and because the grandmother said her daughter's baby was from someone older—"

"You're making this up."

"No. I'm not. She's not mine. I never lied. But she's probably family. And we're keeping her."

"Why? Why claim her at all? If you're gonna make up some stupid story to take the blame off yourself? Too much conscience? What are you saying? A bird on his arm! That it was Father's ghost? Huh? What kind of story is that?"

"Maybe he's not dead."

"You're being stupid."

"No. I didn't make it up. Katie told me. And I didn't know what to think. I still don't know what to think."

He shook his head, looking rock hard. "You still owe me for a jug of home whiskey. A pretty good one too, didn't you think, Hammond?"

George knew better than to answer a question like that in front of his kids. "I'm done with drinkin'," he muttered. "No offense."

"You're gonna let this—"

But I cut Edward off. "There's no such thing as good whiskey. Don't you remember? Mother and all her bottles everywhere?"

"She drank because of you," Edward said, his eyes cold and stormy. I'd never noticed the bags under them before. Just like Mother.

"No," I told him immediately. "I don't know why she drank. But it wasn't my fault."

"Nothing's ever your fault! Is it, Sammy? Is it?" He took a step toward me, and Joe got in his way. But Edward shoved the boy aside, still coming at me.

"You better git," George told him quickly. "Go on. Been enough fightin' for one day."

Edward just stared, like he was trying to decide what to do next.

"Go on," I told him. "No more trouble."

"Yeah," he said. "I'm the one who's trouble." He spit in my direction and jumped in his car. This time he checked, thank God, to be sure nobody was in his way before roaring out of there.

God help him, I prayed. *He's going to kill himself like this—either quickly with the way he's behaving, or slowly with the liquor. Like our mother. Living half dead half the time.*

I watched him speeding away down the dusty road. And then I turned my attention to George.

"Now, Samuel," he said quickly. "I realize I done wrong. I should a' thought more. Won't be doin' that again, I'll warrant you. Seein' the look Joe an' Lizbeth give me, that's enough to—"

"Fine," I told him. "I'm not going to police you. But I'd think you'd care, George. For your kids' futures."

"I do. I do."

"What about Franky?" I asked, still angry.

"What about him? He doin' all right this morning?"

"Good as can be expected. It was pretty hard, though, George, you pulling him out of the hospital for a painful ride, then just leaving him like that."

"I lef' him the very best place he could be. Your Juli—I'd trust her more'n a barrelful a' nurses. Ain't he fine? It'll heal. Takes time, that's all."

"He needs you, George. He needs some of *your* time."

"Yeah, all right. I'll be by this evenin'."

That was not what I meant, and I think he knew it. A few minutes' visit wasn't going to fix the rift I could see between them. But he didn't want to talk about it, he didn't want to admit there was any problem at all. He turned his back and headed away to the barn.

"Be cuttin' hay this afternoon, if you want to help," he said as he was walking away. "Want me to send Sam for you?"

"I'll come. I'll meet you."

"Suit yourself."

He disappeared into the barn, and I stood there wondering why he had to be so stubborn. We'd come so far, at least I'd thought we had, from him nearly losing himself with grief after his wife's death, to managing what had become a good working arrangement for all of us.

Standing beside me, Lizbeth shook her head. "There's times Pa's weak," she said solemnly. And I guess that about summed it up.

TWENTY-FIVE

Julia

His car came racing up our lane, screeching to a stop beside the lilacs. I prayed that Samuel would turn right around from the Hammonds and get himself back here. Edward was mad, I could plainly see that. With his face angry red, he came jumping out of his car, slamming the door shut, huffing toward me at the garden like some kind of mad bull.

"I want to talk to Katie," he demanded. "Where is she?"

I stood up, wishing I had the hoe in my hand. "You might as well just go. You're in no fit shape to be visiting a child."

"Where is she?" he asked again, louder this time.

"Come back when Samuel's here. When you're calm enough not to scare the girl half to death." I tensed inside, realizing what I'd said. I shouldn't have told him Samuel was gone.

"I don't want Samuel here," he growled. "I want to hear what she's got to say without him standing over her. And I figure maybe I've only got a few minutes before he heads back. So you get her and get her quick, or I'll find her myself and you won't be able to stop me."

They were in the house. All the girls and Franky. Emma Grace was taking a little nap, right beside her brother. And Sarah, Rorey, and Katie were in there playing, after promising me they could be quiet and come and tell me as soon as the baby woke up. I hoped she wouldn't wake. I hoped they'd be quiet indeed.

"The kids went to the pond," I said. It wasn't quite a lie. Robert, Willy, and Kirk were there.

"I don't think so," he said. "I don't think you'd send little girls out there without you, now would you?"

"They're . . . they're not alone."

I heard a noise from the house and did my best to ignore it. I had no idea what Edward wanted or what he was so angry about, but Katie didn't need any part of it.

He turned his head just in time to see Rorey's face peeking through the window. She ducked out of sight, but it was enough for him. He laughed at me. "You lie just like your husband," he said. "Maybe you ain't the Christian you seem to be."

He took off toward the house. In desperation I followed him, running to keep up. "Wait!" I called. "Just hold on!" But he wouldn't hear me.

I'd seen something that scared me in his eyes. I didn't want him running in there at those kids. So I grabbed at his arm. "Just stop!" I said, trying to sound brave. "You tell me what's so all-fired important that you've got to go racing around here half-cocked! You can see her. Maybe. Once I know what this is about and you can behave yourself decently. Until then, you're not going inside."

He shoved me away like I was nothing more than a kid goat bringing annoyance. I couldn't stop him. He was to the door and inside before I could do another thing. But I hurried after him, not sure what I was going to do.

Oh, Samuel. Why'd you have to go see George now? Why were we foolish enough not to leave any of the big boys here? What is he capable of? What is he going to do?

He hurried straight through the kitchen and into the sitting room. The girls were in there, just like I knew they'd be, looking wide-eyed and scared at this big man rushing toward them. He grabbed Katie's arm, and she cringed, bursting immediately into tears.

"Let her go!" I demanded.

He turned to me with his eyes blazing. "I'm not going to hurt her. I'm not going to hurt anybody. All I want to do is talk. So you get these other kids and you get yourself clear out of here. I'll be done soon enough."

It had to be from God, the strength I felt. "No." I told Sarah and Rorey to leave the room. They went, but not far—into the bedroom with Franky and the baby.

I stood my ground. "You're scaring her. You're scaring all of us. I will not leave."

"Fine," he said. "Keep your mouth shut."

He turned his face to Katie, and the poor girl crumbled. She tried her best to shield her face from him, but he still held one of her arms.

"Please let her go," I begged.

"Shut up." He shook her, just a little, making her look up at his face. "I want you to tell me just exactly what you said about a picture. Tell me about your daddy, girl. Tell me what he looks like."

She could barely breathe, she was so terrified. But with quick little gasps, she managed to find her voice. "H-he looks like Mr. Wortham, except . . . except real tired and . . . and tall and dark hair and—"

"I know about the hair! What else?"

"I—I think he's mean. Like you. I—I think he's scary."

I thought he was going to hit her. I almost grabbed for her, to pull her away, but he suddenly dropped his hands and let her go. She ran. Straight to me, burying her face in my skirt.

But he wasn't done. "Sit down, Mrs. Wortham. Just sit down."

I did. I took her with me to a chair and held her in my arms. "Please," I started. "Can't you see—"

"Shut up." He tried turning her face toward him again, but she held me tight and resisted, leaning into my shoulder and my mussed-up hair. "Now, listen, Katie," he told her. "We best finish our talking before your crazy Mr. Wortham shows up again. I'll hurt him. If I see him again right now, I'll hurt him, and I don't want to do that, do you understand?"

Katie was crying, and I couldn't blame her. "Please go," I told him.

"Shut up," he said again. "Can't you see I'm asking for help? Katie, I need to know. Was there anything else? I need to know!"

He was different, somehow. Shaken. I couldn't understand it. Katie looked up at him, perhaps as puzzled as I was.

"About your daddy. About that picture. Was there anything else?"

"He had a big bird on his arm," she said. "It kind of looked at me a little."

I could see Edward swallowing down a deep breath. "Right side up?"

"Yes, sir. Because he had his arm up on the tree. This Mr. Wortham doesn't have any bird, and I wished he did, but . . . but the sheriff said I could stay anyway."

"Who told you?"

Katie didn't answer.

"Who told you, girl? About the blasted bird on his arm!

Did Samuel put you up to this? Did he tell you you had to say that if you wanted him to keep you?"

She shook her head. She burst into tears.

"Tell me the truth. Did he tell you what to say?"

"You're like him," Katie cried, shaking her head again. "You're like my daddy was in my dream! All scary and mean. He hit people. He hit my mama."

Edward stared. First at her. Then at me.

He stood and backed up a step. "Did your mama ever say your daddy's middle name?"

"No," Katie whispered. "No."

He laughed, nervously, strangely. "They're both Eddies. Did you know that? Samuel Edward Wortham. And he called his second son Samuel Edwin. Why do you figure he did that? Huh? After calling his firstborn Edward Charles? Why is that? Why'd he give his second son his name?"

I swallowed hard. He wasn't rational. "There's no way we can answer that," I told him. "Please. Go."

"You're afraid of me." He shook his head. "Every one of you. Even Samuel. You're all afraid of me."

"I'm not." It was just a little voice from the next room, weaker than I was used to hearing. *Oh, Franky, no!* My heart thumped immediately. *There's just no telling what this man could do.*

Edward turned toward the bedroom. "It's the hammer boy."

"Leave him alone. You know he's hurt."

He looked at me for a moment and then turned his eyes away. "Yeah. I know."

The baby started crying. Edward walked into the room. Sarah and Rorey were there by the bed, both of them leaned over Emma Grace, trying to calm her.

Franky was sitting up, away from the pillows, pale, sweating, and angry. "You better leave that girl alone," he said. "And Mrs. Wortham too."

Edward just stood for a moment, suddenly seeming paler himself. "What do you think I'm gonna do?"

"God prob'ly thinks you oughta say you're sorry," Franky told him.

I was amazed, but no more than Edward was. I saw something crumble in the man. I saw all the anger fall away. He stood for a second, looking confused, not seeming near so large as he had just moments before. "I just come . . ." he said, stammering over the words. "I just come to find out . . ."

He stopped. He looked at Katie. He looked at me. "Just . . . just go back to doin' whatever . . . whatever you were doin' . . ."

He backed out of the room, and then we heard him leave the house. After a while, his car started, and we could hear him drive away. Only then did Franky lay back down again. I touched his forehead, but he brushed my hand away.

"I'm okay," he insisted. "But I'm sure glad he left, 'cause I'm not sure I coulda got no farther up."

"I hope he don't never come back," Rorey said.

Sarah looked up at me, her big eyes brimming with tears just as much as Katie's were. Baby Emmie just lay there looking at us, as if she were trying to figure out what in the world was wrong.

"I think he'll have to," Franky said before closing his eyes. "He'll have to come back 'least once. 'Cause he knew, when I said he oughta say he's sorry. He knew."

Katie was still clinging to me moments later when Samuel came in the door. He found us there by the bed, Katie and Sarah just drying their tears. It was all I could do to hold back a flood of my own. "Oh, Samuel."

He was a mess—dirty, disheveled, the way Edward had

been. His shirt was torn. But the look in his eyes was so much softer. Wounded. "He stopped here. Didn't he?"

Suddenly I was afraid again. Of Samuel's reaction. Of what had already happened that I didn't know about. "He didn't hurt anyone, Samuel. He seemed confused—"

Sarah jumped forward, taking her father by the waist. "He was scary, Daddy. I was afraid he was going to take Katie away."

Samuel hugged our little girl, lifted her up in his arms and squeezed her tight. "I'll have to tell the sheriff. We can't have him . . . we can't have him terrorizing you every time I have to go away for something."

I didn't like the idea. I don't know why. Surely Edward would just get tired and go away on his own. We weren't holding him here. Nothing was holding him.

We tried to get back to the day's activities. I started dinner. Franky slept. Emmie was up and running, pulling dish towels out of the cupboard and throwing them on the floor. Robert and Willy came home, and Samuel told them to stay by the house the rest of the day. He'd promised to work field with George, but he was going to have to ask Barrett Post for the use of his truck and go into town to talk to the sheriff.

He told me a little about the fight. But not much. Not in front of the kids. He didn't say much when I told him how Edward had been. He sat and put his face in his hands. He didn't want to go into town. Not yet. But he didn't think he had a choice now.

We were just finishing up dinner when Joe came running through the timber to our yard. He came straight to the house all out of breath and burst in without knocking. "Did Harry and Berty eat with you?" he asked, looking around quickly.

We all stared up at him. The little boys had gone home with Lizbeth and had not been back. We told him that.

"They was playin'. We figured they was in the shed." He looked at Samuel. "They didn't come in when Lizbeth rung the bell to eat. We ain't seen 'em since about the time your brother left."

Those boys. They were so fearless, thinking they were more grown up than they were. More than once I'd thought how easy it would be to lose them in the middle of a day's tumult.

"Where have you looked?" Samuel asked Joe.

"Everywhere over to home. That's why I come here. Can I look in your barn? Maybe they's playin' with Whiskers somewhere."

We checked everywhere. Samuel took Willy and Joe with him to double-check the path through the timber, the pond, and our creek.

An anxious hour later, Joe was back to tell me Samuel had sent him to get the Posts and the Muellers to help search the woods. There was no trace of the boys.

I prayed. Sarah wanted to go help them look. When I told her she was just too young, she went upstairs to look out all the high windows. Rorey went outside and climbed a tree.

Franky couldn't rest now. His mind was working on the problem of his little brothers. "Maybe they decided to go to the school," he suggested. "They's anxious to be big enough to go. Or maybe they figgered on walkin' all the way to Georgie Dixon's house. They sure like playin' with him, but the only chance they ever get is on Sunday."

"I'm sure they'll think of all that," I told him. "Try to relax."

"I don't wanna relax. Ain't there somethin' I can do?"

I brought him beans to snap. Seemed silly, but busy hands make for less worry on the mind.

It was hard waiting and not knowing any way to help. Robert was having an especially hard time, because he thought he was big enough to help search, but Samuel had told him to stay with me.

"It's because of Uncle Edward," he complained. "He's afraid Uncle Edward'll come back stirrin' up more trouble. Maybe he took 'em, even. You think he'd take 'em?"

"Not very likely. They weren't with him when he came by here."

"Well, maybe he went back over there, Mom. Maybe he done it for spite."

"Lizbeth or George or somebody'd see him," I said. "Besides, it's your father who he's spiteful toward. If he was going to do anything, he would do it to one of us."

"I think he's hateful. The poorest brother I ever heard of. Why can't he just be like normal folks?"

Two hours passed, maybe more. Kirk came by to see if the boys might have showed up at our place. They still weren't home. And they must be getting mighty hungry by now, I figured. I prayed some more.

Mr. Mueller and his son stopped at our well for water and then went back to searching. Samuel hadn't been home. Maybe he wouldn't be until they were found.

"Is this a bad day?" Katie asked me as I was drawing water to wash Emma Grace's diapers.

"I guess it is, compared to most."

"It was a bad day when Mr. Eddie hit that boy with his car too, wasn't it?"

"Yes. It was. Very bad."

I lifted the heavy bucket and started back to the house.

"Is most days good days here?"

I had to stop. "Oh, honey. We've had some bad things lately, that's for sure. But it's not always like this. And it won't stay this way. They'll find those little boys soon, and they'll be just fine. They're a bit big for their britches, that's all, thinking they can do whatever they set their minds to. Took to wandering this time, a little too far, I'm sure. They'll be found."

She didn't say much more, just looked at me a little uncertainly. Sarah came up beside us and helped me lift the water bucket. Rorey was still in the tree. And Robert was in the barn, busying himself at something.

Suddenly I heard a car. *More searchers,* I thought. *Maybe somebody's found them.*

"It's Uncle Edward back," Sarah said, her face all serious.

"Surely not. Not now." I looked, hoping to see Barrett or Clement Post or someone else I knew coming to bring us some word.

But Sarah was right. It was Edward again. Katie clung to my skirt in a sudden panic, but Sarah remained strangely calm. "What should we do, Mommy? Should I take Katie in the house and sit with Franky again?"

"Yes. Thank you, honey. You do that."

I didn't yell for Robert. He was only a boy. And he'd hear soon enough, anyway. I didn't wait for Edward to get his car into our drive. Just seeing him come up the lane made something hard well up inside me. Maybe he wanted to frighten us again. Maybe he enjoyed that. But we had enough to think about. And I didn't want him here, causing my family grief. I'd make him leave. I'd do something.

Seventy times seven.

The words jumped into my skull, but I could hardly bear them. *No, Lord. He's dangerous. Just seeing him's scaring Katie out of her wits.*

I ran toward the road, not knowing for sure what I'd say or what I'd do but knowing I had to get him to leave before he troubled the girls any further. And before Robert got out here, because who knew what might happen then.

I stood at the head of our drive as he pulled up and stopped, still in the roadway.

"Keep going," I told him. "You're not touching one of these children again. You're not welcome here."

He looked strange, but even so, my hard words didn't seem to faze him much. "Where's Samuel?" he asked.

"He's not here," I said, making sure I was blocking the drive. "Just go."

"I need to talk to him."

"No, you don't. You've already talked to him. You've beat him black and blue and spread all kinds of lies. Just go!" I was serious. Furious. But way down in my heart a persistent little voice repeated, *Seventy times seven.*

I stood my ground, shaking my head and not budging to give him any opportunity to turn in—unless he drove right through the daylilies.

"You can hate me all you want," Edward said. "That's fine, and I don't care. But I mean to find Samuel. Where is he?"

Hate him? The words struck me hard. I couldn't really hate him, or anybody. Could I? I didn't want to. It went against all I was taught and all I believed. It went against that still, small voice urging me again and again to forgive.

"I don't hate you," I said. "I can't. But I'm angry. You've hurt and frightened innocent children. You've attacked my husband when he doesn't deserve it. But God loves you. I know he does. And I can try to do the same, even though I haven't seen you do anything but mock and destroy."

"Just tell me where Samuel is," he said in a quieter voice.

"I can't. He's in these woods somewhere, doing his very best to help his neighbors, something I'm not sure you've ever done in your entire life. He's trying to find two lost little boys, and that's what you'd be doing if you cared an ounce for anyone besides yourself!"

"Didn't know nothing about it," he said without batting an eye. "Besides, there's boys all over this countryside. I wouldn't know which ones you're looking for if they stared me in the face."

"I don't suppose you'd care to know. I guess that's the way you are. But Samuel's got to help. Because he cares! So he doesn't have time for you to be hitting him again, or for any more of your accusations. If you've got anything new to say, just tell me now, and I'll tell him when he gets home. Whenever that'll be."

I couldn't help it. Tears were running down my cheeks. I tried to stop them, but they wouldn't be stopped. Out of the corner of my eye, I could see Robert coming toward us. *Please, God,* I prayed. *Make Edward leave. Make him leave now, before there's any tussle between them. I don't want my little boy hurt.*

Edward didn't say anything. Not another word. He looked at me, he nodded just a bit. Then he turned his car around in the road and drove away, on toward the Posts' house. And I didn't care where he went, so long as he was gone.

Robert came up beside me, and I hugged him with a prayer in my heart. *Thank you, God, for helping me tell Edward one more time that you love him. Thank you for helping me, that he left so peacefully. And forgive me, Lord. Because I'm trying to forgive. But I never want to see him again.*

TWENTY-SIX

Samuel

I didn't know how long I'd been out, calling and calling those boys' names. I was getting more sore with every step, but I wasn't about to go back and bellyache about it now. I just kept trudging on, circling through our timber and then following the creek beyond it. I'd found one track. One tiny little bare footprint in the creek mud, and that was enough to keep me going this direction.

I knew how Harry loved to play Indian. Maybe he'd just taken it a little too far and decided to make camp in the trees somewhere. I could relate to that, though when I was a boy the woods where we played had been barely a fraction of the size of this one.

Strange how the memories circled through my mind as I walked. Dewey and I balancing branches against a low-hanging limb to make ourselves a little lean-to. We'd made a ring of rocks and filled it with sticks too, though we never managed to get a real fire going. I'd pretended to really live there. I'd pretended we were Wampanoag Indians with a bear paws symbol. And nobody could find us if they didn't understand our password and the way we marked a trail. A child's foolishness. A child's escape.

A flock of birds burst into flight in front of me, but I went on, wishing that all of us had ways of letting each other know if we found anything significant. The Posts had had their hunting rifles with them, and Joe Hammond had grabbed his squirrel rifle too. They would fire a shot in the air if the boys were found. But I didn't own a gun, to the amusement of some of my neighbors.

I kept walking, past where our Blackberry Creek joined into Curtis Creek and kept going. I remembered the time Edward had come looking for me; he was none too impressed with our little camp. He seemed angry as usual, kicking our ring of rocks in all directions and calling me stupid for not going home when it started to get dark. That was when he'd shared the pickle loaf. It was too bad there was so much strain between Edward and me now. Just that memory, of him caring just that much, might have been enough to help us move on together.

"Harry!" I yelled. "Berty!"

I wondered how George was faring, and where he was right now. *Why all this struggle, Lord? One Hammond boy's laid up with a broken leg, and now this!*

I thought I heard something in the distance. A motor vehicle, and then it was gone. "Harry!" I yelled again.

After two more twists in the creek, I found a cloth ball soaking in the water. Berty's ball. I knew it. Julia had made it for him for Christmas. I picked it up, squeezed the water out over my head, and crammed it down into my shirt pocket. The sudden coolness felt good.

And I'd needed that sign. I was headed upstream, so they had to be somewhere ahead of me. Had to be.

I hurried, calling their names some more. Finally, I heard

a muffled little sound ahead of me that sounded like crying. I called, but nobody answered. I rushed forward, pushing my way through a bramble bush. And there I found Berty, sitting at the base of a tree in tears. First he jumped, as though I'd scared him, but then he leaped to his little feet and ran at me. I scooped him up, thrilled to find him safe and sound. "Where's Harry?" I asked the little boy, real worry churning inside me. But Berty only sniffed and pointed up. Harry sat above us, high on a limb, looking all around like he himself was one of the searchers.

"Come down," I told him. "And tell me what it is you're doing out here."

"We's turtle huntin'," he said immediately, scooting down expertly toward me. "Lizbeth said we could."

"Not this far." I shook my head. Berty, at least, knew there was a problem. He'd been scared. But apparently he was the only one.

"She jus' said I had to take somebody. She never said not to go far."

One day I figured this would be laughably ridiculous, him thinking she meant for him to take his four-year-old brother on such an excursion. But I was pretty upset with him at the moment.

"You worried your pa and Lizbeth something awful," I told him. "If you want to go someplace, you've got to tell them first. And take somebody as tall as Lizbeth or taller. Is that clear?"

"Yes." He took his reprimand with a smile. "We done real good gettin' so far. Bet that was the bestest explore anybody ever saw."

"All it means to me is it'll take us longer to get home," I said wearily. "Can you walk, Berty?"

"Nope," he said, even though he'd managed to get up and come to me. "I tink my foot's all broked like Franky."

I hadn't looked at his feet. I was surprised now to notice

that one of them had been bleeding, but not badly. Probably scratched on a branch. "That's not broken," I assured him. "No big problem. Does it hurt?"

He nodded. "I'm hungry too."

"You'll have to be patient about that," I told him. "But I'll carry you. Harry, you'll have to walk. Stay close."

I tried to hurry as we started back, yelling every once in a while in hopes I would be in earshot of another searcher. But I got no answer, and pretty soon Harry was complaining about *his* foot, and falling behind.

"Come on," I told him. "You're the one who got yourself out this far."

"But it really hurts," he insisted. "Really bad."

I stopped to look. Harry's tough little bare foot had a splinter, right in the soft arch. I tried to pull it out, but it was hard to get ahold of and hard to see in the shady light.

"Carry me too," Harry said.

There'd been times when I could have. Neither boy was all that big. But I knew better now. "I can't," I told him. "Both of you are too much at once."

"Then carry me!" Harry whined. "Please. It hurts."

"No!" Berty wailed. "My footy hurts too!"

Neither boy was hurt badly, and I was about to make them both walk when I heard a sound way off somewhere to my right.

"Here!" I yelled, just as loud as I could. "Over here! I found them!"

At first there was no response, but I was sure I could hear someone coming steadily closer. I yelled again, wondering why they didn't answer.

Then silence for a moment. Maybe I'd been mistaken. But there was another rustling in the bushes before long, and I knew there was somebody coming our way.

When finally I saw who it was, I scarcely knew what to think. Edward, pushing his way through the pigweed and wild rose. He spoke before I had the chance.

"What a stroke a' luck! All I did was pull over and park where there was plenty of room along the road. Thought I'd be obliging to your wife and walk a ways so I could say I'd joined the search. She's something, that's sure. I never expected to hear you yelling. Trying to be some kind of hero, aren't you, Sammy?"

"How far's the car?"

"You askin' for a ride?"

I would have walked away from him had I been alone. "We need it. Yes."

"Well, your wife won't be able to say I don't care no more. Will it make me a hero too, if I bring you home?"

"If you want to be a hero, we'll call you a hero. Fine. We just need the ride. Please."

He laughed. "You look awful, you know that?"

"You're not much to look at yourself." I turned away from him and coaxed Harry to his feet. "We need to start home. There's people searching for these boys."

Edward was quiet for a moment; I didn't know if he'd help us or not. And I almost didn't care.

"Are these some of the Hammonds?" he asked me.

"Yes. They are."

"Well, I know the way to that farm," he said with irony in his voice. "I was just there this morning. A neighbor of theirs got a little out of hand."

He had to taunt me, even now. I turned, expecting to find the same angry mockery in his eyes. But something else was there, I wasn't sure what.

"They're tired," I told him. "One has a scratch and the other has a splinter. They don't want to walk." I handed Berty into his arms, because he was the lighter of the two. No matter how sore I felt, I wouldn't ask him to take the heavier load.

I lifted Harry onto my shoulders. Seemed like he weighed a ton.

"Okay," Edward said with a little laugh. "Follow me. If I can find my way back to the car, we'll go be heroes."

He wasn't too sure of his way, but I knew by now which direction the road was. We moved quickly, but it still took us a while to break through the trees.

"Thanks," I told him as we went along. "You saved me a lot of walking."

He barely glanced my way. "What are brothers for?"

Those words hung in the silence between us for a long time, until Harry started bouncing on my shoulders.

"I'm ridin' a giraffe!" he hollered. "Looky!"

"Me too!" Berty squealed. "Go jaffey!"

"Haven't you boys learned your lesson?" I asked them. "You went too far. You didn't know your way home. You both got hurt. It could've been a lot worse. You are not to go off by yourselves. Do you hear?"

"But we wasn't by ourselves," Harry argued. "We had each other."

"You know exactly what I mean. You need somebody older. You've been told that many times."

Up on Edward's shoulders, Berty was nodding. "I wanna go home. We was too far."

"You sure were. We're almost four miles from home."

"Boy!" Harry proclaimed. "That's a adventure!"

Edward laughed. "You'll have to watch out for that one when he's a teenager."

Walking along beside him, I couldn't stop thinking about the way Juli and the girls had looked after he'd been there. I wanted to address it, but I knew I couldn't. Not before we got the little boys home. We didn't need another fight.

But the silence was awful. And finally I knew what I had to say, despite the anger I felt toward him. "I'm sorry, Edward, for this morning. I should have stopped you . . . some other way. I shouldn't have hit you. It wasn't right."

"You're hardheaded," he answered back. "Still thinking

you had a right to stop me at all. I was just apologizing. He never told me he had trouble with the bottle."

"You didn't know it's illegal?"

"I think it's a foolish law."

I had to shake my head. "You and me, we know about the bottle, Edward. I can't see why you'd want—"

"I know. It's stupid, ain't it?"

I would never have been that bold. But he'd said it himself. "Yeah," I agreed.

"I'm hungry," Berty complained.

"We'll be home before long," I assured him again.

"Do you know where I went?" Edward suddenly asked me. "After you had the nerve to attack me the way you did?"

"Yes," I said immediately, feeling the heat rise to the back of my neck. He'd brought it up. I couldn't help it. "You went and tormented my family. You grabbed a little girl and shook her, and you shoved my wife. I don't care if you want to fight me. Maybe that's normal, I don't know. But I can't have it, not with the women and children, Edward. I can't."

"I went into that little town called Dearing," he said, ignoring the warning in my words. "I found a telephone in the back room of that little service station they got there. Man charged me a whole nickel to make a phone call."

He paused. He let the silence hang there again for a minute.

"Pa talked on a telyphone once," Harry told us. "He was callin' Aunt Chloe, an' it was really cold."

"I want Lizbeth," Berty whispered.

"I called Mother," Edward said, and the words sunk to the pit of my stomach like they were encased in stone.

He stopped and looked at me for a moment. "I had to ask her."

For a fleeting moment I considered telling him not to

tell me whatever it was she'd said. But I knew he would. That's why he'd come. And maybe the Lord was in it.

"She tried to tell me the same thing she said before. But I told her somebody seen a picture, six or seven years old, with a tattoo like that. She cried, Samuel. She got all upset and cried, right on the phone."

I didn't know what to say, so I didn't say anything. We were just coming out of the trees. The car was down the road, no more than a quarter mile at most. It was a relief to see it.

"Ain't you gonna ask?"

"No," I told him. "Honk your horn when we go. Anybody out searching will head back and see what it's about."

"You're something, you know that?"

I lifted Harry down from my shoulders, not sure I could make it much farther under his weight.

"Don't you want to know?"

"If he's dead, you'll accuse me again," I said. "If he's alive, I've got that to think about, and I'm not sure I want to."

He was quiet. Very quiet as we walked the rest of the way to the car.

"Go real fast," Harry said. "I like fast."

"I want Lizbeth," Berty said again.

I got in the backseat with the boys on either side of me. Edward jumped in front, started the engine, and honked the horn once. Then he stopped and looked at me. "She's not seen him in five years, Sammy. Can you believe that? It's been twenty years since she said he was dead!"

He gunned the motor. He raced down that road like a lunatic, honking the horn the whole way. I hung on to both boys and prayed he wouldn't spill us in the ditch. I didn't know my brother. One day, one moment to the next. I didn't know him. But at least he was feeling something over this news. At least he was touched, I could tell that much. But whether it was shock or anger or what, I didn't know.

We got the searchers' attention. We got George and Lizbeth's attention way before we came up their weedy drive, and they were running to meet us. Lizbeth took to hugging both boys and scolding them at the same time. George hung back, obviously surprised to see Edward and me together. But he thanked us both, and Joe fired off a shot into the air, in case anybody out there might be left wondering what the car horns could mean.

We were on our way soon enough, just Edward and myself, back home. I don't know why he took me. I don't know why I went with him.

He stopped before we got to our lane. He just sat in his seat a minute, not speaking.

"You want me to walk the rest of the way?" I asked.

"You're such an idiot. Just shut up."

I did. I sat there quiet. Finally, he started talking, staring out over George Hammond's cornfield. "You really think she's our sister?"

"I got no proof. But I don't know what else to think."

"I never figured when Trudy said Samuel Wortham that she could be talking about somebody that old."

"You wouldn't. I understand that. But he's only about sixteen years older than you are."

"You're right. He looked like a kid when we were kids."

"He never had much. I guess you know that."

He turned on me, a sudden sharpness in his eyes. "You excusing what he did to us?"

"No. Come on. Let's go home."

He shook his head. "Your wife said I wasn't welcome."

I nodded at that. Maybe I was wrong, even thinking about asking him on the place again. But there was something different between us right now, a chance, maybe, at acting like brothers. "If you can apologize, we'll feed you some supper."

He stared at me. "That kid said that. I oughta apologize. Only he said God thinks so."

"Should listen to Franky. He knows what he's talking about."

"You're all pretty crazy, if you ask me. Talking about God, like anybody really knows."

"You can. If you want to."

"There you go again." He looked out over the field. "Why'd you turn preacher, Sammy? You been preaching to Mom in letters a long time now. She showed me some of 'em. She keeps 'em all in a box under her bed."

That came as a shock. I'd never had any indication that Mother thought my letters fit for anything but the trash can.

He started the vehicle going again. We pulled up to the house together. Julia and the children were glad to know about the boys but far less than thrilled to see Edward. But it didn't take him long to tell them he was sorry, which told me a lot. I'd never heard him apologize before. Ever.

We served him supper. I even asked him to stay the night. He told us about dancing with Trudy Vale and getting a slicked-back haircut to look nice for her. He said he was sorry all over again to Robert and to Katie when he thought he saw them looking at him strange.

I wasn't sure how I really felt, having him there. But he was so much calmer, and careful with his words. He was actually decent company, once he'd decided I might not be a liar after all. He saw the old radio the Posts had given us and was interested in a program. But I had to tell him it had quit in June and I hadn't been able to get it going again. He wanted to fiddle with it. He tried for a while, then I tried with him, with Robert looking on, and finally we got it playing again in time to sit and listen to a program before bed.

With him in the house, I lay awake a long time, thinking too much about his past and mine. Finally I got up, unable to sleep, and found him sitting at the kitchen table.

"Just wishing for a cup of coffee," he told me.

Morning was a long way off, but I started a fire in the stove and got out the canister of "coffee blend"—the rest of our store-bought coffee, plus roasted and ground chicory and dandelion root that Julia had dried and stirred in.

"What are you going to do, Edward, from here on?"

"I don't know. I heard there might be a carnival going through some towns south of here. Thought I might see about getting hired on, travel with 'em a while, you know."

"There's likely to be a lot of folks vying for that job, or any job."

"I know it. What about you? You gonna stick it out here?"

"I think we can. Got a few animals. A lot of land to try to make good with."

"You're lucky, Sammy. Chips don't fall for most folks like that."

"We've been blessed. I know that better than anyone." I put a generous scoop of the coffee blend into the pot of water and put it all on to heat.

"You really gonna raise up that girl?" he asked.

"Don't have much choice, do I? Where else is she going to go? We can't find her mother, and her grandmother wants us to keep her here."

"But what if she ain't family? What if it was some other fool with a tattoo?"

"Named Samuel? Wortham? Looking like me? I'd like to meet him, wouldn't you?"

"No. Can't say what I'd do. Probably land me back in

prison. You know Mother was still afraid? That I'd go looking for Father, maybe kill him after all these years. She was glad she didn't know where he was. Maybe he really is dead this time, who knows?"

"It doesn't matter." I sat down at the table with him. "He's not searching us out."

Edward leaned his chair back, looking at the ceiling. "I can't go back to Albany. Mother told me how mad Jimmy is."

"Why? Why's he mad?" I thought that Jimmy, my mother's husband, and Edward had always understood each other pretty well.

"That's where I got the money. To come out here. Right out of his till."

"You stole it?"

"Well, I didn't ask him. Mom knew. She didn't say it was all right. But she didn't try to stop me, neither. She thinks I'm headed straight back to the pen. That's what she thought when I called. That I was gonna tell her I'd been picked up someplace."

I took a deep breath and swallowed it down. "You will be. If you keep on. You know that as well as I do."

"Didn't drinking ever tempt you?"

"I tried it. But it was stupid."

"Yeah, that's me. The stupid one." He stood and walked toward the door. I thought for a moment he was leaving right then, and I wouldn't have stopped him.

"She's proud of you, you know. For making something of yourself."

"You could," I offered.

"Nah."

I heard footsteps, and I knew Julia was up. She was in the kitchen with us in a matter of minutes, blinking her eyes and wondering.

"Couldn't sleep?" she asked me.

"Nope."

By the light of the one oil lamp, I could see Edward shaking his head at us.

"Go back to bed," I told Juli. "It's all right."

She turned and looked at Edward, and he sat in the chair again. "She's probably up missing you," he told me. "She's not much like Trudy, you know."

"Or anyone else," I agreed.

"I guess if I had what you got, I'd have reason to be faithful. Trudy ain't . . . she just ain't your type."

Juli smiled before she turned and left us.

"I'll be leaving in the morning," he said. "You don't need me here."

"Visit," I told him. "If you want to."

"I might do that. Once in a while." He fished in his pocket and finally pulled out something small. "Give this to hammer boy," he said. "I sure hope he comes out all right."

He pushed a tiny little jackknife across the table to me. "I promise I didn't steal it. Old man in Ohio give it to me. I helped him get out of a ditch."

He stayed long enough for coffee in the morning, but he was ready to go before any of the kids were up. He offered me his hand when he went to leave. And that gesture alone meant more than a lifetime of words. He would be back. Sometime. And that didn't have to be a source of worry.

I wrote to Mother and told her she should be proud of Edward. He wasn't as hostile as before. If he could quit drinking, find a job, things would work out for him yet. Forgive him, I told her, for stealing the money. He thought he was on a mission, and maybe he was. Maybe it was God ordained, to get us together again, and to bring us Katie.

She wrote me back. For the first time ever in my life, Mother wrote me back.

Please forgive me for lying. I love you. Even if you didn't think so. Pray for me.

I did. Every day. And for Edward too. As we went on with the life around us, harvesting the wheat and getting by as best we could, I kept on praying. And Franky prayed. Every day he would take the jackknife out of his pocket and pray for the man who'd given it to him.

I started bringing wood to Franky. First to the bed and then to a blanket on the floor or the ground. He sanded little Emmie's chair that he'd made, and soon she was sitting on it regularly or dragging it along behind her. Then he started carving a wooden cross for Juli to replace the one we'd given away at Christmas. He carved a turtle for Harry, a bug of some kind for Bert. Even though it was weeks before he could walk, he wanted to work. He'd taken the whole business like a man, so I started to treat him like one, regardless of what his father or his brothers thought.

Katie was quiet so often. But we soon discovered she liked to sing. She and Sarah were soon singing together, over in the lilacs or at the base of the apple tree.

I often wondered if Edward had gotten that job with a carnival, and if Trudy Vale had found the success that was more important to her than her own daughter. But especially I wondered where my father might be and what he'd done all those years when we thought he was dead. I never found out. I never had proof that little Katie was actually my sister. But it didn't matter. We all believed it. We all lived it. And that was good enough.

TWENTY-SEVEN

Julia

Hazel's funeral was a solemn affair with only church members and her nephews in attendance. I sang the same song I'd sung for Wilametta Hammond, because Delores Pratt said Hazel had remarked on how well I'd done it in such a difficult time. I found it hard to picture Hazel saying a good word about me to anyone. But apparently she truly had. Herman told me she'd called me her friend.

I knew her family would send us home with her hats, because she'd told us that on her deathbed. But I was surprised to learn she had thirty-seven of them gathered over the years. I kept back two or three to wear to church, gave away more than a dozen to the other ladies, and let the girls have the time of their lives using the rest for dress up.

She'd said something about the Hammonds too, but Herman and his brothers weren't really sure what she'd meant. So they came out to the house one afternoon with Herman's car all loaded with blankets, old clothes, and food that had been stocked in Hazel's pantry. It was an incredible godsend. Cloth enough to remake school clothes for everyone. Food enough for four or five meals for a troop their size, maybe more. We gave some to the church, along with some of the dresses, to help the needs of others.

We never got the money for shoes that year. Sarah wore Katie's and Katie wore Sarah's. The boys all passed theirs along to the next one smaller. Sam Hammond traded work to a neighbor for an old pair of boots, and Lizbeth was wearing what used to be her mother's. So Rorey's were the only ones we had to cut the toes in, because Lizbeth's old ones were far too big. I pieced some sturdy canvas and glued it over the hole we'd made to give her toes some room, even spreading it with wax to keep the water out and polishing it the same color. She hated it, but I picked out one of the best hats to be only for her, for church or for school, and made her a fancy dress using some of the nicest cloth Hazel had had. Then she felt better.

Franky stayed with us all that fall and well into winter. When he could finally walk, he had a dreadful limp and couldn't seem to stay up for long, having more problems with his knee than anything else. But he'd go out and look at Emma's old wheelchair and tell me how glad he was that his leg wasn't worse.

"Emma done what all she set her mind to do," he said. "She told us make the most a' what we got. An' everybody's put on this world with somethin', even if it's nothin' but hardheaded determination."

He was determined, all right. Determined to read. He worked for hours trying to keep a *b* straight from a *d* and an *m* straight from a *w*. Finally by Thanksgiving, he was writing his name. Correctly. It thrilled him, though his brothers were less than impressed.

"Harry can do that," Willy teased. "Prob'ly Berty could too, in a day or less if we was to show him."

They didn't understand the times we had, Franky and me, sitting and reading *The Adventures of Tom Sawyer* and *The Red Badge of Courage*. Schooling Franky was a fun adventure, even though I wouldn't let Lizbeth help much, so she could study on her own to get ready for that test for the teacher training scholarship. I was proud of her.

And proud of Franky. He could add in his head faster than I could on paper and recite poetry he hadn't heard in three years. I didn't mind reading to him, because he understood every word and was always thirsty for more.

Sometimes I felt bitter at Edward for the carelessness that left Franky with a limp that didn't want to go away. Sometimes I was angry at George too, for failing to recognize the gift that Franky was to all of us. It was Franky's own sense of duty that had him going back home before Christmas, not because George was missing him being there or asking him to come around.

But I never forgot the Lord's firm reminders to me. Seventy times seven. I even talked about it to Katie late one night when she was crying and questioning why her mother had left her behind without ever trying to contact her since. We prayed together, to forgive.

And I started leading a church choir, along with Juanita Jones, now that Hazel wasn't around to complain. Sarah and Katie were the only young children to sing in it, and they sang like angels.

A week before Christmas we got a card from Samuel's mother and one from Katie's grandmother on the same day. We made them both paper doilies and pretty Christmas cards of our own design. Katie stuck in a smiling paper doll "just because."

Despite my worries, God continued to provide, and I learned again to relax and expect him to. The blackberries had been enough to give us a taste of jelly through the winter, and I canned wild greens, along with what we could from the garden and peaches from Louise Post's tree. We had apples too, though not as many as some years. And walnuts and hickories. Samuel helped George butcher two hogs and two goats and brought home some of the meat. One day Joe and Robert both came home with a squirrel.

We survived. More than that, we were blessed. We even ended up giving Sukey's calf to a family in town who was far more desperate than we were. A mother and six children came to our pastor for help after having nothing to eat for two days and no way to get anything. The father had gone away to work a barge on a river down south and was killed in a freak accident on his third day there. His family'd had no garden, because the mother had been sick. They had no animals, not even chickens, because they'd already eaten them or sold them for flour to make bread. We ended up taking them a meal most every Sunday we came into town. We had little. But it felt good to give. Emma had known that. Thank God she had passed it on.

Thank God for the opportunity to know Hazel and George and Edward and all the other difficult people we'd ever had to love. God knows what he's doing wrapping up the crazy mix he put on this earth.

"We wouldn't know sweet if it weren't for sour," Grandma Pearl had once told me. "Wouldn't know the answers without any questions, nor God's saving hand without something to be saved out of."

Such is life. A parade of opposites. A jumble of trials, punctuated by moments of the purest bliss. Love and conflict. Laughter and sweat and tears. We saw so much of it all, bringing up little Worthams. And Hammonds. And it was good. I wouldn't have missed it for the world.

Leisha Kelly is a native of Illinois and grew up around gardens and hardworking families. She and her husband, K.J., live in a 130-year-old house with two homeschooled children and a golden retriever.

Have you read the beginning of Samuel and Julia's journey?

They needed a home. She needed a family. What they found was a miracle.

"The writing is beautifully descriptive without being overdone. Overall, Kelly's smooth voice and well-crafted writing keep the pages turning."

—***Publishers Weekly***

In a time of confusion, two families discover a gift of hope. A heartwarming novel.

"Kelly's second novel features a gritty, authentic realism as well as a haunting, beautiful mood that enables readers to feel the characters' pain and rejoice when they overcome life's heartaches."

—***Library Journal***